PRAISE FOR
A PLACE of LIGHT . . .

"There have been many Jewish worlds in this last generation—the Old Left, the Zionist movement, the American synagogue, the Hassidic yeshiva, the Israeli kibbutz, the renewal of Jewish spiritual search among young women and men. Who could have imagined a story that could intertwine all these worlds, give life to them all in joy and pain, create living, breathing, all-too-human beings who move from one to another of these worlds? This book does—with extraordinary vitality and insight."

—Arthur Waskow,
author of *These Holy Sparks:
The Rebirth of the Jewish People*

"[Rhonda Shapiro-Rieser] has . . . a storyteller's heart and has fashioned a compelling book that is at once romantic and grittily real . . . *A PLACE OF LIGHT* DELIVERS BOTH FINE ENTERTAINMENT AND UNIVERSAL TRUTHS."

—Noah Gordon,
author of *The Rabbi*

"Knowledgeably and touchingly, Shapiro-Rieser explores the diverse involvements in Jewish life via two young and searching women."

—*The West Coast Review of Books*

"A COMPELLING AND MOVING NOVEL . . . *A PLACE OF LIGHT* WILL HOLD THE READER FROM THE FIRST PAGES TO THE POWERFUL AND REWARDING ENDING. A WONDERFUL EXPERIENCE."

—Daniel Keyes,
author of *Flowers for Algernon*

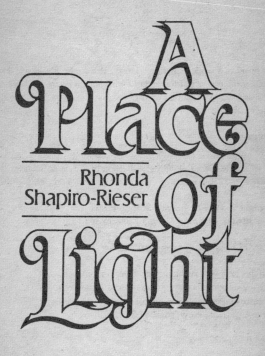

A Place of Light

Rhonda Shapiro-Rieser

PUBLISHED BY POCKET BOOKS NEW YORK

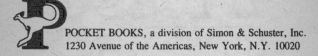

POCKET BOOKS, a division of Simon & Schuster, Inc.
1230 Avenue of the Americas, New York, N.Y. 10020

ACKNOWLEDGMENTS

I would like to thank M. Herring, who got me started long ago; Lady Borton, Marge Nelson, and E. J. Graff, for editing and support; Beverly J. Lerner, whom this book is not about; for technical advice; Ann and Harold Dershowitz, for the warmth of their traditional home and for ferrying the manuscript to the typist. And finally, to my agent, Barbara Lowenstein, for sticking with me.

For my parents.
To my husband.

MADELEINE

MARCH 1948

THE REVOLUTION WAS NOT GOING WELL IN BROOKLYN. Kings Highway shoppers seethed around the pickets in front of Bergman's Clothing Store, barely pausing to gape. The five pickets, worn into sullen silence after only two days, carried signs in various styles of print and hues of red proclaiming their cause. Bergman's low prices were the result of his underpaying and exploiting his labor. None of the five pickets had ever worked for Bergman, though one disgruntled former employee stood off to the side. Those still employed within Bergman's domain sympathized, but had no intention of joining the pickets because, as Bergman was well aware, they were afraid of losing their jobs. The Party Office had hoped to foment a strike among the workers. This having failed, they kept their pickets out in front, to try to draw some attention and circulate some literature.

The sympathy of the Highway clientele was clearly with Bergman; they had already suffered understaffing and high prices in every other store on the block. Knowing this, Bergman displayed himself at his window, immaculately dressed in a suit that he claimed was his own brand but that in truth was not, and waved to those customers who needed a little encouragement before crossing a picket line. Periodically, he opened his door and shook his fist at the

3

subversives while shouting some patriotic slogan. This drew shouts of approval from the more vocal pedestrians.

The frankfurter vendor, a gray-haired man with a three-day growth of beard and a hoarse, abused voice, sensed the crowd's hunger as lunch hour approached. He brought his bicycle cart to rest at the curb, adjusted his disposable paper hat and began the singsong that had years ago destroyed his voice: "Kosher franks. Knishes. Franks and kraut!" A cluster formed around the vendor as people thrust money at him, pressing to grab a frankfurter in return. Even the five pickets wavered as the scent of spice and sauerkraut reached them. But they stood their ground, in principle and in hunger, waiting for lunch hour to swell their ranks.

This battle zone was Madeleine Blumfeld's destination as she and her friend Ruth Kosnik walked together up the subway steps into the bright sunshine. When they approached the store, Ruth, her round face downcast, went to the rear of the throng and squeezed onto the end of a bench by the curb. There she took out the sandwich she'd brought and began to eat with a total absorption that blocked out everything around her. Madeleine accompanied her friend long enough to deposit her purse and books in Ruth's safekeeping; then wordlessly she pushed her way through the hecklers and walked up to Stan Landis, the tall leader of the group. He nodded acknowledgment of her presence and gave her a pack of leaflets she'd helped write. Circulating out from the line, she tried to hand the leaflets to passersby. She didn't have much success. The only person who took a leaflet threw it down and called her a Nazi. She headed back to the pickets.

When Madeleine had taken her place, she glanced down the line. Natalie Irmscher was the only other woman there. Natalie was there because Stan was her lover. She'd dressed for the occasion in a dirndl skirt and peasant blouse pushed off the shoulders. Natalie radiated a voluptuous womanly beauty Madeleine envied. Madeleine was aware that she herself was attractive in her own right. Her face had potential: small nose, high cheekbones, lips just thick enough to be inviting. She could become voluptuous. But standing in line with her proper coed skirt and blouse, her hair pulled back in a ponytail, Madeleine knew she looked not sensual, but cute. She hated it.

Natalie gazed absently in front of her, noticing nothing. Madeleine guessed she was composing a sonnet, or pretending to compose a sonnet. Natalie fancied herself a poet, but spent most of her time playing the part of a poet, which left little time to actually write. Madeleine had seen some of her work. A semester of English Literature at CCNY had elevated her to critic in Natalie's eyes, so she couldn't avoid seeing the work. The poems were pleasant, like greeting cards; but then, so was Natalie. Madeleine had decided that it was Stan's convictions Natalie felt, having none of her own.

The couple lived in an apartment in the Village. Natalie wrote her poetry and worked doing secretarial jobs for the Party. Stan was a sculptor and a Party organizer. The very wickedness of their lifestyle had attracted Madeleine to them. They lived and loved with a freedom she coveted. She'd met Stan Landis her first month at college when he was on campus passing out leaflets explaining the Communist side of the civil war in China. She'd made the mistake of meeting his eyes, and he'd grabbed her with his massive sculptor's hands and shoved a leaflet in front of her face. Intimidated, she had read it. When she looked up from the leaflet, he had begun to speak to her in his gentle bass voice. She'd been mesmerized. That same afternoon she'd accompanied him to a café in the Village where his group, the PPC, Political Philosophy Club, met informally every afternoon. It wasn't until she'd come to the Bleecker Café several times that she realized Stan Landis was actually a card-carrying member of the Party. Around that time she fell in love—not with Stan, but with the Revolution. And the Revolution had brought her to Bergman's.

As she stood in line, the smell of frankfurters reminded

Madeleine that she hadn't had time to eat. A hunger head-ache eased its way up her neck. The hecklers, who were becoming more raucous, irritated her, they and the idiot who had called her a Nazi. She glanced back at Ruth, who had finished her sandwich and was now pretending to read. Ruth irritated her too: Ruth who always sat on the edge of things and waited. A voice shouted again that they were Nazis. Madeleine tensed, prepared for confrontation and took a step forward, but Stan tapped her on the shoulder. He pointed in front of them.

A young man stood before the picket line, hesitating to cross it. The hecklers turned to him, sensing a potential show in his hesitation. Madeleine tried to size him up. He was well built, in his late twenties at least, and though he was pale, he had the body of someone who had done phys-ical labor. His black beard accentuated a pale face and eyes so brown they seemed black. He wore a skullcap, which blended in with his dark hair. And from his hairline a scar ran to his left eyebrow. It was an ugly scar, similar to so many she'd seen on the veterans returning from the war. But the man before her was no veteran. His beard and skullcap gave him away, as did his uniform of white shirt and dark pants. He was a yeshiva boy, someone who had spent his entire life in a religious academy, exploiting the goodwill of others while he sat all day and pored over obsolete texts. Madeleine smiled to herself. Here was some-one she could intimidate easily. His eyes scanned the line and settled on her. She met his gaze and saw the eyebrow under the scar rise slightly.

"Just what do you think you're doing?" Madeleine said.

The eyebrow came down. "I thought I was going to buy a shirt," he said.

He had a strong voice, not what Madeleine had expected. Still, she looked at him with disdain. His face had that undernourished pallor yeshiva boys cultivated so carefully.

"This is a picket line," Madeleine said drily. "To buy a shirt you'll have to cross it."

"I need a shirt."

"I thought it was illegal to have more than one shirt if you studied at a yeshiva," Madeleine snapped. Stan, next to her, chuckled, making her smile involuntarily.

"No," the young man said, his eyes not moving from her. "We're allowed to have two—one to wear while we wash the other—once a year."

Stan chuckled at his remark too, as did a few of the spectators. Madeleine realized they'd become the center of attention.

"Bergman is a blatant capitalist who makes his money by exploiting his workers."

"I don't see any workers."

"You can't cross the picket line."

"Why not?" he asked, his voice slightly louder, playing to the crowd.

"Come on," she said softly. "Jews don't cross picket lines."

"What? I don't think I heard you."

"I said, Jews don't cross picket lines!" That drew boos mixed with scattered clapping and even more attention.

"Oh." The young man closed his eyes and stroked his beard as he chanted in an unintelligible singsong. The throng quieted further. He opened his eyes. "I'm impressed. I can't recall anywhere in the Shulchan Aruch, or even the Mishna Torah, where it states that Jews don't cross picket lines. Perhaps we can study together and you can show me the proof text."

"I'd love to show you what you can do with your proof text, Yeshiva Boy." Whistles of approval followed her statement, egging her on. Her heart pounded, and she felt the crowd closing in on them.

The young man stroked his beard again and then pointed his finger casually upward. "But the Torah does dictate that I need a shirt. Of that I'm sure."

"Buy it somewhere else," Madeleine said.

"Bergman has the cheapest prices in Brooklyn."

"Ah, so that's what the Torah boils down to: the cheapest prices in town. It's cheap because he exploits his workers." Madeleine stopped. She'd have been more effective if she'd left it at the Torah. She hated debating.

As she had known he would, the yeshiva boy ignored the first part of her statement. *"You,"* he accused, "are exploiting *me.*" He turned to the crowd, held up his right hand and pointed to the frayed sleeve.

"I need a shirt," he said. "I can barely afford a shirt at Bergman's. Now she"—he pointed at Madeleine for emphasis—"wants me to go without the shirt I need. And I notice she's well dressed."

The people, now on his side, began to boo. They called out for the Commies to let him pass. Stan scowled at Madeleine. The young man signaled the people to quiet down and turned back to Madeleine.

"Tell you what," he said. "You want me to make a commitment to your worker friends, right?"

"I just want you to stay away from the picket line, Yeshiva Boy," Madeleine said. She hated him. The whole confrontation had become a circus.

"You want me to commit myself to being shirtless." He paused, then shouted so the crowd would hear. "How committed are *you?*"

Madeleine hesitated, confused. She looked at Stan who shrugged. "I beg your pardon?"

"How committed are you?"

"I am completely and wholly committed to the cause of the worker and the Revolution," she said. He was setting a trap, that she knew.

"Do you like me?" he asked, and smiled.

"I can't stand the sight of you, Yeshiva Boy."

"Good," he said, as if she'd answered a question correctly. "I want to learn more about Communism. I won't cross the picket line if you will have dinner with me tonight." The crowd cheered.

"You've got to be kidding."

"I'm serious," he said. "Are you?"

"I am not a chattel. Part of what the Revolution will bring for women is—"

"Now, wait a minute. I'm a pious man with no ulterior motives. I don't want a chattel, I want to discuss political theory."

"From your, what, Shulchan Aruch?" she asked, sneering.

"From Shulchan Aruch, from Marx, nu? You'd miss a chance to gain a convert to your Revolution? Think how far Trotsky went."

"Trotsky was an idiot, and so are you."

"Okay." He shrugged and shook his head. "If you're sure, just let me through to buy a shirt." He pushed past.

Stan leaned over to her. "Go out with him," he whispered.

"What did you say?"

"Look at the crowd. This is human interest. What if you can convince him? Just think of what it could mean tomorrow."

"Stan." Her whisper was hoarse with the control it took not to scream at him. "What the hell are you talking about? He's making fun of us."

"Go out with him—quick, before he gets to the store. That's an order."

The yeshiva student had crossed through and was about to be welcomed by a smiling Bergman.

"Wait!" Madeleine shouted. "I'll go out with you." The crowd applauded as she glared at Stan, who could not keep from smiling. The young man turned back, and Bergman's face fell.

"So what's your name, Yeshiva Boy?"

"Aaron Stern. And yours?"

"Madeleine Blumfeld. I'll meet you in front of the Avenue P Diner at six." She glared at Stan again. "To discuss political theory."

"Fine," Aaron said, and walked away.

"Hey, Stern!" Madeleine yelled. "How come you can't

afford to buy a shirt from a decent store, but you can take me out to dinner?"

Aaron turned and grinned wickedly. "I forgot to tell you. We go Dutch." With that he disappeared among the on-lookers.

Now that the excitement was over, the crowd broke up and Ruth became visible once more. She stood and started slowly away, the signal that it was time for Madeleine to come back to school. For once, Madeleine was grateful to be leaving her comrades. She looked at Stan, who had walked quickly over to Natalie, avoiding her. Then she made her way through the clumps of remaining gawkers and out into the street. She met Ruth at the subway stop and took her things.

"I can't believe that guy," Madeleine said.

"I thought he was kind of cute," Ruth said, giggling.

"Kind of cute. Ruth, get serious."

Madeleine's friend sighed and led the way down the steps. She moved quickly in spite of her hefty build, so Madeleine had to hurry to catch up. They sat next to each other on the train, forced into silence by the roar of the subway. Ruth opened one of her textbooks, trying to make use of the time, but Madeleine stared at the black beyond the window.

She thought about Stan. Who was he to give orders? Party discipline. Well, she wasn't a member of the Party yet, and she was going to make that clear to him the next time she saw him. What if this man was a pervert? Images of her broken body rattled through her head in time with the sway-ing of the train. Madeleine broke the silence.

"Hey!" she shouted in Ruth's ear. "You don't think this Stern is weird, do you?"

"Madeleine, all he thinks about is Talmud. He's a yeshiva boy."

"So? They're maybe exempt from being weird?"

"I wouldn't worry," Ruth said.

"Of course not. You're not going out with him." Ma-deleine settled back to stare at the window again.

Stan had pawned her off, like a prize for good behavior. That wasn't the way it was supposed to be. They were supposed to be comrades. A dozen slogans came to mind, which in turn made her think of Illi. Who, thank goodness, wasn't there. But still, crazy as Illi was, he wouldn't have pawned her off just to make points with the lunch crowd. For all Stan's talk about Revolution, what he wanted was a warm body for the Party. Nothing more.

And her parents wanted nothing more than a doctor or lawyer son-in-law and scads of grandchildren. But Madeleine wanted more. She wanted greatness. Her parents, her sisters, even Ruth kept asking her what she wanted to be. But she couldn't tell them. She sensed in herself a potential for greatness that surpassed the lives her sisters led, surpassed the children and the "better neighborhoods" and the nice cars. It was a greatness that propelled her past the boundaries her father would have liked to set up for her, or the role society expected of her. She was going to take on society and win. The Russians, at least, had known how to dream the great dream, the Revolution. There was her end. There her greatness would be achieved. Someday, she thought, the Revolution would come to Brooklyn. The battle would begin here and she would lead it.

In her mind she saw herself running along Ocean Parkway, dodging barricades, gunshots and barbed wire. Today, she led her Red Army squad on an important mission—up ahead, a key position was still in the hands of the enemy. Stan had tried to take out the gun emplacement, but had failed and lay wounded near his objective off Avenue M. Knowing Stan was in trouble, she raced ahead of her squad as the shrapnel exploded around her, knocking her to the ground; she rose again and kept running. She fought hand to hand, downing three of the enemy, the spirit of the Revolution giving her strength. When she finally reached Stan, he pointed weakly to the bomb he'd tried to throw at the gun emplacement. She scooped it up and ran to the enemy, who were shooting furiously. Just as she threw, she was hit in the arm, but it was too late for the oppressors. The bomb exploded along with the gun emplacement. Bleeding, she dragged herself back to Stan and took him in her arms. There he died, the look of admiration frozen in his dead eyes.

The subway lurched, bringing Madeleine back from her daydream. She felt a little guilty about killing off Stan, but he certainly deserved it today. She smiled and sighed. The train came to a screeching halt at their stop. With thoughts of revolution and vindication still in her mind, Madeleine went to class.

Ruth met her later in the day. They sat together while Madeleine finally ate the sandwich she'd brought for lunch. Madeleine had been friends with Ruth since they were children. As they grew up, Ruth had always let Madeleine mold her according to Madeleine's particular idea or belief of the moment. Madeleine took satisfaction in having gotten Ruth to attend CCNY, something she was sure Ruth never would have done on her own. But Stan and his group had proved too much for Ruth, and now, with Madeleine immersed in the group's activities, they found time for each other only in snatches: on the fire escape at night, between classes, or shouting on the subway.

"Well," Madeleine said, biting into the salami sandwich. "It looks like you go home alone tonight." She brightened. "Unless you want to stay and go out with me."

"No, it's your date," Ruth said. "Besides, I have things to do."

"Oh? Assignments?"

"Sort of," Ruth said. She looked uneasy and began to finger the pages of the book on her lap, but she said nothing more until Madeleine had crumpled up the waxed paper from her finished sandwich.

"Madeleine," she said. "I wish you would stop doing all this stuff. I don't think it can lead to anything good."

"What? Going out with a yeshiva boy? I agree."

"No, not that. All this picketing and demonstrating. Your group. It's just a front for the Communist Party, you know."

"You sound like the rightist papers."

"I don't care what I sound like. You know that group is a front. They brag about it when they're among themselves."

"All right, it's a Communist front. So what?" Madeleine looked smugly at Ruth. "I've been thinking about joining the Party anyway."

Ruth did not look the least bit shocked. "That would be a mistake," she said.

"You just don't understand."

"Explain, then."

"You still wouldn't understand," Madeleine said.

"Try me."

Madeleine threw the crumpled paper in the trash can next to them. "Don't you hate being just what your parents want you to be?"

"No."

"See, I knew you wouldn't understand."

"Madeleine, you haven't told me anything yet!"

"I want to be more than a memorial candle my kids light for me once a year, if they can remember the date. I mean you should see my kitchen, you know? Mama tries to remember all the people that died in the family, but she can't, so every six months her kitchen looks like a cathedral."

"I think that's beautiful," Ruth said.

"It's awful. I didn't know any of those people, and frankly, sometimes I get the feeling even Mama can't remember their names anymore. They're just these candles that burn out after twenty-four hours. I want more than that."

"You want to be famous," Ruth said.

"No! More than that. There are people suffering all over this country, exploited people. I want to be one of the ones who free them."

"How?"

"With the Revolution."

"And how is the Revolution going to free them?"

Madeleine frowned. "You don't try to understand at all."

Ruth looked at her, her eyes reflecting emotions she couldn't articulate, a sadness that Madeleine recognized.

"All your friends," Ruth said, "they talk, talk, talk. How are you going to save the world with talk? I went with you to Stan's place, remember? When you were still telling me they were a 'philosophy club.'" She eyed Madeleine, who shrugged.

"I went with you," Ruth continued, "and everyone pulled me aside with his own opinion on how to save the world. Each opinion was different and each one seemed right. I listened and listened until they all seemed wrong. These people aren't going to be remembered any more than your second cousins. You can't change the world by dreaming and talking. You have to do something."

"I am doing something," Madeleine said. "I'm working for the Revolution."

"In Brooklyn?"

"Of course in Brooklyn. Brooklyn is as good a place as Peking."

"And whose revolution?" Ruth asked. "Stalin's?"

"Why not?"

"He's killing Jews, you know."

"That's propaganda, capitalist propaganda. That's just about as true as the man who called me a Nazi today. Where are you picking up all this?" Madeleine's eyes narrowed. Ruth looked away a moment, then met Madeleine's gaze.

"I'm going to my own meeting tonight," she said. "In all these weeks, Madeleine, you've never once asked me what I was doing with my time. I waited for you to ask, but you've been so wrapped up in yourself—"

"In the Revolution."

"—in the Revolution. Oh, Madeleine. There is no Revolution!"

"There is! Can't you see that? Is everyone so blind? In Russia, in China, in Greece. It's all the Revolution. I'm part of it. Damn it, you're my friend; can't you believe in me?"

"I've always believed in you," Ruth said softly. "I'm just afraid you've spent so much time dreaming you'll wake up to a nightmare."

"I don't know what's gotten into you."

"I've been trying to tell you. I joined the Young Pioneers."

"The Zionists? How . . . when?" She didn't wait for Ruth to answer. "So you're getting all this from the Zionists. Why would they tell you all that propaganda? The Soviets support a Jewish state."

"So far. But they hate their own Jews. And they'll change about us, too."

"You joined the Young Pioneers and you didn't tell me anything?"

"You didn't ask," Ruth said. "And I didn't want to subject myself to another political diatribe. You're really hard to talk to these days."

Madeleine stared at the ground before her. Ruth had gone and done something on her own. She'd never done anything without consulting Madeleine, without some sort of approval. Now she'd gone off and joined a reactionary group. Madeleine realized that she had lost touch with her friend. This was not the Ruth she was used to dealing with.

"The Soviets don't hate Jews," Madeleine said.

"They do. If you would only open your eyes. Ben says—"

"Wait. Who's Ben?"

Ruth blushed. "He's a boy I met."

Madeleine smiled with relief. Clarity had returned, the world was back in order and Ruth Kosnik was still Ruth. She's joined the Zionists because of a boy. Now, that was a Ruth Kosnik reason for doing something.

"Well, this Ben character is wrong," Madeleine said. "Ruth, I wish you'd start thinking for yourself."

"I am thinking for myself, probably for the first time. I'm a Zionist, and I want to emigrate to Palestine."

"With Ben?"

"With Ben."

"And has this Ben asked you yet?"

"Yes."

Ruth gathered her books and stood. "I have to go. I have

homework to do before the meeting. Listen, why don't you come to one of *my* meetings for a change? It would give you an excuse to ditch the yeshiva boy."

"No, thanks. I am not now, nor will I ever be Zionist."

"I didn't think you'd come, but I owed it to myself to ask."

"What does that mean?"

"Never mind," Ruth said. "Have fun on your date to-night."

Madeleine watched her friend walk away. She experienced a new sensation: loneliness. She hadn't imagined Ruth doing anything in these last weeks. Ruth the faithful. Madeleine had just naturally expected her to be around, always.

There was a deeper sense of loneliness, too. She couldn't make Ruth understand. It agonized her to see things so clearly and have them blur as soon as she tried to explain to anyone. It was a vision of herself that she'd had since her childhood. A Joan of Arc, a martyr for a glorious cause. She felt she wasn't destined to have home and family. She wasn't destined for long life. She was destined for greatness.

And Ruth? What if she did go off to Palestine? No. Madeleine shook her head. Ruth wasn't the pioneer or martyr type. Madeleine heard the church bell ring four times. Two hours until she had to meet the weirdo.

Aaron entered the Liberal Rabbinical School of Brooklyn, greeted by the strains of "Three Blind Mice" played badly and accompanied by out-of-rhythm creaks from a ballet room on the floor above. The Liberal Rabbinical School shared its refurbished public school building with a so-called music academy. The school was too small to have its own building, and now after ten years it was still too small. A decade of use had not eliminated the public school odor about the building, a scent of perspiration and crayons still penetrated through the pipe smoke of the seminarians.

Aaron walked down the hallway to the rows of mailboxes outside the library. Box 21 had been his mailbox for three years now. Its brass coating had a permanent thumbprint smudge created by some student who had come and passed on. The brass around the smudge was shinier, a witness to the efforts at exorcising the thumbprint. But the print endured, a dark shadow on the lower left. It made Aaron's box stand out from the others. Something he thought fitting.

Peeking inside, Aaron saw a single thin envelope. His father had written, responding to the letter sent a week ago, and leaving Aaron once more with the burden of correspondence. Aaron knew his father dutifully sat down and wrote immediately on receiving a letter. He often wondered what came first, the writing of the reply or the opening of the letter. It was possible that Yehezkel Stern never opened the letters. His responses never connected with the inane ramblings Aaron sent. It was just as well, because the inane ramblings had no connection with Aaron's life.

If Aaron took the letter out, he would have to open it. If he opened it, he would have to read it and then begin the monthlong process of writing another letter. He closed the mailbox instead, and went into the library. He sat down at his place by the window, the bright light due him by seniority, and opened a text. But he couldn't calm his mind; it kept wandering back to Bergman's and all the far more brilliant things he should have said. Still, he hadn't done a bad job. Aaron chuckled out loud, then looked down to the book to avoid the disapproving stare from the man seated next to him. What he had done at Bergman's was totally out of character—or rather, the concept here of his character. All the seminarians expected him to be pious. They sat with heads uncovered, studying sacred books, and judged his piety.

And why not? He demanded judgment from them, he who sat among them in his ritual fringes and his beard. He sat among these reformers, reminding them of what they had so long ago given up. They accepted him because their rules demanded they accept all forms of religious expression, the traditional as well as the experimental. The Great

Reform demanded openness, but its practitioners weren't really open. Aaron had brought the ghetto into their midst, and they accepted him, because to thrust him away would be to thrust away part of themselves. But he was a relic among the sages of modernity: sages who had actually, at one time, thought to change the Sabbath to Sunday to be more in tune with America. With his fringes and beard, with his head always covered, he reminded them that part of them would never be in tune with America. He reminded them of the ghetto, and of the camps, and of the crematoria. But they kept him and would ordain him as a liberal rabbi and part of the Great Reform because they had a moral responsibility. They only hoped there would be no more like him to follow and trouble them.

Aaron's thoughts went to the letter resting in the mailbox. His mother would have written him thick letters, filled with tales and omens, signs to portend every possibility. She'd written him such letters when he was in the Army, thick letters filled with amulets and warnings that proved powerless against the evil he faced. And maybe in another time and place his father's letters would have been filled with questions about his studies and quotes from Talmud passages.

But Risa Stern was dead, and Yehezkel Stern did not want to know of his son's studies. Aaron had left his father's traditions, the traditions of the Loemer Hasidim. The son had joined the father's enemies, and Yehezkel didn't want to know of it. Father and son saw each other once a year for Risa's memorial service. The meeting, and the graveside visitation, memorialized not only Risa's death, but the death of Yehezkel's dreams. It was during the period of mourning for Risa that Aaron had finally told his father he would be leaving.

Aaron leaned back in his chair, balancing on the two rear legs. The heat from the radiator had reached through his shirt to his skin, distracting him. He rocked back and forth on the chair. His mother had supposedly died of cancer, but he knew better. He had been her only hold on life and sanity.

She'd started dying when he went off to the war. Even Yehezkel had admitted that Risa had known the moment Aaron had been wounded. She awoke screaming from the nightmare, gripping her head in horror.

Risa Stern, half-mad, a superstitious woman who sought enlightenment and found only demons in the darkness. She prayed alone on the Sabbath and went to fortune-tellers during the week in search of gods in whom she could believe. When Aaron came home from the hospital she filled his room with amulets. He still remembered coming out of nightmares, feeling her cool hand across the burning scar and hearing her voice soothing him with incantations he couldn't recognize. She warded off the demon Asmodeus and kept Machlaat from snuffing out his life. She gave him her strength and love until he was well. Then, as if she had taken his death upon herself, she sank into illness—a cancer no one had noticed, and a quiet, surprisingly fast death.

The first week of mourning and its attendant rituals had kept Aaron and his father occupied. Afterward, during the thirty-day period, there was the store to be managed and Yehezkel's life to rearrange, adjusting him to meals that had to be cooked, a house that needed keeping. In the end, Aaron hired a housekeeper. Yehezkel accepted Aaron's presence as a given, and the day came when Aaron knew he must leave now or stay forever. In the clothing store, among the racks of suits, he had told his father his plans.

"Where are you going?" Yehezkel had asked. "Your mother is barely in the grave. Where are you going?"

"To New York," Aaron said.

"I thought you'd stay with me in the store."

Aaron moved a suit back into its proper section. "I'm going to attend a school there. They're giving me a scholarship. I'll get disability from the Army too."

"Are you well enough?" Yehezkel's round face was pale with worry and mourning. "And what school is this?"

"It's called the Liberal Rabbinical School. It's a small place in Brooklyn."

"A yeshiva?"

"No."

"Liberal Rabbinical School." Yehezkel said the name over a few times until the meaning of the words sank in. A brief flash of hatred crossed his face.

"Reform," Yehezkel said. "They are worse than Gentiles. How can you do this?"

"Dad, please try to understand. I can't be what you want me to be."

"You never tried. She poisoned your mind."

"Mother never poisoned my mind. I'm not a Hasid. And I'm not a rebbe."

"You. You won't even be a Jew," Yehezkel said with contempt.

"Well, I'll never be a rebbe, that's for sure," Aaron said, his anger flaring in spite of himself. He held his arms out at his sides. "Look at me! I'm no mystic seer. I don't perform miracles. I don't see into souls. I am not the next Loemer Rebbe."

"You're the only survivor. In you is all of Loem. You can't deny it or turn away. All the Loemer Hasidim are in you, and if you set foot in that place you will murder all the Loemers again. You will do what the Nazis have done. Liberal Rabbinical School"—he spat out the words. "What gives you the right to stop being a Loemer Hasid?"

"I was never a Loemer," Aaron said. "I don't know the town of Loem. Here is what I know, Chicago. I don't know about the Great Rebbe and Miracle Worker, the Seer and Righteous One, Avram Levi." Aaron said the words mimicking his father's voice.

"You mock me."

"No. I'm only trying to make you see."

"I saw!" Yehezkel said. "I saw the miracles of the rebbe."

"You told me tales I enjoyed as a child."

"You had faith as a child," Yehezkel snapped. "I was there. I saw such things. What? You think you will achieve greatness as a reform rabbi?"

"No. But I don't want greatness. I don't want to be a

wonder-working rebbe. I want to be a rabbi, simply that. I can't believe in your tales, and all the witnesses are dead."

"You could have seen with your own eyes if you'd had the courage. If she had let you go."

"Mother saved my life. You still don't see that. You wanted to send me to Loem so I could dig my own grave with the others."

"God would have saved you," Yehezkel said.

"God would have buried me. The Nazis were already there and still you wanted me to go."

"You would have known your Rebbe."

"That's all you ever cared about, isn't it?" Aaron said.

"You have a destiny. You have no right to give it up."

Aaron pointed his finger at Yehezkel. It was shaking. "You, Father. You were the last Loemer. What gave *you* the right?"

Yehezkel looked down from his son's accusing gaze. He touched his own clean-shaven face, proof of the first broken commandment; then he reached up and cradled Aaron's bearded cheeks in his hands. "The rebbe sent me away," he said, his voice beseeching. "Avram Levi sent me away. I would have stayed with him in Loem forever. But he sent me to this exile. Finally. Finally, after years of wondering, I realized what the rebbe had intended. The rebbe was a seer. He knew even then, even when you were a baby."

"Please, Dad. Stop."

"He saw the destruction even then, don't you see? He made me go to my cousin in America so you would survive. So you would bring Loem back to its glory. Don't you see that?"

Aaron took his father's hands by the wrists and pulled them from his face. "Enough. There is no glory. Nobody even heard of Loem in Russia. I can't be what you want me to be. I can't redeem you, Dad. Give it up!"

"She poisoned you. Risa's madness poisoned you. She was an idol worshiper and I allowed it, so it corrupted you."

"She believed more than you did. Even when you wore

the black coat of the Hasidim—even then she believed more."

"In what?" Yehezkel asked. "In gypsies and in fortune-telling cards. I should burn them."

"The cards and amulets are mine. Mother gave them to me and you will not touch them," Aaron said. Yehezkel backed away from the darkness in Aaron's voice.

"She corrupted you. She was mad."

"And what drove her mad? Loem! Loem made her a crazy woman searching for God with gypsies. Loem that never let her sing, or dance or laugh. The Great Loemer Rebbe and all his Hasidim drove her mad. Your infidelity drove her mad!"

Yehezkel looked at his son in horror. "I was never unfaithful."

"You were never faithful," Aaron said. "You could never love my mother completely because you always yearned for your Rebbe."

"I was a Hasid. That's the way of a Hasid."

"Thirty years. She endured Avram Levi's picture on her mantel for thirty years. I endured it for thirty years, those dead eyes staring at me."

"Don't you dare speak that way of the rebbe!"

"Tell me. Do you have a picture of my mother? Do you have a single photograph of your wife?"

"Stop!"

"And yet," Aaron continued, "you weren't completely faithful to your rebbe, were you? She told me. She told me how even in the yeshiva you burned for her. You wanted Risa the Heretic, who danced in front of the yeshiva to lure away yeshiva boys."

"She tempted me."

"You were consumed with her."

"So I married her," Yehezkel said.

"Because the rebbe told you to. Your rebbe gave you his blessing, then sent you away."

Yehezkel turned away. "You want me to say that my

rebbe made a mistake. You fool. His eyes were like flames. His eyes saw a man's soul. You are blind. You never felt his love, the love he had for all his Hasidim." Yehezkel turned back. He struck his chest. "The love he had for me! I was a Loemer Hasid, do you hear me? I ate bread from the Rebbe's table. I danced with him until I saw Heaven open for me! Who am I to fathom the mysteries of such a man? I know what was destined, what I am supposed to do. What *you* are supposed to do."

Aaron sighed, his anger gone. "I'm flawed," he said quietly. "Not with the flaws of Risa the Heretic. It's your faults I carry. You couldn't be a true Hasid—not then, not now. You're the one who shaved your beard. You took off your skullcap, and you stopped praying. You don't have the strength to be a Hasid, Dad. And I don't have the faith to be a rebbe. Mother has nothing to do with it."

"Then be nothing. Don't take all that is Loem and turn it into a Reform rabbi. Why must you do that?"

"Because I can't do anything else. Loem burned to the ground with the Jews of Europe. I'm searching for a way to believe in God in the face of that." Aaron smiled. "I'm taking my fortune-telling cards to go searching among the gypsies for something to believe."

"*Don't* believe, then!" Yehezkel shouted. "Not that way. You have no right to believe that way."

"I'm going, Dad." Aaron walked to the door. "I'll write when I get to New York."

"Don't go!" Yehezkel shouted. "Better to deny everything than go to them. Be nothing rather than that. Please!"

Aaron had left his father, that day, shouting after him. There were no shouts now. Between them now was a strained quiet, endured once a year. Aaron looked around him in the library. These were strange gypsies. Risa's fortune-telling cards lay half-forgotten in a dresser drawer. And after three years, after Kant, after Heidegger, after Buber, he still had no answers.

All he had was questions, and a date with a modern

heretic, Madeleine, the Communist with eyes that burned like his mother's.

When they met, Aaron talked Madeleine into an early movie and paid for both of them. He'd suggested *Anna Karenina,* poking fun once more at Madeleine's politics. But since she wanted to see the film, she ignored his jest and they went. For all his mockery, Madeleine noticed tears in Aaron's eyes when the lights came back on in the theater. After the movie they strolled to a nearby delicatessen.

The two walked together in an uncomfortable silence. Madeleine clutched her purse and stared resolutely ahead. All the bravado of the day vanished when she had to face Aaron alone. Aaron, for his part, walked with his hands in his pockets, watching the cracks in the sidewalk.

"Do you always pick up girls?" Madeleine asked finally.

"Would you believe I've never done anything remotely like that before?"

"No," Madeleine said.

"I never have," Aaron said.

"Then why did you do it?"

"I don't really know."

"You sure have a lot fewer answers now than you did this afternoon."

"I was pretty good, wasn't I?" he said, smiling.

"I thought you were an ass."

"But I'm not."

"Well," Madeleine said. "I admit you are different from any other Orthodox boy I've ever met. Just as obnoxious, but different."

"It must be because I'm not Orthodox."

"Oh, you wear the skullcap to hide a bald spot."

"Honestly, I go to the Liberal Rabbinical School on Thirty-eighth and Avenue Q. You can check me out."

"Then why do you look like an escapee from a yeshiva?"

"I went to one once," he said. "My family was Orthodox."

"And you go to the Liberal Rabbinical School."

"Yes."

"But they don't believe"—she indicated his dress—"in that."

"No, they don't."

"Then why dress like that?"

"Everyone is a revolutionary in his own way."

"You aren't a revolutionary, you're an atavism," she said. Aaron laughed.

When they reached the delicatessen, Aaron opened the door for her. She walked into a blast of heat from the warming tables under the display counter, which was accompanied by an overwhelming smell of corned beef. They sat and perused the menu in silence. Madeleine had figured out that Aaron intended to pay for her, despite his earlier words. She was torn between the desire to order the most expensive item on the menu, just to watch him squirm, and her worry that he really didn't have any money, but would buy anything out of pride.

Her touch of compassion bothered her. It had not been part of the scenario she'd worked out for dealing with Aaron Stern. The other thing bothering her was that Ruth had been correct. Aaron was cute. No. More than that. He was a man, a handsome man, far more attractive than the boys she'd dated in the past. She sneaked another look at him, then compromised and ordered a roast-beef sandwich. Aaron did also, so she relaxed.

"If you really do go to the Liberal Rabbinical School," Madeleine said, "which I'm still not sure I believe, your parents must be furious."

"My mother died a while back," he said. "And you could say my father isn't exactly pleased."

"My father isn't too pleased with what I do either," she said.

"I can imagine," Aaron said. He leaned his chin on his hand. "So tell me about yourself."

"That isn't political theory," Madeleine answered.

"I have to know if my teacher is worthy. Let's start with

an easy question. What does this father of yours who isn't pleased with your revolutionary endeavors do for a living?"

"My father, Vellef, is a house painter—very bourgeois now, with his own firm and paint store. I have two older sisters, both married, both bourgeois. My mother is—"

"Bourgeois," Aaron finished.

The waiter came with pickles and the drinks they had ordered. Madeleine waited for him to leave and sipped her Cel-Ray.

"No," she said. "My mother isn't bourgeois."

"Oh? Is she a revolutionary too?"

"Please stop making fun of me."

"I'm sorry," Aaron said.

Madeleine looked at him a long moment before she spoke. "Well, she wants me to get married—preferably to a doctor; and she lives for her grandchildren, cooks, cleans all day in case anyone should come. You know the type. Even so, I can't think of her as bourgeois." She hesitated, taking another sip of the soda, watching for Aaron's reactions. He just watched and waited.

"She lost her family in the Revolution—Russian Revolution, that is," Madeleine said. "I mean literally lost them. They got separated during a Cossack raid and she never found them again. My father discovered her wandering half-starved in the forest. They made it out of Russia together, got married on the way. She was only fifteen."

"What was your father doing?"

"I don't know. He never really talks about it. I have a feeling, though, that he was conducting his own private war. My father would do that."

"For which side?" Aaron asked.

"Against both."

Aaron smiled. "Your father doesn't sound very bourgeois either."

The waiter returned with sandwiches. The two said nothing for the few minutes it took to satisfy their hunger. Madeleine felt a sense of relief at Aaron's smile.

"What about you?" she asked. "You're not from New York."

"Chicago."

"Chicago? No Jew is from Chicago."

"Well," Aaron said. "I was born in Loem, a small town in Galicia. My parents emigrated when I was a couple of years old and came to New York—naturally. My father worked for a cousin in the clothing business. Eventually, they opened a store in Chicago, so we went there. Very bourgeois."

"You're making fun of me again," Madeleine said lightly, but it didn't really bother her anymore. "What else?"

"I'm twenty-eight. I have one more year of rabbinical school after this. And in spite of my father's clothing business, I still need a shirt. That's about it. I'm a very boring person."

"Somehow I don't believe that. If you don't talk, I'll have to ask rude questions."

"Ask." Aaron bit into his sandwich, turning his head downward as he did. Madeleine noticed the scar once again.

"Okay. Where did you get the scar? Bumping into the Talmud?"

"No," he said still chewing. "Got that in the war."

"Oh," Madeleine said, turning red. She said nothing more and shoved a pickle into her mouth. Aaron noticed her embarrassment.

"Please, don't feel uncomfortable. It's nothing dark and mysterious. I have no permanent damage beyond losing the ability to be a pro baseball player."

"Don't tell me you were planning to play baseball."

"Never. But I do get a pension that helps me through school, and I got mustered out of the Army early. For that, I am extremely grateful. By the time I was wounded, I'd discovered that I really didn't like being in a war at all." He went back to eating, dismissing the subject.

"Why don't you dress like a normal person?"

"I am dressed like a normal person."

"Not who goes to the Liberal Rabbinical School you're not. I suppose you get up at the crack of dawn to say your morning prayers too."

"Somewhere after the crack of dawn, to be honest."

"Why?"

Aaron put down his sandwich. He looked at her, his dark eyes serious. "I do what I do to remind myself that I live in two worlds. Just like you."

Madeleine stopped her reply before it passed her lips. "Lots of times I dress just like them," she said finally.

"But you aren't just like your Communist friends. You're half in their world and half in your own."

"Maybe their world *is* my own," Madeleine said, her irritation returning.

She finished her dinner, concentrating on the food so she wouldn't have to talk. She knew he was watching her, waiting with those dark, deep-set eyes.

"May I walk you home?" he asked after he paid the check.

"That's not necessary," Madeleine said quickly.

"I'd like to," he said.

"No." Madeleine saw his disappointment and softened. "Oh, all right." Then she added, "But just within a block of the house."

"Are you that ashamed of me?" he asked with a smile.

"No, it's not that," Madeleine said. She paused, embarrassed. She knew she sounded like a schoolgirl, but couldn't help it.

"Well?"

"Well, I don't want my father to see you," she blurted.

"Why?"

"He'd approve."

"Is that so bad?"

"Yes. Because it would be a lie," Madeleine said. "I really am a Communist, in spite of what you may think."

"Card-carrying?"

Aaron watched her eyes flash.

"I am not a card-carrying member yet. But I am a Communist. My father would take one look at you and start planning a wedding. That would be a lie. He'd start in about me coming to my senses."

"And that, of course, would be a lie."

"Do you want to walk me home or not?"

As they walked, Madeleine found herself talking again, about family, and school, about some of her favorite books. To her surprise, Aaron had read them. As he walked next to her, she found herself alternately fearing someone would see them and hoping someone would. He was dark and muscular and handsome. He was an older man and he was interested in plain old Madeleine. Still, she made him stop at the end of her block. He turned to her.

"I know you despise the atavistic parts of me," he said. "But is there enough to redeem that you'd go out with me again?"

"Yes," she said quickly, surprising herself. "I mean, well, yes, that would be nice." She giggled. "That would show Stan, wouldn't it?"

"Saturday?"

"Sure," Madeleine said, smiling.

There was an awkward pause between them that in other circumstances might have been filled with a kiss. Then she left him standing in the shadows with his hands in his pockets. When she got inside her building, Madeleine peeked out the windows to the side of the door and watched Aaron as he stood on the corner. She felt uncomfortable, as if he knew she was standing there watching him watch her. Finally, he walked away into the darkness. She made her way up the stairs to her parents' apartment.

When Madeleine entered, Vellef Blumfeld stood, throwing the well-read Yiddish paper onto the couch. He glared at her, saying nothing. She waited patiently for the verbal assault to begin. Vellef, like Stan, the other giant in her life, towered over her, but unlike Stan, her father was thin. His skeletal face now pulled tight into an angry grimace, Vellef Blumfeld was a formidable opponent. They fought nightly. Madeleine, his youngest daughter, had somehow gotten beyond his control. She thought too much for his liking; she dreamed too much; and above all, she was too smart to be a girl. It only got her into trouble.

"So nu, you were out with your Cossacks again tonight?" Vellef asked.

Madeleine smiled. Tonight she'd decided not to get angry. Tonight she had her secret joke on them all. "Papa, my friends aren't Cossacks. They're all Jewish. You know that."

"And that blond muzhik? Did you go out with him?"

"Illi? For goodness' sake, I'd never go out with Illi. He's too strange. Now go to bed. You don't always have to wait up for me."

"Somebody has to wait up for you," he said, glancing toward his darkened bedroom where they both knew Bea Blumfeld pretended to be asleep. "Somebody should lock you up and throw away the key."

He spoke his normal-tone Yiddish. For that she was grateful. When Vellef got really angry, he switched to a pidgin English even she had trouble following.

"I hate to tell you this, Papa," Madeleine said. "But I'm eighteen. I'm all grown up." As if to contradict the statement, she ran up to her father and hugged him.

It took Vellef by surprise. He'd been set for battle. He knew his daughter was manipulating him, but he softened, hugged her briefly, then pulled her away.

"No one is grown up at eighteen," he said.

"You were."

"I was on my own, Maidel." He called her by her Yiddish name. "That is not the same thing. I didn't start growing up until I met your mother. Responsibility makes you grow up. But you, Maidel, you've had none. So you're still a child, or a fool."

Madeleine controlled her anger, remembering her secret. Tonight, without a word, she'd bested him. She kissed her father on the cheek.

"Good night, Papa."

She walked slowly to her room, stifling a giggle. He would probably be up all night, pondering her docile behavior. She got ready for bed, thinking she was tired, but instead she lay awake and thought of Aaron Stern. It would have been nice to talk to Ruth, but her window across the alleyway was dark.

Madeleine's thoughts drifted into and out of the day, then back to Aaron. He had an air of mystery about him, with his war scar and his dark eyes and his black beard. He was black, like the black-hatted Hasidim she saw on her way to school. Slowly, Madeleine floated into sleep.

Aaron Stern walked into his apartment and flopped down on the couch, startling Nathan Schwartz, his unofficial roommate. Nathan, who actually resided in the Liberal Rabbinical School's dormitory, spent most of his time in Aaron's apartment, studying Aaron's library of traditional texts.

"You really did it," Nathan said.

"I told you I would."

"So tell me, how was your Communist?" Nathan asked.

"Very nice. I asked her out again."

"I hope she had the decency to refuse."

"No," Aaron said, smiling. He sat up so he could gloat at Nathan. "She said yes."

Nathan sighed. He stroked the beard he had just started growing and swayed back and forth a few times. "Aaron, what am I going to do with you?"

"I thought I was the big brother around here."

"The fact that you were seven years old when I was born does not make you wise, my friend. I just don't understand you."

"Neither does my father, but he loves me."

"So do I. But the more I study in your books, the more I learn of what you already know from the yeshiva, the less I understand why you are going to that goyishe school."

"Well, now, you seem to have mastered Orthodox prejudices; if only you can master the knowledge with as much speed," Aaron said.

"That doesn't answer the question."

"You didn't ask a question. You asked why I'm going to a Gentile school. I'm not. I'm going to the Liberal Rabbinical School because, unlike the yeshivas I've been to, they let me be the kind of Jew I need to be."

"Instead of the kind of Jew God wants you to be."

"Nathan, don't preach at me. If you think keeping every letter of the Sabbath Laws will bring the Messiah, then you must keep them. I don't. I can't."

"Then why are you helping me?"

"Maybe you'll redeem me," he said. Before Nathan could answer, Aaron leaned over and squinted. "Are those side curls I see?"

Nonplussed, Nathan covered the visible ear with his hand.

"You'd better hide those until you finish the term," Aaron said. "I think the learned faculty of our school would frown— collectively and simultaneously."

"You'd protect me," Nathan said with a chuckle. He took his hand away.

"I certainly would not. I have to make it through one more year—just one more, and I'm home free. Do you think the contemporary and emancipated viewpoint of the Liberal Rabbinical School would allow them to ordain me if they found out I'd totally perverted a boy from a nice Reform background?"

"I perverted myself. You just helped. And I don't care if they throw me out tomorrow. I'm just staying on and finishing the year to be nice to my family—on your advice. And, I might add, as a favor to you."

"Please finish the year. Your family hates me enough as it is."

"They don't hate you," Nathan said. "They hate me . . . I embarrass them when I come home."

"That's because you behave like an asshole."

"Am I supposed to eat unkosher meat?" Nathan said.

"Yes. When in your parents' home. At least for now. My boy, a year ago you ate lobster and several other forbidden foods. Ate them with gusto, as I recall."

"I'm Orthodox now."

"You're overpious now."

"Well, you never had parents like mine," Nathan said.

"I had parents exactly like yours."

"I find that hard to believe. You know, my father doesn't call me his son anymore. He introduces me as his disappointment. I'm not kidding. Does your father say that?"

"My father doesn't say anything," Aaron said. He looked out into the night beyond his window. "He doesn't have to say anything."

"What does that mean?" Nathan asked. But Aaron didn't seem to hear the question. "Anyway," Nathan said louder. "I'm only listening to your advice so I can finish the year studying with you."

"I'm flattered," Aaron said, pulling himself back from the window.

"You should be, you goyishe head. So tell me about your Communist."

"Her name is Madeleine and she's very pretty."

"Jewish?" Nathan asked.

Aaron scowled at him. "Of course she's Jewish."

"With you, who knows? You do crazy things."

"She's pretty, and Jewish, and she's not really a Communist. She just thinks she is."

"Such wisdom he has."

"Are you going to listen or not?"

"Okay. Tell me."

"Her parents are from Russia—not Communists. Her mother sounds lovely and her father sounds fascinating. She has two older sisters—both married, sorry. And I'm in love with her."

The last statement didn't register in Nathan's face until several more seconds had passed. Nathan's round, protruding eyes bulged even more.

"What do you mean, you're in love with her? Never mind. The Holy Bratzlaver Rebbe has ten psalms guaranteed to cool a yeshiva boy's ardor. You just recite them in a shower under cold water."

"I thought I told you to stay away from the Hasidic texts," Aaron said. Nathan shrugged. "You really aren't anywhere near ready for mysticism. Nowhere near," Aaron sighed. "And don't belittle the first brave thing I've ever done. I just walked up to a girl and asked her out. Lust has nothing to do with it." He looked at Nathan, who was smiling. "Or rather, not much."

"Sure," Nathan said. "And I doubt it's the first brave thing you've ever done." Nathan looked at the framed medal on the wall.

Aaron laughed. "You're still in awe of that thing, aren't you? I'm going to have to take it down. You've missed the whole point."

"Don't joke about it, Aaron."

"Don't get patriotic on me," Aaron snapped. "You're not old enough. It is a joke. The whole thing was a joke."

"Okay, okay. Back to your Communist," Nathan said. "Does she like you?"

"Oh, no. Well, she did agree to go out again, so she must like me a little."

"A Communist and a refugee from an Orthodox yeshiva. You two will make a great pair. A match made in heaven."

"Maybe," Aaron said, looking at him. "Just maybe it is."

"Or maybe it was made somewhere else," Nathan said.

"Only time will tell." Aaron smiled.

"That is what I'm most afraid of, my friend."

MAY
1948

MADELEINE LIKED THE KITCHEN BEST OF ANY PLACE IN
her parents' house. It was bright and airy, with large windows overlooking the fenced-in patch of grass everyone
called a backyard. The kitchen smelled of a mixture of
chicken dinners, blintz lunches and waxy sabbath candles.
This was where Bea Blumfeld reigned. While Vellef tended
to be authoritarian everywhere else, the kitchen he acknowl-
edged as his wife's domain. This was the place Bea did her
best to calm the storms between father and daughter.

After rising slightly later than the rest of the family,
Madeleine came into the kitchen and waited quietly at her
seat. She'd come in late the night before, and even Vellef
had given up talking to her. It was less his giving up than
her maintaining a pleasant posture toward him, a tactic she
had adopted since her first date with Aaron. Vellef sat in
his accustomed place, reading the Yiddish paper. Bea worked
over the stove, her long hair piled loosely on her head. She
wore a flowered summer dress and an old pink sweater that
didn't match anything she owned, but it seemed to be her
favorite. She cooked and toasted, not turning from the stove
until the eggs, toast, herring, tea and coffee were all ready.
Then she turned with a gentle swish of her dress. Her face
lit up, pleasantly surprised, as if she hadn't realized her
daughter was in the house.

"Good morning, Maidel," Bea said in Yiddish.

"Good morning, Mama," Madeleine answered in English. Her parents knew English fluently, but insisted on speaking Yiddish. The bilingual conversations had evolved naturally as a compromise.

Bea put eggs and toast in front of Madeleine, and herring and an onion roll in front of Vellef. At her own place she set what was left from both the eggs and the herring.

"You were out again late last night," Bea said. "You had a nice time?"

"Yes, it was nice," Madeleine answered. "We went to a movie."

Madeleine started to get up, but Bea read her mind. Bea rose quickly and fetched a cup of coffee for her daughter, a glass of tea for her husband and a glass of coffee for herself. Then she sat down.

"So nu, Maidel, what movie?" she asked.

"A Communist one." Vellef's voice sounded from behind the paper.

Madeleine smiled. She'd seen *I Remember Mama* with Aaron, but the desire to goad her father got the better of her. "Actually, the movie wasn't Communist." She took a sip of coffee, enjoying herself. "It was very bourgeois. *Anna Karenina*. It's about a married woman who has an affair and then kills herself."

Vellef's paper came down in a hurry, as she had known it would. "So this is the kind of movie a girl sees nowadays? For this I am sending her to college?"

"The college is free, Papa," Madeleine said, quietly beginning to smolder in spite of the fact that she'd started the argument.

Vellef reddened. "You eat, don't you? You sleep under a roof and wear clothes, don't you? I am sending you to college!"

"I work for you in the store."

"Oh, ho, three afternoons a week, during which she reads books. One meal this wouldn't get you! And even in my store she reads Communist trash. For this I am letting her stay out at night? For this—"

"Vellef." Bea spoke her husband's name softly. It was enough. Vellef glared and hid behind the paper, taking his tea with him.

"So which one of your friends took you to the movie?" Bea asked. "Someone I know?"

Madeleine smiled, but her thoughts were bitter. Good behavior seemed to worry them more than bad behavior. She'd tried very hard in the last weeks. Her arguments with her father had been cut in half—the half she could control.

"You haven't met him," she said.

"And what does he do?" Bea asked.

"He told me he was a revolutionary," Madeleine said. She saw her father's grip tighten on his paper, but he remained hidden and quiet.

Bea looked at her daughter. "Is he Jewish?"

"Yes, Mama. He is certainly Jewish."

Vellef put down his paper, grabbed an onion roll and tore it. He began to eat, looking only at the plate before him. Madeleine noticed his efforts at controlling his temper. "Thank God," he mumbled.

Bea glanced at Madeleine and then at Vellef. She opened her mouth slightly, but said nothing. Instead she took a sip of coffee. Madeleine watched to see what her mother would do next. Bea stared off into space, holding the steaming glass in her hand, a feat both parents could do. Madeleine always drank out of a cup, in awe of hands that could hold a hot glass and not burn. No matter what Stan or the group said, her parents were not bourgeois.

"You know, Maidel, that your father and I care about you."

"Yes, Mama."

"And we worry about you sometimes," Bea said.

"All the time," Vellef said, his mouth full of herring. "All the time we worry."

Madeleine's anger dissipated. "I know you worry. But I'm all right, believe me. I know what I'm doing." For a moment she entertained telling them about Aaron. She'd have to soon—even Aaron was hinting at that. But she pictured her mother's smile of relief and her father beginning his lecture about her finally becoming a sensible girl: one who would get married and get pregnant. No. Not yet. She'd figure out a way to tell them that wouldn't give them the impression she'd surrendered to their better judgment. She would never surrender, and when she could make that clear, then she'd tell them. Not before.

"I do know what I'm doing," she repeated.

"Good," Bea said. "Remember that we love you—always." Bea said nothing more. Vellef stared at Bea with surprise that he quickly masked. He too ate in silence. Madeleine had the feeling that something had not worked out according to plan.

When Madeleine finished her breakfast, she cleared the dishes and quietly left the kitchen. She hovered near the door, though, to see if her parents would reveal what they had not told her. Vellef began speaking as soon as she was out of the room.

"That was it? That was all?" Vellef spoke in a tense whisper.

"I can't."

"You can't. I'll handle everything, Vellef, she says. Don't you talk to her, Vellef. I'll handle it, she says. This is handling?"

"Yes. Neither you nor I need to know."

"What do you mean? I am the father. I have a right to know."

"And I am the mother. What happens if we find out? I realized something sitting here, Vellef. It's you. You're the father. You have a right to know. The fact that our daughter has begun to act once again like a daughter hasn't softened you; it's hardened your suspicion."

Vellef grunted. Madeleine felt her face begin to burn.

"And what if I asked her?" Bea said. "What if I'd ask her if she'd been sleeping with this mysterious boy?"

"Shah!"

"What are you ashamed of, Vellef? That she might hear? Or are you ashamed of your suspicions? So listen to me. What if she answers 'yes'? It destroys me and you. You would get all filled with your fatherly honor and that awful temper and probably throw her out of the house. Then you would weep and mourn until I somehow set things straight, which I could never do. Then you'd blame me."

Vellef started to say something, but Bea cut him off. "You let me talk," she said. "Now, what if she tells us that she is still pure? Then we have destroyed her by the accusation. And what's more"—Bea's whisper became a hiss—"you wouldn't believe her."

"I would!"

"No, you wouldn't. I see the suspicion in your eyes. And it isn't our daughter's honor that concerns you, it's your own honor. Only you. So if you want to cross-examine her, go ahead. But I recommend if you want to badger someone, badger your delinquent accounts, not your daughter!"

Madeleine moved to the doorway. Vellef started to speak, but he looked up and saw her. Her face silenced his reply. Then she ran from the kitchen and from the apartment, leaving the door open to catch the echo of her feet on the stairs. She ran without thinking, letting her feet carry her in the familiar path that led out of her building, through the backyard and into the next building, where Ruth lived.

"Madeleine, Madeleine," Ruth said as the two sat in Ruth's bedroom, and she stroked Madeleine's hair. "What did you expect? After all, you're the one who's talking about revolutions and free love all the time."

Madeleine paused in her crying and sat up. "But I'm dating a yeshiva boy!"

"Well, they don't know that! And it's your fault."

"I know," Madeleine said, calming down a little. "I was going to tell them eventually."

"What are you waiting for?"

"I am not like my sisters."

"Not hardly," Ruth said.

"But if I tell them, they'll think I am. I mean it's hard enough to fight them as it is. With any encouragement, Papa would really work to make me like Good Little Debra—who's pregnant again, by the way. Or like Ann, who goes to synagogue and worships status instead of God. I see it in Papa, and Mama too. They want me to top my sisters. They want a rich lawyer's wife with lots of children. Well, maybe I don't want to be a lawyer's wife! Maybe I want to be a lawyer!"

"Lady lawyers get mustaches."

"Ruth, please! It's not funny." Madeleine wiped her eyes with the palms of her hands. "Maybe I should just go ahead and have an affair. They already think I'm loose."

"Don't be silly," Ruth said. "Better go wash your face. We have to leave for school in a little while."

Madeleine went to the bathroom. When she returned, she was composed. Ruth still sat on the bed, staring at the mirror that reflected her image. Madeleine came up behind the two Ruths, startling them both.

"Sorry," Madeleine said. "What are you thinking about?"

"Secrets," Ruth said absently, glancing at Madeleine and then returning to the mirror.

"Mine or yours?" Madeleine asked.

"Oh, so you acknowledge that I may have some."

"You obviously do. Going to tell me?"

Ruth turned to her. "Madeleine, are you still my best friend?"

"That's a dumb question." Madeleine saw her friend's eyes still questioning. She sat down beside Ruth and took her hand. "I am now and will always be your best friend."

"I wasn't sure after all that's gone on in the last few months. You've seemed so different, like another person."

"I'm me," Madeleine said. "And just now who was the first one I ran to? You'll always be my best friend, Ruth."

Ruth took a deep breath. "I have a secret. I want to tell you so you can straighten things out after I've gone."

"Gone?"

"Remember I told you that Ben had asked me to go to Palestine with him? Well, I'm going."

"Are you crazy? There's going to be a war over there!"

"That's why we're going. We want to be married in the Holy Land, and we want to be there when Palestine needs us."

"This is too much," Madeleine said, shaking her head. "You're going to run off to a war halfway around the world with a boy who hasn't even married you yet?"

"Hey, what happened to free love?" Ruth asked. Madeleine's eyes widened. "No," Ruth said. "Neither one of us want to sleep together until we're married—in Jerusalem."

"So you've thought about it," Madeleine said quietly.

Ruth laughed. "Thought about it? We've come real close to doing it."

"Really?" Madeleine looked at Ruth with a new respect. "What's it like?"

Ruth blushed deep red. "I can't talk about it. Besides, haven't you and Aaron—well, you know."

"Are you kidding? Aaron really is a yeshiva boy deep down inside, you know. And he's so conscious of being older. It took him three weeks to kiss me good-night." Madeleine bounced a little on the bed. "That doesn't answer my question. I can't believe you are going to run off with this Ben."

"I love him."

"You were in love with Artie Shatzer too."

"This is different," Ruth said. "Ben was born in Palestine, you know. He's been here studying at the university for three years. Don't get mad, please, but I see in him what I didn't see in your Communist friends."

"Yeh? What?"

"Well, for one thing Ben doesn't talk nearly as much,

and for another, he's done things. Every time he supposedly visits home, he's actually smuggling in illegal immigrants. He's even been in jail a couple of times, and he's worked for the underground against the British. And I don't have just his word for that."

"So you're in love with a hero."

"It's more than that. He's so strong—or, he tries to be so strong and lead all the time; yet when we're alone . . ." Ruth's voice trailed off as she tried to frame her words. "He leans on me. Sometimes he needs me to be strong for him. Me. Ruth Kosnik. And there's more. When I'm at Young Pioneer meetings, I feel proud to be a Jew. I feel like I'm going to help the whole Jewish people, and that feels good. So that's why I want to go halfway around the world with a boy who hasn't even married me yet."

"Whew." Madeleine whistled softly.

"Don't you love Aaron that way, just a little?"

"I don't know. I really don't," Madeleine said. "He doesn't lean on me—at least, not that I notice. Sometimes, sometimes I can make him laugh when I know he's hurting, but he never tells me what's hurting him. I like being with him. He's struggling, just like I am. His father was a Hasid."

"And he goes to a reform seminary?"

"Yeh. He talked a bit about being in two worlds the first time we went out. He really is: maybe that's what hurts him. He's caught between them." Madeleine smiled. "I am too, going off with Stan and helping the Revolution, then having to come home and set the dinner table. But Ruth, can you ever see me as a rebbetzin—a rabbi's wife? Mrs. Aaron Stern, rebbetzin, going to all the synagogue functions and being a pious lady for all the women in the congregation. That's what he'd want me to be. I can't be that. I just can't."

Ruth sighed and stood. "Well, I want you and Aaron to go out with us Wednesday night. You can meet Ben, and we'll give you the final details."

"But how will you get the money to go?"

"We don't need money. They want anyone willing to fight, so they're getting us there."

"But the British, and the Arabs. You could get killed!"

"Will you go out with us on Wednesday?"

"Am I going to meet hordes of your Zionist friends?"

"Yes."

"Terrific. But I'll go. I have got to meet Ben," she said. "Can I tell Aaron what you're planning?"

Ruth thought a moment. "I guess that would be all right. But no one else."

That afternoon Madeleine sat behind the cash register in her father's paint store. It was the slow time of the day and of the three customers in the store, she'd spotted two as browsers, though what one browsed in a paint store remained a mystery to her. Idle, bored and still feeling the weight of the morning on her, Madeleine looked around at the stacks of wallpaper and brushes neatly ordered in the same section where they'd always been. Wallpaper had its place, but paint was her father's real business. Paint cans climbed in piles to the ceiling. Paint cans lined the aisles between paint cans.

Madeleine recalled the major events in her family's life by colors of paint. Her eldest sister, Debra's, wedding came to her in a shade of tawny peach, Ann's wedding in lime green. She remembered the birth and circumcision of her nephew Lennie in muted orange, and her own graduation was powder blue. Vellef Blumfeld was a painter, and much to Madeleine's adolescent embarrassment, he never quite got the paint from under his fingernails. She'd held her tongue for Debra's wedding, but at Ann's she'd felt it a sisterly duty to voice her disapproval of her father's lime-green fingernails. Madeleine considered it an act of charity, knowing that socially conscious Ann would be dying inside as her father led her down the aisle and everyone stared, not at her Saks wedding gown, but at her father's fingernails. That was Madeleine's first and last act of sisterly love for

Ann. Her remonstration caused her father to blush, also for the first and last time in her memory. Thereafter he assigned her to a period of servitude in the paint store. As for Ann, she never forgave Madeleine for the fact that her father reeked of turpentine throughout the whole ceremony.

The fingernail incident had occurred seven years ago, but the period of servitude continued, though now Madeleine received a small stipend. Each Monday, Wednesday and Friday, Madeleine came into the store and sat by the cash register from three o'clock to five-thirty. She then helped her mother lock up, and accompanied her home. Vellef had considered her old enough at the age of thirteen to carry the paint cans to the mixing machine. At fifteen, she'd been allowed to work the mixing machine. Finally, to her secret pride, her father had given her the responsibility for mixing the ingredients that changed peach to tawny peach, or orange to light rust. Of course, such tasks came to Madeleine only when neither parent was in the store, and those instances were rare. Mostly she sat, as she had sat from the age of eleven, reading and dreaming.

The paint store had stood on the corner of Sixty-fourth and Lawrence Streets for twenty years. It still had its original sign out front: WILLIAM AND BEA'S PAINT, INC. For Vellef, that sign symbolized his success and his Americanization. William, the name Vellef had received at Ellis Island, was the official name on his naturalization papers. In the movement of a harried clerk's pen, Vellef's wife, Bina, had become Bea. Hence WILLIAM AND BEA'S PAINT. The INC. was just for show. Through the years, friends and customers had come to think of Bina Blumfeld as Bea, but Vellef somehow always remained separate from William.

In spite of the Yiddish first name, Vellef was staunchly American. As a boy, back in Minsk, he'd been apprenticed to a house painter. In America, Vellef had found work easily, unlike all the former scholars who were forced to pushcarts and sweatshops. Vellef had done well in America and considered himself a loyal citizen. This brought him into frequent conflict with his daughter, especially when she carried "Communist" books into the store with her. Vellef's definition of "Communist" was very broad.

Luckily for Madeleine, her father stayed out of the store most of the time. He went out on jobs with his men, if only to supervise. Aided by an old clerk, Bea took care of the books and inventory. She handled everything except delinquent accounts. Those Vellef handled, and in twenty years it had never taken him more than one visit to receive payment.

As Madeleine glanced at the windowed office across the store, she saw her mother bent over the ledgers, her dimestore magnifying glasses perched on her nose. Bea ran her finger down a column of figures, her lips moving silently. She had stopped using the adding machine years ago, though she still kept it at the corner of the desk. Bea had a gift for figures, a mind as fast and as accurate as the machine that gathered dust beside her. Madeleine thought she might have been a great scientist, an Einstein. But Madeleine had long ago discovered that Bea had no desire for the Nobel Prize and was content just doing her books. Frustrated, Madeleine talked to her about bigger dreams, greater accomplishments, something more than a paint store. Bea had replied that in Russia she hadn't even dared dream of a paint store.

Bea did dream, however, of seeing all her daughters married. Debra and Ann had long since been taken care of, and that left only Madeleine. That particular dream Madeleine refused to discuss.

Madeleine glanced at her watch and then back at her mother. They hadn't really spoken for an hour, both of them kept in silence by secrets. Secret conversations and plans, hers, Ruth's, her parents'. Bea's secret discovered, Madeleine's hidden. The secrets pressed in on Madeleine. She already had too many secrets to bear. Madeleine stood up and walked slowly across the store. She waited quietly until Bea looked up from her ledger.

"I'm not sleeping with anyone," Madeleine said.

"I know, Maidel. If I'd thought otherwise, I wouldn't have gone along with what your father wanted to do. It was a mistake anyway. I'm sorry."

"Tell him."

"That isn't necessary."

"You mean he won't believe you," Madeleine said. "Well, then, tell him that the boy I'm seeing is a rabbinical student."

Bea's glasses rose on her nose as her eyebrows lifted briefly. She looked down at her figures, then back at her daughter.

"You are a strange girl, Maidel. You frighten your father and you frighten me. Maidel"—Bea hesitated, and the lines in her face deepened. "If you had slept with someone, I'd know. And if you'd slept with someone, it would be our secret. Between us."

Madeleine looked at her mother in shock.

"I want you to keep yourself pure," Bea said. "But after this morning I realized something. Your father is a very good man, but he is still a man. Some things men just can't understand. Whatever man you find, I just want you to be happy. Now," Bea said with a tone of dismissal, "the store is too slow to bother and stay. You go with your friends." It was not a request.

Madeleine turned and walked out the door. She was afraid to turn back lest something in the air shatter. "Mama," she called. "I love you."

"That too I know. Now go."

Aaron passed easily among the Hasidim of Williamsburg, but the atmosphere of that special piece of Brooklyn attacked his spirit. Each passing block carried with it sounds of young men and boys chanting Talmud passages in endless study at the countless storefront yeshivas crammed into the ghetto. A Hasid walked ahead of Aaron, scurrying forward in his fur hat, black caftan and white stockings. The smell of the man's sweat clung to Aaron, stinging his nostrils. Williamsburg, land of holy chant and rancid sweat.

The community had risen from the ashes of Nazi Europe, and like the Broken Shards of the mystical tale of Creation, pieces of human souls gathered here. They rebuilt, remarried and reproduced, trying to effect the Tikkun, the Cosmic Mending, by their survival itself. Aaron walked among those survivors, a survivor also, but of a different kind. Hasidic women passed him, adorned in the identical wigs that announced their married status. Aaron, in accordance with custom, surreptitiously observed them. The women barely veiled their curiosity about him. He had the look of a man not yet married. They sensed him, like a cat spotting prey. They had unmarried daughters; they always had unmarried daughters who would be pure and chaste, devoted mothers and rebbetzins. But he didn't want that kind of wife; he had turned his back on a life of study and sect in order to survive. Yet Williamsburg drew him like Jerusalem.

Aaron had come to buy Nathan tefillin, the leather phylacteries used during morning worship. He'd come to buy, and to walk among those who still seemed like ghosts, whose eyes bore witness to the flames of a Europe devoured. He walked until he came to the street of scribes. Signs hung out down the block, advertising the same thing in the same lettered Yiddish. Aaron stopped at the first shop. There was no point in going on, because the first shop was, would be like the second and like the third, like the signs, all the same. Only the names were different. This shop belonged to Simons.

A man, presumably Simons, sat on a bench and hunched over the long table that served as a counter. Pieces of leather thong and black lacquered boxes surrounded him, carelessly tossed into piles. He examined the thongs for blemishes with slow-moving, arthritic hands, and when the bell rang he pretended not to hear. Aaron saw two men in the room behind the counter. An old hunchbacked man sat at a high table with pen and ink; a young man with a sparse beard assisted him. The decades of scribal work had deformed the old man into the perfect posture to hover close to the holy parchments. The young man leaned close also, but of his own accord. As Aaron watched the two men, the one at the counter finally looked up.

"That's my brother," the man said to Aaron, twisting his body slightly to indicate the two men behind him. "His name is Simons too."

The man at the counter was younger than he had appeared when bent over his leather. Aaron guessed him to be in his fifties. Aaron detected a Hungarian accent in the younger Simons' speech. The elder ignored Aaron's presence, remaining absorbed in his work.

Aaron paused before speaking. His Yiddish would betray his origins to anyone with an ear. "I would like to purchase tefillin," he said.

"Galicia," Simons said.

"Chicago," Aaron answered. "But by way of Loem in Galicia."

The man at the counter nodded and eyed Aaron. The furtive appearance he'd had when bent over his leather was belied by the intensity of his slate eyes. He had wound his long side curls several times around each ear to keep them out of his way. His ears looked furry.

"How much?" Simons asked finally.

"Depends."

Simons shrugged and called to the apprentice in rapid Yiddish. The young man hurried to bring sets of tefillin of varying sizes and quality out from the piles around the shop. With shaking hands, he placed them on the counter. The young man looked at Simons and at Aaron, then returned to the old man's side.

"He came to us from a displaced-persons camp," Simons said. "The son of my wife's second cousin, may he rest in peace. May they all rest in peace." He looked behind him and laughed. "My family." Then he abruptly changed his demeanor.

"All kosher," he said pointing to the tefillin. "Guaranteed. You were smart to come to my shop. I guarantee."

"They all guarantee," Aaron said gruffly, entering into a bargaining preliminary because it was expected of him. "Let me see what you've got."

The two men argued over the sets of tefillin, engaging in a bargaining ritual as old as the art of making phylacteries. In spite of his gnarled hands, Simons did good work with the leather. He explained, in the course of haggling, that he'd been a scribe also, before the camps, but arthritis had set in. He still continued to make the leather thongs and boxes of the tefillin, but his voice was wistful. He knew that that craft too would be stolen from him by the arthritis.

Aaron picked up the largest set. He held the two boxes, one in each hand. The black leather thongs felt cool and smooth in his hands. The boxes that would contain the holy parchments had no blemish or mistake. He looked at the box in his right hand. This box Nathan would place on his head. "A frontlet between thine eyes." Aaron chanted the Hebrew command in his mind. Then he held the box in his left hand close to him. "And a sign upon thine arm." Arm and head woven by the leather, with the name of God. The thongs attached to boxes hung down from Aaron's hands and swirled onto the counter.

Yehezkel, his father, had explained it all to him long ago. Aaron remembered his father speaking of the commandment as he slowly wrapped his arm in the thongs, placing one box on his arm opposite his heart and the other box and thong on his head. The words had been whispered to him during Aaron's first time using tefillin, the holy time when he had first come of age. Those were the days when Yehezkel still did such things, though even then his beard was shaven.

That set had been made in Loem, examined for quality and handed to Yehezkel on his bar mitzvah by the Loemer Rebbe himself. When Aaron made his bar mitzvah, Yehezkel passed on this artifact of Loem, and the touch of the Loemer Rebbe, to Aaron. That day Yehezkel Stern ceased donning the tefillin. If it had been possible, Aaron would have given that set to Nathan, the more worthy candidate. But he had betrayed his father enough already. Instead, he wished to purchase a new set, shining with the promise of traditions yet to be born.

Aaron haggled as astutely as Simons might have wished, so by the time they agreed on a price, the storekeeper had taken a liking to Aaron. He demonstrated this by including a plain but adequate carrying bag for the tefillin, free of charge.

"So," Simons said, wrapping up the package. "I don't place you. You been here often?"

"No. Not very."

"You study maybe at one of the yeshivas?"

"Once."

"Once. Once. Once the bargaining is over, a big talker you're not. You got a place to eat for the Sabbath? I got three daughters."

Aaron smiled. "No, thank you. I have a place to eat and a girl."

"Feh! Now you sound like an American. You don't have a girl until you're married. Dating leads to sin. What do you do for a living?" Simons had not yet given up hope for his daughters.

"I give lessons," Aaron answered, uncomfortable with the turn of the questioning. In this place especially, he wanted to be anonymous.

"Lessons, nu, what kind of lessons? To boys?"

"No, to baalai tshuva," Aaron said. A baal tshuva was one who had returned to the tradition after spending most of his life nonobservant, and Nathan certainly qualified in that regard. It was a basically true answer that Aaron hoped would lead to no more questions.

But Simons gazed at him. "This is holy work," he said. "Helping Jewish souls return home. Yes, holy work." He looked down at the packages. "The tefillin, they're for one of your students?"

"Yes. He's going to a yeshiva, and I want him to have a good set."

Simons undid the package, took out the plain carrying bag and replaced it with a richly embroidered one. Aaron thanked him, but he shook his head.

"It's my privilege," Simons said, "and a blessing. Another soul restored. Another . . ." his voice trailed off as he retreated into his own thoughts and memories. Then he began rewrapping.

"Loem?" Simons asked.

"Yes," Aaron said.

"Did your father know Avram Levi, the Loemer Rebbe?"

It was the question Aaron had dreaded, yet the question he had known he would face, coming here to Williamsburg. He waited a moment before answering. "No," he said.

"No? Your father missed a great man. They are no more, the Loemer Hasidim. I met one in Auschwitz. Who knows? Maybe he was the last one. Such fire in his eyes."

"My father never met the Rebbe," Aaron said quickly. He felt coldness in his fingertips. It crept up his palms. "I'm sure he would have told me." The last Loemer died in the camps. Aaron was nothing to these people because the last Loemer died in the camps. Aaron repeated that in his mind, chanting it like a scripture.

The old man in the back had stopped working. Aaron noticed that he was watching the two of them. Why was he watching? Even Simons paused in his wrapping and stared off once more.

"Excuse me," Aaron said loudly. "I'm in a hurry."

"I was just trying to remember," Simons said. He called back over his shoulder. "Moishe! Do you remember that melody the Loemer taught us? I can't remember, and it bothers me." He looked to Aaron also for help.

Aaron remained silent. He knew it, but he wouldn't help them. He was free of Loem, and he wouldn't be shackled again.

"Such a melody," Simons said. "A melody like the fire in the Loemer's eyes." Simons took the money Aaron offered him and went to the cash register. "Moishe! Do you remember? He even sang it during the selection, remember? He went to the gas with it." Simons seemed to be talking to the cash register. "And when he passed by me, I thought I would have that melody in my soul forever. Moishe, what was it?"

The old man continued watching Aaron a moment; then he closed his eyes and began to hum the melody. He swayed as if in prayer. Simons smiled and nodded.

"Yes. That's it. That's it. How could I have forgotten?" He too began to hum the melody.

Their eyes were on Aaron; even the closed eyes of the old man were turned to him. They sang and watched him with eyes that seemed to know all, as if waiting for the melody to reveal his identity. Aaron grabbed the package and walked quickly to the door, not waiting for his change.

But the melody followed him as he walked down the crowded street. He walked faster, trying to escape, but it hung around him, ringing in his ears and burning his eyes. Aaron turned down an alley and began to run, but his breath came in rhythm to the melody, and his heart pounded out time as the melody came faster and faster, demanding that his lips move and his voice sing out. He knew the melody; his father had taught it to him. It was the Loemer Rebbe's melody, and Yehezkel had first heard it sung the day the Rebbe composed it. Aaron ran until, out of breath, exhausted, he collapsed by an overturned garbage can in a narrow alleyway inhabited only by cats. The melody pounded in his brain, and he clutched Nathan's tefillin to him.

"Let me alone!" he screamed. "For God's sake, let me alone!"

"Illi is at it again," Stan said as Madeleine sat down at their table. She nodded her agreement as she heard Illi's shrill voice coming from the other end of the café.

"Who is he berating this time?" she asked.

"The Trots," Stan replied. He cradled a cup of coffee in his huge sculptor's hands.

"Oh, God." She leaned back while the waitress placed a cup of coffee in front of her. She was relaxed, confident that she fitted in with their surroundings. She'd taken the time to change before she came. Her long hair flowed freely over her peasant blouse and almost touched the waistband of her dirndl skirt.

The Bleecker Café was crowded and filled with smoke, as usual. Its clientele consisted of Communists, anarchists, assorted artists and bohemians. Most of the individuals were men. The few scattered women were hanging on the arms of their men like Natalie, who was sitting next to Stan. Madeleine was irritated, but she wasn't sure whether she was angry at the women who were a part of the Revolution only as an extension of their lovers or at the fact that she had no lover here to be an extension of.

"I thought you worked today," Stan said.

"My mother let me off."

"That's probably because she's busy planning your wedding to the rabbi. Do I get an invite for introducing you two?"

Madeleine ignored the remark. "How long has Illi been screaming?" she asked, pointing behind her with her thumb.

Stan looked at his watch. "Almost long enough. I give him five more minutes until he chokes up."

"I still don't understand why you, why we all put up with him."

"Well, not for Illi's talent at debating," Stan said. He looked over her shoulder. "If you give him something to do, he does it. He organized the security for the last rally, and he did a good job."

"He usually does a good job when it comes to rough stuff," Madeleine said. "But Stan, he's nuts."

"No, my dear, he's a comrade," Stan said.

Natalie leaned further on Stan's arm. She brought her

finger out as if testing the wind. "Ah, gloom. I can tell we are thinking about Illi again, aren't we?"

"I'd really like to do something about that son-of-a-bitch," Stan said. "I don't like him; I'll never like him. But he does his work okay."

"And, more importantly," Natalie said. "The boys in the front office want him here." Stan glanced at her, and she said no more.

Illi sputtered to a stop, and his listeners stormed out of the café in a preplanned show of disgust. Illi walked over to their table and sat. His pale face was flushed, and his long blond hair was wet with perspiration.

"You shouldn't let them get to you," Stan said, pushing a glass of water over to Illi. "It'd be a lot better if you stuck to breaking heads and left debating to me."

"I don't just break heads," Illi said.

"Yeh?"

"The bum at the rally was about to bash in someone's head. So we put him in the hospital."

"It was messy," Stan said.

"I meant it to be messy as a lesson to those other fascists. I could have killed him without a mark, too."

"Sure," Stan said. "But Illi, the Trots aren't worth the scenes you make in here. It just makes us look bad."

"That's all you ever worry about. What we look like."

"Well, if you don't like the way I operate with this group," Stan said evenly, "feel free to go somewhere else."

Illi smiled. "But I like it here, comrade. I like being with all my friends." He glanced around the table, then grabbed the glass of water and drank it down. He drank too fast, which started him hiccuping. That made him furious. No one at the table said anything until he appeared to calm down.

"I finished *The Naked and the Dead* last night," Madeleine ventured finally.

"It's about time," Stan said. "What did you think of it?"

They launched into a discussion of the novel. Madeleine

had prepared for the debate that would ensue. Stan, for all his politics, knew very little about literary criticism, and she was determined to beat him once at his own game. Stan won his points, though, less by logic and knowledge than by making her the butt of his wit. Still, she was satisfied. At least with Stan, there was no small talk. No talk of marriages and babies. Here she spoke and was listened to, and felt she had a place in the world.

After Stan drew a crowd, the topics shifted and the focus moved from her, giving her time to sit back and drink her coffee. Illi, who had been sitting silently morose, leaned over to her.

"Comrade," he whispered. "May I speak to you?" Illi wiped a lock of his hair from his eyes. His hands still trembled with the emotion of his former argument. "May I speak to you at another table?"

Madeleine turned to him, frowning. "All right," she agreed, after seeing Illi's determined expression.

The two moved to a booth a few tables away. Madeleine glanced back to see Stan still speaking, but looking in their direction. They sat, and Illi leaned close.

"Comrade Madeleine, I heard about the unfortunate and exploitive circumstances of your meeting with this Aaron Stern. In that light, it puzzles me that you continue to see him. How serious are you about this man?"

"I just like him, that's all. Nothing serious." Madeleine thought Illi was presumptuous to ask about her personal life. But one didn't cross Illi without good reason. There was a barely contained fury in his eyes, always a tension, waiting to be unleashed.

His eyes narrowed. "I'm concerned for you, Comrade Madeleine. You'll have serious decisions to make soon, I'm afraid."

Madeleine sighed. Illi spoke with his "member of the Party" voice. He usually reserved that tone for official business, and gloried in it when he was on security duty.

Illi continued. "I've been impressed with your ability to

think for yourself. Unlike some other women we know, you have the ability to become equal to a man—as it should be. I've already thought of you as a comrade and Party member."

"The Party hasn't asked me yet."

"Soon," he said, smiling. "Soon the time may be right for you to join us officially. But this Stern business has me puzzled."

"How so?"

"Think, Comrade. Your efforts, as noble as they might be, will come to no good for you or the cause. You can't make a good Communist out of a Jew."

Madeleine looked at him; the blood drained from her face.

"Illi," she whispered. "Stan is Jewish, and Natalie, and most of the people in this room. I'm Jewish, Illi. What are you saying?"

Flustered, Illi tried to explain. "I—uh—no, I didn't mean you. I mean Jews. You know. The kind that push Bibles all day. The kind that pray and sway and pray some more while the world burns. While they burn the world with their praying and their money!"

She barely heard him. She saw his face, his eyes looking back at her, trying to make her understand. Cold, furious eyes.

"I don't mean Jews as a class, for Christ's sake!" Illi shouted. He stood up quickly, knocking over a chair near the booth. "I mean—Comrade, you, of all, must know what I mean. Religion is the opiate. You know. I mean that! That!"

Illi looked around at the people staring at him. The café became quiet. His mouth was set defiantly as he raised fisted hands to his chest. "Don't you understand?" he asked Madeleine fiercely. He looked at her one more time, then walked out of the café.

Madeleine sat without moving, staring at the fallen chair. Slowly, the conversations resumed around her. Stan excused himself and came over.

"Are you all right, Madeleine?" he asked. He sat down beside her and took her trembling hand.

"You're not going to believe this," she said, still looking at the chair. "In all my life, no one has ever talked to me like that."

"Welcome to the real world."

Madeleine looked at him, her eyes wide. "He frightened me. God, Stan, he really frightened me."

"We should get rid of him."

"Can we?"

"It may take some doing," he said drily. "But I think we can. I've always wondered how that lunatic found our group and why the boys in the front office kept him here. He doesn't fit in, but he's trying to take over as if"—Stan paused—"as if he'd been assigned to it."

"You mean someone sent him? Who? Why?"

Stan smiled and squeezed her hand. "I've said enough already. It's nothing to worry your innocent little head about. Uncle Stan will take care of everything."

Benjamin Yair took them to a party at a house in Westbury. Though Madeleine knew the neighborhood was restricted, she noticed immediately that the thirty people gathered in the small living room were Jews. They spoke a mixture of Yiddish, English and Hebrew, but the Hebrew had a different sound to it. It wasn't at all like the prayers she heard on the High Holy Days. The sound of this Hebrew was musical and smooth, like Ben, who sat next to her on the living-room floor.

To Madeleine's surprise, Ben Yair was not the monster she'd conjured up in her imagination. He was small-boned and compact, contrasting with Ruth's solid but, as Madeleine noticed for the first time, considerably thinned-down Polish physique. Ben had a youngish face and deep-set eyes highlighted by thick eyebrows. He radiated a calm virility. His soft, flawless English had just a trace of an accent, which he attributed to his birth and rearing in Palestine.

Ben was a third-generation Palestinian. His great-grandfather had come to the Holy Land from Egypt. The family had sent Ben to the United States three years before to study engineering. While he studied, he also organized groups of Jews who wanted to risk running the British blockade to emigrate.

Madeleine suspected it was just such a group meeting in the house tonight, but right now she was more conscious of the two men who sat on either side of her. Aaron sat on one side, pale in his white shirt and looking as uncomfortable as she felt. Ben sat on the other, with his dark-complected, muscular physique showing even through the shirt. Ruth sat next to him, watching him with adoration, listening as if every word he uttered were holy. Madeleine half-listened to the conversations, her mind continually drawn to the two of them. She had seen Ruth undressed many times as they were growing up. Now she tried to picture Ruth and Ben, unclothed, touching each other. Her mind switched to herself and Aaron, remembering those times when he put his arms around her, how firm his body was. She felt an uncomfortable tightening between her legs that made her quickly push the images out of her mind.

The two couples sat in the middle of the floor as people stepped over and around them, occasionally stopping to chat with Ruth or Ben. The crowded, smoky room and the heated conversations reminded Madeleine of the Bleecker Café. And as in the Bleecker Café of the last weeks, there seemed to be an underlying tension, barely masked by the trappings of a party. She hadn't been introduced to the owner of the house, and she had the feeling that no owner would appear. Madeleine noticed Ruth looking at her and realized she'd been staring off into space. She sighed and tuned in on the conversation.

"So you've made it back to Palestine many times in these last three years," Aaron said. "That can't be easy."

"For me, it's easy, since I was born there. It gets harder when I smuggle in weapons." He said it so casually she almost missed the line.

"Smuggle guns?" she asked.

"Revolutions are fought with guns," Ben said. "I assumed you knew that."

"I know. I just wasn't sure you were in a revolution," Madeleine said.

"Ah, yes. Your Communist friends are very particular about the term. At least when it's applied to Jews."

"Ben," Ruth said. "Madeleine is here to find out how nice you are, not how fanatic."

Ben laughed. The room was getting hot. Madeleine felt her own perspiration and saw the wet patch forming on Ben's shirt. She could see his chest hair through the now translucent material.

"Ruth wishes to protect you," Ben said.

"Or you," Madeleine replied, smiling. "But in any case, she doesn't need to. Go ahead. I'd be interested in your theories." She tried to keep the sarcasm out of her voice for Ruth's sake.

"We are in a revolution. We're throwing off the yoke of the British Empire."

"I thought they were leaving on their own."

"They've had their asses kicked out of Palestine and they know it," Ben said. "So just as a parting gesture, they've been confiscating Jewish—only Jewish, mind you—weapons. Then they pull out and wait smugly for the Arabs to massacre us."

Madeleine glanced quickly at Ruth. "Are the Arabs going to massacre you?" she asked slowly.

"No." Ben looked at Ruth, then back at Madeleine. "We will survive and we'll win. And when we do, we will no longer be a remnant of refugees depending on the world's pity. We won't be what the world wants us to be any longer—their victims."

"The world isn't Nazi Germany," Madeleine said.

"Isn't it?"

Madeleine said nothing. The memory of her encounter with Illi was still too vivid and disquieting. But yet, was Ben any better? All he cared about was Jews, and what was good for Jews. He was like her father. Everyone else be damned if it helped the Jews.

"Then we have to build a better world," she said.

"We have to stop dying for the rest of the world. We're a people whose land was stolen. It's time to take back our inheritance."

"To inherit, you have to survive," Madeleine snapped. She said no more, seeing the look on Ruth's face. Aaron had been silent a long time. Madeleine turned to him and saw a vacant stare that had become frighteningly familiar to her. Aaron's stare was not the look of a daydreamer. He watched from clouded eyes that saw into another world very far away from her. She was about to tap him when he turned to Ben, his eyes still cloudy.

"And where is God in all this?" The question was barely audible.

Madeleine, worried, looked to see how Ben would react. He faced Aaron, his eyes soft with an understanding that passed by her.

"We can't afford to wait for the Messiah," Ben said quietly.

"Why?" Aaron asked.

Ben drew his eyebrows together until they were almost a straight line. Then they parted, and he looked at Aaron. "Because the Messiah may have already been gassed at Auschwitz. God needs a push. If there is a God."

Someone beckoned from across the room, and Ben stood. "Come, Aaron, I'll introduce you to a former religionist. You'll find him interesting."

Aaron hesitated a moment, then stood and followed Ben.

"Well, what do you think of him?" Ruth asked as the two men walked away.

"I think he's nice," Madeleine said. She saw Ruth's relieved smile and quickly added, "But he's pompous, he's crazy and he will get you killed if you listen to him!"

Ruth's smile broadened. "He's not really pompous. Poor Ben. He's trying desperately to impress you."

"Me? What on earth for?"

"Oh, Madeleine, how can you be so blind? He knows how much you mean to me. All this"—Ruth casually swept her hand out in a half-circle. "All this is for you."

"Well, I don't understand."

"That I can see," Ruth sighed. "You talked about committing yourself, about how I floated through life without seriously thinking of anything. You were right. You were so right. But now I'm doing something. I'm going to fight and maybe even die—"

"Don't say that!" Madeleine spoke loudly. The room quieted for a moment. Then the conversations began again with everyone studiously looking away from the two young women.

"Let's go into one of the other rooms," Ruth said.

She led the way to a den at the back of the house. The conversations of the living room became an unintelligible rumble as they closed the door. Madeleine looked around the room and spotted a crucifix on the wall. She looked questioningly at Ruth.

"In spite of what Ben says, not all the friends of Palestine are Jews."

"I didn't think you ever disagreed with him."

"I do a lot," Ruth said. "More than you ever disagree with Stan Landis."

"You haven't been around lately to see."

"No. But if it's any comfort to you, that's where I started doing my thinking. That's where I caught your dream, Madeleine."

"Yeh? And that's why you left us, right?"

"Yes!" Ruth said. "I left because I caught the meaning of your dreams. There is more than marriage and babies. But that doesn't mean I have to dream the exact same dream as you, does it? I never had the courage to dream my own dreams, so I let you dream my dreams for me."

"Because I was so brave," Madeleine said sarcastically.

"Yes. You were brave enough to fight everyone. I even

let you do the fighting with my parents when you wanted me to go to college. I wanted to go, but I was afraid to upset my parents' plans for me."

"You didn't tell me that."

Ruth smiled. "I know. I didn't even have the courage to tell you you were right. But I am telling you now. And I've also got the courage to show you my dream."

"Are you sure this isn't Benjamin Yair's dream?"

"It's my own. Ben is part of it, true. But only a part. Come here," Ruth said. Madeleine walked to where Ruth stood, by a picture on the wall opposite the crucifix. "Look at this."

In the picture Madeleine saw an ancient-looking walled city. In one section a dome flashed in sunlight.

"Jerusalem," Ruth said.

Madeleine looked at the picture again, trying to see what Ruth saw. Then she took her friend's hand.

"Look at the picture with real eyes, would you?" Madeleine said. "It's an old walled city. Walled against what? The Warsaw ghetto was walled too. Look beyond the wall. Ruth, there's nothing out there! It looks horrible. It looks like stone and sand. Nothing more. It's dead, Ruth! Dead. Just like the fantasy of a Jewish state."

Madeleine expected Ruth to get angry, but her friend just squeezed her hand and smiled. "I just realized," Ruth said, "that I'm a bigger dreamer than you." She turned back to the picture.

"I see walls bathed in a golden sunlight from the setting sun. I see the walls of the city centered among farmhouses and fields like a tree that sends out its shoots. I see green land and vineyards."

"You see something that isn't there," Madeleine said.

"I will see it and touch it someday."

"Not if you're dead."

Ruth smiled. "Then my children will see. I'll pass the dreams on to them."

"Oh, God, Ruth, don't go. They're going to kill you in that place! I love you too much to let you go."

Ruth took her other hand, so that both Madeleine's hands were cradled in Ruth's large bony palms. "Please?" she said in a whisper. "Please love me enough to let me go. I can't ask my parents that. But you've got to understand, Madeleine. You've just got to."

Madeleine stood for a moment, looking at Ruth as conflicting emotions struggled within her. Madeleine thought of her father and her father's ways of dealing with things, then remembered that one precious moment with her mother.

"I understand," she said. "You do what you have to. I won't try and stop you anymore." She looked back at the picture on the wall. "You just send me a picture when it's as green and beautiful as you say it will be." Then she embraced Ruth as she wished she had embraced her mother.

Aaron sat by himself on the floor, awaiting Madeleine's return. He'd gone over to the group with Ben, but quickly felt that he, with his Orthodox appearance, was not welcome among them. So he had excused himself and returned to his place on the floor. Aaron sat now, eavesdropping on the conversations around him. Those conducted in Hebrew were hard to follow because of the strangely accented words, but he found if he concentrated, he could follow. He listened for a while, then faded into his own thoughts.

If they expected him to argue the point, they were mistaken. To defend God one must have faith, and he had none. His father had told him that the Loemer Rebbe called God to task. "Shall not the God of Justice do justly?" But Aaron was no Rebbe to defend or accuse. He was only a mourner, the sole mourner at a party filled with life. He grieved for the deaths of the people around him. For all those who would be turned into gaping, staring corpses. God knew which ones would die. God knew, and that was why he could not defend God.

Aaron stared at the floor. Images of corpses came into

his head, hazy, barely recollected fragments of memory. The doctors had told him he would never remember, that the memory was gone along with the piece of his brain. But someday, he knew, he would remember it all. He feared that day, as he feared for the people in the room with him now. The din of words seemed to close around him like a wall, separating him from all those who would at least get to the Holy Land, who would actually see Jerusalem.

How his father dreamed of doing that. At Passover, when Yehezkel spoke the words "Next year in Jerusalem," he would close his eyes, reveling in the secret dream encompassed by those words. After a long silence he'd open his eyes, wipe away the tears streaming down his face and whisper once again, "Next year in Jerusalem." Aaron knew his father would never make the pilgrimage. The Jerusalem Yehezkel saw with his closed eyes was Jerusalem filled with dancing Loemer Hasidim. There were no more Loemer Hasidim. They had died in the ditches and camps, and with the Messiah at Auschwitz.

"That's a dandy scar you have," came a voice in Yiddish. Aaron looked up in time to see a young man drop down beside him. "You got that in the war, didn't you?"

"Yes."

"Where?"

"Europe."

"Is gutt. Good, you killed Germans."

"I really couldn't tell you," Aaron said coldly.

"Why not?" The young man looked at Aaron a moment, then broke into a broad grin. "I too have a scar. My name is Shimon. It's my new name. I killed the other. See the scar?"

He raised his arm. A long, ugly scar stretched from his wrist to the inner part of his elbow. It cut across the partially obliterated concentration-camp tattoo. Aaron saw the numbers and looked again at Shimon. He was not an attractive man, his nose long and his lips thick. His face seemed too lined for his age.

"I was in a camp, but I escaped," Shimon said. "Yes, I did. Why can't you tell me you killed Germans?"

"I don't remember."

"How could you not remember? I remember everything. How could you forget?"

"I didn't forget." Aaron ran his fingers through his hair. They touched the skullcap, the sign of his supposed faith. He pulled his hand away. "I just can't remember," he said.

Shimon waited expectantly. Aaron stared at the scar and the number on Shimon's arm. "It was a rough engagement," Aaron said quietly. "I was wounded, and I can't remember."

"How many dead?" Shimon asked.

"Who counts?" Aaron shrugged his shoulders.

"I do."

"On our side, all but me."

"And the Nazis? How many? How many Nazis?" Shimon grinned in anticipation.

"Thirteen. Thirteen Germans killed."

Shimon laughed and clapped Aaron on the back. "Is gutt. You killed them all. I see. You don't have to tell me. I see. You are modest and you killed them all."

"I told you, I don't remember."

"Not remembering killing is not not killing. They're dead whether you remember or not. Bastards! I saw your girlfriend," he added. "She must be proud of you."

"She doesn't know."

Shimon looked surprised. "You never told her?"

"No."

"Then why does she love you?"

Aaron sat beside his accuser. He ran a tongue over dry lips, feeling the roughness of his skin. The number took away his right to refuse. The scar demanded answer to any question. He wished Shimon would go away.

"I don't know that she does," he said finally.

"She doesn't know you if you are silent," Shimon said.

"She knows part of me."

"Not enough."

"She knows the part of me that suffers."

"Does she?" Shimon asked. "She does not know the dead."

"We both suffer," Aaron said. "With different words, we suffer the same way."

"How?"

"We dream," Aaron said. Shimon grinned and said nothing more. He sat next to Aaron, his eyes vacant. Finally he spoke again.

"We Jews can fight. You and I know that."

"Yes. We know that."

Shimon stood as Madeleine came back with Ruth. He looked at Madeleine. "Your lady is pretty. You should have many children by her. Thirteen children." He laughed. "Yes, thirteen Jewish children." Shimon looked around uncertainly, trying to spot a corner where he might fit in. Then he walked away.

"That was a very strange man," Madeleine said.

"He has a right to be," Aaron answered. He turned to Ruth. "This is a farewell party, isn't it?"

Ruth nodded and called Ben over. He smiled as he sat down.

"Well," Ben said. "Now you've proved that yeshiva training can come to good use occasionally. We would have told you in any case."

"What's going on?" Madeleine asked, irritated that the conversation seemed to be bypassing her.

"This is a farewell party," Ruth said. "Everyone here is going to Palestine."

"When?" Aaron asked.

"Tonight," Ruth said.

Madeleine looked at her in horror. Ben caught Madeleine's look.

"Madeleine," he said. "I'll take care of her."

"How can you take care of her? You don't even know her."

"Do you?"

Madeleine reached over and stroked Ruth's cheek. "I thought I did."

"Well," Ruth said, taking Madeleine's hand. "I'm announcing to both of you that I can take care of myself!"

The phone rang, quieting the room. It rang several times, but no one rose to answer it. Then it stopped. In the silence after the ringing, men and women looked at each other, the fear and anticipation seeming to pass from one face to the next. Then, slowly, people stood.

"It's time," Ruth whispered. The whisper sounded loud in the silent room. She hugged Madeleine. "I wanted to share this with you. I wanted to say good-bye to you. I love you, Madeleine."

"I love you too, Ruth." Madeleine held on to her friend, her eyes closed to banish all the people watching them.

"How are you going?" Aaron asked.

"I can't tell you that," Ben said. "There is someone waiting outside for us. I'm afraid you'll have to take the train home. The station is near here."

"I know the way."

"I hope so," Ben said, taking his hand. "And I hope one day it leads to us."

The room emptied as people filed out the door. Shimon passed them, grinning. "We'll show them," he said to Aaron.

Ben touched Ruth on the shoulder. She parted from Madeleine and took his hand. "Next year in Jerusalem," she said. They walked to the door. Ruth turned once and was gone.

Madeleine and Aaron stood alone in the smoke-filled, empty room. She turned to him, not certain what to say or do. For the first time she noticed the ticking of a clock. She located the sound and saw it was late.

"We ought to be going," she said. "But I'm not sure I can face my parents right now."

"Come on. I'll take you out for an egg cream."

"Should we turn out the lights?" she asked. Suddenly the

question seemed ridiculous. She began to laugh. Aaron caught her mood and also began to laugh. Then he put his arm around her, and they both stopped laughing.

Aaron kissed her—a long, gentle kiss. He held her to him awhile. She could feel his heart beating against her cheek as her head rested on his chest. She felt that tightening again in her loins, that nagging urgency she couldn't dispel. Aaron kissed her again, his tongue seeking her out. He kissed her neck, running his beard along her skin, making it tingle. Heat radiated in waves from her thighs, and every part of her skin begged to be touched. She reached down gingerly to touch Aaron and felt the hardness beneath his slacks. He stroked her breasts, then reached inside her blouse to pinch her nipples. As he did, she moaned softly. She heard her sharp intake of breath as he moved his hand under her skirt. She was afraid, but she couldn't stop him, did not want to stop him. She wanted comfort, the surety of his caress. Her kisses pressed against his lips as her heart pounded and she reveled in the feel of his body next to hers. Her breath became ragged; her body convulsed as she sought his lips. Then she relaxed against him. Ashamed, she began to cry.

Aaron held her to him a moment, and she heard his deep slow breaths. He kissed her around the face, wiping her tears away and stroking her hair. "It's all right," he whispered. "I love you. I love you and it's all right." He whispered it over and over, the words comforting, calming her. Then he kissed her once again, gently. Arm in arm, they walked to the door. He paused by the light switch and flicked it off.

JANUARY
1949

MADELEINE STOOD BY THE WINDOW THAT OVERLOOKED the narrow alleyway. Frost had begun to form on the glass, and the frigid air around the window crept out to touch her face. Across the alleyway, Ruth's window was dark. It was always dark. Mr. and Mrs. Kosnik seemed to have recovered from their daughter's sudden departure, but from her window, Madeleine often saw Mrs. Kosnik sitting on Ruth's bed, weeping. Ruth was the heroine of the neighborhood, and the arrival of her monthly letters was considered a neighborhood event. The Kosniks barely had time to peruse her letters for themselves before having to read them to the friends gathered at the mailbox. Ruth's letters were filled with her exploits and tales of heroism by the many refugees turned freedom fighters. Her stories had a profound effect on the neighbors. Every family on the block now displayed the blue-and-white box of the Jewish National Fund in its window. A money box was even nailed to a telephone pole by the street. The neighbors filled the boxes with dimes and quarters and sent them off to the Fund. The land bought with the money would be Ruth's land, and through Ruth, their land.

Madeleine also received monthly letters from Ruth, and she too had to read them aloud to the audiences by the mailbox. But in Madeleine's envelopes were always two letters, the second for her alone. In those, her friend spoke a far less heroic truth. Madeleine glanced back at the letter she'd started—yet another trivial, churned-out response that lay on her desk. Ruth's letters haunted her by day and invaded her dreams at night. Madeleine walked back to the desk and sat down. She opened the drawer that contained the secret letters written only to her.

> *Madeleine, last night I killed someone. I was walking guard duty by the Children's House of the kibbutz. I had my rifle, the one I'd carried for so long without using. Last night I used it to kill an Arab boy, who knows how old? Just a boy. The attack started at night. They usually do—just skirmishes. But this time they broke through the outer lines and into the kibbutz. Flares went up and I saw him heading for the Children's House with a grenade, going to blow up babies with a grenade. Suddenly, I don't know how to describe it, I was filled with hatred and rage. For a while afterward, that was all I remembered—rage. I shot him, screaming at him and emptying the whole clip of bullets. Then I went over to see what I had done. I wanted to see him dead. My God. The back of his head wasn't there anymore—just his face and the eyes that stared at me. Blood everywhere.*
>
> *I wish I knew what to do with this heaviness weighing on my soul. I've killed another human being. I keep seeing his eyes . . .*

That had been one of the first letters. Others followed. Ruth poured herself out in her words, passing on to Madeleine the dark side of the battle for the Jewish state. It was a dark side that Madeleine had sworn to Ruth not to share with anyone.

> *. . . The violence seems to breed death even when the guns aren't firing. I had a miscarriage. I'm not going to tell my mother, but I had to tell someone. I have to make someone understand. I look at this beau-*

*tiful land and I think about my dreams. And sometimes
I think there is so much death, I won't live long. Yet
another day goes by. Funny how I can kill a human
being, but I can't carry one inside me.*

Madeleine wanted to take the letters in her hand and carry
them into the street, shout them at all the people who got
so much pleasure out of Ruth's adventures, who didn't think
anyone over there was suffering. But she couldn't shout.
She couldn't even share them with Aaron. The letters were
too personal, too naked to share.

*. . . I hate Arabs. I hate them. They want to kill
me. They want to kill my baby, if I can even carry a
baby. What's the use of giving birth when someone
is out there waiting to kill your baby? I hate them. I
must hate them because I am killing them. I must.*

It was hard for Madeleine to think of Ruth hating anyone.
But the Ruth of these letters was a different Ruth. The war
had changed her. In all the times Madeleine had dreamed
of battle and glory, she'd never imagined she would be
changed by it all.

Madeleine went back to writing her letter. It was stupid.
All her letters were stupid because she didn't know what to
say to Ruth, how to comfort her, or if Ruth even needed
comfort from her. At least, there was another cease-fire in
Israel. Maybe this one would hold. Maybe all the terror and
the killing would be over for Ruth and she could live the
good side of her dream. Madeleine finished the letter filled
with gossip and funny stories, trying not to reveal the frustration she felt at being far away and safe. Madeleine folded
the letter and stuffed it into an envelope. She licked the
envelope, slicing her tongue and swearing softly.

"Well," she said aloud. "Happy New Year, Ruth. And
Happy Cease-Fire."

If only things settled down in Israel. At least then there

would be one thing less for her to worry about. She seemed to have so much to worry about lately.

Everyone demanded things of her. Stan wanted to talk to her. Illi wanted her to worship at Lenin's feet. Aaron wanted her to like his weird friend Nathan. Ruth wanted—what did Ruth want? Nothing. And that was what made her the most demanding of all. Well, one demand at a time. Madeleine grudgingly got her hat and coat and headed for the subway to Bleecker Street.

People nervously eyed the door as Madeleine walked into the café. She smiled apprehensively and hurried to Stan's table.

"You're late," Stan said as she came up.

"I certainly got a lot of stares when I came in."

Stan chuckled. "We were all afraid that Comrade Illi had come calling. He's become obnoxious as hell. Want some coffee?"

"You treating?" Madeleine asked.

"Yeh, I'll treat."

"In that case I'll have some hot chocolate with whipped cream."

"Being demanding, aren't you?" he said, but he signaled the order.

Madeleine wrestled herself out of her coat. "I came thirty minutes on an unheated subway, just because you wanted to see me."

She took the cup of hot chocolate from the waitress and clutched the cup against her cold-reddened fingers, sniffing the aroma through a runny nose. She really wasn't in the mood for Stan.

"How's your boyfriend?" he asked, blowing on his re-filled coffee cup and watching her.

"Don't start on me, Stan. And that better not be why you wanted to talk."

"Easy, easy. Just let me lead up to this. Please?"

"Okay." Madeleine took a sip of chocolate. It burned her already wounded tongue.

"You know," Stan said, sighing, "I like you a lot. I've got a soft spot for you, my innocent one."

"Sure."

"Ah, it's true, Madeleine. If I didn't really have a soft spot for you, I would have seduced you long ago."

Madeleine looked away from him before she could stop herself. He reached under her chin and gently pulled her head back. "See?" he said. "I just love that. Natalie probably stopped being embarrassed when she was twelve."

Madeleine shook her head free. "Well, I doubt if you would have succeeded."

"Oh, I would have. You and I both know that. But that's neither here nor there. The point is that I liked you too much to try."

"If that's a compliment, thanks."

"So how's your boyfriend?"

"He's all right."

"Marry him."

Madeleine looked at him, waiting for the punch line, but it never came.

"I'm serious," he said after awhile. "This Revolution business isn't what it used to be. Too many free agents. Things are getting rough and they're bound to get rougher. It would be nice if you were out of it. You know—somewhere safe, so your pretty, innocent head won't get broken."

"Are you warning me or threatening me?"

"Why should I threaten you?"

"Why should you warn me?" Madeleine replied. "I like Aaron very much, but you see that I haven't let him get in the way of my commitments to the Party. I'm not stupid. I know things are getting unpleasant." She paused, thinking back to Ruth. "But I believe in the Revolution. I'm willing to risk my life for it. And I'm still here waiting for you to finally make me a Party member. That won't change."

"Everything changes. But you're blind to everything, aren't you, honey? I don't know who's calling the shots anymore, but I put you in for membership a long time ago. Months.

In fact, I was so sure of my mark that I put you in a few weeks after you started hanging around the café."

"So what happened?"

"They don't want you, honey. You front for them much better as an innocent. And if there's going to be a revolution, you might as well get used to the fact that you've been chosen as cannon fodder."

"I don't believe you. Why are you telling me all this?"

"I said, everything changes." Stan stirred his coffee absently. "I am doing, right now, the one, and probably only, decent thing I will do in my life. I'm going to tell you the truth, something I rarely do. And stick my neck out, something I never do."

"I'm listening," Madeleine said.

"What does the name Mikhoels mean to you?"

Madeleine thought. The name sounded vaguely familiar. "I remember. He was the actor murdered by reactionaries in the Soviet Union last year. *Worker's Press* played it up big. So?"

"Reactionaries, shit. Mikhoels was murdered by communist assassins, and Stalin ordered the whole thing."

"Why would the leader of the Soviet Union decide to kill one actor?"

"A Jewish actor, my dear. A signal to start all that blood flowing again. Comrade Stalin doesn't like Jews."

Madeleine blinked a few times, waiting for the feeling of déjà vu to pass. Ruth's words came back to her. "He's killing Jews, you know."

Stan continued. "You've heard our dear friend Illi lately, haven't you? He's started throwing the word 'cosmopolitan' around a great deal."

"Cosmopolitan, yeh," Madeleine said absently, still distracted by the queer feeling in her stomach. Something didn't make sense. "I assumed that Illi discovered a dictionary, and was trying out his favorite new word."

"Wrong. Funny, but wrong. 'Cosmopolitan' is communist talk for 'kike.'"

"That's crazy! And who are you to be saying all this? You're the one who told me—"

"I lied. They told me to lie, so I lied. I lied to you, and to them." Stan leaned back in his chair. "And I lied to myself."

"They, they. Who are they?"

"Honey, the one thing you don't want to know is names." Stan reached forward to casually finger the edge of his coffee cup. "Illi takes his orders from them, says what they want him to say, thinks what they want him to think and above all, does whatever they want him to do. He's with his contact right now."

"How do you know?"

"I've been around. A hell of a lot longer than they think I have."

"So he does want to take over the group," Madeleine said.

"No, my innocent. He wants to destroy our group. And it won't be hard. The House Un-American Activities Committee is grabbing at us faster than they can make the crosses to hang us on, so our fair-weather friends are deserting in droves. Now Illi and his friends want me out of the way. But what I'm afraid of most, my dear, is that either way, HUAC or Illi, you're tainted. That's why you should go get married, like a good girl."

"Stan, I believe in the Revolution. I believe in the Party. And I believe you're nuts!"

"So is Illi, or haven't you noticed? And I venture, he's crazier than me. But a loyal Party member nonetheless."

"Well, so are you," Madeleine said, irritated at defending Stan to Stan. He began to laugh.

"What's so funny?" she asked.

"How I hate to disillusion those naive eyes. Well, can you keep a great big secret?"

"Lay off."

"Lay you is what I should have done." Stan looked at her, his indecisiveness showing on his face. "Love, I really don't think I should do this. But what the hell. I'm a member of the Socialist Workers Party."

"A Trotskyite? You can't be!"

"But I am."

"I don't believe you!"

"You've been saying that a lot. If you're going to survive, you'd better start believing right now." Stan leaned forward again and looked around before talking again. His voice was low.

"Stalin is a maniac. Trotsky knew it. My God, even Lenin knew it. Trotsky almost succeeded, you know; he almost took over for Lenin. But Stalin beat him, beat him out of nowhere. Lenin never wanted Trotsky in high office. Want to know why?"

"Because Trotsky betrayed the ideals of the Revolution."

"Shit, Madeleine. Don't you read anything but what I give you? Don't you think? He didn't take over because he was their Jewboy. Want to know what Lenin said about Trotsky? 'Trotsky is with us. He's with us, but he isn't one of us.' And Lenin wasn't talking about Trotsky's politics."

"Stalin supports Israel."

"He's begun the annihilation of Jews in Russia. And he's already started cooling toward our new Jewish State. Don't you see? Any man who would personally order the death of one Jewish actor, take time out from running a country to knock off one lousy Jew, hates Jews too much to support their country. It's"—he hissed out the last words—"too cosmopolitan."

"I believe in the Revolution."

"Please, don't spout my own propaganda back at me."

"It's not your propaganda," Madeleine said angrily. "It's something I believe. It's my dream, Stan. You think that I only know what you tell me, only believe you. So you can change your tune and fully expect I'll change mine. I may have gotten the dream from you, but it's my dream now. And I think Illi is getting more power and you're jealous."

"You know that isn't true," Stan said softly.

"I'm not sure what I know. At least he hasn't betrayed the Father."

"The Father. What crap. Stalin, the great Father of us all. People are drowning in all the blood he's spilling over Russia. And it's just begun!"

"You can't make me a Trotskyite just by saying you are, Stan. I'm not Natalie."

"Oh, damn," he said harshly. "I don't know why I even bothered to talk to you. I'd forgotten how good I am at my job. You listen to me, Madeleine. The only revolution that's coming is the ax that's going to cut down the Jews. Stalin's ax. That's what he killed Trotsky with, you know. Couldn't stand to have the Jew boy in the same world with him, so he sent a loyal Party member to cut him down." Stan said the last words slowly. He looked at Madeleine until she broke away from his eyes.

"What are you going to do?" she asked finally.

"Well, I'm not going to stay and fight, dear. If anyone finds out, and I hope to God no one does, I won't be tolerated as nicely as the Trots around this café. I'm going to get the hell out of here. Fade into the woodwork and then maybe, if I still believe in anything, I'll resurface in Cuba, or Bolivia, or somewhere."

"You're that worried."

"I am," he said. "I haven't told anyone about this. Even Natalie doesn't know. You can't tell anyone. You can't even hint at it, not even to your boyfriend. If they suspect me, they'll be watching you."

"I think your flair for the dramatic is showing."

"Madeleine, please! Don't tell anyone!"

"All right. I won't," she said. He looked at her. "I promise."

Stan nodded. "And remember. Watch out. You're tainted."

"Look. I won't tell anyone. So don't throw any more propaganda at me."

The room quieted momentarily, and the two looked toward the door. Illi had walked in. He looked at them a moment, then surveyed the room. He smiled to himself; then he walked to an empty table, head lowered, eyes still searching the people in the café.

"There he is," Stan said. "The hope of the Party until his superiors decide he's a liability—which probably won't be long." Stan smiled the sarcastic smile she'd seen so often. "Well, having failed once more, it's time for me to leave." He stood and looked down at her, the smile vanishing. "Please, Madeleine, get out before you ruin your life."

The smile returned, and Stan walked to the door. As he did, Illi rose, and, with exaggerated movements, bumped into him. The larger man stopped. The two stood, Illi looking up into Stan's eyes. Then Illi grinned, shrugged his shoulders and walked past Stan to where Madeleine sat. Stan gave her a last warning look and left.

"Comrade, may I sit down?" Illi asked as he sat down. He wiped a swatch of unwashed hair out of his eyes, which promptly fell back.

"Illi," Madeleine said. "I'm getting ready to leave." Suddenly her irritation and tension came to the surface. "And don't call me 'Comrade,'" she snapped. "I'm not a Party member. You've all been stalling me about my joining. If you don't want me in the Party, don't call me 'Comrade.'"

Illi smiled at her. For a moment his face looked soft, boyish. "I'll always consider you my comrade, Madeleine. You're with us whether or not you carry a card."

"But am I one of you?"

He reached over and patted her on the hand, then quickly drew back, placing his hands on the table before him.

"What did you and Stan talk about?" he asked softly.

Madeleine eyed him. The suspicions Stan had planted began to work on her in spite of herself. "A lot of things," she said.

"Like what?"

"Illi, my conversations are none of your business."

His fists clenched and were instantly flat on the table once more. "I am involved in security," he said.

"That was only for a couple of rallies."

He smiled. "I bet you're still upset by what I said a while ago. Months, it's been. Can't you forgive me? I wasn't feeling well, and it was such a little indiscretion. You know, Comrade Madeleine, I'll admit something to you. I have trouble expressing myself about things important to me and," he added shyly, "to someone important to me. Will you forgive me?"

"I forgive you, Illi. Now I've got to be going."

"Where?"

"Lately all I ever get from you is questions. All anyone gets is questions. My life is my own."

"Your life is the Party's."

"I'm not a Party member. The Party doesn't want me."

"But the Party needs you. You really should devote more time to us."

"I'd rather not have any lectures." She stood up. "I've done all the jobs Stan has given me. He understands that I'm going to school."

"Maybe he's too understanding. It makes him a weak leader," Illi said slowly, looking at his hands.

Madeleine started to say something, but pulled back. "I really have to go."

Illi stood in a swift catlike movement that blocked her way. "I'm extremely concerned for you, comrade. Please, consider me your friend and brother in the Revolution."

"I will, I will. Good-bye." Madeleine hesitated a second, then pushed past him. She could feel his eyes on her back, even after she walked out the door. She walked quickly to the subway, putting distance between herself and the café. Her sweaty palms turned numb in the cold.

The half-hour it took to get back over to Avenue Q gave Madeleine more time to think than she wanted. Things were happening too fast, and she couldn't fathom their consequences. No one was who he seemed to be. She ached to have Ruth beside her so she could talk. Everything hadn't worked out the way Ruth had envisioned, and Ruth wasn't giving up. She needed her support.

Madeleine sought comfort in the sway of the subway car.

This car, at least, had the heater working. Bathed in warmth and swaying, she closed her eyes, clearing her mind of her troubles. She wouldn't even be able to talk to Aaron, because Nathan was with him. Her mind floated to the vision of her daydreams, the image of Stan lying dead in her arms.

Once at Avenue Q, Madeleine walked down the small side street that led to the Liberal Rabbinical School of Brooklyn. Today was garbage day, and unclaimed empty trash cans lined the street, lending their pungent scent to the clean roadway. Three children played hopscotch in the middle of the street, struggling against scarves, coats and sweaters.

When Bea Blumfeld had told Vellef about Aaron, Vellef had been delighted, as Madeleine had feared he would be. The result of his and Bea's more restrained but no less enthusiastic pleasure was a weekly Tuesday dinner invitation to Aaron in addition to a weekly Friday-night dinner invitation. And to make things worse, Nathan Schwartz, Aaron's friend, was also invited. Madeleine had tried, but she didn't particularly like Nathan.

When she entered the building, she saw Aaron and Nathan down the hallway, a text opened between them. Nathan held one side and Aaron the other, as each waved his free hand, or pointed to a place in the text. They looked like a pair of frenetic choirboys. Aaron looked up and saw her. He smiled, holding up his hand to stop Nathan as she approached.

"If it's that important," Aaron said, "we can continue the discussion at Madeleine's."

"Oh, Aaron—"

"No oh, Aaron. I wish to speak also with my lady."

"So," Madeleine said. "You noticed I was around."

"I even notice when you aren't around," Aaron said.

"And how are you?" Madeleine asked, turning to Nathan.

"Fine. Just fine," Nathan said. He closed the text and tucked it under his arm, giving up. "You have to admit," he said to Aaron, "that I have a point."

"If it makes you feel better to have a point, have one—

until we get to Madeleine's. Then be prepared for all the points *I* have."

"I can't wait," Madeleine said.

"You know," Nathan said to Madeleine, "he was much nicer to me when I went to this place."

"Then you needed encouragement," Aaron replied. "Now you need challenging."

"My, doesn't that sound wise," Madeleine said. She wanted to give Aaron a hug, and would have, had Nathan not been there. Such things made him uncomfortable. His rigidity made her uncomfortable.

The only concession Nathan made in his Orthodox regimen was eating at her parents' house. He'd questioned Madeleine about what her mother did in the kitchen. As she answered his questions, she had realized, for the first time, that Bea kept a fairly kosher kitchen. The family's meat came from the kosher butcher. They used the same dishes for meat and dairy meals, but the plates were clear glass. Nathan had approved of that, explaining that glass plates could be used interchangeably. The family had always used different silverware for meat and dairy foods. Bea kept her silverware not in a drawer, but in two wire baskets, putting the appropriate one on the table. What amazed Madeleine most was that she'd grown up never questioning this quirk of her mother's.

"Okay," Aaron said. "Let me get my coat and briefcase, and we'll be off." He walked down the hall as the two stood silently watching after him. Nathan put his hands in his pockets and turned to her.

"You know," he said. "I still get the shivers when I walk into this place."

"So do I. Only for different reasons."

"I know." He paused and looked down at the floor. "So how are you two doing?"

"We're doing fine. But please don't ask me if I'm going to marry him."

"Why not?"

"Everyone's asking but him."

"And what if he did?"

"If he did," Madeleine said, gazing down the now empty hall, "I'd have to think about it."

"You could do a lot worse."

"And just how could I do a lot worse, Nathan Schwartz, matchmaker?"

"Don't get angry. I just mean you won't find a better man."

"What if better men and worse men don't matter? What if what I want out of life has nothing to do with a man?"

"Please, don't get angry," Nathan said. "I just don't understand."

"You don't? Okay. What if it wasn't Aaron and me, but you and me? What if I wanted you to marry me, just like I am—no compromises, no kosher home, maybe no kids."

"I couldn't," he said definitely.

"Why not?"

"Well, first of all, you couldn't really love me and ask me to do that. I'd be giving up all that I am or want to be."

"Exactly. I want to be more than a wife and mother."

"That isn't something tangible."

"To me it is," she said.

"It's not the same."

"Okay," Madeleine said. "Would it be the same if I wanted to be a rabbi?"

"You can't be a rabbi."

"Why not? There's nothing in the charter of the Liberal Rabbinical School that prevents me from entering the program. What if I wanted to be a rabbi instead of a rebbetzin?"

"It's not the same."

"Why not?"

Nathan was silent. Madeleine edged closer to him, knowing that that would threaten him. "Why not?" she asked again.

"Because you're not a man."

Madeleine eased off and smiled. "And that's what it boils

down to for everyone. It doesn't matter what I want to be. Revolutionary or brain surgeon, it doesn't matter. Aaron's dreams, your dreams are more important than mine because I'm a woman."

"The Holy One gave us each—"

"Don't talk God to me! I don't care what God wants. I don't care about a God that gives me the ability to dream, and then says I can't try and make those dreams come true. What I want out of life may not be important to you, or to my parents, or even to God, but what I want is damn important to me!"

"Well, if that's the way you feel, you shouldn't lead Aaron on like this."

Madeleine looked at Nathan, incredulous. "Lead him on? And how am I leading him on? Aaron has always known what I think."

"He's in love with you. Are you in love with him?"

Aaron appeared in the hall. The two abruptly stopped their conversation. "You two look serious," Aaron said. "Another political debate?"

"Definitely," Madeleine said, smiling at Nathan.

With effort, he smiled back at her. Aaron laughed as he put an arm around each of them and headed them toward the door.

"Do we have to walk? It's cold out there," Nathan said.

"Certainly," Aaron replied. "I see it as my duty to heartlessly force you to walk out in the glorious winter air and marvel at the icicles hanging from the trees—"

"He who pauses in the study of Torah to admire a tree has lost his soul."

"Oh, good grief," Madeleine said in disgust.

"Don't worry, dear," Aaron said. "That isn't our Nathan speaking, but a grouchy forefather in the Talmud. And Nathan really doesn't believe that—do you?"

Nathan was quiet a minute, thinking.

"If you become a fanatic, my friend," Aaron said, "I will personally break your healthy Davidic nose."

Nathan grinned. "No. I don't believe it." Then he added ominously, "Not yet, anyway."

"Hopeless," Aaron and Madeleine said together.

As they walked along the park benches that lined the sidewalk, Aaron reached into his briefcase and pulled out unpopped corn, throwing it to the pigeons. He soon had a flock following him.

"They're dirty, filthy, disease-ridden creatures, you know," Nathan said. "My mother used to make me wash my hands if I sat on a park bench in any proximity to pigeons."

"Ah," Madeleine said. "But dirty, filthy, disease-ridden creatures are still creatures of God."

"Very good, Madeleine," Aaron said.

"I thought you'd like that. I don't believe a word of it, of course. Dirty, filthy, disease-ridden creatures are merely dirty, filthy, disease-ridden creatures."

"Hear, hear," Nathan said in agreement.

Aaron clicked his tongue. "Nathan, I'm disappointed in you."

"You said you didn't want me to become a fanatic. Where pigeons are concerned, my mother wins. I will never become a fanatic."

Nathan looked longingly at a bus that went by. The three were walking at a brisk pace, and he was already out of breath.

"You keep this up and I may cease my visits, in spite of Mrs. Blumfeld's cooking."

"Never."

"Well, if you'll slow down a little so I can breathe, I'll tell you what I've been thinking."

"What makes you think we want to know?" Aaron said. But he slowed down. "What you're thinking better be good. We're doing this for your health."

"I've been thinking about Jerusalem," Nathan said.

Aaron speeded up.

"Wait a minute! I'm thinking about going there."

"What about the yeshiva?" Aaron asked.

"I agree," Madeleine said. "What about your dedication to that exploitive training ground?"

"I'm not going now. After I get ordained."

Aaron started walking again, but at a moderate pace. "When did all this come about?"

"I got the idea from what your friend did, Madeleine. I thought about Ruth, and her yearning to go to the Holy Land—"

"You're getting sentimental," Madeleine said. "And you are too impressionable."

"Now, wait. I admit that. I know everyone is imbued with the Zionist spirit, running around with lights in their eyes. We've had two guys from the yeshiva go off to fight the Holy War."

"You say that with sarcasm," Aaron said.

"Yes, I do," Nathan replied. "Well, yes and no. It is a Holy War, if wars can be holy. But there are other kinds of fighting. I don't approve of leaving Torah to carry a gun. God will be influenced by Torah more than by guns, and we need God's help to survive."

"Oh, I get it," Madeleine said. "Sitting here in Brooklyn, in your nice little yeshiva, doing Torah portions while someone supports you, you're doing as much for Israel as Ruth when she's getting shot at." Madeleine flushed with anger. "Of course. I should have realized that before."

Nathan looked at her. "That's exactly what I'm saying. And I'm not going to get apologetic about it because it makes you uncomfortable."

"Nathan, calm down," Aaron said. "Madeleine, calm down. Nathan, go on."

Madeleine stared sullenly at the sidewalk while Nathan continued. "I want to stay here until I'm ordained. Then I want to emigrate."

"Sure," Madeleine said, looking up. "When it's safe."

"Madeleine," Aaron said quietly. "It is never going to be safe there. After this war or any other."

"Safety has nothing to do with it," Nathan said. "I would go now, if I was prepared to study and pray the way I need to. A lot of people are going to Israel to die for the Holy Land. I want to be fully prepared to live for the Holy Land. We've had real experience at dying, but we may start a whole new country without knowing how to live." He paused as they waited in silence for a traffic light to change.

"Okay, go on," Madeleine said when they had crossed the street. Nathan smiled faintly.

"I've been thinking that had Israel been in existence when I started searching, I wouldn't have gone to yeshiva in Brooklyn. I would have gone to Jerusalem, seeking. I'm thinking of teaching in a yeshiva there, or if I have to, starting a yeshiva myself for those who come." He stopped talking and put his hands in his pockets, embarrassed by his burst of intensity.

"Well, what do you think?" he asked finally.

But Aaron said nothing. He looked straight ahead with the clouded gaze Nathan had seen so often. Madeleine too looked at Aaron, the worry clear on her face.

"Well, taking into account how atavistic it is," she said to divert attention from Aaron, "I think it's a fairly good idea."

"Why, Madeleine, I'm truly touched. I'm not sure, but I think you approve."

She glanced again at Aaron, hoping he would reply. But his eyes still looked into a world she did not share.

"I do not approve," she said. "I merely said it was one of your better atavistic ideas. And it will serve to siphon off some of the fanatics from Brooklyn."

The two looked at each other, acknowledging the act they were putting on for Aaron, and feeling, at that moment, a bond of common concern.

"Ah, Aaron," Nathan said loudly. "Watch out. I think she loves me!"

"Like she loves pigeons," Aaron said, finally coming out of his silence. He laughed.

Tuesday dinners at the Blumfeld house had become a duplicate of the Friday-night meal in everything but the candles and wine. Bea took special pleasure in the Tuesday meal when Nathan came along with Aaron. As Madeleine and the "boys" entered the apartment, Bea greeted them with tea. Madeleine offered, as she did every week, to help. Bea, as she did every week, refused.

Madeleine's mother, who now came home early on Tuesdays, had filled the house with the aromas of roast and browning onions. She moved into and out of the kitchen, dressed in her Sabbath clothes, humming tunes Madeleine hadn't heard since she was a child. Sometimes Bea stopped and watched Nathan and Aaron as they pursued the argument they'd begun at the rabbinical school. This was a part of Bea that Madeleine had never seen, one of the many complexities she'd begun to discover in her mother.

Madeleine drank her tea, all but forgotten by the "boys" five minutes after they sat down. Aaron shot her an apologetic glance which made her feel better. At least he noticed her exclusion. She rose quietly and went into the kitchen, where her mother was bent over in front of the oven, worrying about her roast. She straightened up and smiled, seeing Madeleine.

"Such nice boys. It's a pleasure to have them here. You've given me a gift, Maidel. Of all my girls, you've given me the gift with the most pleasure."

Madeleine winced. "I don't see how cooking your heart out two days a week instead of one could give you pleasure."

"No?" Bea looked surprised; then she sighed. "No, you wouldn't, would you?" She glanced over at the brass Sabbath candlesticks that rested on the shelf by the sink. "I came from a religious family, you know."

"You never told me that."

"It was long ago, very long ago. That's why I light candles."

"And why you keep the house kosher," Madeleine added, prodding as her mother's thoughts seemed to trail off.

Bea laughed. "Kosher by my mother's standards it isn't."

"Why didn't you ever teach me, or Ann, or even Debra to light candles?"

Shrugging, Bea looked at the candlesticks. "My family was religious. I am not."

"Then why do you do all those things?"

"You ask too many questions," Bea said.

"Why?"

"I like to."

"That's not good enough," Madeleine said. "I might like to light candles, yet you've never taught me how."

"Maidel, I can see you doing many things, but . . . but who knows?" Bea sighed. "I didn't teach you anything because your father asked me not to."

Bea saw her daughter's look of disbelief and continued. "Try to understand. We'd just come from Russia, and settled into the business, when Devorah came. Your father didn't want me to light candles. But it was all that had been left to me. These . . ." She reached over and gently laid her hand on the candlesticks a moment. "These were supposed to go to my older sister, but I found them in my suitcase when we fled. My mother must have put them there." Bea paused. "She was given to premonitions," she said softly.

"Your father wanted you to be Americans, to blend in with the New Country. That's why your Jewish names are only used at home. To the American world you have American names and faces."

"Do you mean that with all this religious holy American stuff Papa shouts all the time, he's afraid to be a Jew here?"

"I said, try to understand, Maidel." Bea's voice was sharp. "He has no family; neither do I. You, God willing, will never know what we knew, to be cut off from who you were, from those you loved and those who loved you. You can never be the same after that, never trust completely, no matter how much you want to. Your father believes all that he says to you, yet with the deepest part of his soul, he wants to be sure you survive. That his family won't be blotted out again. So, he has made you into Americans. And," Bea said, reaching for the hot pad, "I think he did too good a job with you."

Madeleine heard the door open and glanced at her watch. In order for her father to be home now, he must have closed the shop a few minutes early. Miraculous changes were coming about in the Blumfeld family. She peeked out into the living room and saw her father standing, an ill-fitting black skullcap on his head, listening to the two men. Vellef cocked his head, straining to hear and catch enough to understand, smiling when he did.

Bea walked into the living room. In spite of her protests, the guests insisted on pulling out the table and setting it. Vellef moved over to the couch to read the paper. His refusal to do "women's work" never failed to infuriate Madeleine, and she suspected he continued the behavior just to make her angry. So he sat until they were finished.

"You know," Bea said, after they sat down and the food had been passed, "in the village I came from, there was a yeshiva. Every family that could afford it had eating days. You know what eating days are?"

Nathan and Madeleine shook their heads.

"We would take in a yeshiva boy on a certain day of the week. He would eat with us, like now, on Tuesday; then on Wednesday someone else would take him, and so on. Eating days."

"That's lovely," Nathan said. "I'd never heard of that."

"Yes, well"—Bea looked at her husband—"sometimes things get lost in America. Good things."

"I don't see it as so good," Madeleine said. "Except for the yeshiva spongers who mooched off poor working people, while they did nothing all day but sit and read."

Aaron sighed and rolled his eyes upward. "You're hopeless."

Bea dished out more roast on Nathan's plate before he could protest. "Maidel," she said. "I know you would like to put us all in rags, but not all families in Europe were poor—not even all Jewish families. And in return for meals, the yeshiva boys would give lessons or a talk on the Torah portion of the week. I learned a lot from them."

"You had to," Madeleine said. "Because they wouldn't have let you into the yeshiva." She looked at Nathan. "After all, you were only a woman."

"So," Vellef said loudly. "Have the two of you considered marriage?"

Everyone stopped eating and stared at Madeleine's father. In the astounded silence, Vellef spoke again.

"It's a logical question. You're seeing each other for months now. It would be good to know your intentions in this area."

"Vellef!" Bea said.

"Oy, Vellef already. Don't Vellef me. You're curious too."

Madeleine sat frozen, her fork poised above her plate. Her father had caught her completely off guard. Aaron came to the rescue.

"Madeleine and I have thought about it, Mr. Blumfeld."

"We have?" Madeleine asked.

"I've thought about the subject of marriage. I assume you have some opinions on the matter."

"I certainly do."

"And, Mr. Blumfeld, we intend to discuss it in the near future."

"We certainly will."

"Good," Vellef said. "Very good. I'm pleased for you. Very pleased."

"Papa, Aaron said we would discuss marriage, not get married. I personally think marriage is an exploitive tool to create a whole class of indentured servants."

Aaron rolled his eyes once more.

"What?" Vellef asked.

"Servants. Like people who cook all day and clean up and set tables, while other people read newspapers."

Vellef's face began to darken. "There is work women do and work men do. That's that."

"Oh? Work men do? Like working in the paint store?" Madeleine asked.

"Maidel, please," Bea said. "If I need battles fought, I can fight them myself. With an ally like you, the battle is already lost."

"She doesn't paint!" Vellef shouted. "Only *I* paint. Painting is man's work and cooking is for women. That is how God made things."

"Since when do you talk about God?" Bea asked. "You who haven't been in a synagogue in twenty years, even for the High Holy Days. Since when do you talk about God? You always said you didn't believe in God."

"I don't!" Vellef snapped, feeling himself backed into a corner.

"Then maybe I should paint," Bea said. She faced her husband with her arms folded over her breasts.

Vellef looked at her in shock. "Bea?"

Bea returned his gaze without a hint of pity. "I'll tell you what, Vellef. I'll cook if you'll believe in God. Agreed? Good." She unfolded her arms and tapped Madeleine on the shoulder. "Maidel, it's about time you learned how to bless the candles on Friday nights. We'll start this week." She turned from her shocked daughter to her shocked husband and smiled. "More vegetables, anyone?"

After dinner, Vellef, firing a vindictive glance at his daughter, suggested that the men go outside for a while. The three went downstairs and sat on the retaining wall of the red stone porch. Vellef lit a cigar.

"I usually don't smoke. Bea hates the smell. But a customer gave me a few good Havanas. You would maybe want one?"

Both Aaron and Nathan shook their heads. Vellef looked relieved and put the two offered cigars back into his shirt pocket.

"Madeleine will glare at me all evening for this. She doesn't understand. You know, I've lived with four women for the last twenty years or so. Always women. Women talking, women laughing or crying. Sometimes it's good just to sit with a couple of men for a change."

They sat and watched the boys in the street finishing their stickball game in the chill of the setting sun.

"It's good Maidel met you, Aaron," Vellef said.

"Thank you."

"I'm six years older than Maidel's mother, you know." He puffed on the cigar, holding the smoke in his mouth a moment and blowing it out on the cigar as he stared at its glowing end. "She is very young, my Maidel. She dreams, but she knows nothing of life. She needs someone older, like you."

"I hope so," Aaron said. "I love your daughter very much."

"And you want her to marry you."

"Yes. But I won't ask her—not for a while."

"What about her dreams?" Vellef asked.

"When the time is right, I'll ask her to choose."

"You think she will choose you? It's not very glamorous to be a rebbetzin. Not nearly as glamorous as being a revolutionary."

"Yes," Aaron said definitely. "She will choose me."

"I hope so," Vellef said. "God in Heaven, I hope so."

Nathan watched the two men, remembering his talk with Madeleine just that afternoon. He said nothing, but feared his friend was going to be hurt deeply, and soon.

APRIL
1949

SOMETHING MADE MADELEINE STOP ON THE STREET TWO blocks from the Bleecker Café. If the day had been gloomy and cold, she might not have noticed the dark voice of warning that sounded within her. But the day was filled with blue sky and spring, so on impulse, Madeleine crossed to the opposite side of the street, feeling half-foolish because of her apprehension. In the months since Stan's departure, Illi had been trying to scare her with talk of Stan's turning informer, and the police poised to arrest them all. In fact, now that she thought about it, her inner dark voice sounded a lot like Illi's.

At least Illi was not the new leader of the group. As Stan had predicted, a short time after he left, the group disbanded. Most of them were now plugged into a small storefront headquarters off Union Square. There everyone, including Illi, took orders from Raymond Getz. And that was fine with Madeleine. Raymond was very different from Stan, making him look coarse by comparison. Raymond had cleanly cut black hair and always wore a tie. He'd graduated from Harvard and spoke with a New England accent. He was quiet, soft-spoken and very good-looking, though she was attracted to him only in a comradely sense. It was loyalty that made her blush every time he looked at her.

Though Raymond had been the one to put a stop to Illi's efforts at leading the group, Illi never spoke against him. Illi seemed so attached to the man, so loyal, that a word from Raymond could send him into a joyous frenzy, or a silent depression. Madeleine, in contrast, had no control of Illi, and spent most of her time trying to avoid him. Stan's warnings still rang in her head. Madeleine defended Stan as best she could without revealing what she'd promised to keep secret. Sometimes she had the feeling that Illi's scare talk was just to get some sort of information from her. He hadn't succeeded, she thought smugly.

About half a block from the café, Madeleine spotted the government agents. They stood outside, flashing identification to those who passed by and cornering people as they came out of the café. Madeleine watched her friends being pulled aside and then obliterated from view by the mob of gray suits. She walked slowly, noticing the police car parked on her side of the street. One of the two officers looked up. Madeleine walked slowly by.

Her hands shook in the pockets of her jacket. Someone had informed. Panic rose in her throat. But there was nothing to tell; she wasn't even a Party member. Maybe no one had informed. The whole country had been nervous since the Russians had exploded their A-bomb. Maybe it was just the FBI trying to impress the public.

"Miss?"

Madeleine jumped at the voice and turned around to see a young policeman from the car, the one who had noticed her. Suddenly she felt light-headed. "Yes, Officer?"

"You dropped this, miss." He smiled and handed her an envelope.

"Thank you," she said. "A letter. To my friend. She doesn't live here anymore."

"Obviously," he said.

"I forgot to mail it."

He nodded.

"Well," Madeleine said. "I guess I'll go mail it now." She turned around and took a step.

"Oh, miss?"

She stopped, slowly turned back around and forced a smile. "Yes?" she said.

"I was wondering, do you come by this street often?"

"Uh, not very." Madeleine's head throbbed with each heartbeat. "Why?"

"I thought if you came by here regularly, you could point out some of the characters who frequent that café." He jerked his thumb in the direction of the Bleecker Café. "Just a hunch."

"No. No, I couldn't tell you anything." Madeleine paused a moment. "Uh, what kinds of things have been going on there?" she asked. "It looked pretty calm to me—those few times I've been by."

"Subversion," he replied, very serious. "A bunch of Commies. And now they've killed someone."

"Killed someone?"

"Yes, miss, this is a murder investigation." He unbuttoned his pocket and took out a photograph. "Let me show you this just in case. You might have seen him once or twice." The officer handed Madeleine the photo.

It was Stan. Madeleine saw the picture and knew she'd gone pale. She felt the blood drain from her face.

"You recognize him?"

"Yes," Madeleine said, forcing her voice above a whisper. "He tried to give me a pamphlet once. Is he the murder suspect?"

"No, miss. He's the victim. Could I have your name and address?"

"He's the victim? You mean he's dead?"

"Real dead. Somebody killed him with a cleaver or an ax or something. He took a while to identify. His name was Stanley Landis."

"Stan Landis."

"Yes, miss."

Madeleine stared at the photo. It was an old picture. Stan looked very young. She tried to will her body out of its paralysis, to take her eyes from the photo.

"Can I have your name and address?" the officer asked again. The implication of his question finally moved her. She looked at him.

"Why?" she asked. "Why do you want my address? He just tried to give me a leaflet, that's all."

The policeman laughed. "Oh, don't worry. I doubt if anyone will follow up; but I've got to have the information, since you did recognize the guy."

Trapped, Madeleine heard herself giving her name and her address. She handed the picture back to the policeman, still trying not to give herself away. She said good-bye and walked slowly away.

"Miss?"

The word stabbed her. She halted again and turned.

"Your letter. There's a mailbox right by you."

She walked over to the mailbox and dropped the letter in. She smiled as the officer walked back down the street to his car. She tried to absorb what she'd heard as she made her way down the subway steps at the end of the block. Stan was dead. All she could feel was horror and the tightness in her body. She held her breath as if she would explode and only her breath could save her. Her eyes were already blurred with tears when she saw the grimy sign marked LADIES and pushed through the door. Enclosed by the stall, she leaned her head against the cool dark wood and began to sob. The passing trains below covered the sounds of her grief. She brought herself under control and reached for the stall door, only to begin crying again, terrified at the thought of walking outside.

Stan. Her mind tried to convince her that she'd heard wrong, mistaken someone else for him, but her body believed Stan's death. It knew the truth, and waves of sobbing consumed her. At last, she reached for the stall door and opened it. She greeted her image in the mirror, a Madeleine with bloated eyes and runny nose. She washed her face at the cracked sink. There were no towels. She glanced back at the stall. There was no toilet paper. Her irritation helped her get more control, as she wiped her face on her sleeve and walked out of the rest room.

She didn't want to go back to street level. The police

were waiting there. Instead, she went down the steps to the platform, feeling the wind sting her eyes with dust as a train roared in. She wanted to be far away from this place, from the café. She stepped inside the train, not caring where she was headed.

Madeleine glanced around the car, half-expecting the police. She sat, trembling and trying not to let the trembling show. Illi had murdered him—she was sure of it. Maybe they'd already arrested him; maybe they hadn't. The thought made her shudder. She looked around the car and saw two curious eyes staring at her from beneath a black-brimmed hat. As she became aware of her surroundings, Madeleine noticed the large number of black hats, black coats. She squinted to read through the dirt-clouded window above the curious boy. She'd taken the train that went through Williamsburg.

Madeleine got off the train at the next stop and walked to the platform on the opposite side. It was time to go home. But she didn't want to. She wanted Aaron. As she waited, the platform became more crowded with men in black, holding black books and reading the black Hebrew characters. She wondered if they ever noticed where they were, if the sky was blue, if people died. This had been Aaron's world. In some ways it still was. Yet this was the part of his life he'd never let her touch. She'd never been to Williamsburg. Right above her, waiting, was his world.

The brilliant sun at the subway entrance made her squint. Her eyes adjusted to the glare, and she beheld a flood of Hebrew characters spewing out Yiddish words on billboards, store signs and schools. She had no trouble reading them, and that gave her comfort in this alien place. She saw almost no signs in Hebrew. The few she did see looked odd. After a lifetime of Yiddish, Hebrew words seemed too short, too orderly. The words had the same letters as the Yiddish, but to her they were endowed with the confinement she felt sitting all day in the synagogue on Yom Kippur. Yiddish blossomed into many-lettered words, descriptions, meanings. She derived no meaning from the tight black Hebrew. Once at Yom Kippur, when she was young, she had tried to sound out the words in the prayer book, hoping for some meaning. No understanding ever came. She marveled that the two languages could be so much the same, yet so far apart.

Madeleine felt light-headed and leaned against the railing. Everything had changed in a matter of hours. If it was even that long. She looked at her watch. A little over an hour. Stan was dead. She tried to analyze why she felt it so deeply, but her mind refused to work. She could feel only numbness, fear, desire. Stan had known all along that she'd desired him. Madeleine shivered. She could have known his touch, but no more. She was ashamed at the flush she felt. He was dead. Death, like a black shadow, like the black shadows passing her in the street. No one looked at her. No man would have her here. They looked away at their books, at their God, at Aaron's God. Suddenly she was afraid. She ran back down into the subway. She ran to Aaron.

They sat in his apartment and finally she felt safe. Aaron held her, his arms strong, his body warm beneath the white shirt.

"What are you going to do now?" he asked.

"I don't know," Madeleine said. She snuggled beneath his arm. "Maybe stay on this couch with you forever."

"I'd like that," Aaron said, giving her a squeeze. "I'd like that very much."

"Stan wanted me to leave everything and marry you."

"Considering what's happened, that might not be a bad idea."

"Are you proposing?"

"I'm raising the issue," Aaron said. "I love you."

"Why?" she asked.

"What?"

"Why do you love me, Aaron?"

"What do you mean? I love you because of who you are. It's not easy to say why you love someone. You just love them." He leaned over to kiss her, but she moved back.

"I accidentally wound up in Williamsburg today," she said.

"And?"

"It frightened me. All those glaring men in beards and black coats frightened me."

"I will have to remember not to take you to Williamsburg."

"You carry it around inside you all the time," Madeleine said. "You were the one who told me about living in two worlds. That's your other world, and it frightens me."

"I hardly am the type to make you wear a wig."

"What do you want of me?"

"I want you to love me!" he said.

"No. You want more. I want to be a revolutionary and you want me to be your rebbetzin. I don't believe in God and you want me to keep kosher. Aaron, I think you fell in love with me because of Williamsburg."

"I lived in Chicago, remember?"

"I think you love me because I'm a heretic to all those people."

"That's nonsense!" Aaron said. He sat up and drew his arm away. "I love you, Madeleine. I just do. You can't analyze that."

"Maybe we could, if we ever really talked," Madeleine said. "You're always strong; you never mention any problems. You never really confide in me. There are whole dark spaces in you, and they frighten me. I just wish I knew what you wanted."

Aaron drew her to him. "Shh. Now's not the time."

"No, it's not," Madeleine said. "I have to go soon." She closed her eyes. "And right now I want you to hold me and be strong for me. Right now I want to love you and forget the rest of the world."

Agents Knox and Bach arrived at the Blumfeld house ten minutes before Madeleine did. They sat quietly and politely refused the tea Mrs. Blumfeld offered. Knox, the elder of the two, made his mental notes. In his ten years of experience, he'd spent many moments like this. Nervous parents waiting to see what awful things their favorite children had done. Somehow, the nicest parents seemed to have the worst kids. And with these particular investigations, it seemed as if he ought to go and learn to speak Jewish. He was beginning to think the whole damn Communist Party was one big synagogue.

The girl who came in the door was younger and prettier than Knox had expected. She wouldn't be hard to scare, if only her father let him get near her. Mr. Blumfeld didn't look like the kind that was easily intimidated. Blumfeld had that look about him; he emitted a hatred so deep, so unyielding, that it masked his eyes. Knox could feel the man's hatred, and his power.

The two agents rose when Madeleine entered. "Madeleine Blumfeld?"

"Yes?"

Knox flashed his identification at her. "I'm Agent Knox. This is Agent Bach. We'd like to speak to you." He smiled. Bach didn't.

Madeleine looked at the two in dismay, but she didn't let it show. They were too late. She was too wrung out to react to them. She sat down without saying anything. The two sat opposite her. They could have been brothers with their sandy hair and gray eyes. Bach didn't like her, she could see that. His contempt showed in his eyes.

"Mr. Blumfeld," Knox said, "if you will be good enough to leave us alone for a while?"

"No."

"Mr. Blumfeld—"

Vellef stood, so that he towered above the seated Knox. "Mister, this is my house and my daughter. I don't want to cause any trouble, but I stay with my daughter."

Knox looked at him a moment, his eyes saying nothing. Then he shrugged. Vellef resumed his place on the arm of the couch next to Madeleine. Bach started the questioning.

"Miss Blumfeld, we were informed by the local police that you knew Stanley Landis. Is that true?"

It was obvious by Bach's half-smile that they knew more than she'd told the policeman. "I knew him," she said.

"More than casually?"

"I went to the Bleecker Café pretty regularly."

"That's not what you told the police."

"I don't remember what I told the police. I was in shock."

Bach nodded for no particular reason. "Two days ago Landis's body was found in an alley near his apartment." He reached into his pocket to show her a photograph. She took it, thinking it would be the same one she'd seen from the police. It wasn't. She dropped it and clamped a hand over her mouth to keep from screaming. Then she took a deep breath and forced herself to relax. She picked up the picture without looking at it again and handed it back to the agent.

"He was killed with an ax. Do you know anything about it?"

Bach continued his questions, and Madeleine heard herself answering, but she wasn't sure what she said. Then Knox took over. He had kind eyes, but she knew better. She heard Illi's name from her mouth, and watched herself with detached fascination. The image of Stan's body froze in some horrible part of her mind—some dark room of thought—waiting, she knew, to be released in a nightmare.

Vellef watched them. He'd sent Bea off to the kitchen, and for once, she'd listened to him. He didn't know what would come of this, so he wanted to concentrate on his daughter alone. Madeleine seemed all right, but Vellef knew that that was not the case. Shock, death. Shock. He knew the symptoms as if all the deaths of decades ago were yesterday. The questioners hadn't changed. Whether from the Tsar or Bolsheviks, the Nazis or Americans, the questioners always looked the same. They came into your house and reminded you it wasn't yours. Sometimes they stole; the Bolsheviks had stolen. Vellef kept an eye on the hands of the two in front of him. He tried to pay attention to their words, but his mind kept flashing back in time. Woods. A grave. He looked at his daughter and saw for the first time how much like his brother, Berish, she was. She had Berish in the hollow of her cheek, in the shape of her mouth. Berish with tight lips, trying to be calm and brave, his fear betrayed only to those who knew him. Berish, later, lips no longer tight, buried in a grave without a coffin, as if Russia were the Holy Land.

The older one, Knox: Vellef knew that one. He could kill and not even blink. He could torture and feel nothing. The younger one would be like that soon. Vellef smiled to himself. He too had learned to kill without feeling. He'd paid them back, both sides, for Berish, making Tsarist graves and Bolshevik graves. He had kept making graves until he met Bea. But a long time had passed. He had no desire to kill these men, to fight the wars all over again. The killing had long ago stopped, but he was amazed at how quickly the fear returned. He just wanted these men away from his house. Away from his daughter.

Bea came out again with tea. Knox smiled through his irritation and accepted a cup. After seeing it was permitted, Bach also accepted. Madeleine took her tea with trembling hands. This, Bea could see, did not go unnoticed by the agents. She tried to remember the name of the younger one, but she couldn't. Vellef did not accept tea. He didn't want her coming into the living room or offering tea. Vellef didn't want peace with them, but it was her house too, and even enemies can be softened with a little tea. She'd listened at the kitchen door, waiting for a time when it seemed that Madeleine needed a rest. The men tolerated her interruption because they considered her flighty. Well and good. She'd learned long ago that men were blind.

It was odd. Now she couldn't remember the older one's name either. And when they'd first come, she'd forgotten her English. Suddenly, she'd been standing there listening to them and not understanding a word. She had panicked at first, while Vellef covered for her. She had hurried into the kitchen, her kitchen, to gather her wits. She had reached for her candlesticks and prayed for God to return her English. Of all the things to pray for. Not even to pray for her daughter. But she had prayed as if her English would save her daughter. Now she felt embarrassed by it. She strained to listen and understand what the agents were saying.

Knox decided to give up. It was impossible to accomplish anything with the whole goddamned family sitting in his lap. Besides, he could tell that this one had nothing for him that he didn't already know.

"All right, Miss Blumfeld," Knox said. "That's all for now."

He stood. Vellef and Bach stood with him. He nodded at Bach.

"Don't leave town," the younger agent said.

"Why? Is my daughter a suspect?"

"Yes, Mr. Blumfeld," Knox answered. "Until we have the murderer, your daughter is a suspect."

"Then next time," Vellef snapped, "you should come with a warrant, and maybe you don't expect to speak with my Madeleine without she has a lawyer."

Knox shrugged. Damn Jews. "Fine, Mr. Blumfeld. You're entitled. America is a free country. But remember—" He turned to Madeleine. "Your government takes note of cooperation in national-security matters. It also takes note of lack of cooperation."

"And what does *that* mean?" Vellef asked.

Knox caught the slight wavering in Blumfeld's eyes and smiled. "Nothing," he said. "Just a statement. Thank you for the tea, Mrs. Blumfeld."

Bea hesitated, afraid her English would desert her again. "It was . . . You are very welcome."

Vellef closed the door behind the two men. He stood facing the door a few seconds, then turned suddenly to his daughter.

"This is where your Revolution has gotten you!"

Madeleine ran her fingers through her hair, trying to keep her composure. No more. She wanted no more. "Papa—"

"No!" he shouted. "You listen! They can do anything.

That's what that man said. They can do anything. If they want you to go free, you will go free. If they want you in prison, you will go to prison."

"Papa, this isn't Tsarist Russia!" Madeleine closed her eyes briefly and nodded. "You want me to tell you they scared me? Yes, they scared me. But you don't lecture me now. I haven't got the strength." She started to cry. "No more strength. Not now."

Bea walked over to her daughter. She paused by Vellef and let her hand linger a moment on his arm. Then she helped her daughter to her feet, and walked her into the bedroom.

"Maidel," Vellef called. Madeleine turned and saw the tears in his eyes. "I can't bear it, Maidel. I want you to leave those Communists. I want you to leave and never return."

"I can't think now, Papa."

Vellef looked to Bea, then to his daughter. "You will leave them or leave my house. I can't watch this time, Bea. They will destroy her the way they did Berish, then stand together over her grave. Both sides! I can't bear that." He looked once again at his wife and daughter framed in the doorway of the room. "You will have to decide soon. You will leave them, or you will leave my house."

Madeleine picked up the oversized corned beef sandwich the waiter had set before her. "You know," she said, "one of these days I'd like to have a big lobster dinner, complete with caviar and champagne. I've never had that." She took a bite of the sandwich and looked up at Aaron, her cheeks stuffed like a chipmunk's.

He smiled.

"You're too late on the lobster. Nathan Schwartz, my lobster expert, has become observant."

Madeleine frowned as best she could with her mouth full. "Forget it. I don't think I'd care to eat lobster with Nathan."

"Now, now, he's a nice person."

"He's a fanatic."

"So are you," Aaron said. "Speaking of which, the caviar and champagne don't sound very proletarian."

Madeleine shrugged. She was drowning her guilt at leaving the memorial rally for Stan in corned beef and Cel-Ray. Aaron had taken her to the rally, agreeing not to tell her father. Going to the memorial had seemed like something she had to do, a duty. But the speakers had droned on for one hour before anyone who'd even known Stan spoke. And that speaker was Illi.

The identity of whoever had murdered Stan was still unknown. To her surprise, though, Illi had been cleared of suspicion. In fact, he'd been cleared before she had, which also made her feel guilty. Her suspicion had been founded on her dislike of the man, and Stan's suspicion, rather than a search for truth.

Thankfully, for Stan's memory, Raymond Getz had written Illi's speech and got him off the stage when it was done. She really couldn't figure out how he handled Illi so well. No one else even came close. She swallowed.

"Caviar and champagne will be proletarian when all workers can afford them."

"But you don't sound like you want to wait."

"Ask me again when I'm not so hungry," she said. "Illi didn't do too badly—compared with everyone else. I should have figured beneath all that security talk he was harmless. But poor Stan made him seem so ominous."

"Are you so sure Stan was wrong?"

"Come on, Aaron. The police cleared him, and they certainly aren't partial to card-carrying Communists."

"I guess," Aaron said.

Madeleine took another bite, feeling guilty once again. But Aaron had been right. The rally had been abysmally boring. She'd stood through most of it in the packed room, listening to her stomach growl and feeling droplets of sweat trickling between her breasts. Aaron's proximity to her during the droning speeches had made her mind wander to things which had nothing to do with Communist ideology, something she had not yet learned to control. She wanted desperately to sleep with him. Though she was scared at the prospect—mostly scared at going home afterward—she spent so much time imagining, fantasizing. But Aaron was firm, damn him: marriage, then bed. No marriage, no bed. She wished Ruth were around to talk to, because they could really talk now. But Ruth was off in Israel, pregnant, no less. Still several steps ahead of her. Madeleine had known about the pregnancy for quite some time, and had told Aaron just because she had to tell someone. Ruth had not told anyone else until the danger of another miscarriage had passed. Secrets. It seemed Madeleine never got away from them.

"You're staring off into space," Aaron said, bringing her back to the deli and her sandwich.

"I was thinking of what I'd like to do with you later."

Aaron smiled again. "I think something could be arranged."

"Something, yes. But I want everything."

"You don't know what you're talking about. And you want too much."

She pouted. "You're a prude."

"Yup."

"You're also a brainwashed member of the bourgeoisie. I am not a possession to be deflowered after being properly given to you by my father. What difference does a twenty-minute ceremony and a piece of paper make?"

"To me, a lot."

"You're a possessive prude. Watch out. I might get so frustrated I fly into the arms of another."

"And who would that other be?"

Madeleine thought. "Now, Raymond Getz isn't bad-looking. And he was great tonight. He salvaged the whole evening. I mean when he finished speaking, I was in tears. I noticed," she added drily, "that you weren't."

"I don't like Raymond," Aaron said.

"Hmm. I hear a note of, maybe, jealousy?" Madeleine grinned.

"Don't confuse dislike with jealousy," Aaron said. "I don't like the man, and I am not forgetting that Stan Landis's murderer is still loose."

"And I'm not forgetting that all of us who were suspects—including me, mind you—have been found innocent."

"Not found innocent: cleared of charges."

"Same thing."

"No, it isn't," Aaron said. "And I don't like Raymond Getz because of the way he behaved on stage."

"How can you say that? When he finished talking about Stan he was too broken up to introduce the next speaker!"

"Then," Aaron replied, "he sat down, absolutely dry-eyed, and began to talk to the person sitting next to him on the stage. He didn't believe a word he'd said. He merely manipulated the crowd and watched."

"You know, I get tired of all this all the time. I don't sit here and criticize what you believe in. One of the reasons I cried when Raymond spoke is because I believe what he said. I believe it, and it doesn't really matter whether Raymond does or not. You just can't believe a Communist is sincere."

"I didn't say that. I just can't believe Raymond Getz is sincere."

"Sure, Raymond's a Communist and he's not sincere. I'm sincere, but you keep trying to tell me I'm not a Communist."

"You're not."

Madeleine threw down the fork she'd picked up, drawing stares from the table next to them. "That's all you do. Dump. It's like trash-pickup day on East Fourth Street. You dump garbage on everything I hold sacred."

"Communism isn't sacred, Madeleine; it's an economic system."

"And Judaism isn't sacred either," she said. "The Communist movement has helped millions of people. What the hell has Judaism done? Judaism made my family go through four countries before they got here. Judaism makes my father afraid even in his America. You're worried that maybe one of my Communist friends killed Stan. Well, the God you want me to adore burned up six million of the faithful in ovens. So you tell me which is sacred and which isn't."

"Madeleine—"

"I need some air," Madeleine said as she stood up. "I need some fresh air for a change." She walked out the door of the deli.

The breeze cooled her anger a bit. She glanced inside to see Aaron paying the check. The street was wet from a sudden shower that had passed by without her noticing. The air smelled of wetness and spring. She breathed deeply, remembering the first time she and Aaron had walked together in spring. Aaron came out.

"I'm sorry," he said. "Madeleine, I want you to marry me."

"Right here in the street?"

"No." Aaron smiled. "I'm willing to wait a few months, at least until job interviews are over. I wouldn't want to duck out during the wedding to do a fancy service for a prospective congregation."

"You're serious, aren't you?"

"Yes, I am. How about an answer?"

"Wait a minute, would you? Did you hear anything I said in there?"

"I heard it all. But I also know we love each other. Madeleine, I want you desperately. Marry me."

"And what about what *I* want?"

"I'm hoping that deep inside, you want the same thing."

"I guess you'd have to. It certainly could jeopardize your position if the rebbetzin tried to foment a revolution in the Temple Sisterhood."

"Everyone has to make choices. Some dreams you follow, and some you leave behind because they aren't real. I am reality, Madeleine. I care about you. You can't say that about any of your Communist friends. I'm offering you a life, a good life." He pointed his hand in the direction of the rally. "What are *they* offering? Is sharing your life with me so hard to accept?"

"No," Madeleine said, gently touching his face.

He took her in his arms and kissed her so hard she felt his teeth. His tongue probed for her mouth and she opened for him, meeting him. As he touched her, she felt a thrill accompany his breath hot on her neck. She wanted him; she lost herself, surrendering finally to the desire she'd felt all evening. But Aaron pushed her away. He took a deep breath.

"I just wanted you to realize how long we have waited."

Anger swallowed desire. "You did that on purpose!"

"I want to sleep with you, Madeleine." He reached out and stroked her hair. "I want to make love to you. But you're only nineteen. I won't unless we're married. Not to possess you, to protect you. I love you."

"I know," she said, leaning her head against his hand a moment. Then she straightened. "But—" She glanced behind her toward the rally. "Do you believe in destiny?"

"No."

"I do. I was destined for something, Aaron."

"Be my wife."

"Is that all? Is that all I'm going to be? Just a rabbi's wife with her children? My life devoted to you, to them, to everything but me?"

"Right now, your life is devoted only to you."

"And you're different? You want to be a rabbi. You want a congregation. You want a wife. You want me. Are you any different?"

"Yes."

"Because you're a man."

"No," he said. "Because I've committed myself. I know you, Madeleine, maybe better than you know yourself. I know it's killing you that your friend is in Israel immersed in some great historic cause and you're here in Brooklyn. That's what you mean by destiny. But Ruth committed herself. You're still a Communist between classes, working for the poor yet living comfortably in your father's house. You've never known what commitment meant."

"You want me to commit myself to you."

"That's what Stan wanted too," Aaron said.

"Stan never asked me what *I* wanted either," Madeleine said.

"That's because it wasn't important to him. Stan knew you were a part-time revolutionary. You are something to use, the way Raymond used Illi tonight. Stan used you because he also knew you better than you knew yourself. He finally told you the truth. I don't know why: maybe he was the only one who came to care about you; maybe he saw his own death—who knows? But he did know that these weren't the times for middle-class college Communists."

"You don't think I'm strong enough. You think even Ruth is stronger than I am."

Aaron shook his head. "Madeleine, there is nothing to be strong for. For Illi? For the Party? For all those boring idiots trying to make political points from a man's murder? You don't really believe in all that."

Madeleine laughed.

"What's funny?" Aaron asked.

"I just realized that I've always had men telling me what I really believe, what I really think. It's either been my father, or Stan, or you, or even Nathan. How is it you all know me so well?"

"How is it that you know yourself so little?"

"You think I'm so naive I can't see the pettiness in the Party, the rotten little men mixed in with all the honest ones? Well, I see them. But I believe in the cause, even if it's a bit tarnished. I know myself, Aaron. I'm just beginning to know myself."

"I love you, Madeleine. Come with me."

"If I go with you now, I'll never know." She looked at him, begging. "Give me time—a year—and I'll show you what I'm capable of."

"You're capable of getting killed like Stan, or thrown in prison. Come with me now."

"Let me try, damn it!"

"No," Aaron said. "You'll fail, and they'll hurt you."

Madeleine's eyes became hard. "And if I succeed, then you won't have me, will you? Not the way you want me. That's what you're most afraid of, isn't it? You aren't afraid for me at all."

"I'm terrified for you," Aaron said. "And I'm terrified of losing you."

"Believe in me. Please, believe in me."

"I do. I believe in you enough to marry you. I believe in you enough to know we could be happy together."

"In *your* world. On your terms."

"That's the way the world is!" he shouted. "And one human being isn't going to change the entire world. There's nothing I can do about it except try to make you happy."

"But you don't know how to make me happy, Aaron," she said softly. "I do love you." She touched him on the cheek. He took her hand, but she moved away from him.

"Good-bye, Aaron." She turned and walked away.

Aaron stood, paralyzed by terror. "No, Madeleine, wait!" He called for her, but she ran. She ran away, leaving only the darkness.

SEPTEMBER
1949

"COMRADE MADELEINE, HOW ARE YOU?" ILLI SAID AS Madeleine walked in the door of the Party's Fourteenth Street headquarters.

"Uh, just fine, Illi."

"That's good, Comrade. Very good." Humming, he walked over to a stack of papers by the Ditto machine and began collating them.

Raymond Getz noticed her from his office and beckoned to her. When she came into the office, he smiled and closed the door behind him. Through the glass she could see Illi watching them, a frown on his face. Then he returned to his collating.

"How are you doing?" Raymond asked. He reached over and stroked her hair. In spite of herself, she felt her blood warm. "Staying with Harriet is working out, isn't it?" he asked.

"Harriet's wonderful. I want to thank you for talking her into taking me in," she said. She looked at him. "Now all that's left is my membership."

"Soon," he said, and smiled.

"Come sit next to me." He moved two chairs opposite his desk. He took her hand and sat looking at her a moment, just long enough to make her shy and embarrassed.

"Now, on to business," he said, releasing her hand. "I have a problem. The papers have had three days to exploit the Peekskill Riot. Our newspaper has gotten some infor-

mation out, but we need more people to know the truth."
He stood up and walked to his desk. Then he handed a set
of papers to Madeleine. "I know of very few people left
who have the strength to go over what happened at Peekskill.
It was a nightmare, but the true story has to get out. Would
you work on this for me?"

"Of course I will," Madeleine said.

"It needs editing, then typing onto Dittos." Raymond
rested his hand on hers as she held the papers. "This won't
be too hard for you, will it?"

"I can do it, Raymond."

"Good," he said. "We'll need five thousand copies."

Madeleine, who had been reading the text before her,
looked up. "Tonight?" she asked.

Raymond looked at his watch. "I know it's late . . ."

Madeleine smiled. "I can tell you've never been a secretary."

"But it's essential that we have it tomorrow." Raymond
looked worried; then he brightened. "Tell you what. I'll get
someone to help you, and escort you home. I'd help myself,
but I've got three meetings tonight—all at the same time."

"I'll do it, Raymond. You don't have to—"

"Sure I do." Raymond went to the door and called Illi.
Illi looked up, his eyes on Raymond, his face flushed.

"Illi, I want you to help Madeleine tonight, then take her
home afterward."

Madeleine tried not to let her disappointment show. She
stood up. "I really don't—"

"I will be pleased to assist Comrade Madeleine, Comrade
Raymond."

Madeleine thought for a moment that Illi would salute,
but he turned around stiffly and went back to his work.
Raymond caught the look on Madeleine's face.

"Did I make a bad choice?" he asked. "Illi is a little
strange, but I like him, in a way."

"It's all right, really."

Raymond leaned over and caressed her cheek. "I trust

Illi. That's why he's my security man. I trust him with my most valuable possessions." He kissed her lightly on the lips. "I'm free tomorrow; are you?"

"Yes," she said quickly.

"Why don't we go to my apartment tomorrow night? I'll make us dinner." When Raymond looked at Madeleine, the place between her legs seemed to contract.

She went back to her desk and, except for waving good-bye to Raymond, spent the next few hours in a fog of excitement and apprehension. She had finally committed herself. Tomorrow night she'd prove it. Madeleine vaguely heard the sounds of her own typing as she envisioned what it would be like; what Raymond would be like. He was so different from Aaron. Now, he would make love to her. Now, she could make love to him. Typing and retyping all the Dittos necessary for five thousand copies seemed to draw her deeper into her fantasy world. She'd forgotten Illi was with her. He called to her, startling her.

"Comrade Madeleine."

Back in the present, she answered him. "Yes? Trouble with the machine?"

"No. Not that." Illi cracked the knuckles of his left hand. "You don't talk to me much anymore."

"Don't I?" Madeleine asked absently.

"Not like the old days."

"Oh, well, I'm sorry." She started to go back to her typing and daydreams, but Illi continued.

"I mean, we're the only ones left from the old group. The only ones."

Madeleine looked up, a little more aware. "I guess you're right. I hadn't thought of it."

"But you still have to divest yourself of the cosmopolitan elements in your life."

"That's why I don't talk to you," she snapped. "I'm not a fool. I know what 'cosmopolitan' means, so don't use it with me! Aaron was . . ." Madeleine stopped. The tightening in her throat surprised her. She didn't even want to mention his name to Illi.

"It's getting late," she said. "Please just go and run off the leaflets. I have at least four more of these damn Dittos to type."

Illi's face reddened. He seemed about to say more, but he looked down and began turning the handle of the machine.

Madeleine retreated into her thoughts. She found herself longing for Ruth's company. But Ruth would never approve. Ruth was wrong. They all were, and she'd show them. They were wrong about her dreams, and her courage. Aaron was wrong. Yet thinking of him tightened her throat again.

"I want you, Madeleine."

Madeleine looked up half-expecting to see Raymond or Aaron. But Illi stood before her. "What did you say?"

Illi leaned over close to her. "I want you," he said. His eyes were red, almost bloodshot. "Come with me. Live with me."

"Go away, Illi," Madeleine said, mustering an authoritative tone. To her relief, Illi started to turn away. She looked down at the typewriter.

"No!" He pounded on her desk, sending the Dittos to the floor. "I have a right!" Illi straightened up and waved his hand around the room. "This should have been mine. They promised me. Mine. Not his!"

Madeleine didn't move, afraid to set him off further. She tried to think. "Take it easy, Illi." She tried to sound calm.

"They said he would get followers, and I couldn't. He took everything. But he's not going to get you. I have a right!" Illi paced back and forth in front of her desk.

Madeleine remembered the guard Raymond had had posted outside the door since Peekskill. She smiled with relief. "If you don't calm down, Comrade, I'm going to get Mike and—"

"He's gone." Illi stopped pacing and gave her a sly look. He pushed a lock of stringy hair back on his head. It fell forward again. "Raymond made me head of security. I sent him home."

Madeleine looked at the door.

"And I locked the door," he said.

The fear she'd blocked began to rise. There was a way to calm him; there always had been. "Illi, you don't want to get into trouble, do you? The leaflets have to go out tomorrow."

He laughed, then pounded the desk again and stopped laughing. "I want to be leader. They promised me. I wanted to love you, but they brought *him* in." Illi's voice cracked as he pointed an accusing finger at Raymond's office.

"I can get followers. Believe me, I can. I hate him. I want to kill him. *Kill* him!" Illi leaned on the desk, his voice conspiratorial. "He makes me do things, you know. He always makes me do things. He promised; then he tried to break his promise."

Illi walked over to Raymond's office, keeping his eyes on Madeleine. She tensed, ready to run. She could lock herself in the back room. She just had to make it across the main room. Illi continued to watch her. He lifted his hand and began to stroke the office door; then he turned and leaned his head against it.

"I did everything for him," he said.

Madeleine eased herself out of her chair. Illi stared off into space. "I did everything he wanted me to, but I saw the way he touched you."

She moved around the desk.

"I know him better than you think. He isn't going to get you." Illi looked up just as Madeleine began to run. He cut her off, blocking her way. He stood near her but made no move toward her.

"You Jew bitch," he hissed. "You spread your legs for your kike rabbi, and you did it for *him*"—Illi pointed at the office again. "Now you can spread them for a real man."

Madeleine backed away a step. "Illi, please, don't do this. You don't want to hurt me. Raymond wouldn't like it."

Illi grinned. Then he lashed out, knocking her down with

his fist. The pain exploded in her head, blurring her vision. Illi spoke, his voice suddenly calm.

"He knows," Illi said, "that I have my needs. And you're a Jew slut. You think you're too good for me. Well, you're scum."

"Illi." Madeleine tried to talk through the blood in her mouth. "He'll get angry. You're wrong."

"Raymond will understand."

"But I'm your comrade, remember? The old days."

He stood over her. "Comrade? No. I tried. I really tried, but I couldn't." He leaned down. "You're a kike, a Jew bitch who's only good for one thing."

He unzipped his pants and dropped to his knees next to her. He pulled out his erect penis, then grabbed her by the hair. "Look," he whispered. There was a tone of wonder in his voice.

Madeleine winced but did not cry out. He was so close she could smell his body, unwashed and sweaty. His penis stood out from his pants, ugly. She tried to turn away, but he wouldn't let her.

"Raymond took my manhood," Illi said. "But look. Do you see? He gave it back to me."

Illi touched himself with his free hand, caressing his organ. Then he struck Madeleine with such force that her head jerked out of his grip and she hit the floor. The ceiling light above her brightened and swirled. She prayed for blackness, but none came. With blurred vision, she saw Illi sitting on the floor, taking off his pants. She tried to move. Illi jerked her head up again.

"I'm going to hurt you, Jew bitch. Hurt you good." He let go of her hair and reached for the fastenings of her skirt. She fought him, tearing at his hands with her nails. He pulled his hands away a moment, laughing, then punched her in the breast. She started to scream, but he clamped his hand over her mouth. "Scream and I'll strangle you right now."

Illi ripped at her skirt, then tore off her underpants. Madeleine felt his hands on her, filthy hands that bruised her, tore at her. She tried to fight him again and he hit her, this time in the solar plexus, knocking out her wind and making her helpless. She felt him on top of her, smelled his rancid breath as he tried to shove himself into her. But her body still resisted him. Desperately, he tried to enter her. Then his shoving against her became convulsive, and she felt warm liquid dripping around her vagina, evidence of his failure.

Illi screamed. He straightened to his knees, his face a mask of horror. "No! Raymond, no!"

For a moment, Madeleine thought rescue had come. She looked out through swollen eyes. But they were alone. Illi knelt between her legs, crying out his agony and pumping the now small penis. Madeleine began to giggle hysterically. She tried to stop herself, but couldn't. Illi stopped touching himself. His eyes narrowed.

"You're dead," he said, standing up.

She tried to move. Illi kicked her in the side. "I'm going to kill you, kike. You can go fuck Landis."

Illi ran to his coat. Madeleine knew if she didn't move she would die. She didn't want to die. Not now. Not this way. She managed to raise herself up on her elbows when Illi returned. Not enough. Not nearly enough. He stood above her, naked from the waist down, holding a meat cleaver in his hand. Madeleine looked up at him.

"You're all Trots," Illi said. "You all think you're too good for the rest of us." He smiled and fingered the blade. "They killed Trotsky with an ax, you know. They hacked him up. Stan knew. I saw that he knew what I was doing. I saw it in his eyes." He looked at Madeleine. "I killed him and it was easy. Fun. It was for the Party. It was right."

Madeleine tried to talk. "Police . . . cleared."

Illi laughed. "I told the agents that I would spy for them if they let me go. Raymond was very surprised to see me again. Raymond . . ." Illi looked between his legs and wailed.

Then he lunged for her. Madeleine brought her knees up

and kicked him in the groin with all her strength. Illi dropped the cleaver and fell, screaming and holding his penis with both hands. Madeleine pulled herself to her feet, using the desk behind her for support, as Illi rolled back and forth on the floor. She saw the typewriter on the desk. Now she felt no pain, no weakness, only rage. She picked up the typewriter and held it over her head.

"Die!" she screamed. Illi looked up at her, his eyes wide. She threw the typewriter down toward his head. He reached up to protect himself, but he couldn't break the force of the heavy machine. It crashed into his face.

"Die! Die!" She continued screaming at him as his body twitched. Then she raised her foot and drove it down between his legs. She stamped down again and again until her shoe was bloody and she could no longer lift her leg.

The strength her rage had given her began to ebb. She dragged herself to her torn skirt. As she walked, she was filled with disgust, feeling his semen between her legs. Nausea overwhelmed her. She vomited over and over until her sides ached. Then she slowly moved to where her raincoat stood. A trickle of blood started out from under the desk that hid Illi from view.

She had to get away. She put on the torn skirt as best as she could, then covered herself with her raincoat. She stumbled as she reached the door, remembering that he had said it was locked. She didn't want to go back, to see Illi. She tried the door. It was open. She could have escaped. The thought made her want to cry, but she couldn't. She had to get away before the police came.

Madeleine walked out onto the empty street. She looked around, half-expected flashing lights, sirens, but everything was dark and silent. She walked for a few blocks, using the walls of buildings to support herself. When she thought she was far enough away from the headquarters, she hailed a passing cab.

On seeing her condition, the driver tried to take her to the hospital, but she insisted he take her home. She just wanted to go home. As he drove to Brooklyn, she leaned back against the door, feeling the dull pain coming from her body and her heart as she watched the lights of the bridge flash by.

No police came knocking at the door. There were no calls from the Party. If it hadn't been for the bruises, Madeleine would have doubted her sanity. She thought of going to the police herself, but if Illi had told her the truth, that wouldn't be wise. So she waited. By the time a week had passed, she began to hope that by some miracle, she might be free of the whole thing. Yet not entirely free. The images from that night haunted her dreams. From those images there was no escape.

Every Tuesday, Aaron called the Blumfelds and spoke with Bea. This, Madeleine found out, had been his custom since she'd left home. Bea wanted her to speak with him, but she refused. Bea, in talking, had not revealed the circumstances of Madeleine's coming home. On the second Tuesday of Madeleine's stay, she retreated into her bedroom to avoid answering the phone. She lay on her bed, listening to her mother make small talk, wondering what Aaron must think.

It didn't matter what her mother said or didn't say. Aaron knew that Vellef wouldn't have let her into the house if she were still with the Party. Aaron knew she had failed, just as he'd predicted. Madeleine heard the murmurs of her mother's voice, then heard her name mentioned. She wondered if Aaron wanted her back.

That idea disturbed her. On the one hand, she didn't know if she could ever forgive him for wanting her to fail, and yet she no longer felt worthy of him. She felt soiled. He would probably change toward her, just as her father had. Vellef said nothing about that night. He was subdued and gentle, but he had become distant. They no longer argued. They no longer really spoke.

Madeleine rolled over onto her side and tucked her arm under her head. She tried to recall the last few months.

Somewhere in all the insanity, there had to be something, a seed of some ideal that had been worthy of her faith. She'd been punished for her sins, but she still felt impure. Her heresy had been the belief that the given order could be upset. Her sin had been imagining she had a place in the events of history.

There was no Revolution. It had all come to a trickle of blood moving slowly along a floor littered with manifestos no one would ever read. She was not the Madeleine Aaron had known. She tried to think of those times when she'd loved him, but nothing came—no feeling of pain or love. She felt nothing as she listened to her mother's voice and then heard the phone hanging up. Bea came in.

"You know what I feel like doing?" Bea said. "I feel like going to the shvitz."

"Ma," Madeleine said sitting up. "We haven't been to the steam room in years. You said it went downhill." Madeleine got up from the bed. She did not ask about Aaron. Bea didn't speak of him either.

"Sure, but they have a shvitz at the YMHA, and women get to use it on Tuesdays."

"Are you sure the YMHA isn't going downhill?" Madeleine sneered.

Bea laughed. Her daughter's spirit was coming back. "Want to go? We could sit and talk like the old days."

A shadow crossed Madeleine's face. They both knew she hadn't been out of the house in a week. "I don't know," she said.

"Well," Bea said. "We could stay home and do windows. I bought more vinegar this morning. I leave you to think about that—and maybe smell a little." Bea walked out.

Madeleine smiled and stared after her. The shvitz, the steam room. Now, there was a long-standing Jewish tradition. She had gone to the shvitz as a girl with her mother and sisters. They had gone there every other Saturday night. She'd loved it then. The men and women separated, going to their respective sides, not to see each other until the next day. There were cots for rent, and food, mostly brought by the women, and of course, the interminable pinochle game. It was a magic place filled with locker-room smell, schnapps and herring. Women played cards, ate, nursed babies. They came in all sizes. Some sat with sheets carelessly thrown over them; some didn't bother with sheets at all. Madeleine went naked, glorying in the periodic relief from self-consciousness.

Most of the women were big-breasted and overweight, upholding a Slavic criterion for a good marriage. A woman should get a little plump after marriage to show that her husband could provide. Madeleine was thin, and all the women encouraged her to eat. Sometimes her weight would launch a whole discussion, with her mother noting all the suggestions and remedies, duly trying them out the following week.

Madeleine spent a lot of time listening to the women's talk. Babies, husbands and secrets. It always seemed that husbands and secrets were linked together. When Madeleine got older, Bea encouraged her to listen. She said that the women would teach Madeleine things. So she listened, pretending not to listen. The women pretended in turn she was not listening. That was the way Madeleine learned about men and women. She learned that Tova had been raped in Russia and her parents had married her off to the first man to take her. That was why her husband was such a dolt. Madeleine learned that Leah's husband was a gambler, but treated her well in bed. Most of all she learned that there were things a woman kept from her husband, if only so that she could call something, even secrets, her own.

"I'll take the shvitz to vinegar any day," she called out to Bea.

The steam room at the YMHA wasn't nearly so intimate or welcoming as the shvitz of Madeleine's youth. There were no cots, no homey smells, only attendants in white uniforms. Still, if the steam room was not rich in texture, her memories of another time were. The two women sat alone in the room. Madeleine sat on the second bench, and Bea sat in front of her on a lower bench. Bea faced forward and looked at the floor. Madeleine hadn't seen her mother undressed in years. Her skin was dark, and looked like tan crepe paper. Too many years of sitting in the sun at the beach. Bea's back was rounded from all the years over the ledgers. Folds of fat gathered at her waist. Yet she still had a striking beauty that would never fade. The silence between them was as thick as the steam. Madeleine reached out and touched her mother's shoulder.

"You wanted to say something, Ma?"

"Why do you say that?"

Madeleine laughed and surveyed the steam room, letting her eyes rest once more on her mother. Bea glanced away a moment.

"It isn't the same," she said. "The world changes so fast. But I wanted to come back to a shvitz. I wanted to feel the steam again. It always helped me think."

"About what?"

"About life and the past. And what must be." Bea sighed. "Madeleine, I want you to do a very difficult thing for me. I want you to call Aaron."

"I can't."

"You must. I think even you know that. He loves you. There is no one else for him, and he is still brokenhearted."

"How much have you said to him?" Madeleine asked. Her voice had a sharp edge.

"He knows nothing. And I tell him nothing. I just listen to him. He does know you're home and what that means."

"He won't want me," Madeleine said. "God, Mama, haven't I been hurt enough?"

"You have been hurt too much! Too much. I want you to heal."

"He won't want me when I tell him."

Bea looked at her daughter. "You won't tell him. These things he doesn't need to know. And there isn't any way for him to find out. God protected you from that."

"A secret. Like Tova's secret."

"All women have secrets. All wives have secrets from their husbands. That's the way it is."

"And what secrets do you have from Papa?"

"I too have secrets. They're mine to keep," Bea stared out into the steam. "Mine alone."

"I can't. I don't love him. I don't know if I can love anyone anymore."

"That means nothing," Bea said.

"Don't you see? When"—Madeleine stumbled over the name—"when Raymond looked at me; when he . . . I forgot about Aaron. I just forgot about him."

"You are confused. For this Raymond, you felt passion. What do you think passion is? Do you remember Raizel?"

"The skinny woman with seven children."

"Do you remember what she used to say?" Bea asked.

"She used to cry that her husband gave her babies but no pleasure."

"Yes. Poor Raizel ached with passion. And this Raymond incited passion in you."

"More than Aaron did. That shouldn't be."

"Who knows what should be?"

"I don't love him."

"Love." Bea said the word in English. She spoke it as a foreign language. "Your father is a good man. He's a good husband and, in spite of his temper, a good father. I love him. Now. I love him deeply." Bea paused, her eye glazing.

"Back in Russia, he saved me. He took me with him and protected me. Without him, I would have died. There were many who would have left me to die, or taken advantage. Not Vellef. I knew he was a good man. That was all I needed to know. The ones you 'love'—the men who make your heart race, and your breath shallow—they usually aren't very good men. It isn't important that you love the man you marry in that way. You will love him very much in time."

"But I'd be using him."

"Aaron loves you. He *wants* you to use him. But you must tell him nothing. Men are so strange that way. Unimportant things become important to them. If you did tell him, then in spite of his love for you, he might not accept you."

"Like Tova."

"Yes. Like Tova."

"Mama?"

"What?"

"Are all my dreams dead?"

"Yes."

Bea reached up and took Madeleine's hand. "But new dreams come. I know. I do know."

Madeleine felt the steam slowly suffocating her, though Bea didn't seem to notice.

"I'll call him," Madeleine said.

LYNDA

JUNE
1967

JERUSALEM. THE CITY OF PEACE LAY SWATHED IN CON-
certina wire and sandbags. The ancient walled part of the
city, forbidden to Jews, sounded with the cries of muezzin
calling Muslims to worship. In the new section of the city,
the streets were deserted, shops closed. An occasional olive-
colored uniform moved out from a doorway: an Israeli sol-
dier off to join his unit. Back on the wall of the Old City,
a Jordanian, in the uniform of the Arab Legion, leaned
against a parapet, eying the no-man's-land between Israeli
territory and Jordanian territory. Jerusalem, the Holy City,
was preparing to go to war with itself.

The singing that came from Aish Emes Yeshiva seemed
somehow out of place. The songs told of a Jerusalem "filled
with the voice of joy and gladness, the voice of the groom
and bride." The yeshiva students summoned the biblical
words with a fervor that defied the city's hush. At Aish
Emes, they sang for the Messiah. This evening, in the light
of the setting sun, they also sang for a wedding. Duvid
Cohen stood under the marriage canopy with Ruchel Mey-
erman. It was a family wedding, with the yeshiva as the
only family. Duvid had been an orphan from an early age,
and had come to Jerusalem a year before. Ruchel's family
had refused to make the journey. She was newly orphaned

129

by a family that didn't understand what had brought her to this strange land so far from them, and to a life so alien.

Ruchel had found her own way to Jerusalem. Like the ninety other students at Aish Emes, she was a seeker, and had found a place with Rabbi Nathan Schwartz and his yeshiva for American students. He never turned anyone away. He was teacher, father and mentor to his students. He had married Duvid and Ruchel weeping with the joy of marrying one's own children.

Ruchel felt a twinge of guilt as she thought about Rabbi Schwartz. With him here, she didn't miss her parents. She looked out from the throne the girls had built for her. Tonight she would not feel guilty, no matter what. Tonight she was bride and queen. Duvid, the king, was on the other side of the curtain wall that separated the men from the women. No matter. They'd be together soon enough. She watched the girls dance in her honor. Lynda, as usual, was at the center of the circle, dancing with an abandon that bordered on immodesty. Ruchel smiled. Lynda whirled around, and soon the other women stopped dancing and stood in place, clapping a rhythm for her. She finally noticed she was the center of attention and broke through the circle, still dancing. She grabbed Ruchel's hand, pulling her from the throne into the circle and dancing her breathless and dizzy.

A roar came from the men's side. Ruchel turned to see Duvid's head peeking over the curtain as the men lifted his throne high in the air, dancing with him. The women around her hesitated a moment; then Lynda whooped. She dragged Ruchel back to the throne, snagging helpers on the way. They lifted Ruchel high into the air, where she waved to her new husband with one hand and held on for dear life with the other. There was another roar, and a section of curtain wall came down. Rabbi Nathan Schwartz, his olive uniform standing out in the mass of black suits, grabbed a napkin from the scattered dinner tables. He handed one end to Ruchel while Duvid grabbed for the other end. Then, connected but not touching, the king and queen were dancing around the room. Ruchel looked down into the sea of bobbing faces. Like the rest, Lynda seemed to be looking up at her, but Lynda looked past her, to something else, something Ruchel knew she would never see. Ruchel looked away to keep any sadness from creeping in on this night. Her eyes fell on Moishe Wittenstein, and she smiled. Lynda, then Moishe, two ends of the spectrum. Moishe stood apart from the crowd, trying to pluck yeshiva boys from the group of dancing students. Everyone ignored his efforts.

Finally, when no one had any strength left, the couple were set down side by side. The home-grown entertainment commenced: balancing acts, juggling and a Russian kazatzka done with a bottle on the head. After the entertainment, the king was lifted once again and returned to the men's side.

Ruchel spotted Lynda resting at last. She sat with her chair leaned back against the wall, her chest heaving and her damp hair clinging to her scalp. Ruchel walked over to her.

"You should be on your throne," Lynda said between breaths. "The queen isn't allowed to abdicate."

Ruchel pulled up a chair and sat opposite her. "I just came over to see how you are. A queen can visit her subjects."

"I'm fine," Lynda said. She took a deep breath and let it out slowly. "Just getting my second wind."

"You get carried away, you know."

"That's impossible. This is a wedding, remember? The only reason I look overly enthusiastic is because they look anemic." With her head, Lynda indicated the group of young rebbetzins who sat and watched the girls dance. "Geez. I thought a wedding would finally get their blood running."

"They've been dancing. I can see better from my vantage point."

"They've been dancing. But they haven't been"—Lynda paused for emphasis—"*dancing.*"

"Well, they haven't been dancing like you, but no one does. There's something about you."

"Not me." Lynda smiled. "All we women have it. It's

called animal magnetism. That's why we have to wear long sleeves."

"Oh, stop joking."

"I refuse to. It's a wedding."

Ruchel sighed. She squeezed Lynda's hand, then let go, leaning back in her chair. "You keep me in a constant state of confusion."

"What else are friends for?" Lynda asked. "Anyway, how could I possibly confuse a fellow Talmud scholar?"

"You're a scholar. I just study."

"Neither one of us is the scholar," Lynda said.

"I concede," Ruchel said. "Two months of a Talmud course wouldn't make even you a scholar."

"Yeh. Two months, by the goodness of Rabbi Schwartz's heart, as long as we don't breathe a word of it to anyone connected with the Ministry of Religion."

"There," Ruchel said.

"Where?"

"That's how you confuse me. See?"

"Not at all."

"We study together," Ruchel said. "You work so hard to learn and then still have enough left over to help me. You've only been here a year, yet you tutor the other girls in Bible. You pray the Morning Service as if the Messiah came to visit." Ruchel sighed. "Then that."

"What?"

"Sarcasm. I know you love Rabbi Schwartz, but you just sounded—well—nasty."

Lynda's eyes went cold as she gazed out past Ruchel's shoulder. "Well," Lynda said, turning back to Ruchel with a faint smile. "Let's just chalk it up to me being a complicated person."

"I'll say."

"It comes," Lynda said gravely, "from my father, the Crowel, New Jersey, Rebbe, who used to beat me every day while I recited passages from Torah. He'd had a vision that said if I knew enough Torah, I'd turn into a boy and be heir to the discount-store business that my father, the Croweler Rebbe, ran on the side when he wasn't doing holy deeds. And then there was my mother—"

"Oh, stop!" Ruchel said, laughing suddenly. "For a second you had me going."

"It's time to get going—back to your throne."

Ruchel stood. "Promise me something," she said.

"Sure."

"I'm serious," Ruchel said.

Lynda passed her hand over her face, making her smile disappear. "So am I."

"I mean it." Ruchel hesitated. "Promise me you'll always be my friend, no matter what." Her eyes looked frightened.

"Of course I'll always be your friend," Lynda said. "Is something wrong?"

Ruchel smiled. "No. It's my wedding, remember?" She bent over and kissed Lynda on the cheek. "Take it easy."

"Be happy, my friend," Lynda said.

Lynda watched the girl walk away. Ruchel certainly was a friend, but the kind of friend Jeremy, her little brother, had been. She was close, in need of confiding but never a confidante. The other girls were like Ruchel, fresh out of high school, or with only a year of college behind them. Lynda had come to Jerusalem after graduating from college, so the rebbetzins, rather than the students, were her peers. But Lynda couldn't talk to them. And although they were at the women's school to give advice, most of the girls couldn't talk to them either. The girls came to Lynda with their problems, in numbers that made some of the rebbetzins jealous. Lynda sighed. The tile wall felt cool against the back of her head. She glanced at the small prayer books that lay beside each dinner plate to be sure hers was among them. Then she closed her eyes. She stayed with her eyes closed until she sensed a shadow in front of her. It was Rabbi Schwartz.

He was packed to go. He held his helmet in his hand; his rifle was already slung over his shoulder.

"You're leaving, Rabbi?" she asked.

"Getting ready to. Just making the rounds before I do. Do you mind if I sit down?"

"It's fine with me, but Moishe will have a fit."

"No, I'm safe," Schwartz said. "He's probably off somewhere framing his report to the Ministry of Religion about the curtain coming down." He chuckled as he sat down.

"With all due respect, Rabbi, I don't see how you can stand to have Moishe around."

"He's got a good heart. Besides, after thirteen years in the yeshiva business, I can remember some who make him look like an atheist."

"I doubt that," Lynda said. She wondered why the rabbi had stopped to talk to her. Then she realized that, quietly, he'd gone around to every one of his students. She looked at him, acutely aware of the rifle and the uniform. He was saying good-bye to all of them, just in case.

"You keep your head down, Rabbi," she said softly.

Schwartz laughed. "Of all the people I talked to tonight, you're the only one who's given me any practical advice."

"Pragmatism is my specialty."

There was an awkward silence as Lynda faced Rabbi Schwartz. He had never really talked to her. In a way, Lynda was hurt by his silence. But she also knew she'd come under his spell. Even when she had come to him with her request for a Talmud course, they hadn't talked. She'd gone over the heads of Rebbetzin Lefner and Rabbi Boren, who said that women did not study Talmud. She'd expected to be told the same thing by Rabbi Schwartz. When the rabbi had asked her why she wanted to study Talmud, she'd thought of dozens of eloquent arguments and reasons. But all the effort and logic had come down to two words. She'd said, "Why not?" Rabbi Schwartz had looked at her a long time; then he had told her that he would set up a class the following week. Ruchel had been chosen to study with her, so that she would not be alone with the male teacher, and Rebbetzin

Lefner sat in as a chaperone, doing her best not to listen and not to show her disapproval.

But Rabbi Schwartz hadn't ever really talked to her. What he'd done was revolutionary enough. Women weren't taught Talmud at yeshivas in Jerusalem; hence their unspoken agreement not to speak of the class publicly. Schwartz's yeshiva was still on the fringe of right-wing acceptability in the Ministry of Religion. But still, he'd never talked to her. And now too he sat silent.

"You know," Schwartz said finally, "you're the best student in the girls' school."

"Ruchel is just as good," Lynda said, but she knew it wasn't true.

"She's a hard worker, but you're the best." He leaned back and stroked his beard. "You're potentially better than three-fourths of the boys. You know that, don't you?"

"Yes," Lynda said, looking at him. The coldness flashed in her eyes again, then disappeared.

"What are you going to do with it?"

"Study, Rabbi."

"And after? Do you want to keep studying all your life?"

"Why not?"

"What about a home? A family? Children?"

"Why can't I have both? Are you going to ask *them*"— she pointed to the male side of the curtain—"whether they're going to study or have children?"

"They are commanded to study."

"They're also commanded to have children; I'm not. The Torah says so," Lynda said, irritated. "So my husband can have the children, and I'll study."

"That's nonsense, and you know it," he said. He gazed at her with the intensity that was part of his spell. "Why did you come here?"

"Why not?" Lynda said. "That's a very important question for me, Rabbi."

"I know." Rabbi Schwartz leaned back and stroked his

beard again. "You have to change, to compromise in life. You settle for what you must do, and then hope you're doing the best."

"I'm not sure, Rabbi, that that's as hard a thing for you to say as for me."

"Why? Because I'm a man? There are thousands of other compromises." He looked at the three slanting stripes on his uniform.

"Once," he said, "I believed that the only way for a religious man to fight Israel's wars was with study and prayer. But I was greeted with the realities of life. I compromised. For me, that means I have to kill people. No, Lynda, I don't think it's easier for me to say."

"I'm sorry," Lynda said, softening. "It's just that I don't know why I'm here, and I don't know what I'm going to do. I only know there's this part of me that I'm trying to fill. I don't even know what that part is."

He paused, looking at her. She noticed for the first time how many lines he had around his eyes. The waning evening light and the uniform seemed to make them stand out.

"I shouldn't be talking this way at a wedding," he said. "But I'm leaving soon, and . . ." His voice trailed off as he gazed at the wall above her. Then he turned to her. "I knew a woman, a long time ago. You remind me of her."

"At a yeshiva?"

He laughed. "No. Not hardly. She also asked why not." He leaned forward. "But you know, the whole time she asked that question, she wasn't a very happy person."

"What happened to her?" Lynda asked, fully expecting the reply.

"She stopped chasing phantoms and she married my best friend. They have three children. She compromised. There is some peace in compromising."

"Is she happy?" Lynda asked.

"Yes."

"How do you know?" Lynda asked. An emotion she couldn't name choked her voice. "Just how do you know?"

Rabbi Schwartz straightened slowly in the chair. He looked at Lynda, sadness apparent in his eyes. "Well," he said softly. "This is no place to discuss serious matters."

A dancer whirled near them, stopped and quickly moved away. Rabbi Schwartz stood. "We'll talk when I get back."

He started away. Lynda realized once more where he was going, what might happen. She couldn't send him away like that. She called to him above the music. "Rabbi!"

He turned.

"Don't forget to keep your head down."

Schwartz smiled at her, then moved on to the next student. Lynda watched him, sadness threatening to engulf her. But this was a wedding; God commanded that she be joyful. Lynda tossed back her hair and ran to the circle. She danced slowly at first, then faster and faster. She closed her eyes, dancing to the bride and groom, dancing to God and trying to lose herself in the commandment of joy. The circle broke and re-formed around her, but she didn't notice. When she paused for a rest again, Rabbi Schwartz had already left.

The wedding finally ended at midnight. The night was still and clear, with stars brilliant against a black sky. Lynda stood outside a moment and watched the students break into two groups. The men went off to the dormitory they shared with another yeshiva. The women walked to the two apartments Aish Emes had found for them. She watched them go, grateful to Rabbi Schwartz for allowing her to live alone. So that she could pay her rent from her meager savings, he had allowed her to attend the yeshiva free of charge. She took her meals with the rest of the women, in the women's section of the dormitory cafeteria, also free of charge. He'd known even then that she could not have borne living with the other women. If she'd been forced to live with them, she probably would be back in the States by now. In his own way, Rabbi Schwartz did understand her.

As she walked the empty street, Lynda thought again about their conversation. He wanted her to compromise. She wasn't even sure what that meant. She'd found her way to Aish Emes, but she still didn't know what she sought. Lynda folded her arms across her chest and stared at the sidewalk as she thought. She held her prayer book clutched under folded arms. She started to put it in her purse, but decided not to. Sometimes the prayer book was more of a comfort to hold closed than it was to pray out of when open.

Lynda looked up at the sky. Somewhere in the midst of all that blackness and silence, God lived. When she and her brother were children, they'd had many discussions about where God lived. Once they had even come to blows over it. Lynda had believed God lived in the light from the stars—not the stars themselves, but the light. Jeremy, poor Jeremy, was sure God lived in the blackness between the stars and never spoke to anyone. He'd been jealous when her Hebrew-school teacher, Aviva, had given her the prayer book. And he'd been angry that they made a whole book of prayers for a God who never talked to anyone.

In their separate ways, they were both still searching for where God lived. Jeremy's last letter, incoherent, said he'd dropped out of Harvard Business School and had gone to California. She knew the signs in the letter, the wording, the images. He was into drugs, and there was nothing she could do. Her father must have disowned him by now, since her mother hadn't mentioned him in any letter. Poor Jeremy. And poor Lynda, she thought. It would be really easy to begin to feel sorry for herself. She was twenty-two and still searching for herself. Still trying to find her way between the stars. With a final look skyward, she quickened her pace home.

An air-raid siren woke Lynda in the morning. She lay in bed a moment, paralyzed, listening to the siren and the sound of distant explosions. She couldn't think whether she was awake or asleep and having a nightmare. Mrs. Sheinman, her landlady, pounded on the door.

"Lynda, wake up! There is war. Wake up!"

Lynda moved quickly from the bed to the door and beheld an already dressed Mrs. Sheinman.

"You must hurry," the old woman said in accented English. "I will go to the kitchen and get the food. You go and do as we planned." Then Mrs. Sheinman moved off down the hall.

Lynda, in a daze of fear and exhaustion, stripped off the T-shirt and shorts she used as pajamas. She put on a clean skirt and long-sleeved blouse. Slipping on her sandals, she gathered the bedroll she'd kept ready. She started down the apartment hallway, but doubled back to go to the bathroom. Then she grabbed her toothbrush and ran to the kitchen. Mrs. Sheinman beckoned for her to hurry.

"We must get to the shelter. Can you take a box of food?"

There was a knock at the door. Two men came in. Both were about Mrs. Sheinman's age, and as Lynda remembered, both had designs on the widow. Georgi, who walked with a pronounced limp, took Mrs. Sheinman's bedroll and box of food. Avram stacked two boxes of supplies and carried them to the door. Few words were exchanged. Rumblings sounded in the distance, with accompanying concussions that they felt through their feet. Lynda followed the three to the door, then ran back to get her prayer book. She eyed the bathroom again, but as another explosion sounded, she ran for the door.

In the street, people moved quickly. Lynda spotted a woman struggling with three children. Tucking her bedroll under her arm, Lynda grabbed one child as he ran into the street. He began to scream. Lynda walked beside the mother, speaking softly, but failing to calm the child. Luckily, the ulpan, the Hebrew school for immigrants that served as a shelter, was only two blocks away. The group made its way as quickly as the children and Mrs. Sheinman's pace would allow. A plane sounded overhead, and they all looked up.

"Egyptian?" Avram asked. His eyes were too bad to see very far.

"No," Georgi said. "Syrian." He grinned, revealing several teeth missing. "The Egyptian planes are all gone. That one soon will be too."

They made it to the shelter as a bomb hit near them. Lynda felt the ground shake and almost lost her footing. They walked down the narrow steps to the basement. There Lynda helped the mother get settled in a corner of the large room that usually served as a canteen for the immigrants.

The immigrants, who lived at the ulpan, gathered in language clusters: two Rumanians; six Russians. The four Greeks sat on the raised platform that sometimes functioned as a stage. Lynda envied them a moment. There was no familiar cluster for her. Envious, she quickly moved near Mrs. Sheinman, helping the old woman get comfortable. Rounds came down regularly, shaking the building. Lynda noticed that the windows of the shelter were small and thick, reinforced with metal bars and sandbags stacked outside.

"Our neighbors the Jordanians are shelling us," Mrs. Sheinman said. "Shelling Jerusalem." She shrugged, her large breasts moving up with her shoulders and down again. "What can you expect?"

A woman near them began to cry. Mrs. Sheinman eyed her, then turned to Lynda. "How do you feel?"

"All right," Lynda said. "Frightened."

"Being frightened is okay," Mrs. Sheinman said. "Israeli women are strong even when frightened." She spoke loudly. "Only Egyptian women cry." The woman looked at Mrs. Sheinman. She straightened up and wiped her eyes. When the next round came in, she was silent.

Lynda found a clear space on the floor. She sat on her bedroll and pulled out her prayer book. But she couldn't pray. She was too afraid, too startled by the noise to pray. The prayers demanded a detachment and abandon she could not summon. She was in a bomb shelter in the middle of a war. That was all that filled her mind.

"Excuse me." Lynda jumped at the voice. She looked up to see a young Orthodox man. He was tall and thin, his brown beard sprinkled with red and gray.

"I'm Tzvi Heldman," he said.

"Oh, I've heard of you," Lynda said. "You're the genius of the men's school."

He smiled. "And you're Lynda Jacobs, the genius of the women's school."

"I am?"

"Well, that's what I've heard," he said. "May I sit down?"

"Sure." Lynda moved over to be certain they would not touch. "I'm not a genius," she said.

"Neither am I. I saw you at the wedding, but I never got the chance to say hello. Moishe Wittenstein kept running interference to keep me on the men's side."

Lynda laughed. She looked down and saw the patches of gauze on Tzvi's hand. "What happened to you?"

"Sandbagging. Gentle me got blisters. I figured it was the least I could do."

"Moishe let you leave off studying Talmud to go sand-bag?"

"No. He lectured me endlessly as he bandaged my hands."

"That's one advantage I have in taking a Talmud class," Lynda said. "Moishe stays as far away from me as he can. Is it true he has a following at the men's school?"

"As a matter of fact, he does. Rabbi Schwartz calls them Overpious Anonymous."

Lynda looked up at the sandbagged windows. "I wonder where the rabbi is." Her words hung, unanswerable, in the air between them. Lynda sighed. She looked around the room. Except for the immigrants, Tzvi and herself, the people in the shelter were old men and women, or mothers with children. They were probably all wondering about someone.

Someone turned on a radio; the two listened to the news in silence. Lynda strained to hear the rapid Hebrew coming from the speaker. Mount Scopus was surrounded by the Jordanians, and the fighting was heavy. The fighting was heavy elsewhere as the Israeli Army fought hill by hill to silence the guns firing on Jerusalem. A wave of artillery came down on them, drowning out the radio. Lynda jumped and reached for Tzvi, her first impulse to hold on to someone until the noise and shaking stopped. She caught herself, though, and hugged her knees instead.

"That was close," Tzvi said when it ended. "Very close."

Then there was silence, a silence not of peace but of war, the awesome quiet between bombardments. It frightened her more than the noise.

"I should have joined the Army," Tzvi said. He twisted a bandaged finger into his beard.

"I think it's a little late for that," Lynda said. "And that's not why you came here. Rabbi Schwartz would have told you to go join if he'd thought it was useful."

"The rabbi is very protective of his yeshiva boys."

"The rabbi also knows when an effort is worthwhile and when it's not. You did just as much good filling sandbags."

"I guess so," he said. But his gray eyes told her he remained unconvinced.

A roach crawled by. Lynda moved to kill it. She heard the sound of gunfire in the distance and stopped, letting the thing pass unharmed.

"I just can't believe this is real," she said. "I keep wondering if we'll win, like this was some damn football game." She looked at the ceiling, then at Tzvi. Another round came in, drowning out words.

"It's not a football game," Tzvi said. "We'll win. If we don't, they'll annihilate us. God won't permit that."

"Why not? Why is this any different than the Holocaust?"

Tzvi started to say something, but shrugged and looked down. He sat cross-legged in front of her, studiously scraping sand and dust with his finger. He made a pile in the center of one of the cement squares.

She knew he had no answer. None of them did. She also knew it had been a stupid thing to say. Yet the question didn't seem stupid to her. God won't permit it. Tzvi had spoken with such certainty. The men at Aish Emes, and the women too, had a certainty she envied. She watched him pile the sand for a while, then reached once again for her prayer book.

"I haven't seen one like that," Tzvi said.

"I didn't get it here. It was a gift, back in the States."

"Your parents?"

"Not hardly," Lynda said. "My Hebrew-school teacher when I was thirteen."

"Why do you say not hardly? Your parents cared enough to send you to a Hebrew school."

"Ah, but you don't understand. My parents were also sending me to St. Teresa's Academy."

"You're kidding," Tzvi said. "A Catholic school?"

"It's where a lot of the Jews sent their kids. My parents had not yet been accepted into the ranks and thought my schooling would help. But," she said, "my schooling would not help me marry well if the nuns polluted me and made me a Catholic. Now, my Daddy believed that all Catholics, in addition to being anti-Semites, were fanatics. And the only way to fight fanaticism is with fanaticism."

"So he enrolled you in Hebrew school."

"Not just a Hebrew school—an Orthodox Hebrew school, four days a week. You can imagine how thrilled they were when I came in, in my St. Teresa's blazer complete with cross and coat of arms."

"Whew. How long did you go?"

"To St. T's or to Hebrew school?"

"Both."

"I graduated from St. T's high school. I only went to Hebrew school until my father found I was taking those studies seriously." She looked down at the prayer book. "Shortly after I received this." She stared, saying nothing more.

"Something awful happened, didn't it?" Tzvi asked softly.

"Oh, you could say that." Lynda smiled a thin, humorless smile. "My little brother, Jeremy, had warned me that our parents were suspicious I was getting too—how did he put it?—Jewishy. But I didn't listen. Aviva, that was my Hebrew teacher, invited me to her house for Shabbos, and I had the stupidity to ask my father for permission. That was a famous night. It was the last time I mentioned anything religious in the house. It was the last time I attended Hebrew school." Lynda clutched at the book. "Also the last time I ever locked my door at home. My father kicked the door in and ransacked the room for all the stuff from Hebrew school. Jeremy hid the prayer book for me; that's the only way it was saved."

"He sounds like a nice brother."

Lynda sighed. "Yes. He is." She stared off a moment. "Oh, yes, and it was the last time I ever loved my father."

"That's harsh," he said.

"So is my father." Lynda smiled genuinely this time. "I like you. You listen well."

"I like you too." He looked at his watch. "And we've known each other a whole two hours."

A shell came down close to the shelter. "No," Lynda said. "It's been longer. I'm aging very fast. And now my religious leanings have made me loose."

"Loose?"

"Here I've immodestly revealed my deepest emotions, which in turn may incite your Evil Impulse, and you'll take advantage of me."

"I very well may," Tzvi said.

"I beg your pardon?"

He grinned. "Some of the guys in the yeshiva have been trying very hard to persuade me to meet you. I am, after all, twenty-three and not yet married. They too worry about my Evil Impulse."

"Ah, an old maid," Lynda said. "And I, at twenty-two, am a spinster."

"A perfect match."

"I have to admit, I've heard your name mentioned many times." She leaned closer to him. "By the rebbetzins."

"That serious, huh?"

"Well, considering it's from the rebbetzins, I don't know how serious. Everyone is always afraid that I'm about to leave the fold."

"Are you leaving?" he asked.

"No," Lynda said quietly. "I'm not leaving."

"Good. Marry me."

"Sure."

"Look, with the rebbetzins behind us we can't go wrong. And you said you were worried about my Evil Impulse."

"How about we wait until we can get out of this shelter, and then wait until we get out of this war. Then you can take all the time you want to discuss matrimony while you court me with American-style ice cream."

"Your Evil Impulse?"

"Certainly is."

"Agreed," he said.

By evening, Lynda had gotten over her embarrassment at stepping over a dozen bodies to go to the bathroom. Also by evening, she'd recovered her appetite. Dinner was an incongruous but delicious mix of people's provisions. No one went hungry. Mrs. Sheinman had saved the best of her cooking for Lynda and herself, gladly sharing with Tzvi over his protests. Lynda could see the light of a marriage match in the old woman's eyes. In Jerusalem everyone tried to make matches.

Long after sunset, a man stood up, declaring he couldn't stand it anymore and had to see if Jerusalem was still there. He left the shelter and came back shortly, with a broken nose and a cut over one eye. He testified that Jerusalem was still there. A Rumanian and a Greek rushed to his aid, their physician's bags in hand.

Tzvi had come down to the shelter with nothing but his bandaged hands, so Lynda gave him one of her bedroll blankets, again over his protests. She half-expected him to move to the other side of the room, but he didn't. Except for a brief break to pray the evening service in another room, he lay next to her and they talked, their conversation becoming whispered as the hours grew later.

"Okay," Lynda said finally. "I'm ready. I've known you long enough. What was your name before you saw the light?"

"You mean you don't believe I was born with the name Tzvi?"

"No."

He chuckled. "It was Terry—Terrence when I was called formally, or in trouble. And what was your name," he asked sarcastically, "before you saw the light?"

"Lynda. I was named after myself."

"Nonconformist," he said. "You know, when I think of a yeshiva nonconformist, only people like Moishe usually come to mind."

"Moishe thinks I'm from the Other Side," she said.

"Ah, the Forces of Darkness. Because of the Talmud class?"

"What else?"

"Well, I said Moishe came to mind as a nonconformist."

"Anyway," she said, moving from a painful subject, "do I strike you as a Brucha, or a Ruchel, or a Bluma?"

"No, I must admit you do not. But you shouldn't think you are the only person at Aish Emes with a worldly past. In my younger days, I tried to join a motorcycle gang."

"You're kidding," she said. "How old were you?"

"About sixteen. I had a black leather jacket and everything."

"What happened?"

"I learned the virtue of obedience when I mouthed off to the gang leader. He broke my arm. It was then I decided there were healthier ways to express my youthful rebellion."

"Did you have a motorcycle?"

Tzvi looked at her, eyebrow raised. "No. They were going to steal me one as a token of membership."

"That I refuse to believe."

"And how," Tzvi asked with mock piety, "did you find your way to our Rabbi and Teacher?"

"I came by way of the University of Wisconsin and the civil rights movement."

"Were you a Freedom Rider?"

She nodded. Tzvi looked at her, eyes wide with wonder. She hated that look.

"I was a Freedom Rider," she said quickly. "I hated it most of the time, was scared to death all of the time and wet my pants in the bus once. So don't look at me as if I'm a saint or something."

"Sorry. So what brought you here?"

He was making piles of dust again. Lynda watched as he demolished four small piles, then moved them together.

"One time, I saw this man with a white beard and white hair walking next to Martin Luther King. His beard and hair reflected the sun, shining brilliantly. I got an impression of him just before the fire hose smashed me into a wall."

"I can see how that would make an impression." Tzvi cocked his head skeptically. "A vision?"

"No. Abraham Joshua Heschel," Lynda answered laughing. "As you said, the circumstances made an impression on me. Have you ever read any of his books?" she asked. Tzvi shook his head. "Well, so much for being worldly."

"I told you, I was into motorcycle gangs."

"I've read them all. He kind of led me back to Judaism. After I graduated from college I went back to Aviva, my Hebrew teacher, who was married by then with four kids. Anyway, she put me in touch with someone who told me about Rabbi Schwartz and Aish Emes. And what grave trials brought you here?"

"Alas, I didn't suffer at all. I asked my parents if I could go to Jerusalem and study to be a rabbi. They approved immediately."

"That's hard to believe."

"It's true. They believed that the best thing for me was to lead a holy life and have the blessing of studying Torah. The Gentile girl I'd been dating had nothing to do with it at all."

They laughed, then stopped laughing as the world exploded around them. Tzvi smiled reassuringly and lifted his hand, only to put it down again. She was aware of his presence, his body next to her. She was aware too of a void between them. It would have been nice to hold his hand, to soothe her fears in the touch of another human being. All around them, people held each other, comforted and calmed the terror in the thunder around them. Up until now, at this time, in this place, the life of the yeshiva had seemed natural to her. She'd accepted the separation, the lack of touching, the guarded and walled lives of the students. But here the natural thing was to reach out. Old men comforted young women, and she saw no Evil Impulse there. They sat in awkward silence. He looked at her and she saw that awkwardness in his eyes, along with a fear of his own desire. They both looked away. The shelling stopped.

Tzvi coughed. "Well, how is Talmud going? Rumor has it that you're a real scholar. I've heard Rabbi Schwartz chide some of the lazier members of the boys' school that he'll send them over to you so they can see what a real Talmud student does."

"Well, it's nice to know I've elevated myself to a threat for bad yeshiva boys."

"I didn't mean it that way, and neither did Rabbi Schwartz."

"I wonder," Lynda said. She looked at Tzvi. He didn't answer.

Aish Emes lay in ruins. The yeshiva had been one of the first casualties in the thirty-six-hour shelling of Jerusalem. Half the large study room that just days before had housed a wedding was gone. Around the city, the battle for Jerusalem continued. Mount Scopus had been relieved, but the Old City remained. In a drive born of the frustration of having been closed out of the Walled City in 1948, Israeli troops fought their way to the Temple Mount, fighting hand to hand in order not to hurt the Holy City. As the soldiers fought, other hands carried rubble out of the shell that had been Aish Emes. Yeshiva students crawled over the ruins, looking for books and a Torah Scroll lost in the debris.

"When we find the Torah, you know we'll all have to fast," Moishe said to no one in particular.

Lynda, leaning against a remaining wall, exhausted from hours of picking through rubble, chose to reply. "Shut up, Moishe."

"Don't tell me to shut up. That's using an evil tongue. I'm trying to guard Torah."

Lynda sighed and looked at Moishe, who stared fixedly at the rocks before him. Even resting, he had trouble keeping his body still. He twitched and fidgeted, winding the ritual fringes he wore around his fingers, swaying back and forth as if he were at prayer. She closed her eyes against the anger welling in her. He wore the fringes. He guarded the Torah.

"We have to find the Torah Scroll first, Moishe," she said.

"We'll find the Torah with the help of God," Moishe answered, gazing at her angrily. He realized he was looking at a woman, and averted his eyes, turning red.

"It will have to be with the help of God, because we certainly aren't getting much help from you."

"Evil tongue," he said. He stood up and walked away, calling behind him. "Evil tongue you get from studying Talmud when you shouldn't!"

Tzvi came over and sat down near her. "You shouldn't be so hard on him."

"I shouldn't be hard on him?" Lynda snapped to everyone around her. "He's been so busy ordering everyone around, he hasn't picked up one rock."

"That's not quite true," Tzvi said.

"Everyone thinks he's so pious. Have any of you thought that maybe he's just crazy?" Lynda was greeted by three or four shrugs in unison.

"What do you want Rabbi Schwartz to do?" Tzvi asked quietly. "Throw him out?"

"No," she said. She turned so one shoulder leaned against the wall and she faced Tzvi. "And I'm really not in the mood for you to be sensible."

"I noticed."

She was silent a moment, thinking of the rabbi, so present in his absence. A breeze blew through the open building, bringing the sound of gunfire and the smell of smoke. For all the shelling, the Jerusalem she saw through the broken wall was in remarkably good condition. It made Aish Emes look even sadder.

"I'd hate to be here when he finds out," Tzvi said softly, echoing her thoughts.

"You know," Lynda said, "I've always wondered about him." She looked around her. "How he got here."

"I've heard stories," Tzvi said.

"Really? Tell me." She sat down, straightening her skirt to cover her knees. "I think I could use a story right now."

"Well, I heard he wasn't very observant, but got turned on to Torah by a religious friend of his."

"In Israel?"

"No. The States. Even Rabbi Schwartz says that he got the idea to emigrate from a person he hardly knew. A woman who came over to fight the War of Independence."

"Was she observant?"

"No, she was a kibbutznik. You know Kibbutz Ruth?"

"Not really," Lynda said. "I've never gone kibbutz hopping. I came straight to Jerusalem."

"Oh, you should," he said. "It's great. There's nothing like picking oranges until your arms fall off."

"Sounds romantic and heroic."

"Kibbutz Ruth is a small kibbutz between here and Tel Aviv. It's named for her."

"I gather she died," Lynda said.

"Yes. In the '56 war. A sniper."

"How do you know so much?" Lynda asked suspiciously. She remembered the motorcycle story.

Tzvi smiled faintly. "I really used to worship Rabbi Schwartz when I first came here. I'd heard the story, and wanted to see who this woman was who could so profoundly influence my 'rebbe' when he barely knew her. So I made kind of a pilgrimage to the kibbutz."

"And what did you find out?"

"That picking oranges can make your arms fall off." He chuckled and stood. Lynda stood up with him. "That ended my worship phase and started my profound-respect phase. Much healthier."

"You mean you grew up," Lynda said.

"I guess that is another way of putting it," he said. They were interrupted by Moishe yelling from across the room.

"I think I found it!" he yelled, waving his arms. "I think I found it!"

They ran to where Moishe stood. One of the men, who had rescued a flashlight from one of the offices, peered into the rubble. He nodded, and they all took turns looking down what appeared to be a shallow three-foot tunnel of boards, rock and dirt. At the end of the passage a small grotto had been formed by two huge blocks fallen across each other. Beneath their arch lay the Torah Scroll.

They worked to widen the narrow passage, but debris began to fall around the Scroll. The passage was still too narrow for anyone to make it to the Torah. Lynda sat near the entrance listening as the men argued what to do next. Logic told her that the Scroll was safe, that they would just wait until they could get the proper help to dig it out. But part of her burned with the thought of the Torah under all that dirt. That part of her, so much like Moishe, propelled her to the small dark hole. None of the men would ever fit. She was the smallest of the women. Maybe that was why she was here. For once, even as a woman, she could feel commanded. God commanded her to rescue the Scroll. It became clear to her as she headed into the passage, wriggling her shoulders through the opening. She was halfway through the opening before anyone could stop her. She heard Tzvi's muffled voice above her.

"Let her go. She's the only one who can do it."

The Torah was only three feet away; she could almost reach it. All she had to do was grab the Scroll and back out again. She flushed with the effort of moving by fractions of inches, and with the fever of her task. Maybe this one act was why God had brought her to Jerusalem. The dust and rock trickled down around her face, forcing her to stop and wipe her eyes, but still she smiled. She was getting closer. A metal rod tore at her arm, but she continued. The air of the passage became moist with her breath and sweat.

Blindly, Lynda grabbed for the handles of the Scroll, made contact and pulled it toward her. She tried to move backward, but with the Scroll in her hands, it was impossible. Lynda yelled for the others to pull her out. Hands tightened on her ankles and she began to move.

It was then that she saw the roof of the passage collapse around her. She tried to shout, but the dust and pebbles dribbled into her mouth. A weight came down on the back of her head. She pulled the Torah to her, to protect it. Suddenly words filled her head, hundreds of words. Phrases came and went by so fast she couldn't understand most of them. Hebrew words danced in front of her; ran from her. "Aitz Chaim Hi: She is a tree of life." Lynda heard the words and tightened her grip on the Torah. "Tein Helkenu, give us our portion in Your Torah." She heard the words, felt her portion of Torah in her hands. She wanted to say the Sh'ma, the statement of faith she knew she must say before dying. She heard voices above her, but whether they were from her friends or from Heaven she couldn't tell. She wanted to say the Sh'ma as she was commanded, but she couldn't open her mouth because of the dirt. The commandment stated that she had to say it aloud, or at least mouth it with her lips. But she was suffocating and the dirt wouldn't let her say it. She couldn't fulfill the commandment. Aitz Chaim Hi. Lynda felt pain in her ankles. Some clawed being that she could see in her head was trying to pull her from the Torah. No. She would hold it. Aitz Chaim Hi. She finally had her portion in Torah, her place, her inheritance. She finally had what she'd come for. That was all she'd ever wanted. It was all clear now. But she couldn't breathe and she couldn't say the Sh'ma. She had to fulfill the commandment and get the claws out of her ankles. But they kept pulling and pulling and wouldn't let go.

Then light, air, gentle hands. Lynda spat out the dirt from her mouth and choked. She was dizzy. Someone held her and brushed the dirt from her eyes. She cried as they took the Torah away. The crying washed enough dirt from her eyes that she could see Tzvi holding the Scroll. His body seemed to waver as if a great heat were before them. Maybe he would give it back to her. Slowly she began to focus and think. She had blood all over her shoulders. Someone held a cloth to the back of her head. She saw it was Leah who held her.

"We've sent for an ambulance," Tzvi said as he handed the Torah to another man. "But I don't know how long it will take to get here. I'm going to get a car. Can you make it?"

Lynda nodded, but winced in pain. Her vision blurred again. When it cleared, Moishe was standing over her.

"You're crazy. You know that? Crazy!" He turned to the rest of the group. "She should have left it where it was!"

"She made it out, Moishe," Leah said. "Don't worry."

"Don't worry?" he yelled. "What if it's her period? Huh? Then she's touched the Torah and defiled it? How about that, huh? She should have left it!"

Lynda began to laugh. She laughed as someone began to call out the legal argument countering Moishe's accusation. She laughed and listened to them all and laughed again until she finally lost consciousness.

JUNE
1968

MADELEINE AWOKE WITH A START. SHE'D BEEN DREAMING about Ruth again. She hadn't realized she'd fallen asleep, which made waking all the more jarring. She looked out the window by her seat on the airplane, still seeing dream images against the starry blackness. In the dream Ruth beckoned—not to her, but to Joshua, her son. She called him to a crevice that was both canyon and mass grave. Joshua ran to Ruth as Madeleine stood paralyzed, unable to stop him. Recalling the dream made Madeleine's palms sweat. She turned to Joshua, who sat next to her, and gently patted him on the lap. He grunted in his sleep. Madeleine turned on the light above her head, which seemed intrusive in the darkened cabin. She looked at her watch. It wouldn't be long now. Soon they would be in Ruth's land and she would greet the spirits that dwelt there, leaving her son as an offering. Joshua Stern, at seventeen, was about to become a kibbutznik. He would stay six months with Ruth's family. In that six months, Madeleine knew, he would try to devise a means to stay forever.

She glanced past Joshua to Aaron, across the aisle. Still awake after all these hours, he stared ahead of him. Madeleine knew that he too saw ghosts. At least her ghosts were consigned to the dreams of sleep; Aaron lived with his apparitions constantly. Next to him sat the twins, ten years old, both of them asleep. The whole family was going to the Holy Land. She might have been able to stall Joshua off one more year if Aaron hadn't decided that he too wanted to see Jerusalem. To underscore his seriousness, he'd announced in the congregation that he was taking a vacation—something he hadn't done in fourteen years. With that much ammunition behind him, Joshua wouldn't hear of waiting until he'd finished a year of college.

Madeleine couldn't recall if she'd ever been consulted on the subject of a family tour. But then, they all knew what her opinion would be. She preferred her Zionism at a distance and tried to confine it to the little blue boxes of the Jewish National Fund, or benefits for Youth Aliyah. It had never occurred to her to actually set foot in Israel.

That, of course, was a half-lie. The thought had occurred to her in nightmares, where Israel swallowed her son. She'd had more of those lately, and more remembrances of times better forgotten. The prospect of meeting Benjamin and Ruth Yair's daughter, Yudit, had dredged up everything.

"Still awake?"

Madeleine turned to her son and smiled. "I just woke up. How are you doing?"

He rubbed sleep out of his eyes. "Fine. It won't be long now. Maybe an hour."

"Then you will finally have your dream come true."

He smiled. "Israel."

"No, I was thinking of Yudit."

"Come on, Mom. I'm not coming all this way just for a girl." He looked away. "Besides, she's two years older than me, and she's probably engaged to some muscular paratrooper."

"I thought you told each other the most intimate secrets by mail. Lord knows, you two have been writing long enough. Don't you think she'd tell you if she had a paratrooper on the side?"

"She probably didn't want to hurt my feelings. She probably thinks I'm a nerd."

"I doubt that. She thinks you're handsome."

"No, *you* think I'm handsome. And you're biased."

"Absolutely," Madeleine said. "But that doesn't mean I'm wrong. You look like your father. Believe me, she'll be a sucker for those black eyes. I was."

"I don't suppose you could just leave me when we see the kibbutz," he said.

"We've been through this before, Joshua," Madeleine said, her voice firm. "We're not going to see you for six months. The twins are already miserable. We'll all see the kibbutz; we'll tour around together for a few days to get you acclimated; then we will leave you with Ben and Yudit."

"It seems dumb."

"It may be. But it's what I want, and it's my compromise from wanting you around the whole three weeks we're here."

"Yeh, yeh."

"Don't sulk, Joshua."

Joshua reached for the magazine he'd looked at several times already. Madeleine leaned back and closed her eyes.

She really should just leave him and let him have his freedom, but she didn't want to let him go. Only by seeing him in the country and feeling that he was happy, could she then leave him and live with her fear. She wanted to have images of her son elsewhere than Ruth's kibbutz; somewhere other than the heart of Ruth's dream.

Madeleine glanced over at Joshua. He was now watching Aaron, who stared ahead of him, as if there were a display on the seat back in front of him. Joshua spoke without turning.

"He's getting worse."

"Who?"

"Dad. Ever since we decided on this trip, he's been out of it."

"I haven't noticed anything," Madeleine said.

"Yes, you have. It bothers you too."

Madeleine paused, tightening her lips. "This isn't easy for him, Joshua."

"Why?"

"He's going to meet a lot of . . . ghosts."

Joshua finally turned to her. "Don't tell me he sees ghosts."

"Never mind, Joshua. I can see you aren't prepared to understand."

"I've been trying to understand all my life," he said.

"Well, in case you didn't know," she snapped, "your father and I had a bit of a life before yours began." Then her voice softened. "A good part of that life was connected with Nathan Schwartz." Madeleine smiled. "It certainly makes me feel old. I remember when he got the idea for the yeshiva."

"Dad told me. From Yudit's mother."

"Your father is getting to that age where a man begins to judge his life, and tries to see if the choices he made are the right ones." She patted Joshua on the lap. "It tends to make one moody."

"Is this trip going to be hard on you? I mean going to the kibbutz?"

"Well, it will be interesting." Madeleine leaned back again and said no more. Putting things into words made things worse. The pieces of her past that she had thought buried were all being dredged up. She had been a fool to come along on this trip. This was the kind of thing Aaron did to himself. It seemed as if she'd caught his disease.

She'd spent the morning packing and thinking about ghosts, but ones she'd seen in the flesh. It had been long after she'd thought she was safe. Aaron was the assistant at a congregation, and Joshua had just been born. Then had come the knock at the door.

When she recognized the faces at the door, she almost closed it again.

"I see you recognize me, Miss Blumfeld," Agent Knox said. "Pardon, it's Mrs. Stern now. May we come in?"

Madeleine nodded dumbly, and they walked past her. "You remember Agent Bach, don't you? Good." As Knox spoke, he looked around with thinly disguised curiosity. He noticed the bassinet and walked up to it.

"Beautiful little baby you have there," he said smiling.

"Get away from him," Madeleine said, moving quickly over to where Joshua slept. "Get away."

"Now, Mrs. Stern. I'm not an ogre. I've had a couple of kids of my own. Colicky at all?"

The question didn't register for a moment. "A little," she said.

"You know what me and the wife used to do? Whenever the youngest, he was the colicky one, started fussing, we'd take him out for a ride in the car. Just drove around the block and he was fast asleep." Knox looked up from the bassinet and smiled at Bach, who had been roaming around the living room. Then he looked at Madeleine. "Bach, there, has a wife expecting."

"What do you want?" Madeleine asked.

"Just to talk. May we sit down?" he asked as he sat down. Bach came over and indicated the chair near the bassinet for Madeleine to sit in. He sat down at her side.

Knox smiled. He still remembered her father. With him gone, this would be a piece of cake. "What do you know about Julius and Ethel Rosenberg?" he asked.

"My God."

"I doubt," Bach said, "that God has much to do with the Rosenbergs, Mrs. Stern."

"Now, now, Bach," Knox said, smiling. "Mrs. Stern has married a man of the cloth." He turned to Madeleine. "I hope that indicates a change of heart and mind."

"What do you want from me?" Madeleine looked at her sleeping son, and then at the two sets of eyes that waited. "I left all that," she said. "I left. I don't know anything."

"Are you saying you never met them?"

"Never."

"I can name rallies you attended with the Rosenbergs."

"You know perfectly well how many people attended rallies," Madeleine said. "If they were there, I never knew it, and I certainly didn't meet them."

"You may know others who did, then, Mrs. Stern," Knox said.

Madeleine looked down once more at the sleeping child. "I can't tell you any names," she said softly.

"What was that?" Knox asked. "I didn't hear you."

"I said, I don't know anyone who might have had contact with them."

"I'll tell you what," Knox said, leaning back and smiling. "Why don't you just give us the names of some of the people you knew in the Party, and we'll judge for ourselves."

"I can't."

Knox looked at her. She could name names and she would. It remained only a question of time. He looked at Bach a moment and saw him nod. Straight for the bleeding wound. Okay.

"Mrs. Stern," Knox said. "I don't have time to fool around. Mr. Bach is going to show you something. Two reports from September sixteenth, 1949. You choose which report you want to become public record."

Madeleine took the papers as Bach leaned toward her. One report was from the New York City Police Department, and one from a government investigation. She looked at the first, then the other.

"You know," she said.

"We knew all along."

"How?" Madeleine asked. "How could you know? Did you have me followed? Were you there?"

The horror in her eyes made Knox flinch a bit. These things were always embarrassing. He waited for the look to change to hatred. That always happened. Hatred was cleaner, easier to deal with. But the look didn't change. She stared at him, holding the reports in her hand.

"Which report do you want official, Mrs. Stern?" he said gruffly. "Ours says self-defense by a probable rape victim—unknown. Case closed. The police report says attempted murder—case never closed."

Madeleine continued to stare at him. "Did you—watch?"

Knox looked away briefly. "No, Mrs. Stern. I wasn't there."

"Did you know?"

Bach interrupted. "That is not the issue here—"

Knox shook his head, cutting off his partner. "I knew."

"Oh, my God." Madeleine breathed out the words. She reached down to touch Joshua's back. "Were you with your colicky baby, Mr. Knox?"

"Look, lady," Knox said, his voice raised. "You had plenty of warning. There wasn't anyone that didn't try to warn you. You did it to yourself!" Bach was watching him curiously. Time to calm down. It had been a long day.

"And you let it happen," Madeleine said.

"Which report do you prefer?" Knox asked.

"It says *attempted* murder."

"You didn't kill the son-of-a-bitch, no. You would have saved us a lot of expense if you had."

"Is he free?"

"No. He's in a state mental hospital. He can't even feed

himself. Keeping him alive costs a hell of a lot of money."

"Why don't you do your duty, Mr. Knox, and kill him yourself?"

"That would be against the law."

Madeleine held up the reports. "And this isn't?"

"Both reports are true. We just have different information."

"Wouldn't all these sordid details come out if I was arrested?"

"No, Mrs. Stern," Knox said. "You've got a lovely baby and a nice house, and I'm sure a very pious husband. But I promise you, I won't hesitate to arrest you." He pulled out his handcuffs. "Not at all. I want names. As many as you know. Anyone connected with the Party, anyone who belonged, anyone who attended meetings of any kind. Now if you want to take your baby to jail, fine. It's your choice."

She'd told the agents what little she knew. That had started her seeing ghosts. For weeks she had seen Illi in every shadow, until she found the right state hospital and verified his presence. Then it had faded. All memories and pain had faded away—until now. Her ghosts had reappeared. She saw Ruth in her dreams, and for weeks before they left she'd started seeing Illi in every shadow again. Maybe she could rid herself of the evil spirits in the Holy Land.

She glanced at her watch. Almost time. She leaned over Joshua. "Aaron," she said. He didn't answer.

Joshua reached out and tapped him on the shoulder. He started suddenly and turned. "Shh," he said. "The boys are finally asleep."

"Perfect timing," Madeleine said. "We should land within thirty minutes."

Aaron smiled. "Good! I'll wake them up."

"No, you don't!"

"But we're getting near Israel. I promised."

"They will live."

Aaron frowned, but didn't wake up the children. He stood and motioned to Joshua, who switched places with him.

"There," he said, sitting down and taking Madeleine's hand. "If I can't wake up the boys, I'll have to make do with holding your hand."

"I'm not sure I find that remark flattering," Madeleine said. She squeezed his hand. "What are you thinking about?"

"My father."

"I figured."

"I wish he'd come with us."

"Oh, Aaron, you know he would only have been disappointed."

"I know. But I wanted him to come," Aaron said.

"He spends so much time being disappointed. Why would Israel be any different?"

"Madeleine, that's not necessary."

"I'm sorry," she said. "But after twenty years, I've earned the right to take it personally. Here you are, rabbi of a very successful congregation that you personally built. You have three lovely children—"

"And a lovely wife."

"And a lovely wife, in whom your father is still disappointed."

"Ah," he said. "That's it."

"Not at all." Madeleine faltered. "Well, mostly not, anyway. I take it personally that your father still considers you his greatest failure."

"At least he doesn't introduce me that way."

"What?"

Aaron chuckled. "That's what Nathan used to say his father did."

"You're changing the subject."

"No, I'm not," Aaron said. He squeezed her hand briefly. "I *am* his greatest failure. I'm a rabbi in Centin, Illinois. I am not a Hasidic rebbe. I'm not even a Hasid. For him that's very disappointing, considering he thinks it's the reason for his existence."

"He's made plenty of advances toward Joshua."

"Was that the week my father sounded so bad on the phone I thought he was dying?" Aaron laughed.

"That was the week. He tried to talk Joshua into going to a yeshiva for six months instead of Israel."

"I bet that was an interesting conversation."

"Joshua was gentle, but frank," Madeleine said.

"I can believe he was frank. Gentle, I'm not so sure. He reminds me a lot of you."

"Funny," she said, "he reminds me of you." She kissed him on the cheek. "A gray hair," she said, and touched his beard.

"Nonsense."

"Two."

"Double nonsense. Anyway, I'm entitled. I'm forty-eight, an old man."

"Not hardly."

"That's because you're too young to notice. Wait until *you're* forty-eight."

"I will be most pleased to wait," Madeleine said. "Anyway, maybe by the time I'm forty-eight, you will take me on a real vacation."

"This isn't one?"

"One seventeen-year-old, two ten-year-olds, a crowded plane and a country full of Jews. I was thinking more of just the two of us. In Paris."

"I'm taking you to a kibbutz. Israel is famous for them."

"And a yeshiva, which Israel is also famous for. They do not come close to Paris."

"But they are infinitely more kosher."

Madeleine grunted and leaned against his shoulder. "Well, Ruth wanted me to see the Jerusalem of her dreams. I wonder how the real thing matches up." She snuggled against him. "How are *you* doing?"

"What do you mean?" he asked.

"How do you feel about seeing Nathan again? Nathan and his yeshiva."

"No problem. He's heard that I am the rabbi of a very successful congregation that I built personally. Nathan should be in awe of me."

"Yes," Madeleine said, looking at him. "He should be." Then she closed her eyes.

Aaron kissed her on top of the head, stroking her hair once. Nathan would be waiting for them, to take them to Jerusalem. Aaron wondered how Jerusalem would match his own dreams. Were there dancing Hasidim in the streets of Jerusalem? There were no Loemers. Yehezkel should have come. Deep inside himself, Yehezkel was still a Hasid, still a Loemer, and he could have brought the spark of Loem to Jerusalem. Instead, as always, he laid the burden on Aaron. And as always, Aaron knew he would fail.

A dissatisfaction and doubt had begun to eat away at his soul. What if God was truly the God of Loem? Aaron feared meeting Nathan. Nathan had his yeshiva for Americans. He had his followers. Nathan had sensed his own destiny and fulfilled its command. Yet maybe there was more. God drew Aaron to Jerusalem. And in Jerusalem he hoped to find the truth, to discover his true destiny before it was too late.

Half in sunlight, half in shadow, Lynda stood before the Western Wall. She reached out to touch the stones still cool with dawn, touching the spot where thousands, hundreds of thousands, before her had touched. The stones were smooth, rounded and worn with grief. Lynda rested her fingers in the shadow of a crevice, waiting for the Wall to lend her its strength. She opened her prayer book again to try to pray. Lynda glanced once at the old woman who stood beside her. The rebbetzin. That was all anyone ever called the old woman. Jerusalem was filled with such old women, rebbetzins who were survivors of migrations, pogroms, death camps. Old women with no family, no children, no names. All that remained was the title from a long-dead marriage. They came to Jerusalem, the Holy City of the Holy Land, to die. Yet they lived on. Like their petitions to God scrawled on scraps of paper and stuffed into the seams of the sacred Wall, they wrinkled, shriveled and endured, waiting for God's notice.

It seemed as if the rebbetzin had always been at the Western Wall, muttering prayers and psalms, as much a part of the Wall as the shadows that now moved slowly about them. Once, on Tisha B'Av, the day mourning the destruction of Solomon's Temple and the sack of Jerusalem, Lynda had heard the woman pray with full voice. Lynda had come to the Wall to chant the Book of Lamentations, as was the custom. But as with so many, her heart wasn't in it. She was too filled with the triumph of the united city to mourn. Lynda was drawn, however, to a group of women standing a few feet from the stones of the Western Wall. They crowded around the rebbetzin, listening to her voice, the voice they knew could reach heaven where theirs could not. The rebbetzin chanted Jeremiah's lament. She bewailed the loss of Solomon's Temple as if her children had been at the destruction; as if her own world had come down around her. And perhaps her children were there, in a world destroyed, long gone to the forces of all but her weeping. She finished the lament, then faded back, once more an old woman muttering prayers.

Lynda had never spoken to her. She longed to talk, to find out how it was that the old woman could still believe and pray. But the barriers between them were too high. The rebbetzin, smelling of pickles and garlic, myriad lines cut into her face, her scarf tied around a shaved head, came from another world. She spoke only Yiddish, and a ghetto-accented Hebrew that was impossible to follow. The secret of the rebbetzin's faith lay walled away by time and language.

Lynda looked once again at the Hebrew words that beckoned her. She took three steps backward, three steps forward and bowed as she began the great prayer of silence, the Amida. One began the prayer with this ritual dance which mimed fear of God, the approach to God and finally submission. It was a lie. She could not submit. Lynda silently mouthed the words she had said thousands of times in the last two years. She reached into herself, through herself, letting the words fly from her mouth of their own accord. She tuned out the meanings of the words, meanings that walled her away as surely as the barrier separating the men and women who prayed at the Western Wall. If she listened to the words, she would have to pray to the God of Abraham, the God of Isaac, the God of Jacob. A God of the Fathers, who stood with the men behind the barrier, in a world forbidden to her. The Torah Scrolls stood on the men's side. On the women's side there were no Scrolls. Here, like Sarah and Rachel, women were barren.

So Lynda let the words say themselves; they didn't belong to her anyway. She saw the jumbled letters tumbling to the heavens as she emptied herself. She became nothing and journeyed toward the light she had first known in her vision. She merged with the Holy Wall, with Jerusalem and with the Torah she had once held in her hands. She merged, losing herself in the holy letters of the Scrolls behind the barrier. She rejoiced as light filled her emptiness. Then, as always, the earth drew her back; the air of this world forced her to become substantial once more and return. Lynda became aware of herself as the light distanced itself. She was leaning her forehead against the worn stone, her cheeks damp with tears she had no recollection of shedding. She straightened and hurried through the final words of the Amida, twisting and bowing the lie of submission once more. She moved quickly through the rest of the Morning Service, then closed her book and kissed it.

The rebbetzin had finished her prayers and now recited psalms, as she would do the rest of the day. She chanted with eyes closed even when she turned the page. The old woman looked up once, her eyes full of approval for her young companion. She believed the lie of submission. Lynda smiled back at her and said good-bye, leaving the old woman alone at the Wall.

It was a twenty-minute fast walk from the Old City to the apartment that now housed the women's school of Aish Emes. Lynda arrived, out of breath, and hesitated a moment before the apartment door. The smell of burnt eggs already hung in the hallway. She opened the door quietly and stepped into the vestibule. The living room was halfway through its transition from cafeteria to study hall. Two women cleared tables. As they did, others sat down with already opened texts and began to sway. In each corner of the room, women sat, hunched in pairs or alone, swaying and chanting with eyes closed as they committed the passages to memory.

Lynda moved to the coatroom, where the melodies of the last song in the Morning Service sounded, blending inconsonantly with the chanting coming from the living room. The burnt-egg smell was very heavy in the air. Lynda grabbed a text and headed for the living room. Ruchel noticed her and moved quickly to meet her.

"Quick, let's start. Rebbetzin Lefner is on the prowl for you, and she has that 'friendly advice' look on her face." Ruchel adjusted the scarf on her head. Lynda grinned. Even after a year of marriage, Ruchel couldn't get comfortable with it.

"Why is she on the prowl?"

"You."

"Why me?"

Ruchel cocked her head and looked up at the ceiling a moment. "My dear, when it comes to you, Brucha Lefner doesn't need a reason. By the way, how was the Old City?"

"Tourists still milling around, most of the Arab shops closed. I think there may have been trouble at the Damascus Gate, but I didn't stick around to find out."

"Very wise." Ruchel frowned. "Damn Arabs. I think the Army should go in and make them open the shops."

"A person has the right to close his business, Ruchel."

"Do you have to be so damn fair all the time?"

"Better they close their shops than shoot people," Lynda said.

"Another bomb went off near here. El Fatah and that bastard, Arafat. I think the Army should take care of him too."

"Ruchel," Lynda sneered. "You don't sound like someone who lives Torah very well."

"Oh, no? I've been hearing about lots of people who live Torah, who are going out to settle the West Bank and the Sinai. The U.S. is already making negotiation noises to sell us out."

"You haven't started listening to the Yesharim, have you? Moishe Wittenstein is one of their main advocates around here. That should tell you something."

"Well, I don't think—"

"Ah, Lynda, there you are. You're finally with us."

As Brucha Lefner approached, Ruchel flashed her "I tried" look to Lynda and shrugged her shoulders. Brucha came over, wiping her hands on her apron, her blond wig slightly askew. "I've been waiting to talk to you, Lynda." Brucha gave Ruchel a look of dismissal.

When the girl had gone, Brucha put her arm around Lynda—a gesture so false in its intimacy that Lynda almost pulled away.

"I'm worried about you, Lynda," Brucha said. "You're not taking care of yourself, and you never really recovered from the accident last year."

"I've recovered completely, Brucha."

"You don't eat well. You eat like a bird anyway, and you've stopped having breakfast with us."

"I don't have the time to make it back here for breakfast."

Brucha squeezed her shoulder. "Then perhaps you should start praying the Morning Service here again."

Lynda pulled away from Brucha, slowly and tactfully. "I'm afraid that's not possible."

"Okay, you wanted to pray at the Wall for a while. But the novelty should have worn off by now. It's time to come home." Brucha smiled.

"I said, it's not possible."

"What do you mean, it's not possible?" Brucha raised her voice, then noticed the women staring at the two of them. She motioned Lynda to the now empty coatroom.

"You have some responsibilities, you know," Brucha said once they were alone. "You're setting a bad example."

"I don't think praying at the Western Wall is a bad example."

"No? And what do we do when all the girls want to go to the Wall to pray?"

"Let them."

"You'd like that, wouldn't you?" Brucha jabbed a finger at Lynda. "You're going to be a rebbetzin soon, whether you like it or not. Even married to Tzvi Heldman, you're going to be just like the rest of us, and you're going to have responsibilities. Just like the rest of us." She jabbed her finger to every word, her eyes narrowed with a barely controlled anger.

"I know."

"No, you don't! You'd love to lead them all to the Wall like some Pied Piper, wouldn't you? You always thought you were better than us. You don't think I've heard the things you say? You don't think I've seen the looks you give me?"

"I'm sorry, Brucha," Lynda said stiffly. "I didn't mean to give that impression."

Brucha hesitated a moment, her expression unsure. Then she spoke. "You're dangerous."

"Why?" Lynda asked, exasperated. "Am I a criminal? A murderer?"

"You're selfish. All that closing of your eyes and wavering of your voice. You try to pray like some Hasidic rebbe. You may fool the girls, but you don't fool me."

"It's not a show," Lynda said. She thought back to the old Rebbetzin. "It's not a show."

"Isn't it?" Brucha moved her lips in a tight smile. "Soon, Lynda, you're going to be married, and then pregnant. Maybe then you'll learn that you aren't a man."

"Is that what marriage is? A punishment?"

"For you it will be. For me it's a blessing." Brucha's face softened slightly. "My family is the way I serve God.

This"—she pointed outside the coatroom—"this is secondary. Unimportant."

"The men don't think so."

"The men have never carried a life within them. The men don't know what it is to feel an unborn child in your womb, to know it even before it's born." She looked at Lynda. "My children are my real yeshiva students." Her eyes grew cold once again. "But you'll never understand that."

"I hope I will," Lynda whispered.

"No. There's a blindness in you. You're blinded by envy, by wanting things God didn't intend for you. I feel sorry for the child you'll someday carry," Brucha said. "But I don't care how blind you are, I don't want you leading the younger girls astray."

"Brucha, if people died so we could pray at the Wall, why is praying there leading people astray?"

"The job of this school is to make these girls into good Jewish wives and mothers."

"Not to teach?"

"To teach what a woman needs to know," Brucha said firmly. "That's why I was against Rabbi Schwartz allowing you to study Talmud. I think he led you astray."

"Maybe he kept me on the path, Brucha. Maybe he kept me here."

"And maybe that was a mistake," Brucha said. The door to the coatroom opened and closed quickly as the person behind retreated.

"Are you going to start praying here?"

"I can't," Lynda said.

"Well, you can, at least for next Thursday. Rabbi Schwartz is bringing an old friend to see us. I want our star pupil and future rebbetzin to be here when he comes."

"I don't perform, Brucha."

"You're always performing, Lynda. Just be here, and have a Talmud lesson prepared." She reached for the door as Lynda nodded. "But then, you always prepare, don't you?" She left Lynda alone.

Ruchel peeked in. "Hi. You still breathing?"

Lynda looked past her as Brucha retreated to the kitchen. "Sure. I'm breathing."

Ruchel looked back behind her, then turned again to Lynda. "I wouldn't want to engage in the Evil Tongue, so I will not say what I think of that woman."

"Good."

"Since we're already in here, why don't we claim it and study Talmud together?"

"Okay," Lynda said. She looked at Ruchel and noticed that her eyes seemed tired. She looked slumped as she walked. "Are you all right?"

"Why do you ask?" Ruchel said quickly.

"You don't look well."

"I'm fine," Ruchel said. She avoided Lynda's eyes.

"Sure there's nothing you want to tell me?"

"Lynda, there is nothing wrong!"

They pushed a few sweaters off the small table used for study. Ruchel opened to the portion they were studying and, at Lynda's nod, began to recite. She stumbled often, preoccupied. Lynda leaned back in her chair—the portion memorized, so that she needed no book. She listened, correcting automatically even as her mind wandered.

Images streamed up from the text on the table. Lynda remembered Heschel, the man with the white hair, seen at such a distance. She'd come here because of him. She'd come to Jerusalem to bow to the power of God, to submit and immerse herself in the light of tradition. But somewhere she'd missed the mark. She was not happy. The road before her seemed like a path of stones.

Ruchel finished reading.

"You have recited the text like a great scholar," Lynda said.

"Sure. Now I've got to explain it." Ruchel put her finger on the line to keep her place. "How's your head?" she asked.

"My head's fine."

"Sure?"

"Sure I'm sure. Everybody, including my fiancé, has been asking me if my head's all right. You all must think I have a brain tumor."

"God forbid," Ruchel said, taking her finger off the book. She frowned and looked for her lost place. "It's just that you've been acting funny since the accident."

"How?"

"I don't know. More withdrawn from us."

"You're not going to harp on me for praying at the Wall, are you?"

"No, no."

"If Moishe went off to pray at the Wall, everyone would think he was being extra pious. I want to do something that brings me closer to God and everyone thinks I'm crazy in the head from the war. Maybe it's all of *you* who are driving me nuts! Have you ever thought of that?"

"Yes, I've thought about that," Ruchel said. "It's just"— Ruchel looked up, her eyes filled with tears—"we're afraid you'll leave us."

Lynda reached over and took her friend's hand. "This is my home, Ruchel. This is the path I've chosen. I'm not leaving." Lynda released Ruchel's hand and laughed. "Besides. This is the last stop. If I were to leave, where on earth would I go?"

A different Nathan walked next to Aaron on the Jerusalem street. This Nathan had his edges smoothed over, like the stones of Jerusalem. He was not a pale yeshiva boy, but tan and strong. They walked on the street that led to the other half of Nathan's yeshiva, the girls' school. The sun shone in a brilliant blue sky, the blue of Jerusalem's summer. This had been the second day Aaron had greeted the sun with prayer, rising before dawn to meet Nathan and pray with the young men, the two of them praying together as if no years had passed.

* * *

"You know, I still use the tefillin you gave me," Nathan said.

"You haven't worn them out yet?"

"Sure," Nathan said. "But I keep having them repaired."

"I'm honored," Aaron said.

"No, *I* am. All this, all I am is because of you."

"Let's not get maudlin, Nathan."

"You still refuse to take credit, don't you?" Nathan said, and smiled. "Well, I have a deal for you. Assuming I'm alive and you're alive, when you're ready to give up the brilliant pulpit career—Madeleine assures me you have—why don't you come teach for me?"

Aaron laughed. "I'm sure having a Reform rabbi on your faculty would do wonders with the Ministry of Religion and your Orthodox colleagues."

"I always have trouble with the Ministry of Religion and my Orthodox colleagues. I'm serious, Aaron. My boys need someone like you to challenge them."

"Don't talk to me, talk to Madeleine."

Nathan chuckled. "I don't think I'd get very far. After twenty years she still has nothing to say to me."

"She's being protective and jealous," Aaron said.

"Jealous about what?"

"Vicariously, for me, I guess. She thinks I'm comparing myself with you."

"Are you?" Nathan asked.

"Yes. And I don't stack up very well."

"Aaron, we're grown men. When are you going to stop crushing yourself with your own harsh judgments? According to Madeleine, you've done very well."

"According to Madeleine, I have done well," Aaron agreed.

"So nu?"

Aaron sighed and put his hands in his pockets. "There's something missing, Nathan. Something very important."

"What?"

"I wish to God I knew."

Nathan stopped at the gate. "We're here," he said, opening the gate and stepping onto the stone walkway.

"This is an apartment building," Aaron said.

"Yes, and in a nice, roomy, very expensive apartment resides my girls' yeshiva."

"I see you don't believe in separate but equal," Aaron commented dryly. "It's not exactly the dormitory-and-classroom building we came from."

"I believe in separate and what I can afford," Nathan said. "The men are housed better and have better facilities now. Eventually, I want to have facilities just as good for the women, but when our building was destroyed I was severely set back. I'm a realist, but the men have priority."

"I'm sorry," Aaron said. "I didn't mean to take it lightly."

"You always were my conscience," Nathan said, smiling. "Well, you needn't worry. In the yeshiva business, I have at least a dozen consciences all telling me to do different things. On the one hand, I have Moishe Wittenstein—"

"That boy is crazy."

"I know," Nathan said. "But he's harmless, and at least in the yeshiva he functions. I couldn't turn him loose on the world."

"Amen."

"And on the other hand, I have Lynda Jacobs."

"Don't tell me she's crazy too; I won't go in."

"No," Nathan said. "Lynda isn't crazy. She's Tzvi Heldman's fiancé."

"The young man from yesterday. He's a brilliant boy. So what's the problem?"

"She asks questions I can't answer, and wants things I can't give."

"I see."

"I've allowed her to study Talmud. That's not very common in the city at this time, though I see it becoming more so in the future."

"So how does she study Talmud?"

"Like Tzvi," Nathan said. "But I think that's only increased the problem. I don't know if I can keep her. And I don't know what Tzvi would do if she left."

"What does she want?"

"Oh, I suppose she wants to pray with a prayer shawl and tefillin."

"So let her."

Nathan frowned. "I almost would, if that would put a stop to all of it. She wants to study Talmud; she wants, in fact, to spend her life in a yeshiva studying and praying."

"So let her."

"I can't," Nathan said. He leaned against the doorpost. "Not here. Not with me."

"Why not?"

"That's precisely the question Lynda asks," Nathan said. "Aaron, I may not have started out as a traditional Jew, but I am one now. Like the sages, I believe 'with perfect faith' God didn't intend that. God gave men tasks in this world, and God gave women tasks. If Lynda Jacobs was meant to be a yeshiva boy or a rabbi, she would have been a man. She was meant to be a wife and a mother. One can't overthrow the divine order of things. That will only cause injury and defeat."

"So why all this?" Aaron asked, taking his hand out of his pocket to point at the building. "Why the school, why teach women anything? You sound medieval, Nathan."

"Being a wife and a mother does not mean being ignorant. One of my other consciences, Brucha Lefner, is head rebbetzin around here. Women's ignorance is an article of faith with her—teach them just enough to keep a kosher home and no more. But I don't believe that. I do believe, however, in priorities. If I gave Lynda what she wanted, she wouldn't marry Tzvi, she'd never make a home. And from her there would be no Jewish children, of that I'm sure."

"And what if she leaves?"

Nathan straightened up and shrugged. "I just have to hope she loves Tzvi enough not to. You gambled once and you won."

"I almost lost everything gambling like that."

"But Madeleine came back."

Aaron looked away from him. "Yes," he said softly. "Madeleine came back."

"Well, let's go inside," Nathan said. He looked at his watch. "I don't know when they begin the Morning Service. Maybe we can hear the end. The women sing beautifully."

Expecting guests, the women were gathered in the living room rather than the coatroom. Aaron hadn't seen apartment rooms like this since the forties. He'd pictured the girls jammed in a small New York–style apartment, but the thirty women gathered in the living room presented no problem. And Nathan was right. They did pray differently. The melodies were the same, but the pacing was different, with harmonies added. The sounds of prayer were familiar, yet foreign.

Lynda was there, in the center, with the light from the living room ceiling casting a soft glow on her back. Slowly, her presence drew Aaron's eyes to her, and it was all he could do to keep from taking a step forward. He watched as she threw her head back as if to cry out, but only moved her lips silently as she began to sway back and forth. Others too began to sway, those closest to her swaying in time. Then her voice rang out. The melody was not louder than the rest, but sharper to Aaron's ears.

"Who is like unto Thee, God among the mighty?"

She sang the Hebrew words and lapsed into silence again. It was as if she became physically smaller as she sank inward to herself for the Amida, the silent prayer. Aaron watched transfixed as the others moved back and forth in quick motions, reaching for the power that swayed gently with the girl in the center of the room. Aaron felt a stirring within him that he could only call desire. That it was not physical did not alter its strength. The light about the girl seemed, to his eyes, to come not from the ceiling, but from something else. And he knew, as surely as he had known his destiny lay with Jerusalem, that the light was his. She had captured it. He knew the light, and the room, certain he had seen them in dreams. The desire welled up and threatened to blind him, but he pushed it away. He had to see clearly. In blindness he would lose his destiny and go mad.

Lynda moved through herself to the place beyond her. She hadn't thought herself able to rise above the people around her and free herself from the yearnings she sensed in them. But The Place had found her even here. The Place. One of the names for God was The Place, and she could enter. The letters of the prayers flowed ahead of her, showing the way. Yet as she began to move and merge, to find that moment of peace, something pulled. It went further than the yearnings and pains of the women that sometimes assaulted her. It was stronger. A shadow crept forward, drawing itself between her and the light of The Place. She could move no farther. Even the letters had stopped their flow. Lynda opened her eyes. The shock of coming back to the room from so deep within made even the living room light seem blinding, and the noises of prayer thunder. She turned, seeking the yearning and pain that had pursued her. There, in the shadows, stood their visitor, Aaron Stern.

Madeleine lay awake in bed as the lights of Jerusalem glowed outside the hotel window. Aaron snored next to her, as did the boys across the room. Reuben cried out in his sleep, and Madeleine moved quickly to where he lay in a folding bed, next to his brother. She kissed his cheek, and his mouth twitched into a smile. David lay on the next bed, his leg already draped over and touching the floor. Madeleine lifted him gently and straightened the blanket curled around him. Two, born from the same womb at the same time, yet so different. Reuben had his grandmother's features and Aaron's eyes. David had appeared with red hair and blue eyes. They had intended to name him after Vellef, but instead gave him the name of the red-haired king of Israel. His grandfather's memory was preserved in David's middle name, and in his temperament. Both boys were beautiful.

Madeleine straightened in the darkness and sighed. As Joshua was beautiful. The worst shock of visiting Kibbutz Ruth had been Yudit, Ruth's daughter. Yudit was the image of her mother as Madeleine remembered her.

Madeleine walked over to the suitcase and dressed quietly. She scrawled a note to Aaron. Then she opened the door to the room, and after checking the boys in the sliver of hall light, she slipped out.

Joshua answered her soft knock at his door. His hair was tousled, the way it always looked when he'd been tossing restlessly in bed. A small cowlick stood at the back of his head. He wore blue jeans, but no shirt.

"Mom?" he asked, blinking in the light. "What's wrong?"

"I couldn't sleep. Want to go for a ride?"

"You mean now?" He leaned back and squinted into his room. "It's four o'clock in the morning."

"You have something better to do?"

Joshua looked at her with an adolescent wariness. He was weighing his fear of her mothering him against his desire to be up and talking. Madeleine could read it in his eyes. He grabbed a T-shirt and slipped into the Israeli sandals he'd bought.

"I think we're both crazy," he said, walking next to her. "And so will the desk clerk."

If the clerk thought so, he kept it hidden. He phoned for a cab, and in a few minutes a yellow Mercedes was at the hotel entrance.

"Where to?" the driver asked in thickly accented English.

Madeleine hesitated a moment. "The Mount of Olives."

"Hokay."

"Mom," Joshua whispered. "I don't know how safe that is."

Joshua nervously watched the Arab houses pass by. He looked at Madeleine several times and she smiled at him, saying nothing.

The cabby drove to the top of the Mount overlooking the once desecrated, now rebuilt Jewish cemetery. "I should wait?" he asked.

"Please wait," Joshua said. He didn't know whether the Arabs or his mother made him more uneasy. In any case, he didn't want to be left alone. He followed his mother to where she stood looking down into the Walled City.

"Yes, that's it," Madeleine said.

"What."

"Jerusalem."

"I can see that, Mom."

"I should have waited until daylight." Madeleine looked behind her to the brightening eastern horizon. "But it won't be long now." She shivered once and hugged herself. "Cooler than I thought."

"Mom?"

"Yes?"

"This is all very hard on you, isn't it?"

Madeleine looked at him briefly, smiling, then turned back to the city. Birds began to sing in the distance.

"Yudit looks just like Ruth," Madeleine said. "And the way she looks at you, I don't think you have to worry about a paratrooper."

"Does that bother you?" Joshua asked.

Madeleine watched as scattered lights came on in the New City. "When I was pregnant with you, when I went into labor and realized that in a matter of hours a new person would enter this world, I was terrified. But not for me." She turned to him again. "For you."

"Why?"

"Because there are so many things out there"—she nodded toward the city—"that can hurt you, and frighten you. That can compromise you."

"There are also hopes and dreams in the world, Mom."

"That too." Madeleine smiled. "This was the view in an old picture Ruth showed me long ago. The picture was so ugly. All it showed was an old walled city and barren hills. Ruth told me she saw something else."

"What did she see?"

"What do *you* see, Joshua?"

He gazed at the dome, and the walls against a reddish sky. "I see me," he said softly. "Right down there." He pointed to a street in the distance. "Or maybe out there." He pointed to his left toward the Negev desert.

"Go on."

Joshua smiled to himself. "Living on the kibbutz I'm going to build. We'll discover how to grow roses with water from the Dead Sea. I see rose gardens in the desert." He stopped, embarrassed.

Madeleine nodded. "Ruth saw all this in that old picture. She saw the lights and the city, the farms and buildings spreading beyond the hills. She saw all this when I saw only barrenness. Ruth was a better dreamer than I." Madeleine shuddered against a chill that Joshua barely felt. She turned to face her son.

"Not all dreams come true, Joshua. And even for dreams that come to pass, a terrible price must be paid."

"Mom," Joshua sighed. "I know you don't want to hear this, but I'm not afraid to die for this place. Don't laugh or say I'm too young, or it hasn't been long enough to know."

Madeleine shook her head. "I'm not going to say those things. But Joshua, know this. The price is always something you never imagined you'd have to pay."

"Ruth knew she might die."

"By then Ruth had paid her price," Madeleine said. "I never showed you her letters to me. Maybe I should have."

"What price?"

"Her innocence. She saw most of her ideals drown in the blood of the War of Independence. She became a killer, and she never got over that. It was a price she hadn't ever dreamed she would pay."

"And what price did *you* pay, Mom?" Joshua asked. "What made you so afraid?"

"Sometimes, Joshua, you pay an awful price for a nightmare instead of a dream," Madeleine said. Joshua started to respond, but she shook her head. "I just want you to be very careful. I don't want you to pick illusions for dreams, and I don't want you to get killed."

"I know, Mom."

"No, you don't, Joshua, and that's what terrifies me." She hooked her arm around her son's. Joshua did not pull away. He was almost a foot taller than she, which seemed odd. He had grown fine and strong, a dream of a son. They walked back to the cab. It was dawn in Jerusalem.

Lynda poured Tzvi a cup of tea in Mrs. Sheinman's kitchen. She sat down and blew on her tea as they continued in silence.

"Sorry," Tzvi said finally.

"Me too," she answered.

"Of all the things to fight about. A passage in Talmud." He chuckled. "I hope it's the only thing we ever fight about."

Lynda held back her words. "Me too."

"You just took me by surprise, arguing like that."

"I thought," Lynda said, "that was the way you learned in Talmud. That's the way Ruchel and I do it. You argue points of law."

"Not when the logic is clear-cut."

"It wasn't," she said.

"Let's not start again. Just remember to tell Rabbi Hoffman my analysis, not yours."

"Gee, Tzvi, why don't you come to my class and tell him yourself? You two seem to be corresponding quite nicely through me." Lynda's temper flared again. "You know, yesterday Rabbi Hoffman told me to give you his compliments on my exposition."

Tzvi laughed. "Tell him thanks."

"The only problem is, I didn't study with you. It was my exposition, mine alone. I examined the material and analyzed it—alone. Since I met you, everyone has an excuse for my ability. I'm parroting Tzvi Heldman."

"You shouldn't get so ego-involved. Torah lishma—Torah for its own sake," Tzvi said.

"Oh, really? Is that why you got so upset when I challenged your brilliance just now?"

"That was different," he snapped. "That was still your ego. You don't know enough to challenge me."

"Will I ever?"

"I doubt it," he said. "I'm sorry. Maybe I do have some ego involvement. It's just that I see myself as your teacher." He smiled. "A woman's husband is her rabbi."

"Don't give me all those damned quotes!" She knew he was teasing her, but she wasn't in the mood. She picked up her tea, stared at it and put it down. "You've changed, you know."

"How?"

"You used to be happy about my studying Talmud."

"I still am. I'm very proud of you."

"But you're sure I'll never know enough to challenge you."

"I said I was sorry about that remark," Tzvi said. "But I've been at this longer, and—"

"And you'll continue after I stop, right?"

"I didn't say that."

"You didn't have to," Lynda said. "You didn't see any end to my studies before."

"They won't end," Tzvi said, leaning closer. "They may change, but they won't end. We're getting married. We'll have a family. Things change."

"Only for me, it seems," Lynda said. She looked at Tzvi. "What have you decided to do about the marriage contract?"

"Not that again. It's not important."

"Then don't change the wording."

"You aren't a virgin."

"Neither are you," she said, "but no one is going to chant it out in front of the whole yeshiva."

"If I read that I was pledging to marry a virgin, it would be a lie."

"The intent of that line is my marital, not physical status."

"I'm not sure of that."

"Tzvi, I really don't care if you're sure or not."

"Well, I do! What is this for, anyway? What's the purpose of living a Torah life if we can skim over all the details that make us uncomfortable?"

"Are you practicing sermons on me?"

"Lynda, you and I have an obligation to guard the Tradition. We have a special obligation because we come to Torah so late."

"Ah, yes. Baalai Teshuva. We who have come to the Tradition late are now obligated to become more orthodox than the Orthodox. To live by standards the standard makers considered unlivable."

"That's not true," Tzvi said. "Look at Rabbi Schwartz."

"I don't need to. I said you'd changed. This little fiasco about my virginity didn't come from the rabbi. It came from Moishe."

Tzvi colored and looked down. "Moishe raised a hypothetical issue."

"And what if we went to Rabbi Schwartz and he said to leave the contract as is?"

"Then I'd have to think about it."

"Oh," Lynda said. "I see. The man you once worshiped is no longer holy enough."

"Rabbi Schwartz tends to bend in places I wouldn't, that's all."

"Maybe that's because he's wiser than you."

"Maybe," Tzvi said.

"Oh, so maybe you're wiser than him?"

"I didn't say that."

"You're not saying a whole lot of things," Lynda said. "Listen, Tzvi Heldman. I agreed to marry *you,* not Moishe Wittenstein. You better decide who you are."

"I'm the person who loves you," he said. He leaned back. "Okay, there are things I'm not saying. I'll say them now. Why have you met with Aaron Stern, and why haven't you told me?"

Lynda looked at him and blinked. "I had intended to tell you," she said quietly. "I just never got around to it."

"What did you talk about?"

"We talked about studying Talmud," she said.

"What else?"

"He told me if I ever left this place, he could get me into his rabbinical school."

Tzvi darkened with anger. "That's obscene. He's trying to lure you away."

"He may be trying to lure me away, but I, for one, don't think the suggestion is at all obscene."

"What does he want in return, then?" Tzvi said evenly.

Lynda looked at his eyes and the suggestion in them. "Is that what you think? That the only reason he could be telling me about a rabbinical school is to get me into bed?"

"I didn't say that!"

"No. You always leave it for me to say!" She quieted her voice. "He wants something from me. It's not sex. He hasn't said what he wants, but I know."

"What?"

"He wants me to teach him how to pray."

Tzvi started to laugh, but seeing Lynda's face, he stopped. "Lynda, I love you."

"I know you love me, Tzvi. I just don't know if that's enough."

Aaron walked into the hotel room, which was dim. The curtains were drawn against the noonday sun. Reuben and David stared at him from their beds, and Madeleine looked up from the desk.

"Where have you been?" she asked.

"On a book-buying trip," Aaron said.

"I don't see any books."

"I didn't find any I liked," Aaron said. "What's wrong?"

"Maybe you were too busy talking to that girl to notice any good books."

Aaron looked away briefly, then looked back. "What's the matter with you? Lynda Jacobs wanted my advice, so I gave it to her."

"More than once, according to Nathan."

"What is going on? Why are you having secret discussions with Nathan?"

"You're not the one to complain about secret discussions. And this wasn't so secret. Nathan and I talked in the waiting room at the doctor's office. I called Nathan because you were unavailable."

"What's happened?"

Madeleine glanced at the twins, trying to control her voice. "Well, you may be due to leave Israel in two days, but the boys aren't leaving for another seven. The twins, my dear, have the measles."

Aaron looked at the boys, who stared back in fever-inspired quiet. Then he looked at Madeleine. "But I *have* to be back," he said. "I have a wedding to do, and the Midwest conference." He looked back at the boys. "I have to be back. What are we going to do?"

Now Madeleine was calm, the confrontation over. "You will do what you have done for the last twenty years, Aaron. You will go off to the synagogue and leave me to manage things alone."

JULY 1968

WINDOW SEAT 27A WAS WAITING FOR AARON WHEN HE boarded the plane. So were 27B and 27C. After the crowded flight from Tel Aviv to Switzerland, the empty seats gave hope for some solitude. Aaron sat and looked out at all he would see of Switzerland: rain, a runway and a tower. In the end, all Israel had been was a predawn darkness and land moving swiftly beneath him as the plane took him away.

He and Nathan hadn't parted on the best of terms. For most of the drive to Tel Aviv they had argued about Lynda Jacobs. Aaron regretted that. Nathan had been good to him, and he had taken Madeleine under his wing. That, in fact, was how the argument had started, with Aaron's attempt at gratitude. Nathan had driven in silence until Jerusalem was behind them. Aaron suspected that he would have been silent the whole trip if Aaron hadn't finally spoken.

"I want to thank you again, Nathan. I'm so relieved to know Madeleine has someone to look after her."

"Sure."

"And I want to thank you for finding us a place to stay. I don't know how I would have found the money to put the three of them up at the hotel for another week."

"Sure."

"My, Nathan, I've never known you to be this talkative."

Nathan glanced at him and then back at the road. "I almost didn't tell you about Mrs. Sheinman's place. In fact, the only reason I did tell you is that Lynda told me. So I figured it would get to you sooner or later."

"Blunt, aren't you?"

"Just honest," Nathan said. "And open. I don't want her under your influence any longer."

"She won't be under my influence. You're taking me to the airport, remember? She'll be under Madeleine's influence, and Madeleine is an exemplary rebbetzin."

"Did you have to talk to her?"

"Lynda Jacobs is a fascinating young woman," Aaron said.

"Tzvi Heldman is fascinating. You didn't talk to *him*."

"Tzvi Heldman is brilliant, not fascinating. He's a carbon copy of all the brilliant Talmudists I've ever met. I can tell you exactly what he'll be like in thirty years, every detail, including yellowed fingers from chain smoking."

"Tzvi doesn't smoke," Nathan said.

"He will. He's a brilliant Talmudist."

"And what, precisely, makes Lynda Jacobs so fascinating?"

"She doesn't belong in your yeshiva, Nathan, and you know it."

"No, I don't know it," Nathan said. "Brilliant analysis after meeting with her two times."

"Three," Aaron said. Nathan glanced over at him again, but said nothing. "And I've done one thing you've never done with her. I've actually talked with her. You've let her take courses, bent a rule or two. You've encouraged her relationship with this Heldman; but you've never really talked with her. Have you?"

Nathan was silent. He swerved into the passing lane, then swerved sharply back as a car came toward them. "You're meddling, Aaron."

"There was a time when you didn't mind my meddling. Why can't you talk to her?"

"I don't talk to her because there is nothing to say. I will not tell her to go spend her days as a Talmud scholar in the men's school. I can't. Besides, she wouldn't be happy. She wants to be more than a Talmud scholar. She wants to be a rabbi."

"Let her go, Nathan."

"The girl is twenty-two. She makes her own decisions. There are no chains on her."

Aaron smiled. "If she told you she wanted to go, would you fight to keep her?"

"No."

"That is neither honest nor open. You've been fighting all along, with Talmud classes, and a room of her own, and letting her pray at the Wall, away from the other women."

"I'm helping her fulfill herself within the limits Tradition will allow."

"She's not going to be fulfilled, or content."

"I can't believe that," Nathan said. "You shouldn't either. Madeleine seems quite fulfilled and content."

"Madeleine is different."

"Oh, really?"

"Madeleine had young pipe dreams. She never aspired to any great spiritual height. She was essentially on a lark, and when things got difficult, she quit."

"A lark?" Nathan asked. "Is that why she walked out on you?"

"She came back," Aaron said.

"My point precisely."

"No, not precisely," Aaron said, softly.

"I don't know what you want from me, Aaron. Do you want me to admit that someone like Lynda Jacobs can't be happy and fulfilled as an Orthodox Jew? I don't believe that."

"And to make sure, you don't have to believe that you're going to sacrifice a brilliant, vibrant young woman on the altar of the commandments."

"And what are you willing to do?" Nathan slowed the car a moment and looked at Aaron. Then he speeded up, passing the car in front of him in spite of an oncoming car.

"What is it you want from that girl?" Nathan asked. "I know you too well, Aaron. After all these years apart I still know you. I also saw you when you watched her pray."

"I was fascinated."

"You were obsessed. You didn't even notice my hand on your shoulder when you started to walk in right in the middle of a women's minyan."

Aaron turned to look out the car window to avoid Nathan's repeated glances.

"Aaron," Nathan said softly, "no one can make peace for you. Your father couldn't and Lynda can't. She has a gift—I know that, and that's why I want to keep her." Nathan sighed. "I don't want her to become like you."

"And what the hell does that mean?"

"Sometimes, the Sitra Achra, the Other Side, comes in the guise of genuine feelings to lead people astray. God didn't intend for Lynda Jacobs to be anything but what she is. God intended her to be a vibrant mother and wife, and a teacher. Not"—Nathan looked at Aaron until the car began to swerve—"not a rebbe."

"I know that," Aaron said.

"And not to make you a rebbe either, Aaron."

"I told you a long time ago I don't want to be a rebbe."

"No," Nathan said. "You told me you *couldn't* be a rebbe. Lynda can't fill your own lack of faith. You can only destroy hers. I believe she'll be happy following the proper path. My path. Not yours."

"And what if you're wrong?" Aaron asked.

"That's always been your problem. You always ask what if you're wrong, if they're wrong, if God is wrong. Let Lynda alone. Leave her in peace."

Aaron left Nathan and the Promised Land with that request preying on his mind. Leave her in peace. It was too late for that; the seed was there, and he had no doubt it would take root. Jerusalem had given him his answer. God had not let him survive for nothing. He could wait now for as long as it took. For the first time in his life, he truly understood his father, truly felt his heir. There was time to pursue his destiny. Like the masters before him, he would unveil himself.

And yet that shadow of doubt crept in, destroying his daydreams as he sat in the airplane. What if he were going insane? His dreams at night were filled with voices crying out. Sometimes he heard them in the day, calling him. In his nightmares the voices were the Hasidim of Loem calling him to his place in the grave. There was so much at stake. What if he was wrong?

A man sat down in the aisle seat, pulling Aaron away from his thoughts. No solitude. Aaron realized it was for the best. He had a wedding talk to write, and the silence only led him back to Jerusalem. He took out the notes he'd made and began to work on the talk. As the plane began to ascend, his seatmate tapped him on the shoulder.

"Yes?" Aaron said.

"Pardon me," the man said. "I don't want to sound strange,

but do you know that man in the aisle seat, one row up?"

Aaron looked over. A man with grayish blond hair quickly looked away. "No," Aaron said. "I don't know him. Why?"

"Maybe I'm paranoid, but he's spent most of his time since he boarded staring at you."

Aaron looked again, but the man did not turn around. He looked at his seatmate, shrugged, then turned back to his wedding talk.

In the aisle seat, Illi leaned back and smiled.

Madeleine sat in Lynda's darkened room. She stared at the wall as light peeked in around the window shades and made dancing shadows on the wall. Of all the ghosts that haunted her, Illi was the one she'd thought she'd exorcised. He was the one demon she'd thought she'd rendered powerless. She remembered all the times in the last few years when she'd imagined she'd seen him. They were real. He had been at the airport. Waiting. For her. But he'd trapped Aaron in her place.

A chill shook her shoulders. The phone rang. Voices, hushed and murmured, filtered through the closed door. She heard Joshua, and Yudit, whose voice sounded so much like Ruth's.

"The ghosts will take everything," she said to herself.

There was no escape, sleeping or waking, from the knowledge of what Illi would do. There was no escape, but she pretended to be hopeful in front of the children. She did not cry. She didn't scream. She thought of praying, but couldn't. She couldn't pray to the God who was allowing her husband to be tortured. The God who wouldn't forgive a mistake made so long ago.

Aaron knew now. She no longer possessed a secret. Yet the pain had come back so freshly. All these years, that night had lain in darkness until it was remembered only in an occasional nightmare. She had done what Bea said to do and gone back to Aaron, and things had turned out as her mother had predicted. Aaron had never asked her about the time gone from him. It was as if that time had never existed. He must have noticed the not quite faded bruise, the small scar under her lip, but he never asked. Bea had been right, of course. Her ambivalence toward Aaron had given way to a more mature, deepened love for him. Still, though, a part of her remained distant from him.

He had never asked, even on their wedding night, when she'd wept as he made love to her. Or later, when she realized her responses to him would always lack the joy she'd possessed long ago. She'd been wounded, first by that night, and later by her husband. Aaron had made love to her and had not noticed the difference. Aaron had never asked what had hurt her.

Madeleine came to realize what her mother had known all along. It was possible to love a man deeply, yet have part of your soul rage in anger against him. There was a certain silence that became a gulf never to be crossed. The irony was that Madeleine had discovered the hurt and anger now, at the same time that the thought of losing Aaron racked her with terror.

Illi had finally won. But then, he'd won a long time ago. She had surrendered her life and done everything she was supposed to do. For nineteen years she had devoted herself to Aaron's life, his career. Yet the punishment continued. Her husband was being sacrificed for old mistakes, and old dreams. And Joshua was being lured away by the ghost of Ruth. Even Ben Yair had noticed it.

Ben had been the same, his face a little more lined, his skin dark with years of sun, but still firm and strong. They had walked together on the kibbutz, the culmination of Ruth's dream, the concrete proof of its reality.

"I think maybe my daughter and your son will fall in love," he said as they watched the two walking ahead of them, "if they haven't already."

"And how would you feel about that?" Madeleine asked.

"It would have made Ruth very happy."

"Ruth is dead."

Ben shrugged. "But they are alive, and *they* seem happy. And your Joshua has a fine head. Just talking to him I see that."

"He's only seventeen," Madeleine said. "And he has to go to college—"

Ben laughed. "I'm not negotiating a match. Just making an observation." He pointed to the building on the rise ahead of them. "That's the children's house where Yudit was raised. We did a fine job with her, don't you think?"

"Is that where Ruth killed the Arab boy?" Madeleine asked.

"So she told you about that. Yes, it is," he said softly. "She had a hard time about that, as hard as the miscarriage was."

"You said you'd take care of her," Madeleine said irrationally.

Ben looked away a moment. "I tried. Honest to God, I tried."

"I told her you'd get her killed."

"*I* didn't shoot Ruth—an Arab sniper did."

"Now I have to give you my son."

"It's in God's hands, not mine," he said.

"I thought you weren't religious," Madeleine said.

"I am, Madeleine. Now."

He'd said it was in God's hands, but what a wrathful God hovered over her life. God sent the ghosts, and they would take everything.

There was a knock on the door. Madeleine's thoughts returned to the darkness. "Yes?" she said.

The door opened, letting in a brief flood of light; then it closed. "Madeleine?" Lynda called softly, momentarily blind.

"Here," Madeleine said. Lynda came over to her. She pulled over a chair to sit next to Madeleine.

"The news reported that Aaron and three crew members are hostages, but they let everyone else go. I thought you'd want to know."

Madeleine nodded. "Illi wants Aaron. They'll let the rest go. He wants only Aaron."

"There's still hope," Lynda said. "He's not the only terrorist, and they've made some demands. All this is not just to get Aaron!"

"No. It was to get me. But they will kill Aaron anyway."

"But he's all right," Lynda said, leaning closer. "They brought him to the door of the plane for the newsmen."

"Aaron isn't all right—he's just still alive."

Lynda sighed and watched the woman sitting so rigidly next to her. "The twins are asleep, and Mrs. Sheinman's gone grocery shopping."

"Joshua?"

"He went with Yudit. She has a friend near here who can put them up."

"Of course," Madeleine said, staring at the dancing light on the wall. "Of course he went with Yudit."

Lynda reached over and took one of Madeleine's hands. It was cold. "Madeleine," she said.

"Yes?" Madeleine pulled her eyes from the light dance.

"It's not your fault. None of this. You're tormenting yourself when you aren't guilty."

Madeleine looked at Lynda. She felt herself slowly breaking apart, too weak to fight. The tears came. Lynda gently put an arm around her, staying quiet as she wept. Madeleine cried half in relief, half hating herself for being so weak. Finally, she pulled herself away.

"It's all my fault."

"Joshua told me you were involved with the Party. So were thousands of people."

Madeleine reached for a tissue on the desk and wiped her eyes. "What Joshua doesn't know is that I tried to kill Illi. I tried to cave in his skull, and for years I thought I had killed him."

Lynda's eyes widened as she tried to think of something to say.

"Not a statement you'd expect from Centin, Illinois's, most charming rebbetzin, is it?"

"You must have had a reason," Lynda said.

"Of course I did. He tried to rape me. That was my glorious career as a revolutionary. It all ended in a seamy office where my comrade Illi attacked me. He was also going to murder me." Madeleine paused, then shuddered. "That's what Illi does best."

"Please, don't give up hope, Madeleine."

"I gave up hope a long time ago," Madeleine said. "In that seamy office."

It was hot. The sun bore down on the plane as it sat in the desert. Aaron felt the filth of four days without washing: four days of sweat from heat and fear. He sat back by the lavatory, his hands bound with wire. They throbbed with pain, and the wire was wet with blood. He'd considered pulling hard enough at the wires to slit his veins, but so far the pain had stopped him. So far. His right eye was swollen shut, so he had to turn completely to identify the noises in the aisle. The caked blood on his mustache testified that when it was Illi coming toward him in the aisle, he would be hurt.

Aaron looked out on the brown-and-gray desert, its unremitting landscape as harsh as the sun that beat down on the plane. How appropriate to die in a desert. How appropriate to die now, with all his illusions gone. His life had been instantly reduced to its essence: a death in the desert and sometime after, a memorial. Maybe a new wing on his already insignificant synagogue, where they would hold bar mitzvah receptions. All his life, he'd thought he'd been singled out, first to survive the Holocaust, then to survive the war. He thought he'd missed his destiny. But now he was to meet his destiny: to die a nobody at the hands of a maniac.

And even that had no particular merit. He was an incidental victim. His swollen face attested to Illi's fury at missing Madeleine. He had stalked them for years, waiting for the right moment. Aaron was thankful that Madeleine, at least, had escaped. This time.

He now knew what had happened, why she'd come back to him. He knew it all. Illi had told him what he'd been afraid to ask her. She had come back to him: that was all he'd cared about. He'd taken her back unquestioningly, thinking it an expression of his love. But it was really his fear. He now had all the missing pieces.

The Madeleine he'd fallen in love with had had a newly blossoming passion she could barely contain. The woman he'd married was muted, neither cold nor warm. Even Madeleine's passionate moments had a distance. The joining he'd dreamed of had never happened. Yet he had never asked her. And she had never spoken. Now this man who had hunted her had found him. Madeleine had returned to Aaron not out of love, but out of fear.

Aaron heard a sound and jumped, but the steps moved away from him. Four days of fear had begun to dig into his mind, retrieving fragments of memory which haunted him. They were the same fragments that had nearly driven him insane after the war. Faces, blood in the snow, an iron cross lying over dead eyes. Aaron feared the dying, that moment before death. The footsteps sounded again, this time coming toward him. He braced himself.

Illi stood over him, throwing his shadow against the light. He grinned once—a crooked grin made by a misshapen mouth—then shoved the butt of his rifle in Aaron's side. Aaron doubled over, but made no sound.

"How does it feel to be involved in a historical moment?" Illi asked. When Aaron didn't answer, he nudged Aaron in the spot he'd just struck. "How does it feel?"

"Painful," Aaron said.

"You've been judged a criminal by the People's Black Brigade," Illi said.

"And how many people are in the People's Black Brigade?" Aaron said. He straightened slowly and winced.

"Maybe ten thousand. Maybe just me and him." Illi nodded toward the other man in the plane. "It doesn't matter."

"What happened to the Communist Party?"

"Too weak, too fat," Illi said. He tossed back his head with its stringy gray-blond hair. "Besides, they wanted me dead. It was time to move on. Once I was free, that is."

"So they put you in prison."

Illi laughed. "No, not that. It took me a long time to recover from what your Jew bitch did to me. But I did. I did." He leaned close to Aaron. "I'm half-insane, you know. Even if I get caught, that will be my defense. You get half-insane when you pretend to be a vegetable for years." He stood straight, the fear clear in his eyes. "I almost became one. I almost pretended too long. She made me into a slobbering idiot. But I remembered how much I hated her, and I remembered my destiny." He looked once again at Aaron. "I am going to be the greatest revolutionary the world has known. They'll sing songs about me like they sing for Guevara, and that fat Castro. You'll see."

Illi laughed and reached over to backhand Aaron across the face. "But then, you won't see. But maybe Madeleine will; maybe I'll let her live that long."

"You'll never make it out of this desert," Aaron said. He expected Illi to strike him again, but the man didn't.

"Don't worry about me, Stern. Just think of me as your teacher. I'm going to teach you what I know now. What Madeleine taught me. I'm going to teach you how it feels right before you die." He grinned. "Only we won't be able to discuss it later."

Illi signaled the other terrorist, who brought the plane's navigator back. He sat the man down next to Aaron. The terrorist looked at Illi and said something in Arabic, to which Illi replied in a tone Aaron understood. The other man looked at the two who were seated, then at Illi, the anger in his eyes. Then he shrugged and walked away.

"Company," Illi said. "So you won't think bad thoughts of me." He struck Aaron across the ear with the hand holding his pistol. The blow made Illi seem to spin in a bright light.

Darkness closed in. Aaron welcomed the dark world, hoping it was death. Then he was back in the plane, with the world still, spinning lights around his head. The lights slowed, and his eyes focused. The window outside was dark now.

"Are you all right, Rabbi?" the navigator asked. His accent was barely perceptible.

"Yes, yes, I'm fine," Aaron said automatically. Then he laughed. "I guess I'm hardly fine. But I'll make it."

"I would like to apologize," the navigator said.

"For what?"

"For all this. I feel it is the responsibility of the airline."

"If it will cheer you up," Aaron said, "I promise to complain bitterly when we get out of this." He attempted to smile, but winced at the pain instead. "By the way, I never use my title when I'm a hostage in a hijacking. My name is Aaron."

"My name is Eric." The navigator looked out to the desert. "And I'm not sure we will get out of this."

"Let me tell you," Aaron said, "I have a strong-willed wife who will absolutely kill me if I get myself murdered by these people." The navigator looked at him. "Sorry," he said. "Bad joke."

"My wife is not so strong-willed, I'm afraid."

"Been married long?"

"Two years." Eric smiled, revealing a cracked tooth, the only flaw in a finely sculpted face. "I have a daughter one year old. Do you have children?"

"Three. All boys."

"It's nice to have sons. I . . . ." He paused. "I'm hoping to have sons too."

"And I've always wanted to have a girl."

"Maybe you will," Eric said.

"Maybe," Aaron said softly. He closed his eyes. His head had begun to throb. Closing his eyes made it worse, so he opened them again. Eric was staring out the window into the twilight, and Aaron decided to leave him to his own thoughts. The footsteps he dreaded moved toward him once again.

"Finally with us, Jew Boy," Illi said. "Now that you two are friends, Eric here can watch you die." The other terrorist ran up and grabbed Illi by the arm, shouting in Arabic. Illi pushed him away and pointed the gun at him. The other man moved his rifle barrel to aim at Illi's midsection. Illi shouted, then began to stutter and switched to English.

"I've waited for this for a long time. No one is going to stop me. You owe me, you and your whole chicken-shit outfit. You shoot me and it's all over. All over. You want to blow it, then shoot me. Son of a bitch! Go ahead and shoot!" Illi's finger tightened around the trigger.

The man stared at him in silence. "You—stink," he said finally. He glanced around the plane and in heavily accented English, spoke loudly enough for the crew up front to hear. "You can kill us all. It still won't make your prick work."

Illi cocked the pistol. "You watch it, Sulim," he whispered. "I just might decide I want to see you die too. Slowly."

Sulim watched him again for a while, then shrugged, but his eyes were narrow with tension. "I'm warning you, Illi. You kill only your Jew. No one else. Or maybe it's you who dies slowly."

"Sure," Illi said. He put the safety on the already cocked automatic pistol as the man walked away, but not before pretending to shoot him in the back. He turned to Aaron and sighed, smiling.

"I really like killing," he said.

Aaron looked from Illi to the pistol. He tried to calm the terror. It had been inevitable. He'd been a dead man as soon as he got on the plane. Inevitable. But he couldn't calm himself. He was afraid. Illi put the pistol to Aaron's head as he backed away. Then Illi moved the pistol back, as if measuring the proper distance. Aaron began to say the Sh'ma, trying to say it the way the Loemers would have said it. Trying to become, in his last moments, what he'd always sought to be. But he was afraid, and instead of thinking about God his mind screamed out for someone to save him. Eric sat beside him paralyzed with terror, his eyes wide. Aaron looked away. He did not want to have Illi's face be the last thing he saw. His heart pounded with his terror, making his head ache. He blinked and saw a corpse. A corpse in the snow. A corpse from the past. He heard the click of the safety being taken off. His memory came back to the corpse. He should think about God, not corpses.

"Ready to die, Stern?" Illi reached over and grabbed him by the chin. He lowered the weapon so that it was in front of Aaron's eyes. There was a scratch on the barrel. Aaron stared, transfixed, at the finger behind the trigger guard. The finger tightened on the trigger. Blink. Explosion. Blink. Something wet between his legs.

Illi laughed. He laughed until he had to sit down. Sulim was screaming in angry Arabic. Aaron slowly began to feel his body again. He'd urinated on himself. He took in short ragged breaths as his whole body was gripped with the tremors. Then he noticed that his face and shoulder were also wet. He turned to see why, then screamed. Eric was sprawled back in the seat where the force of the bullet had pushed him. What was left of his face stared, open-mouthed, at Aaron as his blood soaked into the fabric of the seat.

The sunset from Yudit's friend's apartment was spectacular. Joshua gazed out and listened to Yudit as she cooked dinner in the kitchen she'd forbidden him to enter. It was amazing that he could be so happy and unhappy at the same time. When he thought about his father, the fear came so strongly he cringed. With his mother, he was miserable, watching the worry etch new lines into her face, seeing the shadow of despair in her eyes. He would visit, sit with her and say nothing. There was nothing to say. How many times could he say that his father would be all right? After a while his own doubts were bound to show through. He was unhappy sitting with his little brothers, telling them the same things he told his mother. They were worse. They believed him.

Yet finally, after all the years, he was with Yudit. Being with Yudit was living a dream. More than a dream. He tried to tell himself that he could not know her in less than a month. But in truth they'd known each other since they were children. He'd learned to write both English and Hebrew by writing her letters. For years he had poured out his soul to her. Yudit knew about the time he had wanted to run away. She had known the girls he liked and the girls he didn't like. She knew everything, and she had in turn spoken to him through her letters.

The apartment was beyond any dream he'd ever had. Mara, Yudit's friend, was off on reserve duty, and her parents were out of the country. Alone in the apartment, she'd made him tea as he resolutely tried to ignore the situation.

"You were good with your family," she had said.

"You mean I haven't let my terror show?"

"That's exactly what I meant." Yudit had smiled, her teeth white against a tan face. She'd set down her teacup and leaned back on the couch next to him.

"Your father will be all right," Yudit had said.

"I'm not sure I can believe that."

"You must."

"How?" Joshua had turned to her. A delicate gold Star of David lay between the breasts that rose and fell so softly. He'd looked into her eyes. "How can you have hope living here? People die here. Your mother died here."

"You believe what you must believe," Yudit had said. "My mother was killed, yes. But remember, my father was in the war last year. And I knew he was where the fighting was the heaviest. What was I supposed to believe as the bullets were flying around his head? I believed he would come back to me. In spite of my mother's death, in spite of the fact that I know there are no magic charms to protect me or my father from danger, I believed. And so you must believe. You have no right to refrain from hoping."

They'd looked at each other. Joshua had leaned forward. He'd reached to hold Yudit with trembling hands. He'd felt her next to him, soft, real, more wonderful than all his dreams of her. The nightmare of the day and the nightmare of his father had receded with her touch.

Then they had made love. Joshua remembered now, losing the distance between what he had always dreamed and what was. They were the same: dream touch, real touch; dream land, real land. That night, his father's nightmare had overwhelmed him and he'd wept in her arms. At dawn, after sleep, they had greeted the morning by making love.

His mother didn't know, of course. No one would know. Not for a while. Now he wanted to relish each moment and share with no one but Yudit. He turned from the sunset and grinned.

"You know," he called, "I never imagined you snoring when I read your letters."

Yudit came into the living room and grabbed him around the waist. "I don't snore," she said.

"You certainly do, but I love it."

"Does it ruin your image of me?" she asked.

"Nothing could ruin my image of you," Joshua said. "You're sure I'm not too young for you?"

"I can't believe that for all these years you've considered me an old woman. We're barely two years apart." Yudit looked up at him. "Besides, how you call it, cradle robbing is fun." She laughed. "Look at you blushing."

"Is it too early to ask you to marry me?"

"Yes. But only a little. Besides, how are you going to marry me from America?"

Joshua pulled himself from her embrace. "I'm staying here."

"Shhh. You're speaking foolishly. You'll have to go back, if nothing else, when this is . . . settled."

"Don't be so practical."

"And then you must come back," she said. "And then you must do your Army duty. And then we can get married."

"I thought you said I was only a *little* early."

"You are," Yudit said. "It's only three years or so." She

smiled. "And if you're very good, I will take some time away."

"Ha. Time off for good behavior."

"What?"

"Never mind." Joshua sighed. "I am going to stay. I've known it all along. It's all beshert, like my grandfather says. Beshert—destined."

"I'm not sure I approve of destiny," Yudit said. She turned and went back to the kitchen. Joshua followed.

"Smells good. What is it?"

"Lamb stew, made like my grandmother makes it. A secret recipe I will not disclose until you are a member of the family."

Joshua grunted. "You said you don't approve of destiny. But it doesn't need approval; it just is." Joshua stuck his finger into the stew to taste it, and experienced the double pain of burning his finger and getting his hand slapped by Yudit. "Tastes good," he said with finger in his mouth. "But hot."

"I will accept many things," Yudit said, as she sliced cucumbers. "I will not accept that my mother was destined to die."

Joshua listened to the sound of the knife slicing through the cucumber and making a rapid tapping on the counter. "I don't think much before I blurt," he said.

"Either that, or you think too much."

"My grandfather believes in destiny—my father's father."

"How does your father feel about it?"

Joshua grabbed a cucumber slice and popped it into his mouth. "I don't know. That's what I've been thinking about a lot. I'm trying to think how my father feels out there. What he's thinking. I wish I could know. Maybe that would put me in touch with him." He waved his hand. "Ah, I don't know."

"I do," Yudit said. "During the war, I would get up and watch the sunrise because I know my father loves to be up with the sunrise. Then I would think, Well, wherever he is, we are both watching the sunrise." Yudit paused, then began chopping the tomatoes.

"I wish I knew if my father liked the sunrise. I've thought out all the possibilities—you know, just in case."

"That's reasonable."

"I know exactly what to do if, God forbid, he doesn't come back, because my father has never been around. I love him, but he's never been a part of us. He was always at some congregant's house, or leading services, counseling, meetings, a hundred things. My father's schedule is to be out of the house by eight, come home for supper and be gone again until late at night."

"What about Shabbat?"

"Ah, the Sabbath. Time of rest. He'd be home, with at least five other people he'd invited to Shabbat lunch. Everyone in the congregation told me over and over how lucky I was to have a father who cared so much. They told me how loved he was. Of course the congregation loved him. He gave so much to them, so much love and time to them, that he had none left for us. I doubt my father even noticed the sunrise!"

Yudit had stopped cutting and was staring at him. He smiled bashfully.

"I hate myself for all this coming into my head," he said. Then his voice wavered. "I just mean, what if he dies out there? I never knew him." He looked at Yudit, but before she could move to him, he turned and went back into the living room. The sun was gone, and clear bright stars became visible in the sky. He glanced back and saw Yudit framed in the doorway.

"I'm sorry," he said. "I've had these daydreams that he comes back and suddenly we talk—father–son kinds of things. I tell him I'm in love with you and that I'm emigrating, and he hugs me." Joshua's voice dropped to a whisper. Yudit came close and took his hand. "And he tells me he's proud of me."

Joshua looked up and sniffled. He coughed to stem the tears. Then he turned quickly and took Yudit in his arms, holding her tightly.

"It doesn't matter," he said. "I'm staying here. This is where I belong. It's my life, my dream."

The body of the navigator was still in the seat next to him. After twenty-four hours, it smelled of congealing blood and the beginnings of decay. Illi had not come back since the murder, and no one had brought food or water. Heat created thirst, and thirst was suffering. Aaron needed the suffering as expiation for his untold sins.

Aaron slowly moved his head to look out the window. They were still there. Thousands of Loemer Hasidim in a line stretching beyond the horizon and starting with the black open pit that stretched to a mass grave. They had been marching to the pit and falling in. Endlessly they came, beckoned to him and fell. The grave never filled. He had watched for hours to see if it had filled, knowing that it would not be filled until he entered. Aaron turned away from the window. He was losing his mind, of course. He understood it and viewed it with a certain amount of detachment.

When he'd finally stopped screaming, something had slipped. Some part of him entered not a grave but a void. Truly he was afraid of the void which was neither life nor death. It was black and visionless. But he stayed there a long time, because there, at least, he could hide. Dawn, though, had forced him back into himself. Then he had glanced out the window and seen his vision. Then he knew for sure. His father had been right. He had denied his destiny. The sign he had sought had come to him—too late. Yet the sign was not the vision but the girl, whose soul could have made him a Hasid, a rebbe. He'd thought she would lead him to his path, but she was God's condemnation.

Aaron stirred in his seat. He smelled of blood and urine

and sweat. He was rancid, decaying, and he had lived for nothing. He'd been so sure of himself when he'd first spoken to the girl, so sure of his success.

"Why did you want to see me?" she had asked that first time. They were in the Independence Park, walking the winding sidewalk that ran through it.

"Impulse," he'd said. "I wanted to talk with you—away from the yeshiva."

Lynda had nodded, her hands in the pockets of her skirt. "And away from Rabbi Schwartz."

Aaron smiled. "That too."

"It's amazing," Lynda said. "I never thought the legendary mentor of our headmaster would have been a Reform rabbi. Rabbi Schwartz will lose a lot of points with our fanatic contingent."

"Does he lose points with you?"

"It depends," she said, "on you." A soccer ball rolled to her feet, and she kicked it to a waiting boy. "What was behind this impulse, Rabbi?"

Aaron shrugged. "I got to know Nathan Schwartz a long time ago. I started talking to him when we were both at the Liberal Rabbinical School." He saw Lynda raise her eyebrows. "Oh, he didn't mention that? He attended a Reform seminary for a year. But he didn't belong there. I saw that, and we talked, then I began tutoring him."

"And where did *you* get your learning? Surely not from the Liberal Rabbinical School."

"Don't sell the school short. I received a great deal of learning there. But the type you're interested in came from a yeshiva in Chicago."

"You weren't ordained from there, though," Lynda said, half-asking.

"No. I left before I had to face that possibility. I joined the Army during World War Two."

"And afterward, you went to the Reformim," Lynda said, using the Hebrew plural without realizing it.

"Yes," Aaron said, smiling. "To the Reformim."

"Why?"

"Because I didn't belong in a yeshiva."

"Why?"

The morning was already hot. Aaron headed over to a tree by the sidewalk and to its shade. Lynda followed. She looked so ordinary in the sun, yet still not ordinary. There was still that lingering light, though he couldn't see it properly. When she was near him it was almost as if he could feel an energy, an excitement stir within him. But he had to be careful. Aaron leaned against the tree.

"It started with my mother, Risa, I guess. She didn't belong either. She was a wild flower that wilted and died under the heavy hand of the society my father loved. The Hasidim. That's where it started."

"And where did it finish?"

"In the war," Aaron said. "Do you believe the six million died because of their sins?"

Lynda didn't answer immediately. "No," she said.

"Do you believe God is all-merciful, all-powerful, all-knowing?"

"Yes," Lynda said.

"Yes?" He looked at her.

"I try."

"Me too," Aaron said. "But all I can do is try. I can't dismiss the suffering and the injustice as God's will. I can't accept the religious law that keeps you from doing what you could so easily do as holy. You don't belong in a yeshiva that locks you behind walls, Lynda."

"And where do I belong, Rabbi?"

"I'm not sure. But certainly not here. Not at Aish Emes."

"At the Liberal Rabbinical School, then," Lynda said.

"Possibly," Aaron said calmly, as his heartbeat quickened. "They would accept you."

"The yeshiva accepted me. What's the difference?"

"They would ordain you," he said. "With my sponsorship. There are more women entering each year. It's not easy, and I admit they've done their best to discourage women. But no one could give you a tougher time than you've had here. Afterward," he said, "I could give you a job. A start."

"Let's walk," Lynda said. She said nothing more.

Aaron saw a paper bag on the sidewalk and started to kick it out of the way. Lynda blocked him.

"Don't do that!" she said. She called in Hebrew to see if it belonged to anyone, and shortly, a red-faced boy ran up to get it. Lynda rebuked him, then sent him away.

"Since the war, terrorists have started placing bombs and booby traps in earnest." Lynda looked at Aaron a moment. "In Israel you quickly learn that an unbidden gift may blow up in your face."

"Do you mean me, or the bag?" Aaron asked.

"You say I don't belong here, knowing I've spent two years of my life at Aish Emes, and that I'm engaged to be married. What if all this is merely a temptation—"

"And I'm the Satan."

"Yes. You are, aren't you? A Satan, an adversary?"

"I don't want to be your Satan. I want to be your friend."

"But friends don't set out to ruin other friends' lives. I'm engaged. Rabbi Schwartz and Tzvi trust me."

"And what is their trust?" Aaron said. "They trust you to bury what you're feeling for their sakes. To become a good wife and mother like Brucha Lefner."

Lynda winced.

"This whole way of life allows them to sacrifice you for their own faith. Letting you grow your way, become what you have the potential to become destroys their world. They want you but only behind a wall. Tell me, if you married this Heldman and then you decided to give up the traditional way of life, what would he do?"

"I won't give it up."

"If. If that happened. What would he do?"

"He would divorce me," Lynda said. "But you, Rabbi Stern—what do you want from me?"

"Nothing," he lied. "Just as I wanted nothing from Nathan." Aaron shrugged, afraid to go on.

"I'm not sure I believe that."

"I saw you pray," Aaron said. "I don't know what it is: maybe God; maybe destiny. But I had to talk to you. I had to tell you these things. To give you a choice."

The next meeting they had had been at her request. They had talked more, and her suspicion of his intentions had gradually disappeared. By the third meeting he knew she'd taken the bait.

Now it was all over. He'd been wrong again. God had taken what was to be his, the light, and given it to the girl to be walled away in some yeshiva. Seeing Lynda had been the sign not of his deliverance, but of his destruction. In truth, he had been a Satan, an adversary to lure her away from the life he so sought. Nathan had been insurance, a chance at redemption when all else failed. Lynda had the soul of a rebbe. In these last years, he'd come to hope that somewhere within him too, as his father had always believed, there was a rebbe's soul. Yet, with all his searching, he had found only emptiness. When Aaron had seen her he'd felt the need well up in him, a desire only she could satiate, and the knowledge that God had given her the gift meant for him.

But God had shown him his desire only to condemn him, only to give him the sign that he was not God-chosen, God-protected. Maybe once, but no longer.

"Get up!" Illi stood before him. Aaron looked up blankly, jarred from so deep within his mind. "I said, get up!"

Illi pulled Aaron to his feet and pushed him to the front of the aircraft. Sulim was placing explosives at the doors and scattering them around the floor. The pilot and co-pilot eyed Aaron from the cockpit. Illi pushed hard, causing Aaron to trip.

"What are you going to do?" Sulim asked in English.

"Kill the bastard. This time for real."

"Our demands have been met," Sulim said.

"Only the money," Illi said.

"The organization agreed that that would be sufficient."

"*I* didn't!" Illi said. "We'll get everything. Everything. They wouldn't have given us the money if I hadn't killed the other one."

"We've negotiated," Sulim said. "We aren't going to have any friends out there"—he pointed to the desert—"if we go around killing more people."

"Shut up," Illi said, not even looking at the other man. His eyes were on Aaron.

"You had your chance to kill the Jew; you didn't take it. Now it's too late, Illi. We blow the plane and let the hostages go—according to plan."

"No," Illi said. "I missed her this time, but she's going to suffer. He's not going to get away like she did. He dies!"

Aaron dared to glance at Illi. His eyes were red and fevered. Sweat had broken out on his forehead.

"I will not allow that. It's contrary to our orders."

"We kill him," Illi said. "We kill them." He pointed to the cockpit.

"No!"

Illi laughed. "What do you think this is, some goddamned war with a Geneva convention? Our weapon is fear. Terror. When we're finished with them, millions of people will be terrified."

"We're freedom fighters," Sulim said.

"We're terrorists. What's the matter, Sulim? Aren't you man enough?"

"I'm more of a man than you're capable of being," Sulim said.

Illi ignored him. "Kneel," he said to Aaron.

Aaron went down on his knees. A piece of glass from the floor bit into his leg. He felt the barrel against the back of his head, as he looked at the crew watching their deaths through him.

"Think, Illi," Sulim said, now pleading. "If we kill everyone, they will cut us down out there."

"Don't be an ass. They need us. Learn from me, Sulim. Learn. I am master. Terror is invincible. I am invincible."

Aaron felt the chill of the barrel through his hair. Coldness. Memories fought through the void that had begun to engulf him. Cold and snow. He'd killed three German soldiers with a grenade. Yes. Then there were snipers, everyone dying. Aaron felt the barrel of Illi's pistol pushed against his head, pushing out what he did not want to remember. Laughter. Yes, he remembered laughter, then more shots. Blood running into his eyes as he fell to the ground. Long ago. Yes. He was lying in the snow looking at the black boot by his head. They were killing the wounded. He looked up and saw the German laughing, saw the killer's eyes and the iron cross hanging from his neck. A Nazi. Yes.

Illí pushed against Aaron's neck a final time and laughed. "Now, Jew Boy, I'm going to kill you."

Memories beaten back for so long came in a torrent. Cold and snow and pain. There was the sound of boots crunching the hard-packed snow, and the sound of laughter. Then rage. The demon unleashed in him. Rage and killing hatred.

Aaron screamed. He threw his weight back against Illi as the gun went off, then dived for the open door of the aircraft. He hit the sand and felt a sharp pain in his shoulder and in his wrists tied behind him. He rose, stumbled, rose again and ran as the sand turned into snow, and rage consumed him. He heard the sound of the gunfire and knew it was his rifle cutting them down, one by one. As he ran, the snow filled his shoes, freezing his toes, but still he pursued them. The one with the iron cross was still alive. Aaron heard the whine of bullets, but ran on, shooting. He reached the top of the hill and stopped. He stood looking down at his prey, a corpse with spittle freezing on his chin, an iron cross draped across his face. Aaron cried out with triumph. Then an explosion blew him off his feet. He rolled down the hill as the snow turned back into sand.

Boots. More boots, but brown, not black. Aaron's vision blurred as the man in the uniform and kaffiyeh bent over him, cutting the wire from each wrist.

"I'm Captain Daoud," the man said. "You are safe now." He signaled to one of his soldiers, who gave Aaron some water from his canteen. Aaron nodded, too exhausted to speak.

"You are safe now," the captain repeated. "We will take you to a hospital." The captain looked out at the smoke rising over the hill. "God has graced you. You are the only survivor."

AUGUST 1968

THE AROMA OF FRESH ROASTING ALMONDS AND SUN-flower seeds filled the Jerusalem alley. The scent, thick as incense, drew Lynda from her path to the yeshiva and captured her, making her mouth water. Unable to resist, she crossed the alley and took a place in line in front of the small nut kiosk. Lynda glanced at her watch, then at the line. If she didn't hurry, she'd be late. But she sniffed again and stayed, craning her neck to see the bins. Luckily, this being midweek, the line was short and relatively orderly. On Friday, when she normally bought nuts, the crowds fanned out from the kiosk into the alley, blocking traffic as people pressed against the bins to grab a delicacy for the Sabbath.

Midweek business was brisk in sunflower seeds, to which most Israelis were addicted. One of the first talents Lynda had acquired was the art of eating sunflower seeds Israeli style. This involved quickly shelling the seeds with teeth and tongue only, and spitting out the husks. Hands were used only to convey more seeds to the mouth. After two years, her expertise was such that she could shell several seeds at a time. Lynda stepped up to the bin to order a bag of seeds, but the smell of roasting pistachios engulfed her in a sweet, seductive fragrance. She couldn't afford pistachios. Even as she thought it, Lynda reached into her purse, pushing the prayer book aside, and reaching for the five-pound note she'd tucked away.

When she came through the line into the alley again, Lynda held the still warm bag to her chest with one hand. They tasted even better than they had smelled. Buying them had been a tremendous lapse in discipline. Wednesday wasn't Shabbos, and even on Shabbos she confined her treats to almonds. The five-pound note had been reserved to buy the Malbim's commentary on Genesis. Now she didn't have enough money for the text. Lynda smiled as she chewed on another nut. Right now, pistachios were far more fulfilling than the Malbim. In fact, buying them was the first satisfying thing she'd done since the Sterns had left.

Madeleine had made arrangements to leave as soon as they'd heard of Aaron's rescue. The Saudis, to no one's surprise, had kept him a few days before agreeing to transfer him to a hospital in the United States. Flying him to Israel had been unthinkable. The day he arrived in the States, Madeleine had made plane reservations. They had gone the next day. Not long after, Mrs. Sheinman had left for England, the sudden quiet in the house making her long for her own grandchildren.

Lynda had spent the weeks since studying all day at the yeshiva, trying to bury the temptations of Aaron Stern. She would come back to the empty apartment only to brood over them once again. The attempt to restore her life, to pretend that the Sterns had never entered it, was failing miserably. Lynda walked down the alley, eating her pistachios and brooding. She'd be late again. People were starting to notice. She had to sort things out somehow, and make a decision.

"You settle," Madeleine had said, before she left. They'd been in her room packing up the clothes and souvenirs. "You settle for the realities you have, for the things you can hold on to."

"I'm not sure what's real," Lynda had said. She picked up the carved stone mezuzah and carefully wrapped it in tissue paper before placing it in the suitcase. "Given the nature of the world, you can hardly say that life at Aish Emes is real."

"It's real enough for Nathan Schwartz and your fiancé."

"True," Lynda said.

"Then it's real enough for you." Madeleine closed the suitcase and zipped it. She looked at Lynda, then sat down on the bed. "You've been with me these last few days, Lynda. What do you think?"

"I think you're very brave, and I admire you."

"That isn't the message you should have gotten from all this," Madeleine said. "I've been thinking about what's happened, asking why." Madeleine tossed her head back and faced Lynda. "Maybe it was to show you something. Maybe all this was to show you which path you should take."

"And which path is that?"

"I'll tell you what a friend told me long ago. Marry your yeshiva boy."

"Aaron didn't think I should," Lynda said.

Madeleine nodded. "I never asked you about those meetings." She smiled. "At first it crossed my mind that Aaron was having an affair."

Lynda's mouth opened in shock, and she shook her head. Madeleine waved her protests away. "Sit down," she said.

Lynda sat. "I never. We never. We just talked."

"I said it crossed my mind, I didn't say I accepted it as a premise. No, I realize my husband didn't have an affair with you, but that doesn't mean he isn't trying to seduce you. Not physically—some other way." Madeleine looked to the window a moment. A bird landed on the sill, taking a crumb in its beak.

"Why would he want to do that?" Lynda said, not sure how to phrase the question.

"Aaron is forty-eight. He's been looking at his life, measuring who he is against what his dreams for himself were. The funny part is that Aaron has done well. He built the synagogue practically from the ground up. They love him. But he sees something lacking."

"What?"

"Hasidim," Madeleine said. "His father wanted him to become not just a Hasid, but a rebbe. I think the older Aaron gets, the more his failure to achieve his father's dream for him affects him. He's gathered a congregation together, not Hasidim."

"But what could I do for him?" Lynda asked.

"Nothing," Madeleine said. She sighed and stood opening another suitcase. "You can do nothing for him—in the real world. But sometimes Aaron isn't in the real world. Sometimes he's in that fantasy world of his father's, where all things are holy and the Hasidim dance until dawn."

"I don't understand," Lynda said.

"When he saw you, he saw something; whether it came from this world or from his father's fantasy land I don't know. I don't really understand it myself." Madeleine began to put the twins' shirts in the suitcase. Lynda rose to help her. "He said that the women around you gathered themselves like Hasidim. He thinks you can give him the essence he's always been lacking."

"I can't give him what I don't have," Lynda said.

"I said you could do nothing for him. He can only ruin your life."

"Maybe," Lynda said. "But maybe he can give me an opportunity too. He said he could get me into the Liberal Rabbinical School."

"You can't do it, Lynda."

"You don't even think I should try, do you?"

Madeleine put the last shirt in the suitcase. She stared down at the contents. "All that happens when you fight them is that they hurt you. And the pain never stops. I don't want you to wind up the way I did."

"I think I want to become a rabbi," Lynda said. "Maybe I have to try and see."

"If you fail, you'll have nothing," Madeleine said. "Why? Why is it so important, for God's sake? Why a rabbi?"

"I don't know!" Lynda paused to quiet her voice. "I don't know. No one ever asks a *man* why."

"Sure they do. I've asked Aaron a dozen times."

"And what did he answer?"

Madeleine laughed. "He didn't. But you have to. Because you're getting ready to destroy the life you've built here."

"Nathan Schwartz said you were happy, Madeleine."

"I am," Madeleine said.

"Your eyes aren't happy," Lynda said softly. "Even before this they weren't happy."

"I came to the land where my dearest friend died—"

"And where the dream she built lives."

"But Ruth is dead," Madeleine had said evenly. "Another sacrifice. I would have been happy if I'd settled for dreams I could have a long time ago."

"And Ruth?"

"Ruth is dead. Her dream bled her like a vampire. Don't follow the wrong path, Lynda. If you leave here you'll fail, but it will be too late to come back. You'll have nothing."

Lynda finally put the pistachios away and hurried to the yeshiva. The sky was a brilliant August blue, and the sun made her hair damp with sweat. Summers in New York weren't like this—never this hot and beautiful. In two years she hadn't thought of New York much. It was as if she'd always been in Jerusalem. But could she remain? Madeleine and Aaron were two sides of the same coin, but where between them lay the truth? To go over to the Reformim would be an insult to Aish Emes and everything she'd believed for two years. Lynda stopped in the middle of a street without realizing it. She was jarred from her thoughts by the policewoman shouting angrily at her. She smiled and moved on. Heat, bustle, ancient city. If she married Tzvi, she would have Jerusalem forever.

Ruchel was in the coatroom waiting for her. Lynda sat down at the open volume of Talmud by the empty seat. "Is that the equivalent to the cup for Elijah at Passover? Keeping my place in case, by some miracle, I show up?"

"Just demonstrating my faith in you," Ruchel said. She looked down at her book, but not before Lynda noticed the quiver in her smile.

Lynda waited, as she always did, for Ruchel to begin, but the younger woman stared at her text. Finally she looked up. "Can I talk to you?"

"Sure."

"I mean, really talk."

Lynda leaned back in her chair and swung the door shut. Then she closed the text. "Go ahead, Ruchel."

"Duvid and I are having problems."

"Somehow I gathered that. I'm not sure I'm the best qualified to be a marriage counselor, though."

"You're my friend—that's more important." Ruchel sighed, her lip quivered once more. "Duvid is thinking of divorcing me."

"What?"

"And I think I agree with him," Ruchel said.

"What's going on?"

"I'd been around a bit before we got married. I was kind of a rebellious kid," Ruchel said.

"Weren't we all. I think it's the prerequisite for seeing the light."

"I ran away with this guy when I was seventeen. I got married."

"Oh, boy." Lynda let out a soft whistle. "Was he Jewish?"

"Yes."

"Civil marriage only?"

"Yes and no. We got married in Denver, in a civil ceremony. But when we got to California we wound up in this commune. I don't even remember where it was—I was pretty strung out on drugs. Anyway, there was this guy there, he claimed to be a rabbi."

"Oh, boy."

"Well, he claimed to be the Messiah once, too. At the time, I believed him on both accounts."

"So?"

"So to make the marriage 'messianic,' Allen and I signed a marriage contract. This guy was into Kabbala or something."

"Let me finish," Lynda said. "You both signed a contract that was witnessed. And you lived together—"

"Until my parents found us and annulled the marriage."

"But you never got a religious divorce."

"No," Ruchel said. "So by Halacha, Duvid and I are committing adultery. And . . ." Ruchel's voice broke. "And I'm pregnant."

"Damn," Lynda said. "You told him the whole thing and he's going to divorce you."

"What else can he do? It's a forbidden marriage."

"Duvid has another option," Lynda said.

"What?"

"He can forget about it, and so can you."

"How could we possibly do that?" Ruchel asked.

"How can you possibly bring all this out in the open? My God. You signed some piece of paper when you were seventeen and strung out on drugs, and because of that, you're going to ruin your life and the life of that child you're carrying? If you make this public, the child is a momzer, a bastard. Do you realize what that means? No marriage for him, no yeshiva. Nothing. The child would be stigmatized his whole life. This is Jerusalem, for God's sake!"

"No! It's wrong. We can't make that decision ourselves. We have to talk to someone. We have to get a rabbinical decision."

"You have one! Right in the Talmud. Look it up yourself. Just forget about it. No one has to know—can't you see that?"

"God knows," Ruchel said flatly.

"God knows," Lynda echoed. "God knows that you were never really married back then. God knows you and Duvid love each other."

"I didn't get a divorce."

"You're going to ruin your life over something so trivial?"

"Trivial? You call God's word trivial? Is the Torah trivial?"

"Yes!" Lynda said. She paused, seeing the shock on Ruchel's face. "No, not Torah, but this, what you're doing now. This is trivial. It's so trivial, and you both are prepared to destroy your lives over it. Forget you even talked to me, and I'll forget, and we'll dance at your son's bris."

"I can't forget. It's a forbidden marriage and I'm carrying a momzer. How can I forget that?"

"Of course. You can't," Lynda said sarcastically. "None of us can because we've seen the light. God's shown us the path, so we have to be holier than all the rabbis. We have to wave our holy books in everyone's face until they all see how purified we are, how far from our past sins."

"Lynda, please."

"I know what will happen. You'll go to Rabbi Schwartz, and if he tells you the same thing, then you will go to someone else—right?"

Ruchel looked away. "We hadn't planned to go to Rabbi Schwartz. He's too involved."

"You mean he might be lenient; you might not have to martyr yourselves for the faith. It sickens me, you know? You want to be so holy and so observant, even God has to be in awe of you!" Lynda brought her fist down on the Talmud. It stung her hand.

"We have an obligation!" Ruchel said.

"Oh, yes. We must make up for our past lives by seeing to it that no rabbi is strict enough for us, no judgment hard enough. You, me, all of us." Lynda picked up the book.

"You've turned this into a weapon. Here! You want to use this to destroy your baby? Then pick it up and hit yourself with it!" She slid the book across the table so that it hit Ruchel in the belly.

Ruchel stood, wide-eyed and shaking. "I'm sorry. I thought you were my friend. I thought you would understand how important . . . I'm sorry I talked to you!" Ruchel shouted to Lynda as she ran from the room.

Lynda heard the door to the apartment open and close. What did they expect from her? Only that she be one of them. She would become one of them if she married Tzvi. If.

Suddenly the room, the coats, the women chanting stifled her. She couldn't breathe. She walked out to the main room and saw the women staring at her. Then she turned and walked out the door, slamming it closed behind her.

Lynda walked until dark, pausing to watch the beggars and the old men with runny eyes who sat reading psalms and selling amulets to ward off evil spirits. This was Jerusalem, filled with troubled souls seeking peace. She walked the main square as people rushed by to homes, lives, beliefs. On the corner a mongoloid boy in his teens sat, clinging to a pole, rocking, his eyes vacant. He wore the black hat and side curls of the Hasidim. Lynda smiled at him, but he had been taught well, and lowered his eyes at the sight of a woman. She watched him until his father left the shop and took his hand. The boy, with his slanted eyes, had seemed a foreigner, someone who didn't belong in Jerusalem. But as father and son walked away, Lynda realized that he did belong. She was the stranger.

Long after dark, Lynda walked into Mrs. Sheinman's empty apartment. She walked down the darkened hallway to her room. She turned on the light and took off her clothes, neatly folding them. Then she stood nude a moment and contemplated stretching out on the bed. There had been a time when she'd slept nude; when she'd slept nude with other men. But that time was long gone, so she felt self-conscious. She put on a robe.

For the first time in a year, Lynda craved a cigarette. She smiled to herself. All her habits assailed her tonight. Mrs. Sheinman smoked. Lynda went out into the living room, looking for a stray cigarette. She found a whole pack and took that as an omen. She sat down and lit the cigarette, reveling in the rebellion. Then she realized that she had not even thought to pray the Afternoon Service. It was now time for the Evening Service and she sat in a robe, smoking a cigarette. She leaned back against the chair. Rabbi Hoffman said women weren't obligated to pray, so for once, she'd listen to Rabbi Hoffman. Besides, she didn't want to encounter the black shadow that had haunted her since seeing Aaron Stern. She wanted to forget about God, smoke cigarettes and walk around the house nude.

Instead, she finished the cigarette and drew a bath. She ran the water deep, something she would never do if Mrs. Sheinman had been there. Deep water to remove the desert dust of Jerusalem. Lynda dropped her robe and stepped into the water, sitting back as the warmth washed the tension out of her. What did she want? Too many things at the same time. She wanted to belong and not be lonely anymore. But she didn't want to pay the price. In her room, hidden from everyone's eyes, including her own, was a prayer shawl she'd bought. One day, she'd locked the door and taken it out. Then, blushing and sweating, she had wrapped herself in the garment, the ritual before prayer. She'd felt wrapped in God's wings, yet all those with whom she sought fellowship would have thought her perverse. "A woman will not put on anything pertaining to a man." Torah. God's word.

Yet God's word seemed also to be in her vision of a year ago. Of course Torah was Torah, and her vision, everyone said, was the product of a bump on the head. But it had spoken the truth. All she wanted was her portion of Torah, of God. She didn't want to be more religious than the rest of the Jewish people put together. She had seen the light, really. Her vision had been bursting with light, and the place she went when she prayed was a place of light. She wanted to wrap herself in holiness, to touch it and be touched by it.

She wanted to make love to Tzvi, to be able to hold him, to comfort him should bombs ever fall on the city again. But even after they married, he wouldn't embrace her publicly. Even then, Torah, as Tzvi saw it, would keep him from ever reaching out to her. She loved a man she'd never touched, never really talked to. Tzvi didn't know about the prayer shawl; he didn't know about the place of light. When she was still in the hospital, she'd told him about the vision. She had watched his eyes mask as he smiled.

Lynda pictured herself married to Tzvi. She'd have a yeshiva wedding, with all those present doing their best to make it a good wedding. Her parents would refuse to come— not that she could blame them. She'd become a stranger to them, living in a foreign world they couldn't understand. Or maybe, she thought, they understood it too well. She sighed, sinking deeper in the tub. Her eyes moved down her body to her loins, and she felt a rush of sexual tension. She'd marry Tzvi. They'd disappear for seven days, and then Tzvi would return to the yeshiva for a party. It was custom. She would stay home. It was custom. After a month or so, she'd return to classes with her head duly covered, like Ruchel.

The couple came into her mind. How hard it must be for poor Duvid, she thought bitterly. So many times he made love to his wife, trying to think pure thoughts of Torah, all wasted on a forbidden marriage. Lynda almost smiled as her anger left. In the warm water she was detached, pensive. She let her thoughts flow with the currents she created with her hands in the tub. Tzvi too would make love to her with his thoughts on Torah. Or would he succumb and think of her, her alone? Within a year she'd be pregnant. From that time on she'd be pregnant often, studying when she could, teaching when she could get someone to look after the children. She'd be a yeshiva rebbetzin.

That was Brucha Lefner's curse. Lynda would be a rebbetzin like the ones at the yeshiva. Maybe it would take twenty years, but she'd become just like them. At first she'd fight. She would still go to pray and study. But, Lynda already knew, slowly the life would work on her with its ways, wearing her down until her dreams and her visions faded. She'd become like them, living for her husband's work, redeemed by her husband's prayer, losing all but the identity: rebbetzin.

Madeleine had told her to settle. But Madeleine had pained eyes and past regrets. Were Lynda's dreams so false? That was her fear. She didn't know how to tell which dreams were truth and which were demons. Madeleine had tried. She'd left home and family in pursuit of a dream. It had been a demon instead. Maybe this life, the yeshiva life, was the demon. Lynda closed her eyes, and a picture came of the old rebbetzin by the wall who finally had been left to her prayers and seeking. Lynda relaxed and let her mind wander into and out of drowsiness. The old rebbetzin. Lynda could see her praying. The old rebbetzin, who turned and had her own face, lined and worn, standing alone.

The doorbell rang, startling her. She jumped out of the tub and grabbed her robe, holding it closed as she ran to the door. Through the peephole she saw Tzvi. Lynda took a deep breath and opened the door. Tzvi came in, saw her and lowered his eyes. Quickly she pulled the robe close together and tied it.

"I was taking a bath," she said.

"So I notice. They told me you left the yeshiva in the morning and didn't come back. They were worried about you."

"They can stick it."

"What happened between you and Ruchel?"

"What happened is between us," Lynda said. "Let me go unplug the tub."

She went into the bathroom and Tzvi followed, moving on to her room and opening the door wide. Lynda came in and sat across from him on the bed.

"Mrs. Sheinman isn't here," she said.

"I'd forgotten."

"Would you rather go in the living room?"

"No, I guess this is okay," Tzvi said, looking down. "If it helps, Duvid spoke with me today about a delicate subject."

"I see. And what did you advise him?"

Tzvi stared off and began to stroke his beard. That reminded her of every rabbi in the yeshiva, and it angered her. His eyes were red with too much studying in too little light. That also angered her.

"I didn't know what to tell him," Tzvi said. "I honestly didn't know."

"I told Ruchel to forget it. They both should forget all about it."

"That was a dumb thing to say. No wonder she got upset."

"I was dumb? The whole issue is stupid," Lynda said.

"It's a forbidden marriage."

"It's also a real live child in Ruchel's womb, and a former marriage that wasn't morally a marriage to begin with."

"And when did you become empowered to make rabbinical decisions?" Tzvi said, his voice cold.

"When everyone else became so blind. The rabbis told a momzer to move to another town and not to talk about it. To forget it. I read about it," she said drily, "in a book you've heard of. The Talmud."

"So, now you're a rabbi and a Talmud expert," Tzvi said. "There are other things in the Talmud about forbidden marriages."

"And I'm sure you will search until you find the harshest ones. It's stupid."

"Tradition isn't stupid. Torah isn't stupid."

"Then Duvid is stupid, and cruel."

"Not cruel," Tzvi said. "He's in agony over this thing. This is the wrong country to have bastards in."

"Only if everyone knows. Can't you see that simple fact? He's going to divorce her. They're both such fanatics that they will go to rabbi after rabbi until they find the one who will make them suffer. And you, you're no better."

Tzvi said nothing for a moment. He leaned against the bookshelf and put his hands in his pockets. "No. I'm no better," he said. "I've decided to keep the marriage contract the way it is. And we'll keep the truth to ourselves. Are you satisfied?"

"No," Lynda said. "No, I'm not. Maybe I should be grateful that my future husband decided not to humiliate me in front of the whole yeshiva, but I'm not."

"Why not?"

Lynda smiled. "You're asking *my* question. Why not? Because I don't know if you can live with that, Tzvi. There will be some precept somewhere in Torah that you let pass. I'll tell you what," she said, standing up. "I'll let you off the hook."

She went to the window and opened it. "I'm not a virgin!" she yelled. She hung out the window screaming it over and over until Tzvi pulled her back.

"Thank you," she said, suddenly calm. "That's the first time you've ever touched me." Tzvi dropped his hands to his side. "You know," she said, "you're as crazy as the rest of them."

"And you?" he asked.

Lynda sat down on the bed. "No," she said, looking down at her lap. "No, I'm not. I've tried, but I can't be like you. I can't hurt other people, hurt myself like that."

"What are you saying?"

She heard the fear in his voice. "I think . . ." Lynda felt herself losing control and welcomed the loss. "I think I'm going to leave you." She began to cry, surprising them both.

She cried with racking sobs. Then she felt him lifting her, holding her. She didn't open her eyes, afraid, as she pressed her face against him and felt his warmth. He held her, surrounded her with his body, then lifted her face and kissed her cheek. She clung to him, her breathing returning to normal. Tzvi kissed her again on the lips. For the first time she felt how soft his lips were.

They moved to the bed and lay together, touching, holding. He kissed her, and his hand caressed the tension between her legs. Tzvi untied the robe and folded it back. He stood and began to undress. She opened her eyes and told him no, but he silenced her protest with a touch to her lips.

They made love; she joined with him and thought of herself on Solomon's couch. The Song of Songs ran through her mind, its holy love song heightening her love for Tzvi. They made love as if they had done so a hundred times before. When they had finished, Tzvi said nothing. He kissed her again and put on his clothes, his back to her.

"I've got to go," he said.

"Tzvi," she said, touching him. He turned around, his eyes red with crying.

"I've got to go!" He walked away from her and out the door.

Lynda didn't go back to the yeshiva the next day, or the day after. She had read the future in his eyes that night. It took two days to prepare her belongings for shipping to the United States, and to buy a ticket. In that time she often reached for the phone, but never dialed his number. The phone never rang. She wrote him a letter, putting into words what his eyes had said. She mailed it knowing Tzvi would not receive it until after she was gone.

At dawn on Friday, the day before the Sabbath, Lynda walked to the Western Wall. The old rebbetzin was there, alone, as the sky brightened over the plaza where Lynda stood. Lynda wanted to touch the Wall once more, to feel the stones against her fingertips. But she couldn't face the rebbetzin. She hung back and listened to the old woman's voice crying out her prayer. Just before the old woman stopped praying, just at the time when the rebbetzin would turn and see her, Lynda walked away and hailed the cab that would take her to the airport.

The cab picked up three other passengers, whose talk and laughter covered her silence. She watched Jerusalem pass by and welded its images in her mind. On the road to Tel Aviv, she took out her prayer book. In the rush at the airport, no one noticed when she left it behind.

KNESSET
YAAKOV

CENTIN, ILLINOIS

SEPTEMBER
1979

LYNDA STEPPED ON THE BRAKE ONLY AFTER THE CAR'S bumper had grated against the curb. She switched into reverse, freeing the bumper. The grating noise gave her goose bumps. She looked around. The car was in its accustomed place in the hospital parking lot—the spot reserved for clergy—but she couldn't remember having driven to get there.

Last night she had dreamed of Jerusalem. It was the first dream of the ancient city she could remember having since she'd left it, so long ago. Jerusalem had called to her in the dream, murmuring in Hebrew as she walked its streets. Even now the dream images were so sharp she could barely distinguish them from memory. Yet the dream had not been a pleasant one. At the Western Wall she'd stood, as in a vision, clothed in ritual garments, and waited to receive revelation. But the Wall had burst open and its giant stones had crushed her.

Lynda pulled herself back from the images. She moved the rearview mirror down to check her hair, now short, and the minimum of makeup she wore. She looked into her own eyes, lured once more to the Jerusalem of vision. Then she glanced at the wedding ring on her finger.

Elliot had held her, calming her trembling with the warmth

and strength of his arms. The feel of his body next to her had finally drawn her from the dream, away from Jerusalem and into a gentle lovemaking. She had dozed in his arms after that, secure for a time.

Elliot, of course, did not believe in dreams, or in the nightmares he had so frequently he didn't even wake from them. Elliot confined his faith to the operating room, to his hands and to the miracles he compelled them to perform. Lynda shook her head. Now was not the time to think of dreams, or of Elliot.

Lynda got out of the car, not bothering to lock it. She entered the hospital and headed for Cardiology on the fourth floor. Cardiology was Elliot's domain, and the place where one of her congregants lay dying.

When Lynda opened the door to Abe Katz's room, she bumped into the private nurse the Katz family had hired.

"He's absolutely impossible," the nurse said, glaring at Lynda. She pushed her way out the door.

Lynda watched her go, then looked at the old man on his bed. He was pale and jaundiced, looking frail against the equipment working to procure him days and weeks of life.

"Okay, Abe, you can quit pretending. She's gone."

The old man opened his eyes. "I hate that woman. Hovers over me all the time to see if I'm still breathing." His eyes brightened, looking at Lynda, and he managed a feeble smile. "Hello, Rabbi. Come to see if I'm dead yet?"

"Yes," Lynda said, putting down her briefcase. "But you're not."

Abe started to maneuver to a more comfortable position, but winced and stopped. Lynda moved quickly, adjusting his pillow and covers.

"Don't peek," he said.

"Why, Mr. Katz, it hadn't occurred to me that you had anything to hide."

Abe laughed. "Don't kid yourself, Rabbi. When I go, I'm going with full faculties."

"That's supposed to refer to your mental capacities," Lynda said.

"That just shows you don't know everything," he said. "You look pretty today. New suit?"

"No, it's not a new suit," Lynda said as she pulled up a chair and sat down. "I wouldn't bother to get a new suit for you, even if you are a rich old man."

Abe laughed again. "I love you. You're as mean as me. With all these stupid smiling vultures, it's so nice to have someone nasty around. Marry me."

"I'm already married."

"So nu? I'm dying. What difference would it make?"

"To my husband," Lynda replied, "a great deal."

"I thought you were, how you call it, liberated."

"Not that liberated. Besides, it wouldn't do to antagonize your personal physician."

"I think you two planned this so you could keep my money in the family."

"Abe," Lynda said, in mock astonishment, "are you planning to leave me money?"

"Not a dime, and if I die, I might demand a refund from your husband."

"One of your most endearing qualities, Abe, is generosity."

"I'm already being overly generous. Have you seen what Dr. Klein—a rabbi's husband, mind you—charges? He's a pirate."

"So are you."

"I know," Abe said, smiling contentedly.

"Listen," Lynda said. "Aaron will be by to visit you tomorrow."

"I don't want him," Abe said.

"Come on, Abe. He's your rabbi, and your friend."

"No. Not anymore." Abe's bluish lips tightened as he gazed out past her. "No, I don't want him to visit me. You keep him away from me! When he comes, the air is thick with death."

"Abe, take it easy," Lynda said, leaning over and taking his hand.

The old man didn't seem to hear her. "When he comes,

I can feel death touching me. It suffocates me. He's a thief come to take my soul away, but I won't let him. You hear me!" Abe gripped her hand with a strength she found surprising in so frail a man. Then he relaxed, and his eyes cleared.

"Tell Aaron to stay away," he said.

"I will."

"I don't want to have nothing to do with no goddamned fool who's going to spend the rest of his life decaying on Miami Beach."

Lynda paused a moment, then realized that Abe had no memory of his previous words. "He said nothing about Miami Beach," she said, smiling.

"Anybody who's ass enough to retire at sixty is ass enough to go to Miami Beach."

"He's been in the pulpit a long time," Lynda said, defending Aaron. "It's time to do something else."

"Feh. Sixty-two years I've been in one business. You do what God put you on earth to do. You don't retire." He said the last word with a sneer. "Besides, he isn't going to do anything else. You know it like me. His eyes are dead."

"That's harsh."

"It's only truth. Once he was my rabbi; not anymore. Once his eyes had fire in them." Abe looked at her. "You should have seen him. After the desert, he was like Moses. But no more. No more. You know what I've prayed for, Rabbi? I've prayed to God to give my death to Aaron Stern. I want to live, and he wants to die—so let me live! But God doesn't answer me." Abe began to cry. "God doesn't answer me and I don't want to die."

"Shhh," Lynda said. She moved over to his bed and cradled his head against her as he wept. She whispered to him softly in the few Yiddish words she knew, the words of his childhood, and held him until he drifted off to sleep. Then she settled him on the bed, wondering where his dreams were taking him.

* * *

Elliot Klein slouched back in the easy chair, sipping a Coke. He was still in his surgical greens, and his shirt clung to his chest where sweat had dampened it. He knew he should have showered and changed, or at least changed, but he'd been four hours on his feet. He wanted something cold and fizzy. So he sat, thankfully alone, in the doctors' lounge.

Elliot looked up at the ceiling. Lynda was up there with Abe Katz. She went to the man free of the dread that consumed Elliot. Sometimes he waited until late afternoon before entering Abe's room, hoping the old man would be asleep. Sleep masked the death overtaking Abe's failing body; eyelids hid the accusation in the man's eyes. If Abe happened to be awake, Elliot hid behind his doctor's facade, trying not to hate Abe for showing him once again that death would not be defeated, or denied. That he, Shana and Isaac Klein's miracle boy, could not always perform miracles.

Elliot sighed and closed his eyes. He lifted the Coke to his lips and drank until the tickle in his throat became a burn. Then he rested the bottle on the arm of the easy chair. Except for Lynda, no one in Centin knew he was a miracle boy. In the neighborhood where he had grown up, everyone knew. It had been a neighborhood of resettled camp survivors and their children. Elliot was the walking miracle, incurring jealousy as well as admiration from the families around him. His parents, after surviving the camps, after finding each other once again, had found him, their only surviving child. He was the baby who, against all odds, had been born in the camp and smuggled out to a Catholic family. It had taken two years after the war to find him. He had only wisps of memory of the family that had taken him in, and a recurring nightmare where a figure in black was drowning him. When he became thirteen, he had demanded a conversion ceremony in addition to his bar mitzvah. He had wanted the ritual bath to wash away any taint of baptism. Lynda would have called that an act of faith. But it had nothing to do with faith or God. He believed in neither. It had to do with knowing who he was. The walking miracle.

Miracle boys became doctors, healers, passers-on of the gift of life. If Shana and Isaac Klein were afraid the Jews would disappear, then their son would heal Jews, snatch them from the grip of death with his knowledge and skill. If the eyes of his neighbors called into question his worthiness as a survivor, then his brilliance as a surgeon would justify him. He had spent most of his life renewing the miracle, and so had spent most of his life alone.

Until he met Lynda. He was completing his residency, and she, though he didn't know it at the time, was finishing rabbinical school. He'd taken to attending cultural affairs, having become tired of dating nurses and undergraduates in search of husbands. The cultural events, however, had become variations on a common torture. Instead of standing alone at parties, he stood alone, or walked alone, or sat alone at concerts and plays. Or he wandered in galleries featuring art he didn't like. The art gallery had been no different from the others—until he'd spotted her. She too was alone, but unlike Elliot, she seemed comfortable. He watched her as she smiled graciously at the people who approached her, then disengaged and moved on. She was pretty, he noted, her dress striking. What caught his eye most, though, was that she was a woman and not a girl. She looked good.

He looked good too; he knew that. His red hair made him look like an Irish Catholic, but that could be overcome. He was dressed a little too formally for the occasion, as was the woman. Perhaps she was a kindred spirit. But she disengaged so nicely so often. He realized, as he walked behind her, that he was not the only man there looking for something more than art.

He moved when she moved, staying behind her, his hands in his pockets, wondering why he, Elliot Klein, a well-dressed, good-looking doctor, could think of a hundred ways that that small woman could humiliate him. He stopped and stared at a painting, trying to frame his approach. He felt a tap on the shoulder and stiffened.

"I'd appreciate it if you would stop following me."

Elliot turned, his face already red. Her eyes looked through him, and the humiliation he'd sought to avoid sank to the pit of his stomach. "I really wasn't following you," he said, knowing he sounded more stupid than he looked.

"Oh?" she said, crossing her arms. "What would you call it?"

Elliot sighed and took his hands out of his pockets. "I'd call it trailing behind you, trying to build up enough courage to tap *you* on the shoulder. You beat me to it."

"And what were you going to say after you tapped me on the shoulder?"

"I was going to tell you I'd appreciate it if you'd stop following me."

She continued to look through him a moment, making him feel naked. Then her eyes softened and she laughed.

"My name is Elliot Klein," he said. "Can I start over?"

She held out her hand. "My name is Lynda Jacobs."

Her handshake was firm. He matched it. "Since it's too late to be suave and sophisticated, I might as well admit that I can't stand the stuff hanging on these walls, and I don't know enough about art to fake an intelligent conversation."

Lynda surveyed the room. "Me too. Want to get a cup of coffee?"

Elliot recovered some of his lost dignity on the way out and recommended a nearby Italian coffeehouse. As they walked, Lynda Jacobs revealed herself as a graduate student in Jewish Literature. He mentioned his residency, and thankfully found her only reasonably impressed. He stopped a moment at a flower stand and bought her a rose.

"Thank you," she said, sniffing the flower.

"I'm the one who should say thank you," Elliot replied.

"Why?"

"For being an adult. Do you realize you have not men-

tioned your sorority, your dorm or your Psych Three-oh-
two class the entire time we've been talking?"

"Things that bad?"

"I'd begun to think I was a century older than the rest of
the world. I don't guess you have that problem."

"I was in that awful gallery too, remember?"

By the time they were seated in the coffeehouse, Elliot
had decided Lynda had real possibilities. He liked her. The
thought of finally liking a woman was pleasant and stim-
ulating. The waiter came and brought the coffee and cannoli
they'd ordered.

"So you're doing work in Jewish Literature," he said.
"All of Jewish Literature?"

Lynda looked up. "No," she said, her voice light, belied
only by the brief shadow that passed over her eyes.

"What, then?"

"Holocaust Literature."

Elliot's palms began to sweat. "I didn't know there was
much."

"Oh, yes," she said, biting into her pastry. He noticed a
subtle stiffening of her movements that puzzled him.

"My particular thesis," she said, "has to do with starvation
and its effect on creativity." She smiled at him. "Proving
whether the starving-writer cliché is indeed true." She took
another bite of the pastry. "Most of my work, of course, is
done with posthumous writers."

He didn't like her anymore. "Oh," he said, his voice
cold. "You must love your work."

"Did I say something wrong?"

"Not at all," he said, containing his anger. He set down
his coffee cup, afraid she would notice his shaking hands.
"We have a common interest," he said softly. "My sister
and brother died in the camps."

The color drained from her face. She looked down a
moment, then at him, her eyes already red. "I'm so sorry,"
she said.

"Sure. No problem." He wasn't in the mood to soothe
her guilty conscience.

She sat there looking down as he tried to figure out a way to extricate himself and go home.

"I owe you an explanation," she said.

"You don't owe me anything." He raised his hand to get the check, but she gently pushed it down, her eyes seeing into him.

"Yes, I do," she said, and took a deep breath. "I should have guessed that would happen someday." She kept her hand on his arm. The warmth of her, and the penetration of her gaze, irritated him.

"I don't study Jewish Literature," she said. "And no decent human being would do a thesis like that."

"Then why the hell did you say it?"

"Because that kind of story is guaranteed to cut off questions. It's like telling people you're a coroner. Nobody asks you about your work. And most men don't bother to call me back for another date."

"You want that?"

"With most men, yes."

"And with me?"

She hesitated. "No. I could like you, and I've already behaved like a barbarian."

"No disagreement there." Elliot looked at her. "What the hell do you do that requires such a horrendous cover story? Don't tell me you're a spy."

She smiled briefly and her gaze softened. "You want to hear what I say when I tell the truth?"

"I can't wait."

"I am not a grad student. I am in my last year of rabbinical school. I am going to be a rabbi. Furthermore, I do not want to spend the night discussing religion, nor do I want to discuss why I am becoming a rabbi, nor why you do or do not believe in God. And I have no intention of going to bed with you."

"Whew."

She took her hand off his arm. "Now you can get the check."

Elliot leaned back in his chair. He waved away the approaching waiter and looked at her. "Not so fast. I think I like you."

Lynda married him ultimately, reluctantly. She was filled with doubts about their ability to survive a marriage. His parents had been horrified when he gave up a position at Mount Sinai Hospital in New York to follow Lynda here, to Centin. They believed he had turned his back on his destiny. In truth, he believed it too. No one here knew he was a walking miracle, and the one thing that could again justify his existence Lynda denied him. A child—a new life, and a new generation to put distance between the Jews and the gas chambers. A child, to fill the space where his brother's and sister's lives should have been. If he left no heirs, death would win the final battle.

Elliot reddened with shame, thinking about the child. Last month he'd grown desperate enough to force himself on her, to demand a child or he would leave her. He hadn't intended to threaten. He didn't believe the threat. But Lynda had believed. In silence, with a body as cold as death, she had given in to him.

For all of it, there had been nothing but the wound he'd caused. This morning she'd awakened from a nightmare, trembling, her face the mask of a stranger. She had dreamed a dream from the part of her soul that was a stranger to him. She had dreamed of Jerusalem. He held her, afraid she would fly away to that far place, to the city where he could not dwell, to the God he could not trust.

Elliot remembered the morning as he heard the door to the lounge open and smelled the fragrance of Lynda's perfume.

"Hi, beautiful," he said, letting the memories retreat once more.

"How did you know it was me? Your eyes are closed."

"Your aura of sanctity penetrated my eyelids."

"Uh huh."

"That and the perfume you're wearing." He opened his eyes, surprised once again at how beautiful she was. "I love you," he said.

"I love you too," she said. She walked over and gave him a long kiss that reminded his body of the morning. Then she put down her briefcase and pulled over a chair.

"I take it surgery went well?" she asked.

"Of course. Dr. Elliot Klein performed the bypass. How could it fail?"

"Anyone ever tell you you're a conceited son-of-a-bitch?"

"Yes. You have, several times," he said. "Done with rounds?"

"Doctors make rounds, dear. Rabbis make visitations."

"Correction. God makes visitations."

"How would you know?" she said softly.

"Not nice, and spoken in too serious a tone."

"God is my job, remember?"

"Only too well," he said. "Anyone up there besides Abe?"

"No one I have to visit yet. But I do have a congregant in labor."

"Good. I hope it's a boy," Elliot said. "You get more money for officiating at a circumcision than for doing a little girl's naming."

"Abe Katz was right. You are a pirate."

"I'm looking out for my wife's best interests, that's all." He paused a moment. "How is Abe?"

"You haven't seen him yet?" Lynda said. "No, of course you haven't."

"I don't usually get to see him until the afternoon," he said avoiding her eyes. She read him too well.

She looked at him for a moment, then spoke. "He's beginning to slip away. He's still sharp as a tack, but he faded for a while today and didn't remember what he'd said."

"Damn."

Lynda frowned and stroked his arm. "He's eighty-three, Elliot. He's lived a full life, and now he's dying."

"I know he's dying. I'm his doctor, remember?"

"It's not your fault. You aren't God."

"I ought to be! I have a better record of saving people."

The Coke machine clicked on. Lynda reached for the bottle on the arm of the chair and drank from it. She held it out to Elliot, but he shook his head, so she put it back on the wet ring it had left.

"I'm sorry about last month," he said.

"Let's not talk about it."

"I was insane to threaten you."

"I don't want to talk about it, Elliot," Lynda said. She looked at her watch. "I have to go. I'm running late." She picked up her briefcase and stood.

"I do love you, Lynda," Elliot said. "More than anything."

Lynda paused at the door. "I wish that was true," she said. She opened the door.

Elliot jumped up from the chair, knocking over the bottle. "Wait!" he said, trying to grab at the bottle. "Shit, it completely slipped my mind. I have to talk to you."

"I don't have time now."

"Yes, you do. It's about Aaron Stern."

Lynda closed the door she had opened, and turned. "What about Aaron?"

"Ken Gold talked to me today and asked me to talk to you. And like a fool, I almost forgot."

"Forgot what?" Lynda asked, irritated.

"Aaron's a very sick man."

"How sick?"

"Leukemia."

"Oh, my God. Does Madeleine know?"

"No. Aaron made Ken promise not to tell her. What has Ken worried is Aaron's response to the whole thing. Ken wanted to hospitalize him and start treatment a week ago. He hasn't heard anything from Aaron."

"Somehow, that doesn't surprise me," Lynda said. "How much time does he have?"

"Not much if he doesn't receive treatment. Months, weeks—less if he goes into a crisis and they can't pull him out."

"And with treatment?"

"He could live years."

"I suppose I'm the chosen one to talk Aaron into living."

"That's what Ken was hoping."

"Aaron won't listen. He probably won't even speak to me. I haven't been his favorite person for some time now. And I think he's in the process of making sure I never succeed him at Knesset Yaakov."

"You don't know that for sure."

"Wrong, Elliot. Only *you* don't know it."

"So fake it. Inspire him like you do all those followers of yours."

Lynda sighed. "You'll never understand, will you? I don't fake it. You can't pretend to give a man his soul."

"You damn well can, if it means keeping him alive!" Elliot said angrily.

She shook her head, then reached up to kiss him gently on the lips.

"Don't pity me, Lynda."

"Okay, I won't."

"You'll talk to him?"

"As soon as I can." She pushed open the door.

"I love you," she heard him say as the door closed behind her, leaving her alone in the hallway.

The antiseptic odor in the hospital suddenly seemed more noxious than ever before. Lynda felt her forehead break out into sweat and saliva pour into her mouth, and she moved quickly to one of the side bathrooms, trying to will discipline into her body. But once she was in the bathroom, her stomach rebelled and erupted, leaving her shaking.

Lynda made her way from the stall to one of the sinks, the odor of antiseptic and freshener still too heavy in the air. She avoided looking at her white face in the mirror as she washed, then dabbed water on the back of her neck. She took towels and leaned against the wall, letting it support her as she dried her face with shaking hands. The bouts of nausea had started days ago. She'd have to see someone soon to confirm what she already knew: she was pregnant.

Today, as yesterday and the day before, she'd meant to

tell Elliot. But he would be happy, and she'd hate him for it. She should hate him now, but she couldn't. He'd demanded of her only what she'd promised him. Lynda reached down and picked up her briefcase. It was hand-tooled, a gift from Elliot on her ordination. At that time, she'd allowed herself to believe their lives would work. It hadn't seemed so unreasonable to plan a child. She'd even wanted a child; but that was then. Things were different now.

Lynda walked out of the bathroom and hurried from the hospital. The Indian summer breeze cleared her head as she breathed deeply of the warm air. She'd made it through the Liberal Rabbinical School after five years of battling teachers and fellow students. Twelve women had entered the rabbinical school. Only three had made it to ordination. Of those three, only she had chosen the perilous road of the congregational rabbinate.

It had been a given that she would take her place beside Aaron. It had all been too easy then, too easy to make promises she couldn't keep. She had stayed on at Knesset Yaakov, preferring its familiar walls to the upheaval of finding another place. She was good at her job. Most of the membership of the last few years had come because of her. They came and participated because of her. Had she been a man, not even Aaron could have stopped her from becoming the head rabbi.

But she wasn't a man. Aaron didn't want her around after he was gone, and her pregnancy gave him the weapon he needed to destroy her completely. In spite of all her dreams, when Elliot threatened her with desertion she'd made the woman's choice. In her mind, Lynda could hear Brucha Lefner laughing.

She'd sought to take the sparks of Jerusalem, gather them and make them flame. She'd exiled herself from the ancient city to free herself of its walls. But here, in this modern city, she had found new walls: the walls of the rabbinate. She'd been trapped, crowded in by so many people with so many needs. There was no room to nourish sparks of holiness. Once she had prayed; now she led services. Once she'd thrown her soul into studying the Holy Word; now she taught classes.

When she had first come to Knesset Yaakov, she'd thought herself free to pursue her destiny, to seek the light. She had found time to pray, even if it was alone in the sanctuary, late at night. In those moments she had remembered the wholeness she sought. But later, there was no time. The congregation waited, a jealous lover. Hundreds of people wanted her to inspire them, to lead them to God, or prayer, or to their own souls.

Aaron too had expected her to save him. He'd given so many parts of himself to so many people, there was nothing left. He'd brought her to Knesset Yaakov to inspire him, to give him back his soul. It was an unspoken promise she'd made in the time of easy promises. But Aaron was just one of the hundreds. She had no time. She no longer knew the way. She couldn't teach Aaron to pray when she'd forgotten how herself. She couldn't help Aaron find God when she'd wandered from the path. Her soul was withering after trying so long to be free. Now she'd made another promise—to find a way to make Aaron Stern want to live.

Lynda toyed with the idea of going to Madeleine. But Aaron would never forgive her for that. And neither would Madeleine. There was some great silent wrong Lynda had done Madeleine. It remained shrouded in mystery, but one of the first brutal realities Lynda had discovered on coming to Knesset Yaakov was the reality of Madeleine's antipathy. The woman Lynda had thought would befriend her barely concealed her hatred. There was no talking to Madeleine. There was no talking to Aaron. Yet something had to be done.

And maybe she had to do something about the pregnancy. Lynda shivered at the thought, yet even as the chill ran through her, the thought remained. If she were not pregnant, she might still have a chance. She had stayed at Knesset Yaakov too long to leave. She was a woman with too much seniority in the rabbinate and no place to go. She couldn't ask Elliot to follow her to some congregation in some tiny town where the nearest hospital was in the next county. If, even there, she could get a job. She was a woman, and she was pregnant. But no one knew. No one need ever know.

NOVEMBER
1979

EACH FRIDAY NIGHT AFTER SERVICES, MADELEINE MADE Aaron tea. She filled the silence between them with the comfortable sounds of rattling cups and the teapot's whistle. The month was marked off by the cakes she used with the tea: Honey Cake Sabbath, Sponge Cake Sabbath, Carrot Cake Sabbath and finally, Coffee Cake Sabbath. Tonight began the first Sabbath of the month—Honey Cake. Madeleine sliced the cake down the middle and then along the width in three-quarter-inch pieces. At hundreds of Friday nights, Sisterhood functions, receptions and teas, she had always cut honey cake that way.

She arranged the cake on a plate, and placed the plate on the tray which held the steaming cups of tea. Madeleine made the same tea, never swayed by the fad of new and herbal teas. The tea for Friday night came from the stockpile of tea left over from Passover. It was a science to gauge the cycle of the year so that the tea would just run out by the next Passover and none had to be thrown away. It was all part of marking the cycles of time, the years that flowed one into the next with comfortable familiarity. Until now.

Madeleine paused a moment, glancing out the window

as the autumn wind scraped branches against the house. A storm was coming. She turned once more to the tray, picked it up and carried it into the living room. Aaron had built a fire in the fireplace, adding cedar chips, which sent a pungent fall-like aroma intó the house. Madeleine put down the tray and sat, staring at the flames, until Aaron finished the letter from Joshua and Yudit.

Aaron looked up and smiled. His smile made her notice again that he'd lost weight. His mouth seemed overly large for his face. Aaron folded the letter.

"How about that. She's pregnant again. We'll have four grandchildren, and the twins haven't even started yet. We're going to have some kind of clan."

"Don't count your grandchildren before our younger sons are even married."

"They'll get around to it, I'm sure." Aaron reached for his tea, then took a piece of cake. "Let's go visit them when the baby is born. We'll have the time."

"No."

Aaron sighed, put his cake on the saucer and leaned back expectantly. He was waiting, she knew, for her to fill the silence between them with news and gossip from the congregation.

"The sanctuary needed vacuuming," she said, reaching for her tea.

"I noticed that myself. John's assistant is out with the flu."

"He's out with the flu a lot. Dora Hirshberger thinks he's a drunk."

"And you?"

"I know he's a drunk."

"I'll talk to John," Aaron said. He ate his cake and stared at the fire. A log fell, sending sparks flying through the metal screen. Aaron watched them, trying to control the focus of his eyes as the flames wavered. The sparks seemed to hang suspended, frozen, waiting for him to gather them. They beckoned to him—the first time he'd been called by light and not darkness. He'd never thought of death as a being of light. Gentle death. He knew he should tell Madeleine what the doctor had said. But since making death's acquaintance once more, he felt self-contained, a part of him secreted away for a tryst, waiting for the gentle being of light to take him away. With the finishing of the death begun so long ago, he'd have peace, rest from his father's dreams and his own nightmares. At one with death, he would no longer have to watch Lynda as she gave the light she denied him to others. He had his own brilliance now—his death. He felt finally like a holy man, distanced from the cares of the world. This was the way the Loemer Rebbe must have felt each day of his life. All that remained was a return to Jerusalem, to die on holy soil. Aaron pulled his eyes from the fire. Madeleine had been watching him.

"How was my sermon tonight?" he asked, straightening up on the couch to break the spell of the flames.

"Fine."

"Just fine?"

"You want more?" Madeleine asked, sipping her tea. She saw the momentary confusion on his face. She was deviating from the script, and from their Friday-night ritual. She gave in.

"Sam Waldman thought it was marvelous," she said. "Nate Hirshberger dozed. Everyone else thought it was nice."

Aaron took another slice of cake, though he didn't want it. He always took two pieces. To do otherwise would threaten his secret. He forced himself to bite and swallow. "Sam thinks everything I do is marvelous. I guess the sermon wasn't so hot."

"It was fine."

"Well," he said, "I'm too old to change my style now."

"Too stubborn maybe, but not too old."

"Well, soon the question will be academic," he said, and patted her hand. She moved it. "I see you still don't approve."

"My approval or disapproval has nothing to do with it. I wasn't consulted."

"We talked," Aaron said.

"After you made up your mind." She shook her head and waved away his reply. "No. Let's not talk about it anymore. Only you can decide when you'll stop working."

Aaron sipped his tea, grateful she had dropped the subject. He felt a bout of dizziness, which he fought. "I'd like to leave them with a really good sermon. Just one before I leave—one as good as the sermons Lynda gives."

"She doesn't speak so well," Madeleine said.

"She doesn't do anything well as far as you're concerned. I will never understand what you have against the girl."

"No, you never will," Madeleine said. "And she's not a girl. She wasn't a girl when you met her. She is a grasping, ambitious woman who has used us to get ahead ever since she first met us." She looked at Aaron. "Are you going to make her discipleship official? Is she going to take your place?"

"The board decides that."

"*You* decide it, Aaron. I'm not a fool."

"Things haven't been so clear-cut since Abe Katz entered the hospital and Stuart Levine took over as president."

"You'll still decide. Do you want her?"

"I don't know. I think not."

"That surprises me," Madeleine said.

"I'm full of surprises," Aaron said, smiling. "But I haven't made up my mind yet. I have to think of what's best for the congregation."

"Of course," Madeleine said sarcastically. "Always what's best for the congregation."

Aaron looked at her, his eyes narrowed. "What's the matter with you? Is it so awful to think of relaxing and enjoying life a little while we still can?"

"No, nothing wrong. Maybe we should get a condominium in Miami."

"If that's what you want."

"No, Aaron. That's not what I want."

"What, then?"

"I don't know," she said. "I've spent so many years living

with what you wanted, I don't know how to find what I want for myself."

"Madeleine, you never knew what you wanted."

Madeleine set down her teacup and folded her hands in her lap. She looked at Aaron for a moment before speaking. "Sometimes I wonder if I've ever gotten through to you. If I've ever touched that dream world you built for yourself where I don't know anything I'm not told, and I never feel pain."

Aaron avoided her gaze. "I know you've suffered," he said softly. "Maybe sometimes I just try to spare you more."

"I don't think so. I really don't."

"That's unfair."

"Maybe," she said. "You know when I'm suffering, but you've never let that interfere with your plans."

Aaron shook his head. "I really don't know what you're talking about. I'm trying, but I don't understand."

"I know you saw Ken Gold. And I know you aren't well. I have been waiting for you to tell me something."

The blood rushing to his face made him dizzy again. "If it was serious, I would have told you. I have anemia, that's all. Anemia from being overtired. That's all. There. Do you feel better?"

"Yes, Aaron. I feel much better. Thank you for being honest with me."

Aaron glanced over at her but could not read her eyes. He looked at the letter from Joshua.

"Think about a visit to the kids. Just for a little while. Then we can do whatever you want to."

"No," she said. "I know you too well. You want to go back to Jerusalem and see Nathan Schwartz. You want to spend the rest of your days, and mine, teaching in that damn yeshiva, playing the rebbe to a bunch of fanatic boys."

"That's not true!" Aaron snapped. "I just want to stay awhile with my son, my daughter-in-law and my grand-children."

"You should have thought of spending time with your

son twenty years ago. I doubt Joshua would know what to do with your company."

"I want to make up for that. I want to see my grand-children. That's something you should want too."

"They can come here."

"It's difficult for them to arrange, with the kids," Aaron said. "You want me to be honest; how about you? You just can't bear the sight of Joshua—admit it."

"How dare you say that?"

"That's what he thinks. He thinks you see him as a cripple without the leg."

Madeleine tensed, ready to defend herself, but stopped. Instead, she gathered the teacups and the cake plate. She stood and looked down at her husband. "It won't work, Aaron," she said.

She took the dishes back into the kitchen. The kitchen had never been the refuge for her that it had been for her mother, but it offered some protection. Aaron would not follow her there. She busied herself with cleaning up, and soon heard him making his way upstairs. She sat at the kitchen table, veiled in silence as she listened to Aaron's steps above her.

If anyone had problems with Joshua's missing leg, it was Aaron. She'd adjusted, as she adjusted to every boon or misfortune, though it had taken a while. The first visit home from Joshua had been the worst. Right after the '73 war. Watching him come down the corridor of the airport, look-ing thin and scarred. He hadn't fully recovered, but had come home just to prove to her he was alive. He still wore his uniform, pants leg pinned up. People stared.

"I want them to know who I am," he'd said. At home he'd taken off the uniform and put on an old sweat shirt. He'd looked, then, much more like Joshua, and it hurt even more to look at him. Madeleine had retreated to the kitchen, but Joshua, violator of tradition, had followed.

"Please, Mom," he said. "I'm still me. Look." He smiled and fingered the cowlick on his head. "See?"

Madeleine looked at his hair, but her eyes were drawn to the leg and then away.

"I shouldn't have come home," he said softly.

"No," Madeleine said, looking up. "Don't say that."

"I'm not a cripple."

"Oh, Joshua, it's not that."

"Then what is it?"

She reached down and laid her hand gently on the stump of Joshua's leg. "I'm afraid that land will take you away. Consume you."

"Mom, I made it. I survived."

"That land only consumes survivors."

"That land is Israel. It's not some demon conjured up from a dark place. It's farms and cities, and blossoming roses. It's a place of refuge." Joshua took his mother's hand. "It's where my dreams live. Remember? We talked about dreams once."

"And I told you how badly dreams could hurt you. But you didn't listen."

"Oh, but I did. That's how I survived." He tightened his grip on her hand, let go and leaned back in the chair.

"I don't understand."

Joshua closed his eyes a moment, and she noticed a small scar on his eyelid. He looked at her. "When I came to after surgery, when I realized that I'd lost my leg, I wanted to die."

"I should have had the courage to come and be with you."

"But you were there. You were. For the longest time, I was miserable; I didn't speak to anyone, not even Yudit. Then I remembered the talk we had." He smiled. "When we two crazies went off at four in the morning."

"I still don't understand."

"You told me that dreams exact a price, and the price is never what you expected to pay. Do you remember?"

Madeleine nodded.

"I'd expected to die gloriously to save my people," Joshua said, a bitter smile on his face. "I'd expected to win every-

thing or lose everything. Yet always, somewhere in the back
of my mind, was what you'd said." He slapped his leg. "I
never expected this. You were right, though. And I knew
that you'd survived. You'd paid a price—something I guess
I'll never know about—but you had survived. Then I realized that I could too." He leaned over and kissed her.
"Thank you for saving my life."

She let it go at that, leaving him his illusions, not wanting
to disappoint him. She didn't tell him that she was a coward.
She'd never had the courage to do what he'd done. To go
on. But if it was all a lie, it seemed to be an inspiring one,
so she let him continue to believe in her. He knew she didn't
think of him as a cripple.

Aaron was trying to manipulate her, to make her go back
to Israel, not for Joshua, but for him. He couldn't ask,
couldn't reveal his need for her support so openly. For all
their time together, she'd never touched him deeply enough
for him to need her. Once she'd thought she could pry him
from his father's world, from dreams of Loemer Hasidim
and nightmares of a failed life. Instead, she'd been sucked
into Aaron's limbo of silence and half-truth. She had become
an extension of him, part of a world haunted by the ghosts
of unfulfilled dreams.

Aaron thought she'd be happy in Miami Beach. Maybe
he was right; maybe she, Madeleine Blumfeld, who had
dreamed of changing the order of the universe, would find
happiness on the beach, playing cards and doing needle-
work. She had done nothing in her life to deserve more.

And hanging over them both, like the shadow of a bird
of prey, was Lynda. Lynda Jacobs Klein, someone who
should have been no more than an ornament in Aaron's
world, had become the center, the pillar supporting a de-
cayed facade. After the hijacking, Madeleine had been ready
for Aaron to need her strength and to lean on her. But Lynda
had taken him away, convinced him that she was touched
by God, and that God had finally given him a disciple to
make him a rebbe. Lynda had forged a chain so strong,

Madeleine couldn't break it. Then Lynda had bled Aaron dry in order to take his place. She would succeed; she would triumph. Madeleine hated her.

Almost as much as Madeleine hated Israel. She'd never go back there. It was Ruth's land. Her son had followed in Ruth's footsteps, building on her vision, and having her grandchildren. Madeleine looked at the picture of the three grandchildren, perched on the windowsill. The eldest girl looked like Yudit, who was an incarnation of Ruth. The eldest girl, thin, with the big troubled eyes of coming adolescence, was named Ruth. This Ruth stood with her brothers Asaph and Motti, all of them looking out at the stranger who was supposed to be their grandmother. But they were closer to the grandmother who had died before they were born than they were to her.

Madeleine had been lonely for thirty years. She stared at the picture, seeing Ruth as she had been, her only friend, walking out a door, gone forever. Madeleine reached out and touched the children who were a part of her, part of Ruth, joined. Then she pulled her hand away. No. It was Ruth's grandchildren who stared out at her, living Ruth's legacy. They weren't really hers. She had given them nothing.

Madeleine heard the creaking of the bed. Aaron would soon fall into an exhausted sleep. It was more than anemia. She knew, but she was afraid to ask—terrified of illness, death; afraid of Aaron's finally needing her. She was no longer strong. At the age of fifty, she realized she had no destiny. She was not one of the chosen. Ruth had been chosen, and Lynda. Madeleine finally knew what had attracted her to Aaron. They were the same; they both dreamed dreams unnoticed by God.

Dawn came softly to the sanctuary. The rising sun lit the stained-glass windows above the Ark that housed the Torah Scrolls, and made colors dance slowly on the pews.

Aaron leaned forward, resting his arms on the pew in front of him. He watched the windows brighten as the sun pulled shadows around the Ark. The brass border of the Ark still reflected the Ner Tamid, the lamp, that hung before it. He reread the words engraved on the Ark: AITZ CHAIM HI—She is a tree of life to all who take hold of her.

How many times had he taken hold of the Torah Scrolls in thirty years? He couldn't count. The words, he knew, meant more than that. They were heavenly commands he had not been able to fulfill. To take hold of Torah, of God, and make a tree of life.

But he did not desire to live. Death, his holy companion, warmed him in embrace, illuminated his soul. He felt joy. Today he would pray. He had come at dawn to be greeted by God, to pray like a holy man as Death showed him the path to Heaven. Filled with rejoicing, Aaron reached for a prayer book.

A cloud covered the sun outside and the sanctuary dimmed. Aaron looked up from the book he had just opened. Shadows passed across the sanctuary. He looked down once again and began to sing "Ma Tovu"—"How goodly are thy tents." Halfway through the prayer, he stopped in horror. He had sung the words in the Loemer melody. Aaron quickly turned to another part of the Morning Service, and again he couldn't remember the proper melody. No prayers came from his lips, only melody. Aaron called on Death to help him, to send light and release for his soul. But the sanctuary was silent, except for the melody resounding in his brain.

The Ark was shrouded in shadow. Aaron saw in its midst the desert vision, and the lines of Hasidim assaulting him with their song. He collapsed against the pew and wept. Even death gave him no rest.

He knew when Lynda entered the sanctuary. The door opened, and he felt her presence like a bleeding wound. He raised his head.

"Leave."

"I can't," Lynda said. "I know."

He hid his eyes once again, protecting himself from her gaze. "Go away."

"You have to go for treatment. You can't just die."

Aaron sat up. He wiped away his tears. "God is murdering me. I bind myself, a willing sacrifice."

"And what about Madeleine?"

"Madeleine will be better off without me."

Lynda walked over to him. He was terrified she would sit near him, but she took a seat across the aisle. She leaned over to him as he fought to regain his composure.

"My mother was a very superstitious woman," he said, staring at the Ark. "She was terrified of death, yet I think she courted it like a lover. She used to come to the synagogue at midnight, when the dead are supposed to rise and pray. My mother would come, in spite of her fear, to commune with them, to find out what secret terrors the future held."

"Did they speak to her?"

"I don't know," he said. He tried to look at Lynda, but quickly turned away. "I never asked her."

"You could live for years with treatment."

"That doesn't appeal to me," Aaron said. "I'm tired of trying to cheat death. I'm tired of looking for messages in my survival that aren't there. If I was supposed to die in the desert, God failed. If I was supposed to live, God failed again."

"Or *you've* failed," Lynda said.

"Yes," Aaron whispered. "That too."

"Maybe God gave you a choice, a destiny to pursue."

"Only a measure of destiny," Aaron snapped. "Not enough!"

"How do you know?" Lynda said. "And who are you to judge?"

Aaron watched the alternation of shadow and light against the windows. He turned to Lynda. "I thought you were my destiny," he said. "I've also come to the synagogue at midnight."

"And what did you see?"

"Of the dead, nothing. But once, I saw you."

"That was a long time ago," Lynda said.

"What did you see?" he asked.

"Nothing."

"Don't lie to me!" he shouted. His voice echoed back to him in the empty sanctuary. "Please, don't lie to me. I watched you pray, your head covered by the prayer shawl, and tefillin wrapped around you. It was so dark, except for where you were. The light from above the Ark surrounded you like a second prayer shawl. You turned around once, but you looked right through me, and suddenly I wasn't sure if I was really there, or going mad. You led the congregation of the dead in prayer. Don't tell me you didn't see anything."

"I've never tried to see, Aaron," Lynda said. She looked from him to the Ark and back to him. "That was so long ago, I'm not sure I even remember." She closed her eyes a moment. "I opened myself to my blindness and let my soul guide me. I felt, Aaron. I felt what you felt that night."

"I felt nothing!"

"I can't help you. No one can help you, because you would rather have visions of Hasidim than images of God." Lynda stood up. She moved into the aisle and leaned against the arm of the pew.

"You want me to tell you how to pray," she said. "I can't. I don't know how anymore. I've lost my way in this place, Aaron, just like you. I'm not a rebbe to grab your soul and give you salvation. I can't deliver the faith that is seeping out of me. And you did this to me, Aaron."

Aaron pointed at the empty seats with a shaking hand. "I see you with them. I see their faces when they look at you. I see their eyes."

"Some. They frighten me. I'm afraid I'll fail them someday because some day there will be nothing left to give."

"I want them to look at *me* that way. I want the Hasidim you stole from me!"

"There are no Hasidim! Damn it, Aaron. The rebbe your father dreamed of never existed."

Aaron stood up. Dizziness made him sway. "I saw you in Jerusalem." He rubbed his eyes to clear them. "I saw what was mine."

"You can't steal my soul. You can only find your own. Live. Make the right choice this time."

His legs trembled as he moved toward her. "You have what is mine," he said. "I won't live an outcast and see you take my place." He grabbed hold of her arms, gripping so hard she winced. "Give me my Hasidim. I will destroy you. Give me what is mine!"

His grip loosened against his will. He watched, surprised, as the floor came up slowly to meet him. He tried to get up, but his arms and legs no longer obeyed him. Lynda knelt down.

"Aaron, lie still. I'm going to get help."

Then she was gone. "Don't go," he called to the empty sanctuary. "Don't leave me alone. God, don't leave me alone!" He lay back as darkness engulfed him.

Madeleine watched from her chair as Aaron slept. A long, thin tube trickled nourishment to him as his body fought his will and tried to survive. Her mother had kept the same vigil over her father, sitting, waiting and praying for a recovery that never came. Bea had kept the woman's vigil, as now Madeleine, her daughter, did. Madeleine, who once had thought herself so different from Bea, had become just like Bea. Her mother was gone now, having died in her sleep. Bea Blumfeld, the bearer of other people's burdens, had died a burden to no one.

Madeleine kept her vigil alone. Visitors came to the house, but no one entered here, a dimly lit sanctuary where the still living rabbi lay in state. There was no friend to break the taboo, to come and hold her hand. She had seen to that. She'd made only the right friends at the right time. Now the time was wrong, and she was alone—except for the agony of Lynda's daily visits. That woman came, refusing to acknowledge Madeleine's anger, or her silence. Lynda came each day, saying nothing, bringing offerings of coffee or some other food which Madeleine always refused.

"Why did you go to her?" she asked, as she looked at Aaron. "Why did you tell her and not me?"

Aaron's sleeping form gave her no answer. She loved him. Watching him as death overtook him made her realize that. She had shared too much of her life with him not to love him. She remembered her passion for him, once felt so long ago. But the Aaron of her memories was the Aaron she had run from, the man who had parceled himself out, piece by piece, until only his shell remained. Now that too was dying, and she was afraid.

When Vellef Blumfeld died, Bea's life had not greatly altered. She stayed in the same house and continued to run the business that she had, in essence, run from the beginning. But Madeleine was a rebbetzin; she had no business separate from Aaron. What would she be if he died? Thirty years had left her with nothing. Even their house belonged to the congregation.

Aaron wasn't responding to treatment. For days she had come and talked to him, whether he was awake or asleep. Days of trying to pull him back from death. But she knew it was useless. Aaron had never loved her enough to change his path for her. Desperate, she'd even considered asking Lynda to speak to him, but then she remembered that Lynda had sent him here, driven him to the death he so desired. His disciple had finally overcome him.

There was no point in staying. Madeleine sighed and stood. With one last look at her husband, she left the room. The hallway was busy with the noises of visiting hours which had begun after she arrived. She glanced down the hall, fearing that someone she knew might be there. Her dread increased as she saw someone walking toward her. His gait was uneven, and familiar.

"Joshua?" she asked. "Joshua!" She ran into her son's

arms as he hugged her and kissed her cheek. His face was covered with a black curly beard she had not seen before.

"I didn't recognize you with the beard," she said.

"Yes, you did," he said. "Surprise."

"Is Yudit with you?"

"No. The twins called after you sent them back to school. We talked and decided it was time for me to make a trip home." He held her at arm's length and looked at her. "How's Dad?"

"The same," she said. He looked so much like his father with the beard. She half-expected to see the scar parting his hair.

"Ma?"

"Hmmm?"

"I said, what's the prognosis?"

"Who knows? He doesn't get better. He doesn't get worse. Do you want to see him now? He's asleep."

Joshua glanced at the door and then back at his mother. "Let him sleep right now. I'll buy you a cup of coffee. There's something I want to talk to you about before I speak with him."

They found a vacant table in the cafeteria. Madeleine took a sip of coffee and put it down. "What do you want to talk to me about?"

"First I want to know how you're doing."

Madeleine pulled the cup in toward her. She turned it in slow circles as she spoke. "I sit and wait. That's how I am. The doctor asked me if Aaron had a strong will to live. I told him, No, Aaron doesn't want to live at all."

"I don't believe that," Joshua said.

"When you sit and wait for a while, you will."

"I don't intend to," Joshua said. He smiled and pulled a letter from the pocket of his jacket. He handed it to her.

She opened it and frowned at him. "I don't read Hebrew that well, remember?"

"It's from Nathan Schwartz. It's a letter appointing Dad a senior faculty member at Aish Emes. Nathan's place is big now, you know, one of the biggest in—"

"No. Absolutely not. Aaron can't go off to Israel. He's a sick man."

"But he can!" Joshua said, his smile broadening. "I talked with a couple of doctors. He can get treatments at either Hadassah or Sharei Tzedeck, and it will cost less than here."

"No."

"Ma, let's give it a chance. Teaching with Nathan might pull him out of this. Let's give him something to live for."

"He *has* something to live for. Us. You and me and the twins. But we aren't enough, Joshua. We never have been. Why do we have to invent something?" she asked. She twirled the cup around as coffee lapped over the edges. "Why can't he live for us?"

Joshua leaned back in his chair and crossed his arms on his chest. "I don't know," he said softly. "As a kid, every time I wanted him and he wasn't there, I wondered what everyone else had that I didn't. But I'm not going to let him die because of childhood resentment."

"Good, Joshua. You take him to Israel. You take him to his yeshiva in Jerusalem where all his imagined disciples are waiting. But let me alone. Leave me here."

"I know you don't want to go. But he needs you there. He's dying."

"So am I! You look at me, Joshua. Look hard. I won't go to that place, not even to save Aaron's life. I won't spend my life in the shadow of death, living out Aaron's final dream. All I have ever been is a sacrifice on the altar of my husband's visions. No more. I had dreams of my own once!" Madeleine halted as her voice became choked. "I don't want to end my life as some goddamned yeshiva rebbetzin. Do you understand?"

Joshua leaned over and took her hand. "Ma, I—"

She pulled away from him and stood. "I have to get some air," she said. "Stay with your father." She left the cafeteria and hurried down the hall.

When she was out the door of the hospital she broke into a run. She ran for three blocks before she realized there was no place to go.

DECEMBER
1979

DURING THE MONTH OF DECEMBER, THE CITY PIPED
Christmas carols along the streets of Centin's shopping area.
Elliot walked past the shops, kicking the slush left from an
early snow, angry at the melodies echoing on every corner.
They dredged up half-memories and buried images from his
past. Faceless people had sung those songs to him in another
language. They had taught him Their Songs for Their Holiday. He'd laughed and clapped with delight. Now, he
remembered and was ashamed. Other Jews conducted self-examination at Yom Kippur and sought forgiveness. He
examined his life in the season of Their Holiday. He did
not seek forgiveness. He forced the season to remain nameless, like the faceless people who had kept him safe.

Elliot stopped at another corner where the music was
accompanied by the ringing bell of a Salvation Army worker.
He glared at her until the light changed. Then he made his
way past the shopping district. It took him an hour to reach
the house. He stood by the oak tree in the front yard and
watched, but Lynda wasn't there. He'd hoped to get a glimpse
of her through the window. The house keys jangled in his
pocket, but he didn't go in.

It hadn't occurred to him before that their marriage might
be ending. Even when he'd threatened Lynda, that thought
hadn't really occurred to him. If he'd believed, truly, that
Lynda might leave him, he never would have forced the
decision on her.

No. That was a lie. In the season of self-examination he must tell the truth. As surely as those seasons followed one on the other, haunting him, he would have forced her to choose. The wind blew the tinkling of bells his way. He wouldn't be free of them for the whole month, for his whole life. Elliot glanced at the house he'd given up the right to enter.

The memory of his last entry was still painfully clear in his mind. He'd walked into the house, past the unlocked door and the unlit hallway, filled with dread and premonitions of what was to come. The heat in the house had burned his numb cheeks, purging him of hope.

"Are you home, Lynda?" he'd called, knowing she was, but receiving no answer. He hung his coat in the closet and walked into the living room. He shivered with a chill when he saw her.

Lynda had been sitting on the couch. In her lap were a letter and a torn envelope. She did not look at him or acknowledge his presence.

"It isn't what it seems," he said.

Lynda held up the letter. She looked at it, then at him. Her gaze was the familiar hated one, penetrating him and making him feel naked. "Mount Sinai Hospital," she began softly, "would be very much interested in receiving a résumé from you."

"I'm not going to send them a résumé," Elliot said. He was afraid to move closer to her gaze.

"Of course you're not. We're going to stay here and live happily ever after."

"That's what I want, yes."

"You know I'm pregnant," she said.

Elliot sighed. "I've known for some time. You aren't very good at hiding things."

"Neither are you," she said.

"It was a whim. It means nothing."

"Did the whim occur to you before or after you got me pregnant?"

"You don't really think that, do you, Lynda?"

"I don't know what to think anymore," Lynda said. "I do know that Aaron won't speak to me and that any chance I have to influence the board will be gone when they find out I'm pregnant. And I do know that you are looking once more to the East, to the great East Coast practice you gave up for me."

"I love you, Lynda," he said. He came over and sat near her. "Can't you understand? That letter is something I needed to do. I just wanted to know if I was still good enough for them."

Lynda shook her head. "I'm so tired of it, Elliot. I'm tired of living with your worthlessness and having to share your burden of survival. You think because you save lives here in Centin, you're less of a man than someone who saves lives in New York City. You're sure that your survival makes you less of a human being than those who died. Well, I'm tired of being part of the sacrifice you are compelled to make on the altar of the dead."

"I'll throw the letter away. I'll do whatever you want me to."

"I'm carrying your child, and it's ruining my life."

"I wanted it to be our child."

"You want a hell of a lot!" Lynda snapped. "I'm carrying your child and I feel violated by ghosts from the gas chambers."

"Please try to understand—"

"Have you ever tried to understand me?"

"You never let me understand," he said. "You walled away most of your life. Don't forget about your ghosts— the ones from Jerusalem. You keep searching for God and not looking around to see if anyone's with you."

"Oh, the atheist has gotten religion."

"Maybe I have, or could have, if you'd loved me a fraction as much as you love all the jackasses in that congregation."

"That's what you want from me. I have to love you best

of all. I have to want you most of all. I have to choose you over everything and let you impregnate me just so you can feel worthy. I have to tell you over and over that you're a decent human being. Well, you aren't a decent human being, Elliot. You're just another ghost of Auschwitz, and now I've let you pass it all on to another generation. God help me, I even considered having an abortion for a while."

"What are we going to do?" Elliot said softly.

"I don't know," Lynda said. Then her eyes narrowed. "I don't like you anymore, Elliot. And right now, I don't want to be near you."

"Lynda, I don't think I can live without you."

"You can. You'll always survive, Elliot." She looked at the letter, crumpled it and threw it at him. "Get out and take your East Coast practice with you. If I have to leave this place, I'm leaving alone. I've done it before. I've left what I loved because it tried to chain me. I can do it again. Now get out of here!" She stood. He reached for her, but she flung his hand away and struck him across the face.

That had been a week ago, and since then he had been paralyzed. He took off work, unable to continue, and wandered the city. Always he ended up here, before the house, watching. And always, as now, he remembered her hand across his face, and her eyes. Elliot turned from the house; then, slowly, he began the long walk back.

The hierarchy of the current scions of Knesset Yaakov ritualized itself in the semi-annual Sisterhood luncheons. Each round table of ten represented various strata within the synagogue community. At the head table, where Lynda sat, were gathered the ten families whose male members made up the synagogue board. Occasionally, depending on the fortunes of her family, a woman would move from the head table to the next level, where Madeleine sat.

Madeleine hadn't always sat at the second level. Before Lynda came, Madeleine had been the one at the head table, the one who gave the blessings and the occasional speech at the luncheon. Her departure from the public scene had been abrupt. At first she'd been resentful, but she had soon realized how much she'd hated performing at the luncheons. Her relief was a small favor from Lynda—one Lynda probably hadn't thought to give.

Madeleine noticed a burnt odor in the air. They'd burned the noodle pudding again. After hundreds of luncheons, the cooks still burned the noodle pudding. Madeleine watched as Irma Levine, the current Sisterhood president, noticed the odor and moved swiftly from her chair to the kitchen. Irma very seldom spoke to her now, seeing little profit in conversing with a retiring rebbetzin. The women did not speak much to Madeleine at the luncheon, as if they were already obeying the laws of mourning—not to speak to the mourner unless spoken to. But they were premature. Aaron had chosen life—or at least, Nathan's yeshiva. Madeleine didn't know what secrets were contained in the Hebrew script of Nathan's letter, but Aaron had read it and wept. The reflections of death in his eyes had faded and he had begun to respond to treatment.

Now he was home, slowly coming back to life. He and Joshua attended to the details of the move. Aaron had insisted she come to the luncheon, smiling and talking about its being a break for her. Still weak, his hands trembling, he'd taken her arm and told her to enjoy herself. He lived his fantasies once more, dreaming of Nathan's yeshiva and his waiting disciples, and of course his wife to come and stand by his side. It was easy for him to imagine that her greatest desire at that moment would be to attend the same damn Sisterhood luncheon she'd dragged herself to for thirty years.

Joshua, at least, had the decency to feel guilty. She'd tried to forgive him, to get back the closeness they'd once had. But he'd chosen his side. He was dragging her back to Jerusalem, and she really didn't want to be around him. So he spent his time with his father, probably doing those father–son things they should have done long ago. Aaron barely walked into the synagogue anymore. It was as if he'd buried it.

Madeleine noticed that her fork was spotted and that there were stains on the tablecloth. Automatically, she made a mental note to tell Aaron, but realized he was no longer interested. The mumbled sounds around her blended together: women's voices, the clatter of dishes as they were removed. Talk of diets, doctors, pregnancies floated by— so many things she had heard so many times. Yet there were new subjects.

"Well, I just don't know. She's a woman, after all."

"So are you."

"Well, I certainly wouldn't want to be a rabbi."

"And if Stern is so thrilled about her, how come he hasn't said anything?"

"Look, she's taken over the whole synagogue. Take a look at the back three tables, would you? Who cares what he says?"

"I do."

"Well, I think she's done a fine job."

"Eh, not so hot. Not like Rabbi Stern."

"Who's saying not like Rabbi Stern? You spent the last twenty years trying to get rid of him."

Madeleine colored slightly and stared at her plate. She knew who belonged to what voice.

"I never. Oh, there may have been a few times I didn't agree with him. And actually, I still think he's pretty strange. I mean wearing a skullcap all the time."

"Shah. He's a sick man."

"And who ever heard of a reform synagogue with a kosher kitchen?"

"Don't speak badly about him; he's sick."

"But I always liked him."

"Well, she's going to do the same things he's always done. She went to a yeshiva, you know. They never lose that. She'll do the same thing."

"If she's here."

"I say why not? Why not? What's wrong with a woman finally running this place? God knows we've raised enough money for it."

"Well, if Stern doesn't back her with the board, she hasn't got a chance."

"And what if she gets pregnant? Tell me that?"

"You got pregnant and you lived."

"I'm not a rabbi."

"Besides, she's gone all these years with no children."

"Yeh? And do you want a rabbi that doesn't like kids?"

"Shah, she'll hear you."

"Maybe there's something wrong with her."

"Maybe there's something wrong with him."

"Shah! She's getting up to do the blessing."

Irma had come back from the kitchen and was rapping her glass for silence. Madeleine watched as Lynda stood. There was something different about the way she carried herself. She was pale and tired-looking. Madeleine nodded to herself with satisfaction. She was no better than Aaron after all. She was letting the congregation bleed her just as he had. But yet there seemed to be something else, something Madeleine couldn't identify.

Lynda stood, waiting for quiet. Madeleine heard the comments on Lynda's attire slowly fade into silence as everyone waited for the blessing over bread. But Lynda stood as the silence grew heavy over the hundred women gathered. Unaccustomed to silence, they feared it as an omen of disaster. Madeleine watched Lynda with interest. Her eyes seemed to gaze at a distant object, but when Madeleine looked, she could see nothing. Finally, Lynda opened her mouth and softly began to sing. It was a song they all knew from Friday-night services, a song asking God to grant peace to the world. Lynda closed her eyes and sang the song. When it was over, she began it again. Silence reigned at Madeleine's table, and at the head table as well. But then, softly at first, the song came back to them. Madeleine turned and saw the

women at three of the lesser tables in back singing with
their eyes closed. She looked from them to Lynda and back
again, trying to discover what had transpired between them.
Slowly the song grew, spreading from table to table, getting
faster and louder as some women began to clap in time to
the music. It spread until even the head table sang, lips
smiling while eyes showed suspicion of the woman who led
them. Then, when the melody was at its loudest, Lynda
silenced them. In the absolute quiet, she lifted the woven
loaf of bread and began the blessing. For the first time that
Madeleine could remember, all the women said the blessing
together. Then the mood broke, and voices began their
discord of speech once again. Lynda sat down as Irma leaned
to her.

The waiter brought Madeleine's gefilte fish. She forced
herself to make conversation and to be once again Knesset
Yaakov's charming rebbetzin. She was good at it, talking
of doctors, pregnancies and rumors spicy enough to be interesting, but never hot enough to be gossip. She knew the
right people, and for thirty years had kept the powers in
balance. There was no need to continue the act, except from
force of habit. Maybe there had never been any point to it
at all. Maybe it had just been another game she played to
convince herself that she had value. It had been a lie. She
was Aaron Stern's wife, no more. She would follow him
while he pursued his own dreams.

When the waiter brought the soup, Madeleine looked up
from her conversations and glanced at the head table. She
watched as Lynda stood, nodded to Irma and moved off to
the door of the banquet hall. This was a departure from
routine. On impulse, Madeleine rose and followed her. It
was the impulse of spotted forks and stained linen, the
impulse of thirty years' experience in finding out things
Aaron should know. Madeleine saw Lynda out in the hallway, leaning against the wall. Then Lynda straightened.
She walked to the office wing while using the wall as sup-

port. When she went into the bathroom, Madeleine waited outside. Lynda came out and saw Madeleine, her face growing paler.

"A virus," she said softly.

"I see," Madeleine said, looking hard at the woman.

"I'm just going to rest a minute in my office; then I'll be right back."

"I'll make a cold compress for your head."

"No! No, you don't have to do that. I'll be fine."

"I'll get the compress; then we'll talk," Madeleine said.

Lynda averted her eyes, but not before Madeleine saw her fear. Madeleine went into the bathroom, wet some paper towels, then brought them into Lynda's office. She closed the door behind her.

Lynda had poured some tablets into her hand. She took two and put back the rest. She accepted the compress Madeleine gave her, put it on her forehead and leaned back in the chair.

"Thank you," she said.

Madeleine watched her a moment in silence. She was pale, her hand still shaking from the sickness. She seemed so vulnerable that Madeleine was tempted to leave her in peace. But she couldn't do that; too much had passed between them.

"How long have you been pregnant?" Madeleine asked.

Lynda didn't move or speak for a moment. "Three months," she said finally. "More or less."

"The nausea will go away any day now," Madeleine replied automatically.

"So they tell me," Lynda said. She raised the compress briefly and looked at Madeleine. "I haven't told Aaron."

"I doubt that withholding the information will make much difference in his decision. I don't think he wants you."

"That must please you," Lynda said.

"It doesn't please me or displease me. I knew it was inevitable. You came here under false pretenses. It had to catch up to you."

"Aaron tried to steal my soul and couldn't. That's false pretenses?"

"You came here to be the disciple and tried to become the master."

Lynda sat up. The compress dropped from her forehead into her hand. "Doesn't anything about what you've said bother you? All this has nothing to do with whether or not I'm a good rabbi. Whether or not those people out there need me."

Madeleine laughed. "You play Aaron's games too, don't you? They don't need you, Lynda. They don't need anyone. You'll leave and they'll forget you. Aaron will die, and they'll forget him. You get up in front of them, like you did today, and you pretend to be holy. You play at giving them God, but you will lose in the end because you've forgotten—they don't need you at all."

"And what do *you* need?"

"I need the pieces of my husband that you stole."

"What you want is what you let go. I stole nothing."

"I could have saved him, after the desert," Madeleine said. "I could have pulled him away from those insane dreams of his. But he didn't want me. He had you. You were going to give him back his soul and make him a rebbe. He came back from the desert too strong for me to help him."

"With strength he stole from me!" Lynda said.

"You let him believe in you."

"No," Lynda said. "All the times he visited me in rabbinical school, all those years, I tried to tell him that I didn't have any answers for him. He wouldn't believe me."

"But you still came here."

"I needed a job!"

"You should have stayed in Jerusalem. I told you that. You should have settled for the life you had. But no. You had to become Aaron's disciple."

"I was never Aaron's disciple, Madeleine," Lynda said softly. "I was yours."

"Don't lie to me," Madeleine said.

"Look at me, Madeleine. You know I'm not lying. I came here thinking you knew that. I'd wanted us to be friends." Lynda leaned back in her chair. She looked out the window and watched the snowflakes through tear-blurred eyes; then she turned back to Madeleine. "I should have told you long ago. But I was hurt when you hated me so."

"I told you to stay in Jerusalem," Madeleine said.

"But you also told me your story."

"Too much of it."

"Maybe," Lynda said. She wiped her eyes and gazed once more at Madeleine. "Maybe you did. But once I'd heard it, it became a part of me. Once I knew how you had suffered, what you'd dared to do in a time when you couldn't hope to succeed. Once I heard your dream, I couldn't stay in Jerusalem and let my own dreams die. Aaron merely offered me a path to follow."

"I was a coward. You and I both know that."

"No. You've used that accusation as an excuse to be Aaron's shadow all your life, but it isn't true. He's not the strong one: you are; you always were."

"You really believe that."

"Madeleine, I have eyes."

"This doesn't change anything."

"Yes, it does," Lynda said. "The truth changes everything."

Madeleine stood. Her confusion stifled her words before they reached her lips. "We have to go," she said finally. "They'll miss us at the luncheon."

Lynda stood. Madeleine opened the door for her. "You go first. It will be too suspicious if we're together."

Lynda smiled sadly. "Of course," she said. "Not together."

Madeleine watched Lynda walk down the hall. Suddenly she didn't want to return to the luncheon. She didn't want to be the charming rebbetzin anymore. She walked out of the synagogue, leaving her coat and purse behind, not caring, for once in her life, what anyone thought.

Lynda jerked her head up. She'd nearly fallen asleep at her desk. The rumbling in her stomach had brought her out of a doze that probably would have sent her crashing into the cup of coffee by her hand, thereby spilling her total lunch. She'd missed breakfast too, because there had been no time. The Religious School board had scheduled a coffee meeting in the morning to finalize the curriculum for the next year. After it broke up, the singles-group president came in, and it took her half an hour to talk him out of resigning. Then the Golds had called, and she'd dashed off to the hospital, where Nita Gold was undergoing emergency surgery. She'd gotten back in time for Abe Katz's funeral. Guiltily, Lynda remembered her relief at not also having to spend time doing his hospital visits. She looked at her watch. It was now four and she still had correspondence to do, not to mention the two boys coming in for bar mitzvah training.

Lynda sipped the now cold coffee. If she could finish with them in time, maybe she could grab a bite to eat when she spoke to the Reverend Mr. Barret about the upcoming interfaith service. Then again, maybe not. She still had to meet with the senior-member study group and hadn't prepared the lecture. The youth group met after that. Lynda had the feeling it would be a quick pizza and all night in the office again.

Everything was getting done, though. In addition to her own schedule, she'd maintained every one of Aaron's programs. He might remain silent, and Stuart Levine might push for a candidate search, but they'd all have a hard time matching her performance. For now, Knesset Yaakov was hers. She looked out her window at the street and the city beyond. Within these walls nothing could touch her. And nothing beyond the walls really mattered.

She'd buried her wounds under countless duties, endless

needs. All else—Elliot, Madeleine, even the baby—was distant memory. Everything real was listed on her daily schedule. It filled her time and her mind, easing her distress, numbing her soul. Lynda glanced at the rabbinical texts on her shelves. Once, long ago, she'd studied the holy words, immersed herself in the black characters and thereby had renewed her spirit. But there was no time for that now. Lynda shook off the melancholy that crept into her thoughts. This was her synagogue, the walled world of her creation. Here she controlled her destiny.

The intercom buzzed, bringing her back from her thoughts. "Yes, Christina?"

"There's a man here to see you. He's from Israel."

"What does he want?" Lynda asked, looking once more at her watch. She didn't need interruptions in her schedule.

"He's on a fund-raising tour for the Yesharim Settlers."

"Tell him we're not interested in fanatics, especially Jewish ones." Lynda clicked off the intercom. It buzzed again.

"Sorry, Rabbi," Christina said. "But he says he knows you. His name is Tzvi Heldman."

Lynda took her finger off the intercom button. It was damp. She looked at her books and then at the door. Then she signaled Christina again. "Tell him I'll be out in a moment."

She wanted no ghosts from Jerusalem. Not now. Yet one stood beyond the door, and she would have to open to him. Tzvi. She would greet him amid all the books and words her soul had forgotten. And he would know.

Tzvi turned when she opened the door. He was even thinner than when she'd known him, but his skin was tan rather than pale. He wore an ill-fitting black suit of European cut, and he held a black fedora in his hands. A crocheted skullcap was on his head.

"Hello, Tzvi."

"Hi," he said. "It's been a long time."

She pointed to the skullcap. "Is that the one I made for you?"

"Yes," he said. They stood looking at each other until

Christina coughed. Lynda beckoned to her office, and Tzvi walked in. She closed the door behind her.

"Is this all right?" she asked, pointing to the closed door.

He looked puzzled for a moment, then smiled. "Sure. I'm not that crazy anymore."

"Please sit down," Lynda said, realizing too late she still used her formal voice. "Please, Tzvi, sit." After he did, she settled herself in her desk chair. "How on earth did you get here?"

"I'm fund-raising for Yesharim. I knew you were here, and I knew I had to come and see you." Tzvi put his hat on her desk and glanced around the room nervously. "Nice library," he said. He looked at her. "This is the first time I've been back in eight years. Everything has changed."

"Many things, but not everything," Lynda said. "Are you really a member of the Yesharim? What happened to teaching at Aish Emes?"

Tzvi shrugged. "Rabbi Schwartz and I parted ways," he said. "I was ordained from a Yesharim yeshiva. I do teach," he said, "but that's between guard duty, patrols and working in the fields. The movement is growing."

"So I've heard. I can't say it pleases me."

Tzvi smiled. His beard was thicker than she'd remembered it. "You weren't pleased then," he said.

"I told you not everything changes. So you're going to bring the Messiah by kicking every Arab out of Israel."

"Yes," Tzvi said formally. "Jews must own every piece of our God-given territory. The Jewish land must be wholly Jewish; then the Messiah will come. And I don't think anything else will bring him."

Lynda smiled. "You're crazy."

"As crazy as the rest of them," he said. "At least, that's what someone told me a long time ago." Tzvi reached over and fingered the brim of his hat as it lay on the desk. "This is a nice place. Are you the head . . . rabbi?"

She ignored his hesitation. "For now. Aaron Stern is very ill."

"I'm married, you know. Three children."

"Me too. Married. No children."

"I could see that by the name on the door," he said. "You look tired. At least, more tired than the last time I saw you." Tzvi reddened a moment and looked away. "Is this what you wanted?"

"Yes."

He looked at the volumes of Talmud. "So you finally got your Talmud."

Lynda nodded. "But now that I'm a rabbi, I don't have much time to study."

"Neither do I. It's amazing how things twist around," Tzvi said. "I really didn't expect to come and find you so . . . successful. It confuses me."

"Well, go talk to Moishe Wittenstein," Lynda said, laughing. "He'll straighten you out."

"He's dead."

"Oh," Lynda said, feeling her stomach tighten. "How?"

"A terrorist attack on one of our settlements. About a year ago."

"I'm really sorry to hear that," she said. She looked at him, at a loss for what to say.

"Well," Tzvi said finally, "I really better be going. I have a busy schedule." He stood as she did and walked to the door, but he turned suddenly.

"I wanted to see you again," he said, his eyes earnest. "I wanted you to know that I loved you then, and that I never stopped loving you." His words came out quickly, almost in a blur. "And I wanted to tell you—I wanted to say that sometimes when I've been in the fields for days, or when there's a raid, I wonder. You know? I wonder about it all."

"I do too," Lynda said.

"Once, after we'd gotten legal claim to some Arab farm, the soldiers were evicting the family as we were praying the Morning Service. We had to pray loud to cover the Arab woman's wailing." He paused. "I mean, don't get me wrong. I believe in what I'm doing, and that it will someday help even that Arab woman. But sometimes, sometimes I wonder if I didn't go about it the wrong way." He walked over to the shelves and gently touched the Talmud volumes.

"This used to be my life," he said. He turned to her. "Back in the yeshiva, I felt closer to God. Now I'm doing God's work, but I feel so far away. I think of you, and the way we were, and I just wonder what might have been."

"I understand," Lynda said. He looked at her. She touched him gently on the sleeve. "I do understand. They were my life too."

They were close. Too close, she knew. Tzvi bent to her, but pulled himself straight. "I really wish I'd stopped loving you," he whispered. He backed away a step. "I have something of yours that I've kept too long." He reached into his pocket and brought out a worn blue prayer book. He handed it to Lynda.

She took his gift in her hands, afraid the book would fall apart with her touch. "How did you get this?"

"You'd written the yeshiva address on the inside cover. The cab driver who brought you to the airport dropped it by the yeshiva about a week later. I've kept it all this time," he said. "Even after I got married, I kept it, like a photograph. It reminded me of the part of you I could touch."

Lynda held the prayer book in tightly closed hands. She looked at Tzvi. "It's a part of me I've missed."

"Are you happy?"

"Yes, I am, Tzvi," she lied. "I really am."

"That's all I wanted to know. I'll be going now."

"Let me walk you out."

He shook his head. "No." He reached out and took her hand. "Be happy," he said. Then he was gone and the door to her room closed once more.

She would have thought him an apparition, had it not been for the prayer book she held in her hands. It had not aged in the intervening years. She opened the book and slowly turned the pages, seeking, in the ancient characters, the part of her soul she had so long ago lost.

SNOW COVERED THE CITY PARK, WHICH WAS EMPTY THIS time of year. The seesaws had been removed, and only a slight impression in the snow indicated the existence of a sandbox. Madeleine sat on a swing, bundled against the elements, and swung back and forth, creating new crevices in the snow with each slow arc. She watched the sparkles on the trees, remembering Brooklyn walks with Aaron and Nathan, remembering Ruth.

Joshua had gone back to his family and returned again. This would be the final trip home. The next journey they would all take together. In the midst of packing her life away, Madeleine had come upon Ruth's letters, a yellowed packet bound with a brittle rubber band that had broken when she pulled at it. Joshua, catching the letters as they fell, had asked to read them. She'd given him permission, then fled here, to the park.

Madeleine moved back and forth in slow repetition. Back and forth the way she'd done thousands of times with the children when they were growing up. She could almost hear Reuben's squeals of delight. As she glanced at the empty swing next to her, she remembered watching, helpless, when David fell and broke his arm. She wondered if the swing, now sitting under its own pile of snow, was the same one. The pond was the same. Madeleine looked to it, seeing once more the image of Joshua running into the water to catch a duck. He'd caught a crayfish instead, but was just as pleased.

Perhaps it was enough: to have raised children, to have seen her sons into adulthood and have yet another generation pass from her. It might have been enough, Madeleine thought, glancing up at the hill overlooking the park, had it not been for that place. Knesset Yaakov sat on the top of the hill. The synagogue's board would meet this month. Aaron's last official act. In another few weeks, they would be in Jerusalem.

Madeleine had dreamed, the night before, of Ruth. Ruth was young and alive, and so was she. They were in a room, the one in Westbury. When they said good-bye, it was not Ruth who walked out the door, but Madeleine. Yet not Madeleine. The being of the dream was Ruth and Madeleine at the same time.

The dream had awakened a lonely ache Madeleine had long ago buried. How odd it was, after all these years, that she could still mourn for Ruth, the friend of her youth. Maybe it was because she'd never thought of herself as having grown older. In spite of the lines around her eyes, in spite of the slight rounding of the once flat belly, Madeleine saw herself as she had been then. As she had been at eighteen, with the world before her. Maybe she missed Ruth so because Ruth had been the only person she'd loved completely. Madeleine sat, moving back and forth on the swing, trying to sort out Ruth from memories of Ruth. Which was the real person, and which the ghost? But it all blended together. She had loved Ruth the most, but had shared the least with her. A moment in a room, grudgingly given. Tears shed too late. Then nothing.

Footsteps crunched the snow behind her. Joshua wiped the snow off the swing next to her and sat down. He pushed the swing back with his legs, but thought better of it and slowly came to a stop. Madeleine let her swing be still, so they sat barely moving.

"I haven't seen this much snow in a long time. It's pretty."

"You never used to think so when you had to shovel the walk."

Joshua looked out at the pond. "Didn't I catch a duck there once?"

Madeleine smiled. "Almost."

A dog padded across the playground area. He stopped near them and lifted his leg against a pole; then he padded away, leaving a yellow depression in the snow.

"What a simple way to mark boundaries," Joshua said. "I'll have to mention it to my friends on the Golan."

"Yes, but another dog comes by and urinates in the same place," Madeleine said.

"What do you think happens on the Golan?" Joshua said, smiling. The smile faded. "Only instead of piss, we leave blood." He turned to her. "I want to thank you for letting me read Ruth's letters."

"I hope they didn't tarnish your ideals."

He shook his head. "Just when I think I'm all grown up, you treat me like I'm seventeen again."

"As I remember, you were a bit to handle at seventeen."

"Well, my ideals were tarnished a long time ago. The letters, in fact, have shined them up a bit."

"Oh, and how could that be?"

"Ruth was a pioneer. She was there when the state began, but she wondered too. She had doubts. The legend of Ruth Yair doesn't have any room for doubts."

"And what about the legend of Joshua Stern?"

"I have doubts every day," he said. "I had doubts up on the Golan. I have doubts when I see my children. I'm sick of hating and killing, too. But I've never said anything because I've always thought it was my problem. But she wondered too; she saw the dark side of the dream and tried to face it."

"The dark side won, Joshua. She's dead."

"She must have loved you very much to write those things to you. I've never even talked about it to Yudit."

"I was safe. I was far away."

Joshua sighed. "Ma, maybe she wrote to you because she could trust you to understand."

"Don't get maudlin," Madeleine said. "I hope she didn't save my replies. They were insipid."

"I didn't think so," he said.

"You read them?"

"Yes, and they were damn funny. Magnificent, now that I see the context."

"You're a biased critic, and damned impertinent, reading your mother's letters."

Joshua smiled. "You belong to history now." He shivered and hunched down in the swing.

"You're cold," Madeleine said. "Let's go in."

"No. Not yet."

"Well, here, take my hat. I'll wrap up in the scarf."

"Ma, it's got a pink pompom on it."

"What? The hero of the Golan Heights is afraid his manhood will be diminished by a pink pompom?" She handed it to him and watched as he put it on. He grinned at her.

"I have this idea," he said. "I want to bring the letters to the kibbutz."

"I guess Ruth wouldn't mind, by now."

"And I want to bring you."

"I'm *going* to Israel, remember? I'd like to forget, but I assumed you would remember."

"I mean to the kibbutz. To live there. It's driving distance from Jerusalem. You could live on the kibbutz and Dad could teach at the yeshiva."

"I'm a little old to pick oranges, Joshua."

"I don't want you to pick oranges. We don't even grow oranges. I happen to know of an administrative position open. You'd be great."

"I'm not a socialist."

"Let me tell you, socialists make lousy administrators, and an occasional Marxist can set you back twenty years.

Besides, you were a Communist for a while; you can handle it. It'll be like old times."

"I'm not thrilled by old times. And I'm sure Yudit would be thrilled by having her mother-in-law move into her house."

"You wouldn't. I have connections. You would move into an absolutely tiny, but adequate apartment."

"On a kibbutz?"

"Times have changed. I've talked it over with Yudit, and Ben, and the committee that decides such things. Everyone is awaiting your approval."

"Why do you want me, Joshua?"

"Because I love you, Ma. And because you possess a rare kind of wisdom. You see both shadow and light. You represent a part of Ruth Yair's legend that we'll need if we're ever going to make peace."

"I've given up on trying to save the world. I found it couldn't be done."

"Then don't save the whole world. Just work on a corner of it. Be with your grandchildren. Teach them like you taught me one morning in Jerusalem."

"No," Madeleine said. "Thank you for the offer." She stood.

Joshua looked up at her. "When are you going to stop running away?" he asked harshly.

"You want someone who doesn't exist. I'm not some brave wisewoman, Joshua. I'm a coward. I always have been. Running away is an integral part of my life."

"Well, stop it. You're hurting too many people."

"I'm not hurting anyone."

"*I'm* finding it pretty painful."

"You'll have to adjust," Madeleine said. She started to walk away, but turned. "You're just like your father, you know. Has it occurred to you that I don't want to be some damn kibbutznik? I don't want to be part of your dream."

"I don't want you to be part of it either. I want to give you a gift, Ma. Freedom. As much as it's within my power to give. But you'd rather fester in Nathan's yeshiva. I think that's a high price to pay for the right to abdicate from life again."

"What are you talking about?"

He stood too, and faced her. "I don't know what happened to you when you were young, but whatever it was—whatever—it isn't worth renouncing your life. You've let that one thing rule you. Some great dark secret that you keep hidden because you're afraid if it sees the light it won't be so bad, and you won't have an excuse to abandon everything that starts to be meaningful."

"You have no right to talk to me like that!"

"Yes, I do!" Joshua slammed a fist against his artificial leg. "This gives me the right. You said I'm like my father. What you don't see is how much you're like him. He abandoned us for some shadow world of his own making, and you abandoned everything but us for the same reason."

"So to prove I care, I should run to Israel, singing pioneer songs. That's Ruth's world, not mine."

"Ma, Ruth Yair is dead. Her world ended in nineteen fifty-six. I'm not a part of her world. I didn't even know her."

"You had her grandchildren."

"No. I had *your* grandchildren. But you didn't want them. How do you think my children feel? They've been given to a dead woman. That's who you've hurt by running away—three kids who think you don't care about them."

Madeleine sat back on the swing. "I never meant that," she said softly.

"And what did you mean?" Joshua bent over and took her hand.

"I didn't think I was important to them."

"You're so important to so many people, yet you can't see it. I want to give you a chance, before it's too late. I don't want to give you my dream—I want to share it with you. Just like Ruth shared with you in those letters. Don't turn yourself into yet another sacrifice at that yeshiva. I don't want you to come to the kibbutz for me, or even the kids. I want you to come for you. And if you want to leave, that's okay. I just want to give you the chance to dream again. For yourself."

Madeleine sighed. "I don't know. I never dreamed of life as a kibbutznik."

"No?" He smiled. "What did you dream about?"

"Being great. I dreamed I was destined to carve a place in history."

"Well, we could use another lady Prime Minister."

Madeleine smiled and squeezed his hand. "I'll think about it. Now, why don't you head home before even the pink pompom on your head turns blue."

"You're not coming?"

"I want to stay here a little longer. You go."

She heard the uneven crunch of snow move slowly away. She rose and walked to the edge of the pond. A leaf, still red with fall, was frozen in the ice.

In the distance a bird sang. Surprised, Madeleine listened, but couldn't identify the call. She closed her eyes a moment. It seemed she was not alone, yet when she looked, there was no other person in the park. In all her visions of greatness, she had never seen herself on a kibbutz. But then, who knew what Ruth's dreams had been before she chose her path? Madeleine hadn't bothered to find out about those dreams. She heard the bird again, calling to her. She smiled as she gazed in its direction. "Whither thou goest," she said, "I will go."

The Ner Tamid, the Eternal Light, symbol of God's everpresence, cast its glow over the sanctuary. Shadows moved in time with the figure before the Ark. It was midnight, the time when even the dead are heard by God. Lynda stood, swaying beneath the Ner Tamid, wrapped in her prayer shawl. She prayed, reaching into the words of her prayer book as she had done so long ago, seeking The Place of Light. There was no other refuge left her but The Place she had almost touched in Jerusalem. She came as if beckoned, to stand at the head of an empty sanctuary, to pray alone amid the spirits gathered in assembly.

She made offerings with her lips, a sacrifice of the soul. She had abandoned her path for nothingness, had run from The Place to this world. Lynda was dimly aware of the tears against her cheek and the dampness of her shirt as she struggled to remember what she had been, to remember the Lynda who had prayed at the Wall of the Great Temple.

It seemed that she was at the Wall, standing once again with the old rebbetzin. Lynda moved her lips silently, letting the old woman's voice carry her beyond herself, letting the rebbetzin's tears give her the strength to go beyond the shadow her life had become. She moved through herself as the Holy Letters spoke with her lips. She was above the sanctuary and past the Wall. She moved unencumbered by Lynda, who remained struggling before the Ark. She was the wind blowing through Jerusalem, a breeze whose breath was the breath of God. She felt joy at the soaring, and tried to move higher, farther than Jerusalem, to a holiness she had not yet known. But instead, ever so gently, she floated downward, again into the struggle that was Lynda.

Madeleine paused in the shadows just inside the door of the sanctuary. Tentative, she moved to a seat by the steps leading to the Ark. She watched Lynda, uncomfortable with the intimacy of her observation and with the silence of the sanctuary.

Aaron used to come here, fleeing from his ghosts—or pursuing them. She didn't know which. Once, she had come to watch him weep, and cry out at the silence. Now, whether it was the time, or the place, or something changed within herself, the sanctuary felt different. She shivered with a sense of presence, as if she would see Ruth, or a thousand Madeleines who might have been.

Elliot had asked her to come. She couldn't refuse him. And what better place to begin again than this room of might-have-been? Tonight, in this place of ghosts, she would see if they both could survive.

Lynda closed the prayer book and kissed it. She turned, seeing Madeleine.

"Hello," Madeleine said.

"How did you know I'd be here?"

"Elliot told me."

"How did he know?" Lynda asked.

Madeleine smiled. "You underestimate your husband."

Lynda took off her prayer shawl and folded it. She placed it on the lectern by the Ark and, reluctantly, put the prayer book on top.

"Tell me," Madeleine said. "Were you praying for your baby?"

Lynda looked away and said nothing.

"I thought not. My, how like Aaron you are. Elliot told me you're in danger of losing the baby if you don't take it easy. I'd hoped you were praying for guidance, but I knew better."

"You don't know me at all, Madeleine," Lynda said. She moved down the stairs and sat on the bottom step opposite Madeleine. "You've spent a great deal of time trying not to know me."

"Of course I don't know you, and neither does Elliot. You read like an open book and assume your soul is secret. I've lived with someone like you for thirty years. That's how I know you wouldn't pray for anything so mundane as guidance."

"So what would I pray for?"

"You'd pray to enter that world you sense, the one that's so much higher than this one. You want to be next to the God you've sensed from afar, and you think with just a little more effort, a little more soul, you'll reach Paradise forever. Am I close?"

Lynda stared at her through narrowed eyes. "Why are you here?"

"I could say it's because Elliot asked me to come. But Elliot didn't get me through the door. Up to it maybe, but not through."

"So why?"

"Because it's time," she said. "Time to reclaim myself. This seemed like a good place to do it. I wronged you. I want to make up for that."

"By persuading me to become a good wife and mother? I didn't believe that line back in Jerusalem when you tried it the first time."

"You weren't pregnant in Jerusalem."

"I don't want to be now," Lynda said.

"You know why? Because you don't want to be on the other side again."

"Other side of what?"

"Of God. Remember back, Lynda. Remember your fiancé in Jerusalem. His world was just like Aaron's. But you left. Why?"

"Because I wanted to be a rabbi."

"What else?"

"Nothing," Lynda said quickly. But Jerusalem came back to her, and memories of her last night with Tzvi. She sighed and rubbed her forehead. "I didn't want to take second place to Tzvi's God."

Madeleine nodded. "All my life," she said, "I've lived with an adulterer. I took from my life, and the lives of my children, to give Aaron time to go to his mistresses—the congregation and his God. So here I am." She lifted her hands and shook her head. "Empty. And so is Aaron."

"I can't give it up," Lynda said.

"You have to give it up in order to find it. If you lose your baby, do you think you will ever find what you're seeking? The burden will destroy you."

"And how is it you are so wise?"

"I'm not," Madeleine said. "My son is. Maybe that's why I'm here. To finally let go—of the wounds, the ghosts, the dreams that should have died long ago."

"I can't give up my dreams."

"Then don't. Give up your blindness instead. You've imprisoned Elliot in the life you fled."

"I can't . . ." Lynda stopped and rested a hand on her belly.

Madeleine leaned forward to touch her. "Are you all right?"

"Yes," Lynda said, leaving her hand on her belly. "It's something I ate, or didn't eat."

"Feels like bubbles in the abdomen?"

Lynda looked at Madeleine in surprise. "Yes. Tiny bubbles."

Madeleine smiled. "That's your baby talking to you."

Lynda glanced down at her lap and pulled her hand away. She felt the bubbling again and rested the hand once more on her abdomen. The hand felt nothing, yet something was there.

"The doctor told me it was indigestion," Lynda said.

"He's never carried a child."

"That's my baby?"

"That's your little girl," Madeleine said. "Or your little boy. That's you nurturing yourself until you birth a new human being." Madeleine hesitated a moment, then stood and moved over to Lynda, sitting by her on the step.

"Don't become another Aaron," Madeleine said. "He was so blind, he never saw anything to show him how precious this world is, how holy. If you seek some supernatural ecstasy and fail to see how holy that churning in your womb is, you'll never find God or yourself. Listen, and you'll hear your baby talking to you, singing from the womb, with dreams not yet dreamed."

"So what do I do, Madeleine?"

"Nothing. For once, do nothing. Have some faith in God."

"God wanted me to be a rebbetzin in a yeshiva."

"If you really believe that, then you have no business here. Poor Aaron wanted to be a rebbe, but he never had the faith. I watched him parcel out pieces of himself because he never had the faith to keep his soul together."

"And what about them?" Lynda said, looking out to the empty seats.

"God doesn't demand human sacrifices, and neither should the congregation. If you give them one, you're leading them astray."

"You know, you talk like a rabbi," Lynda said, chuckling.

"Please, spare me from that."

"Tell me, what do you believe in?"

Madeleine shrugged; then she looked at Lynda. "I believe that Aaron, in his own twisted way, was right. There is something special about you. I believe you'll succeed. And, I guess, finally, I believe in destiny. My destiny."

"And what's that, Madeleine?"

Madeleine laughed. "I still don't have the faintest idea. But I'm damn well going to find out."

Aaron walked through the halls of Knesset Yaakov, viewing the place as if he were a stranger who had entered his own body. Everything was familiar, yet he was detached from it all. He'd come in on his secretary's day off. Lucille's tears reminded him that an end to his reign might mean an end to hers as well. He should feel sorry for her, and he did, but in a distant, detached way.

The books were almost packed. Aaron had thought he'd be able to do that himself, but he was too weak. John had set his assistant, the one who was a drunk, to help with the packing. He did a poor job, but Aaron let that pass. There would be books at the yeshiva. Aaron smiled to himself. Living and dying at the same time had a satisfying fullness about it. Getting up in the morning was a holy, renewing event. The death he sought was still there, in the distance, beckoning. Nathan's place was merely an appropriate halfway house, a part of his leaving this world. And maybe, in the eyes of a disciple, he would find redemption. Contentment flowed through him.

He felt a tightness in his loins as his body remembered earthly delights. He and Madeleine had made love last night, something he'd thought himself incapable of. She'd moved him with a womanly passion he'd thought existed only in his younger fantasies of her. He hadn't wanted to make love. He had wanted those things of this world behind him. But she'd clothed him in a desire that his body still recalled. When they had finished, he'd reached over to wipe a tear from her eye, but she had told him nothing.

Later, when he was sure she slept, he'd gone down to the basement. He had rummaged through packing crates until he found the box that held his mother's fortune-telling cards and amulets. He had sat in the cold, shuffling the cards, turning them over, one by one. But they had denied him an omen. He could not understand them, and he had no gypsy there to give him visions.

His father's prayer shawl and tefillin were in the crate also. Aaron had wanted to touch them, to wrap himself in them. But his hands wouldn't obey his desire. The holy objects had been touched by the Loemer Rebbe. They had been made for the man his father once was, a half-starved Hasid, a Jew lean in the things of this world. Aaron was still too heavy with life and with the passion he had to kill.

He had started shivering with the cold. The artifacts of his parents kept him a prisoner. Aaron tried to forget the cold and seek warmth and light from that other world, to release the desire that chained him to life. But he had chosen to live a little while longer. Nathan had come, offering him redemption, and he had snatched at it like a drowning man, hating himself for wanting life once again. "Come and find God with me, my friend," Nathan had said. Aaron looked at his fingers numb with cold. The chill would smother his desire, punish him for forsaking the angel of death.

Soon the pain in his hands had subsided and he'd dozed. He had awakened to see the prayer shawl on the floor, the cards all around it. The card of death, the one he'd sought, stared at him. The black of the empty eyes pulled at him. He wanted to go; he wanted to join with it, the desire welling in him as it had in Madeleine's embrace. Death sang the Loemer melody, soothing fear. He reached for the card, but found his hand already closed. When he opened it, an amulet fell across the card, covering the face with Hebrew lettering, forming words of accusation against him.

He had gathered the cards and amulets, locking them away in the box once more. He'd picked up the prayer shawl and folded it with hands so numb they could not feel the material. He'd stood and hugged himself against the cold, waiting, expecting someone. It had seemed he should know for whom he waited, but no image came to him. With a sigh, he had made his way up to warmth once more.

In the light of day, he wasn't sure whether he had done those things or dreamed them. Whether the madness that had gripped him in the desert was now taking him once more. He touched the wall of the synagogue hallway. This was real. This was his creation, and it would live beyond him.

Aaron made his way back to the office. He started to go into the sanctuary, but he found he couldn't enter. The memory of his last visit drove him away. Her presence still lingered there. He could feel it, malevolent, blocking his path. Aaron shuddered and backed from the door. He would take care of her at the board meeting next week. He would correct the mistake he'd made so long ago. If Stuart Levine expected opposition in his fight to remove Lynda, he would not find it with Aaron.

He walked back to his office. On his desk was an amulet, one of his mother's. He stood still, looking at it, feeling his heartbeat against his ears.

"I found it in the pocket of your robe," Madeleine said.

Aaron jumped, startled, then looked to the window where Madeleine stood. "You frightened me," he said.

"What does it say?" she asked.

"What?"

"The amulet," Madeleine said. "The big writing, not all the tiny script."

Aaron walked over to the desk and stared at the letters that had accused him the night before. "It says 'Aitz Chaim Hi l'machazikim bah.'"

"'She is a tree of life to all who hold onto her,'" Madeleine said. "Why did you bring that up with you from the basement?"

"I thought you were asleep."

"I know," Madeleine said. She came around the desk and sat in front of it. "I'm not going to Jerusalem with you, Aaron. Joshua invited me to stay at his kibbutz. I'm going to take him up on it."

"Somehow, I can't picture you sowing the fields and reaping the harvest."

"No, I guess you couldn't. You've got me having tea with the nice rebbetzins at the yeshiva."

"No," Aaron said, shaking his head.

"Tell me, in all these years, have I existed, once you walked out the door? Can you really picture me doing anything?"

"Don't belittle yourself, Madeleine."

"I'm not." Madeleine reached for the amulet. She fingered it, turning the parchment over in her hand. "A tree of life," she said softly.

Aaron sat at the desk, now that the amulet had been removed. He felt its mockery in the room. The air was heavy with the shadow from the letters, and he prayed she would put it away. But she stared at it, turning it over and over. Then suddenly he knew. He wouldn't be able to change her mind. She'd let him go to Jerusalem alone. He would be free, free to pursue death his own way.

Yet instead of joy, he felt panic. He hated the fear that built up inside him. Now he could go to Jerusalem unencumbered, but he didn't want that. He closed his eyes and pictured an empty room, an empty bed. There would be no one to keep the madness away. No one to help him if he cried out. No one to keep him alive.

"Don't go," he said in a whisper. "Madeleine, don't leave me. Everything else has left me."

She looked up from the letters in her hand. "It's too late, Aaron. I'll come when you need me, but I won't be your shadow anymore. Joshua believes in me. I don't know whether his faith is a lie or truth, but I want to be with someone who believes in me." She hit her chest with her hand. "Me."

"It's too late to be a revolutionary, Madeleine."

"It's too late to be a rebbe, Aaron."

She gazed at him and it seemed that the letters were reflected in her eyes. Aitz Chaim Hi. A part of him heard the words out of the silence in her eyes. A part of him gently dissolved as he put his head in his hands and wept. Then Madeleine was there, holding him, stroking his head and keeping the darkness away. "God help me," he said. "I've wasted my whole life."

"No," she said. She lifted his head. "Your father wasted his life. Look around you, Aaron. Look at what we have, for once, instead of what we don't."

He took in a ragged breath and let it out slowly. "What do I do now?"

"Go to Jerusalem."

"Will you come with me?"

"No," she said, straightening, but leaving her hand on his shoulder. "Maybe later, after I find out who I am."

"Do you really think you can do that at Joshua's kibbutz?"

"No, I'm not sure. But I have to start. You do too. So I'll start by confronting Ruth's dream, and you begin with Nathan."

"I don't know if I can face him."

"Aaron, nothing has changed, except maybe your blindness." She patted him on the shoulder and sat down. "Now," she said. "What about Lynda?"

"What about her?"

"Get her the job."

"This is coming from you?"

"Yes. I finally decided I like her."

"I can't do that. She's pregnant," he said.

"How did you know?"

Aaron smiled, looking down at his still trembling hands.

"I've been around here for a long time; there isn't much that gets by me. Also, my secretary's sister is the receptionist for a certain obstetrician in town."

"You didn't tell me," Madeleine said.

"You didn't tell *me*. Why?"

Madeleine shrugged. "A number of reasons. Get her the job anyway."

"Why should I?"

"Because she deserves it," Madeleine said. "And because we owe her."

"I'm not so sure of that," Aaron said. "Besides, if this is what I've done in my life"—he gestured out toward the rest of the synagogue—"I don't want to see it split apart, which it will do if she's the rabbi."

"Aaron," Madeleine said, shaking her head. "Open your eyes and see. This is a congregation, not a monument to you. It's going to grow and change no matter what you do." Madeleine reached into her purse. "And it's about to split anyway."

"What do you mean?"

"Since very little escapes you, I suppose you know that the younger members are threatening a breakoff if Lynda isn't hired."

"This synagogue will survive a few malcontents. It always has."

"I wouldn't call seventy families a few malcontents," she said, and handed him a list. "I talked to Colin Shur. That's how many names he gave me. He's been very busy organizing. They are prepared to walk out and offer Lynda a job. They even have a building where they can meet temporarily. Frankly, Colin has his heart set on being a synagogue president. He'll be disappointed if Lynda gets the job."

Aaron looked at the list. "I can't believe they'd do it for Lynda."

Madeleine stood up. She put on her coat, then tossed the amulet onto his desk. "Of course they would; they're her Hasidim."

"What?"

"They see what you saw in Jerusalem. What I tried to deny. Lynda is the rebbe, you old fool."

"No!"

"I'm going to face the truth, Aaron. Lynda is the rebbe, and Ruth was the hero. That's not the way I wanted it to be, but that's the way things turned out." She sighed. "We're just the followers. We were too blinded by our dreams to see. So for once, look at your life and follow the intended path."

Saying no more, she closed the door behind her. He stared at the door, then around the office. It was empty of his presence. The shelves and walls were bare. On his desk the amulet lay, its delicate letters written by some nameless scribe. He thought back to Williamsburg to the scribe who had sung the Loemer melody. Aaron closed his eyes and listened, and noticed, for the first time, how sweet the melody was. He remembered the desert and his vision. He had survived. He had left the Loemers in a grave in the desert that no one saw but he. No. He had carried them with him, refusing to let them die, refusing to allow the rebirth that comes from death. Preserved by God as an agent of life, he had instead always chosen death.

Aaron listened to the sweet melody that came out of his silence. It brought him joy, the joy he'd seen on the face of the scribe. He heard the wordless song and finally understood everything. He understood this world and the next and sensed a place beyond him, a place of light.

Then the feeling was gone. The office was his office again, bare but for the amulet, and the sweet remembrance of a knowledge so vast his mind couldn't contain it, his joy couldn't hold it. Aaron breathed deeply. He reached for the phone and dialed Stuart Levine's number.

Lynda stood in her study. It was Friday night, the time when the Queen, the Sabbath, visited her people with the gift of rest. The sanctuary was filled, Lynda knew, with people waiting to see Knesset Yaakov's new head rabbi. But before she greeted them, she took the time to greet the Queen in silence, alone.

Yet not alone. Lynda walked over to her desk. Aaron hadn't come to say good-bye, but he'd left her a gift. She opened the embroidered bag and took out a prayer shawl. She held it in her hands. It smelled slightly of age, and of worlds past. Aaron and Madeleine were gone now, to new lives, but the gift was with her, and the presence of friendship that still lingered.

Elliot waited outside with the congregation. Her baby waited within her, growing strong. These also were her portion in Torah. Aitz Chaim Hi. A tree of life. Grabbing hold, she would proceed down the path God had destined for her. Lynda wrapped herself in the prayer shawl. The weight of it felt good on her shoulders. She placed a skullcap on her head and walked to the door. She began to hum a melody Aaron had taught her long ago. It was a haunting melody that she loved. Aaron had said it was composed by the Loemer Rebbe himself.

Still humming, Rabbi Klein went to lead her people in prayer.